ARK HORTON

PORTALS &
PANTHEONS

SECRET OF PANTHEONS - BOOK 2

Table of Contents

Dedication

Not even a book has enough words to describe the love I hold for my family, but hopefully they'll read my words and know they matter more to me than any story I could tell.

To Sebastian, Penelope, Astrid, and Mike.

Portals & Pantheons touches on cultures and mythologies from around the world. Some of the names and terms maybe unfamiliar. Below is a guide to how to pronounce these things.

- Bree Castille —BREE cass-TEEL
- Cailleach — CAH-lee-ahh
- Calliope (Cal) — kuh-LIE-uh-pee (KAL)
- Corbin — CORR-bihn
- Delia Pace — DEEL-ee-uh PAYSS
- Finn MacCool — FIHN mack-COOL
- Liz Castille — LIZ cass-TEEL
- Maia — MY-uh
- Nemesis — NEM-uh-sihs
- Oisína — oh-SHEE-nuh
- Pavlina Sirin — pahv-LEE-nuh SEER-in
- Reynaud — ray-NODE
- Selkie — SELL-kee
- Sphinx — SFEENX
- Thanatos — THA-nuh-tose
- Themis — THEE-mihs
- Ylva Heidelberg — IL-vah HIE-duhl-berg

ONE

The End of Summer

Pavlina Sirin's luck was a slip of smoke that might dissipate if she paid too much attention to it. This belief colored the perfect moments she shared with her niece, Harper. The eleven-month-old sirin loved her tetya so much that Pavlina's heart struggled to contain its joy. Whenever the two were in the same room, Harper's infectious laughter and twinkling eyes softened the serious lines on Pavlina's face. The magical history teacher forgot all about unit plans and state standards as her niece showed off her newly acquired walking skills by giddily toddling towards her tetya.

That afternoon, Pavlina's boyfriend Finn had driven them up to Savannah for one last visit before the new school year started. Since they were both teachers at Annie Lytle Magical Magnet High School, they had a lot to do to prepare. Pavlina was hoping that she could help Finn put together a more inspirational learning environment than the one he'd presented the previous year. He might be an intelligent and stunning immortal Irishman, but he had no idea how to create an inviting atmosphere for his students. His grumpy "I've been doing this for ninety years" attitude didn't help either. She hoped that he would do better this time around.

Pavlina scooped Harper up the moment the babe's shaking fist grasped onto her skirt hem. Once Harper made it up to her tetya's lap, she tugged at the older sirin's dark wavy hair. Pavlina's sister Luda chided her daughter, but Pavlina didn't mind.

"She doesn't know any better," she said. "This is how she expresses her love and it makes her happy." *And she's a sirin like me. How long until those cherry lips sigh under haunted eyes?*

Half of Pavlina hated to leave her beautiful niece behind; the other half was ready to go. However much she loved Harper, each tender moment reminded her of the dark future that would one day dim the child's ceaseless light. This knowledge coiled itself into the braid woven of Pavlina's past trauma, and as she bid her family goodbye, she was glad Finn was driving them home. Yet the ride offered her no relief from this sorrow. In fact, her dread increased.

Flinty clouds pushed out the light of day. It wasn't until the last ray of sunshine disappeared over the marshy horizon that Pavlina noticed the nausea roiling in her guts. When a cold bead of sweat slid down the fluff of feathers on her back, she knew why her mood hadn't improved. Death had sent its calling card.

Pavlina placed a palm on her love's arm. "Finn, let's stop at that gas station," she said, pointing at the exit sign.

"Bathroom break coming right up," he replied.

"Not for that." Her serious tone got his attention. "It's my sense again."

Finn responded with a heavy nod. He pulled off the highway and parked in front of the gas station's convenience store. When they got out of the car, Pavlina looked around in every direction while Finn kept his eyes on her.

"Anything?" he asked.

Pavlina shrugged. "I still feel it, but it's vague. Something on that street, but… There's nothing there." *Yet.*

"Let's get some coffee."

They entered the convenience store where they filled their cups—hers with the last dregs of a strong black pot and his with a pumpkin spice cappuccino from the machine.

"It's still August," Pavlina said. "Has pumpkin spice

9

season already started?"

"I don't know, and I don't care," Finn answered. He took a long sip and closed his eyes to relish the flavor. Licking his lips, he opened his eyes and cast a warm gaze toward Pavlina. "It's delicious and certainly better than that bitter stuff in your hands. Who drinks their coffee black anymore? What are you trying to prove?"

Pavlina rolled her eyes. "Some of us like the flavor of coffee and don't want a million fillers to mask it." She took a sip, and a sludge of grounds slid over her tongue, causing her to cough.

Finn laughed and reached for her cup. "I believe you like black coffee, but I know you deserve better than burnt garbage. Let me—"

The squeal of tires outside stopped Finn. Nausea rolling up Pavlina's throat surged forward. She vomited in her styrofoam cup just as a loud crash blasted from the street. *I knew it.*

Pavlina and Finn raced outside.

Smoke, grey and stinking of burnt metal and plastic, plumed from each hood of two cars wrapped around each other. A middle-aged man staggered out of his vehicle. The occupant of the other car didn't.

Pavlina tapped Finn's shoulder, her eyes never leaving the tragic scene in front of her. "Call 911."

The sirin approached the crash. Her sense of death increased with every step.

"I don't know how it happened," the man said, each word slurred.

His wrinkled clothes and reek of alcohol didn't escape Pavlina's attention. *Liar. You know exactly how it happened.*

Pavlina peeked into the window of the occupied car. A teenager, barely older than Bree, lay on her steering wheel with a cracked and bleeding head. *Shit. This isn't fair.*

Black wings sprang from Pavlina's back, shredding the delicate white fabric of the nice blouse she'd chosen to wear during her trip to Savannah. Like so many other outfits, it would never look the same, even with stitching. Black feathers raced down her chest and arms. "Hello," she said.

The girl only stared into nothingness with dull, unblinking eyes.

"I know I look scary, but it's okay to come out of there. I'm here to help."

A spirit lifted from the teenager's body, shaking her ethereal head in the process. She stepped through the wreckage. No tangle of steel or crunch of gravel slowed her down.

"What happened?" the girl asked. "I'm running late. My mom needs me home to babysit so she can get to her next shift."

"I'm so sorry about this, but—"

The spirit made to turn her head, but the sirin

grabbed it just in time. "No, don't look back. You don't want to see. That's never a good idea."

The teenager's lips quivered. *She's starting to remember.*

"Did I...? Did I...?" She lifted her translucent hand in front of her ghostly face. Her features pulled together, trying not to cry, but celestial tears fell anyway. "I can't be dead, I..."

Pavlina nodded. "You had so much life left to live."

"No," the girl said. "Well, yes, but..." She paused, looking down the darkening expanse of road in the distance. "Kayleigh and Brandon. Mom. They're going to miss me."

Such a good kid. Why did it have to be her? "What's your name?" Pavlina asked.

The spirit turned back to the sirin, clearly wondering why she wanted to know. "Amber."

"I'll talk to them myself tonight." Pavlina took the spirit's hand and held it between her calming palms. "Okay?"

"You will?" Amber asked.

Pavlina nodded. "Yeah, you'll have to tell me where to find them, but I can do that for you."

The ghost considered it. "The cashier inside is Blake. He knows where I live. He can tell you."

"Okay, I'll ask him in a little bit," Pavlina said. "But first, let's get you where you need to go."

Pavlina held her hands above like a ballerina. A

 12

shimmering white circle passed between her arms like a bubble. It floated a few feet away from the pair and stopped, before expanding so they could both fit through.

"What's on the other side?" the girl asked.

Pavlina smiled at the spirit. "I like to think of it as a waiting room. It's quite comfy, actually. Which god do you worship?"

"Um… I never really chose. Is that bad?"

The teenager trembled with panic, but the sirin squeezed her hand to calm her. "It's not bad. Just means one was assigned to you based on your heritage."

This did nothing to calm Amber. "My heritage? Mom always called us mutts." Her reddish brown hair, faint freckles, and hazel eyes indicated that she was maybe of Celtic or Gaelic descendance, but many Americans had ancestors from just about every continent on the globe, and that could be true for her.

"Then you have a lot of options." Pavlina gave the spirit a comforting smile. "Come on, I'll show you."

Finn was still on the phone, waiting on emergency responders to show up. Pavlina waved in his direction, knowing he couldn't see Amber but the black harbinger wings and portal were obvious. *I'll be back. Just making a pit stop in the afterlife.*

Pavlina held Amber's hand as they stepped into the white portal. The cloudy but glittery expanse of souls drifted around the pair, most of them with uncertain expressions, but some with hopeful ones.

The pavement gave way and Pavlina threw her arms around Amber so that she could lift her more easily as the sirin's wings flew past the swirling souls to the white chamber beyond. People of every race, gender, and magical predilection sat or paced around the floors in boredom.

A long reception desk with thousands of angels, vestals, loas, and the like waited for them. The pair approached a daimon, one of the Keres by the look of her.

"Hello, my name's Phoebe. How can I help you?" the daimon asked with a comforting smile.

Pavlina placed a hand on Amber's shoulder. "Amber here didn't choose a god and her heritage is uncertain. Can you help us out?"

"Of course!" The daimon reached out a hand with long, recently manicured claws toward Amber. "Let me see your palm, dear."

Amber bit her lip and looked at the sirin with an uncertain expression.

Pavlina nodded. "It's okay. I won't let anything bad happen to you."

The teenager laid her hand in the daimon's with her palm up. Phoebe traced the criss-crossing lines on Amber's hand, nodding and humming the whole time. She released it and pulled brochure after brochure

from under her desk. She laid one of them in front of Amber, who edged closer in newfound interest.

"Valhalla is a possibility," Phoebe said. "Depends on whether they find enough of a correlation between a car crash and a battle."

From behind Amber, Pavlina shook her head at Phoebe. *Please don't remind this kid of how she died.*

Phoebe pulled out another brochure. "Tír na nÓg is a great contender because of all your Irish ancestry, and that gives you the option to watch over your family as a guardian until you come back."

Amber's eyes widened and her face lit up. "You mean… I can make sure my mom and sister and brother are okay?"

"Absolutely!" The daimon returned to her previous cheery demeanor. "It's part of the deal. You can even be reborn into that family at any time too. So, you might wind up your niece or grandnephew or cousin, even."

The teenager's nose scrunched up. "That's kinda weird but… I kinda like it, too."

Phoebe nodded. "It's a pretty good option, and it's not too long of a wait because a lot of the residents in that afterlife choose to come back after a few years or so."

Amber picked up the pamphlet and read through it, touching the images on its glossy pages.

Pavlina tilted her head at Amber. "Do you want to

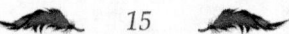

look at the rest of your options?"

The teenager looked once more at the brochure's cover. "No, I'll take this one." She turned to Pavlina. "Please let my family know I'm okay."

"Of course."

Pavlina said her goodbyes and walked back through her portal, which disappeared into smoke once she returned to the mortal realm. Sirens and flashing lights surrounded the site of the crash now.

Finn was explaining what happened to a police officer, but rushed to Pavlina the moment he noticed her. After her wings retreated to their hiding spot in her back, he wrapped his arms around her, and she sank into his embrace.

"Are you okay?" Finn whispered and laid a kiss on her forehead. "Is the girl okay?" He kissed her again.

Pavlina stepped back so he could see her face and know the truth of her words. "It's going to be just fine."

"You were there for a while," Finn said.

A police officer approached the pair. "Is this the first responder you told me about?" she asked Finn.

The Irishman nodded, and Pavlina explained everything she witnessed.

"I also have instructions from the deceased to let her family know she's fine."

The cop shook her head. "Hmm... We prefer to handle that ourselves."

"Perhaps I could come with you?" Pavlina asked. "I can't deny a request from the dead."

"Well… I don't see why not."

At that point, the sirin noticed the middle-aged man standing near an ambulance, wrapped in a blanket and talking to anyone who walked by him. *You asshole.*

"I hope you tested his blood alcohol levels," Pavlina said.

The officer grunted. "We did. Not that we needed to. You can smell it coming off him."

"Throw the book at him, please."

Finn lay in bed well past midnight staring at the downy black feathers forming an upside-down triangle on Pavlina's back. He held back from tracing it with an adoring forefinger. He didn't want to wake his gently snoring girlfriend. She'd had an emotionally demanding day.

As much as she loved her family, and as much healing as she'd experienced since Harper's feather day, none of that dispelled Pavlina's grief. Not even Finn's love could make up for the loss of a husband and a child, nor the absence of Bree and Liz. Then there'd been the girl in the car crash that very night.

Finn hadn't seen the girl, since he wasn't gifted with the ability to see newly-dead spirits. All he'd witnessed was Pavlina shifting to her sirin form, not fully but enough, so that she could guide some unseen person through a portal to the afterlife.

The first time he had seen his love do something like this, they'd been wading in tunnel water, trying to avoid zombies. At that point, Pavlina had shown the terrifying creatures mercy, but it had mostly been to protect the living. Every time since then, he'd witnessed the gentleness she put into this side of her life. She cared. For a moment, she truly loved the departing as her own family. Given how regularly this happened, he understood why grief always shadowed her eyes.

Afterward, she grieved. Pavlina held it back as long as she could, but at some point she always gave in. Trembling and crying, she'd curl into his body. Because she put so much of herself into making sure some stranger's transition to the afterlife was as painless as possible, she took them into her heart, only to lose them—just like she'd lost everyone else.

Finn wondered how many times she'd done this during the time they'd known each other, and he simply hadn't known. He could only guess how many times it had happened over the century and a half of her life. This would have jaded him, but Pavlina's heart was as superhumanly strong as her body, able to lift the emotional burden of loss as well as the physical.

As a legendary warrior, Finn had seen his own

losses, the men and women who had fought with him, those he defeated… his wife. Though, the last one wasn't exactly true. He hadn't seen her die, he'd just experienced her sudden absence from his life. Some druid had kidnapped her, and he'd never found her. She'd be dead by now, but at least his daughter Oisína had earned immortality.

Moving to the edge of the bed, he checked his phone for messages. *Nothing. Still.* He hadn't heard from Oisína since she'd left with Cal, the dimension-hopping bookdealer she'd fallen in love with while still trapped in her book prison. *That's a good thing. She's being safe.* His mantras of her safety did nothing to hold back the tide of worries about anything that might have happened to her. He stemmed that wave by returning his gaze to Pavlina.

She was a dark flower he never knew he needed until he saw her unsmiling face almost a year ago. He couldn't have known she would lie on his mattress, which sagged in the middle, and sleep without any issue.

Over the summer, Plavina had decided to stay at his place, instead of her much more comfortable cookie-cutter home. Too many reminders of Bree and Liz traced the edges of every surface, and she found it impossible to remove them. *More people to grieve. I'm glad I stayed.*

Finn's alarm clock blinked. *12:30 AM. Not as late as*

some nights we've spent together, but I'll have to get used to early mornings in a couple of days. There was no use, though. Finn's stomach rumbled, and his mind raced. With a sigh, he relented to his wakefulness and sat up.

Pavlina stirred and mumbled, "What's happening?"

Finn rubbed her arm. "Just getting a midnight snack. Go to sleep, darlin'."

Pavlina turned to face him and peered at him through a sleepy squint. "I don't want to. I had a bad dream." She sat up and rubbed her weary face. "What if Bree doesn't show up, Finn?"

"She'll show up," Finn said.

"But what if she doesn't?"

"Then we would miss her, but she would be fine in her world with her parents." Finn squeezed Pavlina's shoulder and gave her cheek a kiss. "She'll show up, though. She made a promise, and Bree doesn't break those."

Pavlina nodded. Bree held on to her integrity, even when it meant risking her life. Truth and fairness mattered to her, more than almost anything, but never more than family—and she'd made it clear they were part of her chosen family.

"I still want to share a midnight snack with you." Pavlina slipped off the edge of Finn's bed with one fluid motion and he followed her.

Living in a small, cheap rental meant that no room was more than a few steps away. The two of them fit

in the kitchen like sneakers in a shoe box. Finn leaned over the counter separating the linoleum floor from the living room's carpet, watching Pavlina on the other side as she pulled out some green grapes from the freezer.

Finn lifted one nostril with disgust. "Ugh… healthy food. I'm already immortal, woman. What are you trying to do to me?"

Pavlina handed him a small bowl of the grapes. "If you don't want things that are good for you, then why are you dating me?" She gave him a wink, and he replied with a laugh.

She seems to be feeling better. "Well, I suppose you're right." Finn popped a grape into his mouth. *Gods, these are great frozen. Like tiny popsicles.* "I'll stick to eating all the food you've stuffed into my kitchen."

"I'm going to change your life, Finn MacCool," the sirin said. "One room at a time. Next stop? That corner of the living room you call your *study*." She pointed at his weathered recliner, a new purchase from a nearby thrift shop. Stuffed behind it were piles of books—some on magical application, but most were dollar store romance novels with frayed covers and dog-eared pages.

Finn gasped. "That's my favorite spot!"

"Those books could be in something called *a bookcase*," Pavlina said. "I know being as old as you are, new technology might frighten you, but—"

Finn tossed a frozen grape at the sirin. She tried and failed to catch it with her mouth.

"Okay, fair point. A bookcase would class things up," Finn said. "Wouldn't be such a kip of a place."

"Oh!" Pavlina snapped her fingers. "I think I remember this one!" She tapped her temple, thinking. "Kip means dump, right?"

"You're getting better at this," Finn said.

"I'll miss spending all day with you in our little dump," Pavlina said, walking around the counter to stand close to him.

"We'll still have the night." Finn gave her a sweet peck on the lips. "Let's make the most of this for now." He wove his fingers into her hair and kissed her slow and deep.

Her body leaned into his, the silk of her slip caressing his bare chest. *Could I ever stop wanting her like this? It doesn't seem possible.* Yet, over the centuries, all he could remember about his long-dead wife's face was that she had brown hair and eyes. Pavlina wasn't immortal like he was. One day, she would die and he'd be alone again. He sniffed back a tear at the thought.

Pavlina broke away from their embrace. "What's wrong?"

"You had that vision of dying alone. I won't let that happen to you. I don't care if you're bedridden and as wrinkly as a wad of tissue paper."

The sirin nodded. "I know that's what you want,

 22

but…" She sighed. "It's rare that we get what we want, especially in that last moment."

"No, no." Finn shook his head, the tears flowing now. "I'll be there. I promise. I'll be there."

"Yes, of course. I'm sure you'll love me as long as I'm alive. Maybe even after." Pavlina put her soothing palm against his cheek and wiped a tear with her thumb. "But the vision of my death doesn't mean you left me. It's just a snapshot in time. You could have gone to the store or even another room during that moment."

Then I'll never leave your side again. "Who will be your sirin?"

Pavlina smiled. "Sirins don't get a sirin. Because our afterlife is our greatest treasure, we get an alkonost."

Finn gasped. "Alkonosts guide sirins to the afterlife? I thought they just helped people find treasure." *After all that judgment I saw at the feather reveal, they still deal with death themselves.*

Pavlina shrugged. "Some of them can do more. Only the purest of heart can help dead sirins, and there are far more of them than there are of us. So many will never get the chance, even if they wanted it."

Things made even less sense now. "But if there are so few sirins, who takes care of all the dying? You can't possibly keep up."

"You think only the Russians have death harbingers?" Pavlina chuckled dryly.

She handles death like a day job. "I see. Another product of the Council of Pantheons."

"A good one," Pavlina responded.

Finn nodded. *Not like the Chosen One internship. Not like my sentence.* "It's late. We should go back to sleep."

"But I'm hungry."

Pavlina's hands drifted to his waist and tugged at the elastic band on his grey sweatpants. She lifted her face to kiss his ear. "Just one more snack?"

Finn groaned. *Gods, this woman.* She kissed him again, this time pulling at his bottom lip with delicate teeth.

"Anything you want," he whispered. His hands grasped her waist, squeezing her before roaming everywhere they could. He crushed his mouth to hers and drank her in. Just like their first kiss, she still tasted like chrysanthemums.

Pavlina ended the kiss and pulled him towards his bedroom. Finn stumbled like a drunkard, unable to think or move properly after the way she'd touched him. He knew the way their bodies would move together, the primal, crashing dance they'd share— better than any he could remember.

In his bedroom, Pavlina pushed him onto his bed. "Good boy."

Summer had been a nice break from the depressing

environment of her new home, and an adventure Bree hadn't expected to enjoy. When this reality's parents had told her they would be renting a cabin in Virginia for the summer, she hadn't known it would be at Fairy Stone State Park.

The swimming, fishing, and horse riding had all been fun, but nothing delighted her more than hunting for fairy stones. It was a huge attraction to the park for many and a popular pastime. By the time the Castille family returned to their home in Jacksonville, Bree had quite a hefty supply.

They came home with only days before the school year would begin. As soon as she unpacked her bags, Bree began her back-to-school preparations, which wasn't unheard of for her. This had always been an important part of her life. Though, by the reaction of this reality's parents, it wasn't the way their "Gabby" had done things.

Their family was an odd one. The previous school year, Bree had been picked by the Council of Pantheons as that century's Chosen One, the most sought after internship in the world. It should have been the best thing to happen to her. Instead, it made her the target of a secret, nefarious sect in the Council of Pantheons, and they planned on sacrificing her.

Fortunately, her principal had found this reality where another version of her parents were alive, but her and her sister's doppelgangers had passed away a few years beforehand. So now, she lived with them, and they all pretended they were adequate substitutes for the departed.

The dead girl who shared Bree's face didn't have much in common with her. Bree and Gabby had many differences besides the nicknames they'd chosen for Gabriella. One key thing that separated them was that Gabby was more concerned with friends and boys than she was with school.

After days ensuring that Bree had coordinating outfits for the first week, her school materials were clean and organized in their proper places. Bree felt ready to tackle any big project.

That night before the first day of school, in the gentle lamplight of her bedroom, she sorted her fairy stones into tidy lines according to shape, color, and size on her dresser. She had a few from her original reality that Principal Cailleach had given her tucked into the pencil pouch in her backpack. They would run out at some point though, leaving her with no way to portal over to her school's reality. Bree intended to charge the ones she'd collected that summer when she got to Annie Lytle High. She had at least a few months' worth of stones sitting on the wooden surface in front of her. *After these run out, I'm sure they'll have more ready... Probably...*

The door creaked and Bree turned from her collection to see her sister's sad face at the doorway.

Bree waved her sister in. "What's wrong, Liz?"

Liz closed the door behind her and sat on the end of Bree's bed. She looked up with tired eyes. "They're at it again."

"More fighting?"

Liz nodded.

Mami and Papi never fought like this. Liz had the worst room in the house, the one next to this reality's parents; she heard *everything.* Each fight was always some version of their usual quarrels. Their father worked too much, only coming home long past dinner. Their mother did nothing all day except distract herself from her unending grief. Their grandmother spent most of her time watching videos of people yelling about conspiracies. The more she watched, the angrier and more distrustful she became.

Bree sat next to her sister and wrapped an arm around her shoulder. "They'll get over it. They always do."

Liz shook her head. "This one was different. It… hurt…"

Hurt? "What do you mean?" Having come closer to her sister, she could see red rims around her eyes. *She's been crying.*

"It was about us," Liz said.

Pain lanced Bree's heart. "Oh."

"They were calling us Gabby and Betty again, of course." Liz leaned her head on Bree's shoulder.

Bree nodded. These parents tried their best to get their nicknames right, but the occasional slips continued to happen. Bree doubted they would ever stop.

"And they said—"

A soft knock at the door interrupted Liz. She inhaled sharply, as though caught breaking a rule. Bree squeezed her sister's shoulder. "It's okay," she whispered to her sister. To the door she spoke in a clearer voice. "Come in."

Their mother opened the door, slow and steady, as if opening a tiger's cage. She ducked her head through the crack with an apologetic expression on her face before stepping into the room.

"I'm just checking on you girls," this reality's mother said. "The first day of school can be nerve wracking, especially with Covid still going on."

Liz's sickle cell anemia put her at great risk of dying from this disease. This meant that the family had to keep their distance from the rest of the world. When Bree experienced Independence Day for the first time, something that didn't exist in her reality because all countries were united under the Council of Pantheons' rule, she'd watched the display from a comfortable distance far away from the crowds. That meant Bree would leave for school, but Liz would stay home.

"Bett—I mean Liz." Their mother grimaced at her own mistake. "Do you want to wear that dress I got for your birthday?"

Liz nodded without enthusiasm. "Sure."

Their mother's careful smile wavered. That July, Liz had burst with delight over the dress made of candy-patterned fabric. It even had pockets. Her response this time sounded like she didn't care at all. *She's really hurt.*

"Do you…" Their mother sat down on the chair at Bree's desk. "Do you not like it anymore?"

Liz's eyes widened and she waved her hands. "No, no, it's great."

"I can get you another one," their mother continued. "Maybe you can come with me to choose one. Or maybe you don't need a first day outfit anyway. You're taking virtual classes, after all."

"The dress is great," Bree interrupted. *But you broke her heart with your stupid fight.* "She's just tired."

"Oh, of course, I understand." Their mother's features didn't match any of her words. "I can tuck you into your bed, Liz."

Over my dead body. "Can she stay in my room tonight?" Bree asked. "I'm so nervous about school tomorrow that I think having Liz here tonight would keep me from having bad dreams."

Their mother bit her lip and drew her worried eyebrows together. She looked at Liz and then around the room. She'd already lost this reality's children. Every last thing terrified her that something bad would happen to these almost replicas as well.

"I suppose," she said at last. "As long as you actually sleep. I'll be checking on you."

Bree nodded. "We will. I promise."

Their mother got up from her seat and took a few steps toward the door, but stopped to look over her shoulder at the sisters. "I know you're not Gabby and Betty but I do care about you."

"We know." Bree smiled at their mother as she walked through the door, closing it behind her. *Of course you care. But you'll never love us. Not really.*

Liz got under the covers, and Bree slipped in next to her. The girls curled up on their sides, looking at each other with the weight of this reality in their eyes.

"You excited about your first day back there?" Liz asked.

There, of course, meant their home reality, the one with magic and people that really loved them. They'd never let the parents in this one know, because they'd prevent her from going back to a world that was too dangerous for her to live in.

"I wish I could take you with me."

Liz offered her big sister a sad smile. "Maybe when Hermes and all his evil god buddies aren't trying to kill us."

Bree wanted to guarantee her sister that would happen one day. She and Liz could leave this reality where these strange doppelgangers of their dead

parents were in charge. The Castille sisters longed for the familiarity of their home reality. It was simply too dangerous for them to go back with such powerful beings intent on sacrificing Bree as their Chosen One.

Bree gave her sister a hug. "I love you, Liz."

"I love you too," Liz said, hugging her back.

"Let's try to get some sleep." Bree turned over and pulled the cord on her lamp, blanketing the room in darkness. She drifted off and dreamed of Ms. Sirin, Mr. Finn, and the magic that hummed in her home reality.

TWO

The Welcome Back

The last time Bree had come to the ruins of what had once been Public School No. 4, or Annie Lytle High School in her original reality, she'd been led there on emotional instinct. She hadn't had a plan, only a longing to feel home—her real home. This time, after making big promises to Mr. Finn and Ms. Sirin that she would return for the new school year, she had spent hours coming up with a way to sneak in and out of the facility.

Bree wasn't sure how she'd managed to get through the barriers so easily before. The fence was high, and today there were security vehicles at every corner of the barbed wire barrier. Bree had heard that a nonprofit group was committed to preserving the building and raising funds to renovate it. They suspected that the first day of school would draw superstitious vandals and they'd pay for guards that day. Bree hadn't realized there would be quite this many.

How will I get past these people without them seeing me? The irony was that even a pinch of magic would have worked wonders in this situation. Her brain flipped through one impossible solution after another. I could cast a sleeping spell on… *No magic, Bree! What about making a doorway with a steel beam? Oh, right. More magic.* She sighed, turning the charged fairy stone in her pocket over and over, wishing it could do more than open portals.

There was no use trying to find a cheat. Opening the portal farther away wouldn't work, because she'd come out on the wrong side of the school's protective wards. She'd have to get past the fence the old fashioned way—sneaking in. Bree scurried from bush to bush and post to post, trying to twist her short frame to fit behind them. *I feel like… What did the mother here call him again? Oh, yeah. That Pink Panther guy.*

Then Bree spotted it. A small gap in the fence under the busy interstate overpass.

Being short is useful for once. Bree squeezed her body through the constricted pathway. The road above her thundered and shook. Shattered glass, torn styrofoam, and what Bree assumed was drug paraphernalia littered the ground beneath her. Her heart pounded as she wondered if this would be her last moment alive in any reality. *I made a promise.*

That promise seemed further away than ever when she got to where the gap should have been, but saw that it had been an optical illusion caused by a tree's shadow. If the ground wasn't made of various pieces of jagged garbage, Bree would have banged her head against it. Instead, she slid down the hill supporting the overpass and stared up at the tree between her and the fence.

Maybe if I climb in this and then drop down on the other side... Bree shook her head. *If I break a leg in this reality, I'll be caught. If I do it in that reality, I won't be able to leave the school for the hospital.* Bree puffed out a frustrated breath while weighing all the risks.

She cursed her luck, but couldn't blame the people who'd put up all these blockades. These were volunteers trying their best to keep vandals away. It was a cause she could get behind; anything to keep this former school from falling apart even more. *But I'm not a vandal. I'm a student and this is my school.*

Bree turned the fairy stone over in her pocket, weighing her options. The slam of a car door turned Bree's attention, and she saw one of the guards posted at the perimeter scanning the area. Bree looked around her surroundings, trying to find somewhere to hide.

"Hey! Is someone there?" the man called out.

Too late. If he sees me, he sees me. Bree tossed a fairy stone at the fence, and chanted, "Fairy Stone take me to the Annie Lytle of my home." The man noticed her at last and blinked in astonishment. Before she had to do any explaining, Bree leapt through the opening.

The magical reality pulled her through, as if it couldn't wait to hug her. Bree didn't take a moment to enjoy the familiar buzz of its atmosphere.

"And now we close just as we rose!" The portal wavered for a moment. "And now we close just as we rose!" It shrunk, but rubber-banded back. *Okay, let's try one more thing.* Bree fished around in her other pocket for a new fairy stone and held onto it as she formed a circle with her arms above her head. *I hope I don't look like an idiot right now.* "And now we close just as we rose!"

This time, the portal snapped shut at once. Bree laughed and tucked her fairy stone into her pocket. "Didn't do so bad, did—" She turned to see Principal Cailleach standing behind her. The principal's arms were crossed over her chest and her lips puckered with disapproval.

"I got impatient and shut it for you," the woman said. She yanked Bree's arm with some urgency and rushed her across the school grounds to the main building. "You were supposed to come through a portal on the grounds, not on the sidewalk at the front entrance. What if one of Hermes's allies had seen you?"

Students watched Principal Cailleach drag Bree along. *They probably all think I'm in trouble.* Bree looked at the administrator's determined gaze, aimed at the school's entrance. *Maybe I am.*

The moment they made it inside, Principal Cailleach let go. Bree rubbed her sore shoulder as she explained, "That wasn't really an option. They had people posted everywhere. The front was the only place I wouldn't be seen by people in the other reality." *Except I kinda was.*

"Then you should have stayed home," the stern woman said.

Bree cocked up one eyebrow. "Are you suggesting I should have missed the first day of school, Principal Cailleach?"

"If it means not getting caught, yes." The principal sighed, rubbing her forehead. Then she cast her snowy glaucoma eyes at Bree, holding a rare warmth in them. "You know I've missed you, but not at the expense of your wellbeing."

And she doesn't even know about crawling under the interstate. "Well, I'm here now, and we have all day to figure out a better solution."

Principal Cailleach nodded. "Let's get you your schedule and map." She rushed down the hall, expecting Bree's much shorter legs to keep up with her stride.

Through panting breaths, Bree called out, "I'm a sophomore. Do I really need a map?"

Without turning around or slowing down, Principal Cailleach answered, "Some things have changed since you were last here." She stopped behind a parent volunteer and yanked a map out of his hand. She thrust it in Bree's direction.

Bree took the map, keeping her astonished eyes on the principal. "Like what?"

The principal let out a sharp exhalation, marking her impatience. "To ensure no one could remember where all our security measures were placed, we had to rearrange the campus."

"You mean like move the classes into different rooms?"

"No." Principal Cailleach rushed over to a line of tables with boxes of papers atop them. Bree chased after her.

"Well, what *do* you mean?" Bree asked.

Having made it to her intended destination, the principal took the time to look directly at Bree when she said, "Look at your map, Miss Castille."

Bree did as she was told. The blueprint was nothing like the school she knew. For the first time since her principal had dragged her inside, Bree took a long look at her surroundings. Nothing seemed familiar at all. "How…?" she whispered.

The administrator handed her a slip of paper with

a schedule of classes. "Bell rings in seven minutes. I'd spend that time figuring out how to get to your first class."

Before Bree could say anything like a goodbye, the principal had rushed off to attend some other matter. *Well, it's the first day of school. I'm sure she has better things to do than escort me all morning. It's not like the Chosen One hiding from the Council of Pantheons warrants that much attention.*

Bree's eyes scanned the page to the first line of her A day schedule.

"Advanced Placement Magic in the Humanities," she read aloud. She scratched her head. "I thought AP classes didn't start until junior year."

Tabitha Huey, Bree's unrequited freshman year crush, walked up to her at that moment. Looking down her perfect nose at Bree, she said, "I guess the usual rules don't matter when you're the Chosen One."

"No, I'm sure it's not because of—"

Tabitha scoffed and crossed her arms. "Everything got turned upside down after you took your little sabbatical with the Council of Pantheons or whatever." She scrunched her nose. "They even permanently suspended Jamar because you made up some lie about him threatening you."

"That isn't what—" Bree didn't get to finish that statement. Tabitha stormed away.

Sabbatical with the Council of Pantheons? That's how they're explaining my absence? And Jamar did much more than threaten me. Bree shuddered at the thought of the boy who posed as her friend, but had aided the man bent on sacrificing her.

Bree rolled her eyes. *I've got more important things to get to right now.* After looking up the room number for her new homeroom, she made her way down the familiar, yet much-changed hallways of Annie Lytle Magical Magnet High.

Fresh students with unfamiliar faces entered Finn's room with hesitant steps and nervous expressions. As they sat down at their lab tables, their eyes widened in wonder. Last year, the Council of Pantheons had relocated Finn to Jacksonville, FL to serve the end of his century-long community service as a public school teacher. That was hard enough, but they'd also done it mere days before the school year began. This year, having received the same two weeks of preparation time that the other teachers received, Finn had gone all out to impress his new Magical Application students.

Posters illustrating and summarizing the properties and correspondences of the most common magical crystals took up most of the upper back wall. An accurate, but scaled down display of the light up constellations labeled with their astrological significance hung from the ceiling. This was very much against the fire safety protocols Principal Cailleach had stressed over and over again to the teachers. *But if I'm going to be trapped in a windowless room, I have to have something to brighten the space.*

In previous years, when Finn had time to set up his room, he would display his prized pixie collection. Knowing how much that would upset Bree, however, he kept it at home. She didn't have any classes with him this year. It made sense; most of his classes were freshman level. Still, he couldn't help feeling disappointed, despite assurances that Bree would likely spend some time after school with him.

For the first time in decades, Finn had convinced a principal to put some school funds into backing a Magical Automaton Club. *Principal Cailleach isn't the worst boss to work with. After all, she did help us save Bree.* Students who took part would create little fighters from materials like metal, gears, and charged crystals. Upon completion, they'd put those fighters into a ring and animate them like tiny little mechanical dolls. The automatons would be under their creator's control as they fought to win against the others. *Bree's going to love it.*

Once everyone was seated, Finn handed each student a syllabus. Like every other year he'd taught, he witnessed the shock on young faces as they flipped through the thick document.

After handing the last student her syllabus, he leaned back against his desk and crossed his arms in what he hoped was a casual fashion while taking attendance. Pavlina had spent the last few months convincing him that he'd get more commitment from students if he came off as friendly. The unnaturalness of this act bristled against him more than the tweed jacket he wore.

"You may feel daunted by the packets, but don't worry, that's not your homework," he said. Soft, cautious laughs bubbled around the room, but the students still cast anxious looks in his direction. Finn sighed.

"Raise your hand if you know someone who had my class last year." A quarter of the students poked their palms above their heads timidly. "Now, how many of you heard about what kind of teacher I am before coming into this classroom." Every student raised their hands, except for a boy resting his head against one palm with unfocused eyes pointed at the classroom door.

Finn uncrossed his arms and clapped his hands. It echoed through the room startling everyone, including the boy who seemed half asleep. *Feck. I didn't mean to be that loud.* "I guess my reputation precedes me. That's understandable."

The magical application teacher looked around at the young students sitting at their lab tables. "Take a moment to think about something you've done that you're not proud of, and then think about how you'd feel if everyone knew what you did and judged you for it."

Guilty expressions fell upon the class, even the boy who had previously been close to sleep. *Do they understand? Maybe I need to explain more.* "I wasn't my best self last year. This is my ninety-second year of teaching, and I was... tired... last year." Finn smiled at his class. "But one thing I've never lost in all these years is my love of watching you all learn about this big, magnificent, magical world you live in."

The air in the room lightened. *I do believe I've inspired them!* Then the air conditioner fan kicked in, and he realized the sense of relief had more to do with cooling temperatures than inspiring words. *Ah. Well, I guess it's back to business then.*

"Now, let's crack open this syllabus or, as I like to call it, our teacher student contract." He flipped through the pages of a copy from his desk. "You'll be initialing every page before you sign the last page."

A crackle over the intercom interrupted him. Finn sighed. Of course. *I forgot about this part.*

"Welcome students of Annie Lytle Magical Magnet High School," said Principal Cailleach in her cool voice broken by age. "I trust by now that you've all made it to your classes. If you still haven't arrived, there are volunteers stationed all over school, including the hallways that didn't exist last year. Please ask for their assistance."

A wave at his door's window caught Finn's attention. *Bree!*

Finn took a step toward the door but halted. With a quick look back at his class, he said, "Er... I'll be right outside. Please continue listening to Principal Cailleach."

He bounded over to the door and closed it behind him. Without thinking, he threw his arms around Bree. "Thank the gods, you're back!"

Bree mumbled something against his arm.

Finn stepped back. "What was that?"

Bree gasped like a fish on a deck. "I was saying..." She inhaled sharply. "...that I couldn't..." She held her hand to her chest as she steadied herself. "...breathe."

Finn scratched the back of his head and laughed sheepishly. "Sorry, Bree. Pav—er Ms. Sirin and I didn't have a chance to hang around the entrance to see if you came. I've been worried all morning about whether you'd make it." *More like worried for months, but no reason to upset her.*

Bree smiled. "I made a promise, Mr. Finn."

Finn nodded. "And you always follow through on those." He saw the map and schedule in her hand and the backpack still on her back. "Are you lost?"

It was Bree's turn to look sheepish. She unfolded her schedule. "I've got AP Magic in the Humanities."

Finn's heart glowed with pride. *Of course she's already in AP. Such a smart kid.*

Bree's eyebrows scrunched together. "What's that look on your face, Mr. Finn? You feeling okay?"

Finn shook himself back into professional mode. "I'm fine. I'm not sure where that class is. Can I see your map?"

Bree handed the other paper over. Finn looked over the schedule still in her hands to get the room number and then back at the map. He traced his hands over the newly labyrinthian hallways of Annie Lytle.

"I did everything that made sense," Bree said. "Where I should have turned left, I did. I counted the doors. I looked at the room numbers. I don't know how I could be this lost."

She took the logical steps. That's Bree. "I'm sure you did everything by the *How Not To Get Lost* book. But that may be your problem."

"What do you mean?"

Finn took a quick look back into his classroom. His students were standing with their hands over their hearts as they pledged allegiance to the Council of Pantheons. He returned his attention back to Bree. "I have to rush back. So, let's make this quick. Follow me." He walked as fast as he could without breaking into a sprint.

"Mr. Finn, I can't keep up with you."

Finn turned around to see Bree puffing and

clutching her side. *Ah, yes. My long legs and her short ones.* "No matter. We're here."

Bree looked around, clearly confused. "This is just a wall."

"Rooms don't just go missing; do they?"

Bree nodded in resignation. "Well, no, but—"

Finn knocked on the concrete blocks shining with a fresh coat of white, glossy paint. A door appeared one inch at a time, as if someone painted it stroke by stroke. Bree's mouth hung open.

"Why didn't anyone tell me about this until now?" Bree asked

"They didn't show you at the front entrance?"

Bree shook her head. "Principal Cailleach pulled me inside, gave me this map, and left."

"Well, I hope the rest of your day is less confusing," Finn said.

A man with a curly mop of red curls topping his head and perfectly groomed facial hair opened the door. He somehow made the stylish tailored suit look casual with his easy manner. Up until that moment, Finn had only seen the teacher from a distance. Back then he'd wonder if the man was a supermodel pretending to be a teacher. Face to face, he felt even more convinced that he was too polished to work in a public school.

"This is Bree." Finn rested his hand on her shoulder. "She got a little lost."

The man nodded at Finn with a patient smile on his sympathetic face. "That's been a recurring problem for my class today. I think only half have arrived so far." He looked down at Bree. "Hi, Bree. I'm Mr. Reynaud. I'm very happy to meet you. I've heard fantastic things about our Chosen One."

Bree smiled at her new teacher. "Nice to meet you too." She turned to Finn. "Thanks, Mr. Finn. I'll see you later." She stepped into the class with Finn watching after her.

Mr. Reynaud's eyes focused on Finn, shifting from kind to annoyed. "Please get back to your class so I can get back to mine."

Finn felt heat rise up his cheeks. Embarrassed, he said, "Right. I'll do that—" The door closed in Finn's face.

Pavlina missed her crows, Corbin most of all. *Sure, I'll see them after school, but still.* She'd always treated Principal Cailleach's rule about Pav keeping her murder out of the school building as more of a "don't let me catch you" warning than a firm rule. Now, the sirin didn't have windows to sneak them into her classroom.

Most of the teachers at Annie Lytle were moved into inner classrooms. Some of them were even in hidden rooms contained in pocket dimensions, which were previously only used as panic rooms for the wealthy. *How did Principal Cailleach pull this off with our school's budget?*

Being away from her crows during school felt like temporarily missing a limb. As much as Pavlina loved teaching, she found herself counting down the hours until she could step outside and connect with them again. More important than that, though, was the one name penciled in for the first class right after lunch. *Bree. Magical History 202.*

Like every school year, Pavlina had impatiently waited for her class list during the two weeks of preparation before the school year. This year she felt much more urgency than in the past. Anything could have happened to Bree during her summer break. She could have even changed her mind about coming back to Annie Lytle. *After all, this is a dangerous reality for her.*

Principal Cailleach passed out the class assignments the Friday before the school year officially started, much to the relief of every teacher in the school. *Annoying. Even if I didn't need to know about Bree, I could have used more time to differentiate my curriculum.* Pavlina still managed it though.

Her new students seemed eager to learn, which pleased her, but she was still impatient for lunch the entire period. Just like last year, Finn partnered with her for lunch duty. She could feel her face brighten when she saw him. He glowed at her approach. *I can't be too mad at Principal Cailleach. She cares more than any boss I've ever had.*

When Pavlina got within earshot of the man she loved, he leaned in to whisper, "She's here."

Her chest and shoulders lifted, no longer weighed down with her worries. She held back the joyful tears that burned at the corners of her eyes. *Can't look weak in front of my students. Especially on the first day of school.*

"Look." He pointed at a table in the corner where Bree sat alone, picking at a salad without a shred of interest in eating. Her head hung so low that she didn't even notice which teachers had lunch duty. "She has lunch during our shift. So, at least we'll see her on Mondays."

Though Bree's presence overjoyed her, Pavlina frowned. "She's all alone. She looks so sad."

Finn nodded. "It's hard being the Chosen One. A lot of kids are too scared to approach her and others are jealous."

"Well, I'm going to do something about that." Pavlina took a few steps in Bree's direction before Finn pulled her back. She tugged at him. "Let go."

"Pav, please use your head instead of your heart." Finn's features held every ounce of empathy. "I want to rush over there and hug her myself, but if either of us do that, she's done for."

"What do you...?" Realization trickled in one drop at a time. *The surest way to make sure she doesn't make*

one friend here is if the other students see her receiving
preferential treatment from her teachers.

It hurt not to rush over. Her body longed to move
forward. Her feet ached to continue their trajectory.
But Pavlina forced herself to hold back. "I see what
you mean."

Knowing there was nothing she could do to help
Bree at that moment lowered Pavlina's shoulders from
their former hopeful position.

"You'll see her next period," Finn said. "It will be
okay."

Pavlina nodded and forced a smile. *I'll find a way to
sneak in a hug.*

From the corner of her eye, she saw Tamsin, a
student of hers from last year, cross the room. She sat
next to Bree. The Chosen One, who had been shuffling
lettuce around on her plate just moments ago, smiled
at her old friend. Tamsin reached over for a hug. *I can
imagine Tamsin's excited squeal from here.* Pavlina had
heard it countless times the previous school year.

The two girls chatted away. Then Tamsin pointed
at Finn and Pavlina. Bree's smile widened. Excited,
she waved at the teachers who had done everything
in their power to protect her—who loved her as their
own family. Pavlina waved back. Her heart glowed.
Finn waved beside her.

"See?" he asked. "She's going to be fine. We all are."

Bree turned her attention back to her friend. The two

continued laughing and catching up with each other.

"Yes," Pavlina said. "You're right."

Principal Cailleach entered the cafeteria, bringing her personal frosty climate with her as usual. In the several years Pavlina had worked under this principal, she had always noticed the cold, but chalked it up to her emotional response to the stern woman. When Pavlina learned her boss happened to be a winter deity, the chill made much more sense. *She may be cold, but she loves these students. It's just a tough love.*

The principal panned the room as she approached the two teachers on duty. When she got close enough, she looked at Finn first. "I'm glad to see your first lunch duty shift this year is going much better than last year's."

Finn winced.

Well, she's right. He did egg on Bree, which started that food fight. But then again, maybe I was too tough on him. Pavlina gave his back a discrete pat of assurance.

"Well, I suppose we should leave the past behind us." Principal Cailleach's face softened—a rare occurrence. "You more than made up for one slip up." The principal turned her focus to Pavlina. "I'm mostly here to talk to you, anyway."

This has to be related to Bree. "How can I help you?"

The principal's features shifted to her usual serious tone. "The Council of Pantheons is already asking questions about Bree."

Pavlina's breath caught in her chest. "Questions?"

"Nothing serious," the winter goddess explained. "Not yet. They just want to know where she was all summer. They said they're reassigning her to a new representative, because the previous one no longer works for them."

"They didn't have questions about where he went to?" Finn asked.

Principal Cailleach shook her head. "I don't think they were even aware of the extent of his involvement with her. He was only supposed to give her a mission and designate a mentor. Nothing else."

Finn looked far from content with that explanation. "So they didn't know it was Hermes pretending to be Herald Casmilus?"

"Apparently not," the principal said.

"But... He showed up at the meeting about Finn's daughter," Pavlina interjected.

"That was with a chorus of oracles," the wintry woman explained. "They wouldn't know Hermes in his masked form. Besides, even if they did, the Council of Pantheons asks certain questions of them and they're not permitted to give them anything but the answers to those questions. They can't volunteer information outside of that."

"Why?" Pavlina asked.

The principal waved a dismissive hand. "The Greek pantheon doesn't want to be bothered by mortals for long. Oracles are just tools to them, temporarily tolerated ones. Besides, they don't want mortal opinions swaying godly judgments."

Why would anyone want that kind of position?

"I just wanted you both to be fully informed of the situation, because we need to prepare to face whatever consequences await us." Principal Cailleach followed Pavlina's gaze toward Bree. "I know you both must be eager to spend time with her. Especially you, Ms. Sirin, since she once lived with you as your foster child. But have patience. Give her some space. She likely has much to process."

The principal hurried out of the cafeteria to whatever important matter was next on her list. Pavlina and Finn shared a look full of questions and worries. *The last thing I want to do is give Bree space, but I'll try my best.*

Pavlina caught sight of Bree looking at her. Screw it.

The magical history teacher put on the sternest expression she could fake and pointed in the direction of the cafeteria's exit. The two wandered over there, but not without students watching with curiosity.

Once they were out of view, Pavlina threw her arms around her former foster daughter. "Oh, gods, I've missed you so much!"

Bree nuzzled into the hug. "I've missed you too, Ms. Sirin."

"I didn't know if you'd make it."

Bree pulled back from Pavlina so that she could look her in the eye. "Nothing could keep me from you and Mr. Finn this year."

Past the doorway, Pavlina spied Finn shaking his head. *He knew I'd cave in.* She settled her hands on Bree's shoulders. "If anyone asks, I was getting onto you about your clothes or something."

The Chosen One smoothed down her t-shirt over her jeans. "What's wrong with my clothes? I checked the dress code before getting ready."

Pavlina laughed. "Make something up so no one thinks I was giving you special treatment."

"Oh, yeah." Bree shook her head and laughed. "I don't want to be any less popular than I already am." The teenager waved at Pavlina and returned to her table.

Finn smirked as Pavlina approached him.

"What?" she asked him.

"Nothing." Finn's cocked eyebrow told her differently.

Pavlina crossed her arms. "I waited as long as I could."

"I'm sure you did, my love."

THREE

The Swing of Things

A month into the school year, it still thrilled Pavlina when Bree entered her classroom—a strange mixture of delight and despair. Every time Bree showed up, it reconfirmed that the girl was still alive and in Pavlina's life. It also reminded her that she had to settle for quick hugs and conversations in private, so that there could be some semblance of normalcy in the teenager's life.

As the Chosen One, Bree was subject to unfair judgments from the rest of Annie Lytle's students. Since it was a magnet school, most of these teenagers were ambitious and they were jealous Bree had somehow snagged the internship they all wanted. *They probably all think they're too smart or skilled to die in the quest like the others. Bet they wouldn't be so eager if they knew it was all a sacrificial trap.*

Slowly but surely, the painful practice of keeping her distance worked. Though the group of friends that Bree had accrued didn't hold more than a handful of students, their comradery was true. Tamsin, who had always struck Pavlina as a little superficial, surprised her with empathetic depth and the lengths she would go to for a friend. Now, a small but diverse group surrounded Bree wherever she went, protecting her from the glares and shaking heads.

Now, Bree sat down with the rest of the class. *She may not live in my house anymore, but she'll always be my daughter in my heart.* Pavlina brought up her presentation, and waited for everyone to settle and get out their notebooks.

"Today, we will continue our discussion of the Great Fire of 1901." She watched the young eyes around the room light up with fascination. *Teenagers love a good tragedy.* "The damage caused by the fire led to some pretty ingenious inventions to prevent desolation on that scale again. For instance, underground tunnels were built connecting several banks downtown as possible escape routes."

Bree's gaze met Pavlina's at that mention, both remembering last year's harrowing experience of surviving zombies and a massive alligator while trapped down there. *Even throughout that, the four of us bonded and our lives changed forever.*

"Perhaps one of the most intriguing results came from the Toomer house." Pavlina clicked over to the next slide, displaying the enormous estate owned by the former fertilizer tycoon. "Having lost his home in the fire, Wylie G. Toomer built a new one and incorporated a number of revolutionary spells in the process. Ones we still use to this day."

Tamsin raised her hand just as Pavlina opened her mouth to continue the story. "Yes, Tamsin?"

"Why was he named after a tumor?"

Pavlina blinked. "He wasn't. His name was spelled T-O-O-M-E-R."

"Ohhhh." Tamsin erased several sentences and rewrote them.

Pavlina cleared her throat and continued, "He created a spell for fire resistance that has saved countless lives throughout history, but this didn't stop the—"

"So, like, how does someone get rich off fertilizer?" a student blurted out, interrupting the magical history teacher.

"Please, raise your hand before speaking, Donovan." Pavlina gave the student a firm look that she hoped would stick this rule in his brain. "Jacksonville used to be called Cowford. So you can imagine that it was largely agrarian here and fertilizer was important to the local population."

The boy accepted that, and had no more questions.

Pavlina took a deep breath. "Now, back to the point. What Mr. Toomer forgot to do was properly repair the foundation. 90 years later, it simply lifted off its foundation and drifted onto the St. Johns River, splitting the whole building in half in the process."

Bree raised her hand, and Pavlina's heart glowed. "Yes, Bree?"

"How does a building split in half?" the girl asked.

Pavlina shrugged. "I'm not sure. I just report history. I don't know the full mechanics of it. That would be a good question for Mr. Finn, perhaps."

Pavlina returned to her presentation, clicking over to the next slide. It displayed the house on the river, barely held together with slap-dash materials. "Mr. Toomer had died long ago when this happened, but a descendant of his still lived there. The whole family has a history of magical excellence. So they were able to put it back together again."

Tamsin raised her hand again. Pavlina fought back the urge to sigh. *I just want to get through this lesson.*

"Yes, Tamsin?"

"Is this the house you can see near the Buckman Bridge?" she asked.

That's more like it, Tamsin. "Yes, it's the floating house there. The family still lives there. They have to take a boat onto shore when they need to run errands or go to work now."

Tamsin's eyes widened. "Wow! I just thought it was like pretend or art or something."

"It's very real." Pavlina smiled. "Magic can do pretty much anything."

Pavlina picked up a stack of papers. "Anyway, get out your textbooks. I have some study guides about the spells and inventions inspired by the Great Fire. You can find all the answers in your book. If you have trouble, let me know."

The magical history teacher counted out the worksheets and gave groups of them to the person at the front of each row to pass down. As usual, Bree sat at the front of her row. Pavlina stopped a little longer at her desk.

"Hey, do you have plans to see Mr. Finn after class?" she whispered.

Bree nodded. "Yeah, Magical Automaton Club starts today."

"Ms. Sirin, I left my textbook at home. Can I borrow yours?" a student in the back blurted out.

How many times do I have to tell these kids? "Yes, Brian. As I've said before, you can borrow one of the books in the back. They're an older copy with different page numbers. So let me know if you have trouble finding the chapter."

Pavlina looked down at Bree again, prepared to finish what she was saying before. The teenager was deep into filling out her study guide. *Well, I guess catch*

up time is over.

The girl sitting next to Bree raised her hand. "Ms. Sirin, can we have our worksheets now?"

"Oh, yes, coming over."

One after the other, the students asked for assistance in finding the answers to their study guides. Pavlina didn't hesitate to come over, but she never gave them the direct answer. She only pointed out the passage they needed to read and lent them clues, hoping that the knowledge would stick if they figured the answers out for themselves.

Bree never asked once for any help. She finished the study guide with ease, long before the class ended. She walked over to the pile of books on magical history in the reading corner for early finishers and read up on the St. Augustine Lighthouse hauntings.

When the bell rang, Pavlina kept her eyes on her former foster daughter. As Bree walked out the door, the two exchanged warm expressions. *Gods, teaching her every other day isn't anywhere near enough time. I wish I could at least get to show her affection without the other kids thinking she's a kiss up.*

Much to Finn's delight, not only had the afternoon come for the first meeting of the Magical Automaton Club, but Bree had decided to join as he hoped. *It's*

right up her alley. She can't turn down a new application of magic.

Bins of supplies, carefully organized for easy access, lined the back wall of his classroom. On the lab tables, he'd distributed instructions. Before anyone could get started building, however, he had a presentation to give about the purpose and rules of the Magical Automaton Club, as well as his exciting future plans for the students who participated.

A few students shuffled in, all of them looking tired from another day at a magical magnet high school. *I'm certain more kids signed up than this.* Bree was the last to come in. She walked to her table with a lonely, anxious energy he could sense in his bones. Being the Chosen One was isolating, and she wasn't friends with anyone in this club.

Finn sighed and hoped it didn't show his disappointment with the low turnout. As usual, he clapped his hands to get everyone's attention. "So glad to see you all at our first Magical Automaton Club meeting. I have a lot of exciting things to share, but based on the reactions I usually get to my infamous packets, I'll just share a slideshow and you can jot down what you think is important to remember."

Bree raised her hand. "I was kind of hoping for a packet. I-I like them."

The smattering of students in his room nodded their heads. Finn smiled. *There may not be a lot of students here, but I have the best ones.*

"Well, I can print out the slides. Give me a second." Finn counted the kids in his room and hurried to his laptop. *Glad I sprung for my own printer. I hate waiting in the front office for copies with a heap of other teachers.*

As the warm sheets of paper piled onto the printer's tray, Finn brought up the first screen of his presentation. It displayed a photo of a golem from days gone by, made of clay with a rounded exterior shape and geometrical features within—nothing like what they'd be making in their club.

When the papers came out, Finn realized he'd forgotten to choose the collate setting. He shuffled the papers into piles and fumbled with his stapler as he tried to organize them into packets.

Bree rose from her chair and patted Finn's arm. "Let me help you with that, Mr. Finn. I'll gather the papers and you can staple them. Okay?"

"You don't have to…" *I don't want to embarrass her.*

Bree lifted an eyebrow. "If I want to get home on time, I do. My parents think I'm in a study group right now. They know when I should be back."

Bree plucked the papers up with ease and quickly straightened the packet for Finn. One after the other, the packets were done and the students walked up to grab them as they were created. In no time, Finn was ready to present.

"Now," he said with a smile. "We're ready for a

little history of automatons. I know that's usually Ms. Sirin's topic, but it's important that we understand the origins, so we can do this correctly."

At that moment, his class door creaked open and Pavlina stepped in with a shy smile on her face. "Did I hear my name?"

What is she doing here? "Er... yes..."

"I hope you don't mind," Pavlina said and sat down at a lone lab table in the back. "I'm just so excited about this club I wanted to sit in." She pointed at the projection. "And maybe offer my magical history knowledge if you need it."

Though Finn expected Pavlina's presence had more to do with proximity to Bree than it did to helping with his club, he still loved having her there. "Sound! Your expertise is greatly appreciated."

"Mr. Finn? What's that?"

Finn turned his attention from his girlfriend to an Asian boy pointed at the projection behind him. "That's a golem," Finn answered and looked down at his club roster. "Harold?"

The boy blinked. "I'm Ben. I was in your class all last year, remember?"

Feck. "Right, right. Just joking around, because your name is really Bao."

Ben rolled his eyes. "Well, at least you remembered that."

"What's a golem?" a redheaded girl in the back

asked.

Finn opened his mouth to speak, but Pavlina cut in.

"A golem is a clay figure Jewish sages once used to protect their community from persecution from Pantheon-worshiping purists."

"Yes," Finn said, taking back control of his lecture. "While we won't be making golems ourselves, I wanted to show them as they inspired experts from other cultures to create magical automatons for many purposes." He gave the class a mischievous grin. "We'll be using them for battles against other schools."

"Nice!" Ben called out.

The rest of the students erupted in excited chatter. Normally, Finn would do something to quiet them down, but he wanted to soak in this moment instead. He'd made these young people excited to learn, and Pavlina was smiling at him the whole time. Bree was too.

When the class finally settled down, Finn pressed the spacebar on his laptop, bringing up an image of metal-framed automatons. "Now, let's take a look at typical models used for fighting."

The excitement Bree had felt in Magical Automaton Club was a faint memory by dinner. Her happiness always abated whenever she returned to the grim, magicless reality where she spent her nights and weekends. The only reason why she ever returned was to be with Liz. As much as magic was part of her bones, her sister was part of her spirit. If not for that, Bree would have been happy to sleep on a rusty old cot in the basement with the stench of glawackus dung heavy in the damp air down there.

That evening, Bree could tell Liz was having the same thoughts. While this reality's parents nicked each other with sharp but passive aggressive conversation, the sisters shared knowing looks over their spoonfuls of canned vegetable soup that had been quickly heated in the microwave.

The family dynamic here was more than strange. This was a careful charade. The not quite parents, grandmother, and daughters acted as if they had reclaimed a piece of the past, but it was a warped and fragmented facsimile everyone felt unhappy with.

With all the snide remarks between her parents, Bree decided she'd rather go to bed hungry than listen to another minute of it. She was sure her sister felt the same. After a nod from Liz, Bree opened her mouth to ask permission to leave the table. This reality's father spoke before she could.

"Anyway, how is school going, Bree?" he asked.

Bree settled her spoon in the quarter-full bowl of metallic-tainted broth. "Um, you know, it's school. It's fine."

"Progress reports should be out soon, right?" Their father tilted his head to the side. He did this when he wanted to seem agreeable, but he always had some follow up remark that made Bree nervous.

She resisted wiping at the sweat forming on her hairline. "Yeah, I think so."

"Better be good," he said. "I haven't seen you doing any work."

"Well, Andrew Jackson doesn't require homework," Bree lied. She hated misleading people, but in order to go to her other reality, she'd had to make a habit of it.

Bree had no idea what Andrew Jackson High School's homework policy was. The teenager preferred to do her studying in private. She didn't want anyone asking her why she was writing an essay about a broken house on the river that only magic kept afloat for its residents.

Fortunately, Principal Cailleach was good at creating paperwork that looked official. As long as her parents didn't look too closely, they'd never suspect a thing, and Bree was certain they didn't care enough about her to investigate further. Only Liz cared, so only Liz knew the truth. Though Liz approved of Bree's choice, Bree could tell her little sister was jealous of her frequent trips to their true home reality. *Gods, I can't imagine being stuck in this house all day every day.*

"As long as you bring home good grades, I don't care about their rules," Mr. Castille said. "Even one C, though, and I'll be talking to your principal."

Bree nodded. "Yes, sir. Honor roll or bust."

"Can we go upstairs?" Liz asked. "I'm getting tired."

Their father nodded, and the sisters headed to their rooms, but Liz came into Bree's at the last second. The two girls let out sighs of relief together.

"One more minute of that and I would have died right there," Liz said as she plopped down on Bree's bed.

"At least grandmother was out with her friends tonight."

Bree didn't know if she could have handled the old woman ranting about how masks were an infringement on her rights. *She's probably somewhere with a bunch of people not wearing a mask right now.* The older Castille looked at her sister, fretting about all her time alone with their grandmother.

Liz continued venting, unaware of Bree's worried stare. "If they're going to fight, can't they just get to it? I'd honestly rather listen to them yell than needle each other like that."

"Either way sucks." Bree sat next to her sister. "I wish they had some fighting room they could go to so we didn't have to watch it."

"Speaking of fighting!" Liz sat up with a bright smile on her face. "How was the automaton club?"

Bree laughed and tapped her fingers together like

a plotting villain. "Excellent." She recounted the slideshow of the different types of magical automatons and timeline of how they'd build them.

The whole time, Liz's eyes grew wider and wider. "What are you going to do after you fight them? Does the winning student get an A or something?"

"Well, no, it's not a class, it's a club. You don't get graded for it."

"So, it's just for fun?" Liz asked.

"It's for fun, but we'll also have battles with other schools," Bree said. "If we win, we can get a trophy!" *And it will be displayed with all the others I loved so much on my first day at Annie Lytle.*

"Other schools?" Liz cocked her head to one side. "Are you going to have to travel outside of Annie Lytle?"

Bree had been trying not to think about that. Mr. Finn had been adamant that they'd find a way so that she could participate safely, but she was pretty certain it was a lost cause.

The Chosen One chewed on her lip and fiddled with a stray thread on her pillowcase. Its imperfection rankled her. "I'll at least be able to do the ones at Annie Lytle. That's enough." *Liar.*

Liz placed her hand on Bree's, stopping her nervous twiddling with the thread. "It's okay to be disappointed. I mean, I'm jealous of you getting to go at all, but I know what you get isn't enough either."

Raised voices downstairs turned their attention to the door. Bree held her breath, waiting to see if it would die down or grow louder as their parents made their way upstairs. When the yelling stopped, Bree let herself relax.

"Let's face it," Liz said. "The only way either of us could be really happy is if we were living with Ms. Sirin again." Her shoulders slumped. "I miss her so much."

Bree wrapped her sister in a gentle hug, careful not to hurt her tender abdomen. "Want me to tell her that?"

Liz nodded. "Can you give her a note from me?"

"Of course." Bree kissed the top of her sister's head. "She'll love that."

The yelling rose again, this time accompanied by thundering footsteps coming up the stairs. They each watched the door, waiting for their parents to reach their room. When a door down the hall slammed closed, Bree whispered to her sister that she should get to her room before they came out again.

Liz sprinted out and Bree walked over to her carefully organized row of fairy stones. She was running out of the magically charged ones and would need to bring these to school so they could charge. *So two things on my to-do list: charge some fairy stones and get a fake progress report from Principal Cailleach.*

FOUR

The Exchange Student

Given the quality of the essays she'd received about the Toomer house, Pavlina wasn't certain that moving on to the next part of the curriculum was a smart idea. Unfortunately, Duval County didn't care about that. Teachers were expected to push through a timeline, whether or not students had time to learn anything.

At least some of them read through the St. Augustine Lighthouse materials in the back. Pavlina gave Bree a proud smile, unseen by the teenager. Unfortunately, Bree still had some difficulty making friends. Her one friend in this class had been out sick for days. Since Pavlina had a seating chart, that meant there was an empty desk beside Bree, seeming to isolate her further.

Pavlina brought up the first slide of her presentation, a striking photograph of the St. Augustine Lighthouse. "Okay, so today we're starting our unit on St. Augustine. The haunted history of America's oldest city goes back to Spanish colonization, but I thought we'd start with a tourist attraction before digging into the distant past."

The slide flipped to an image of a translucent man wearing slouching denim pants. His cotton shirt had its long sleeves rolled up to the elbows, but his clothes were mostly covered by a tattered apron. Most notable were the bits of brain matter leaking from his broken skull, only partially obscured by his paint-stiffened hair. He posed for the photographer with his chin raised, not willing to part with his dignity even after death.

Many of the students winced. Bree didn't, however, and Pavlina knew why. The teenager had spent many years with ghosts for neighbors. She may not have liked the experience, but she certainly had grown accustomed to spirits with gory injuries.

"Peter Rasmussen was a hard-working lighthouse keeper in the late 1800s," Pavlina stated and pointed up to his open wound. "It was his work ethic that led to his death. He was painting the lighthouse when he fell. Even when a harbinger tried to take him to the afterlife, he refused, wanting to make sure the lighthouse received adequate care." *Or to ham it up for the tourists.*

Bree raised her hand, and Pavlina nodded.

"But there were a lot of keepers that came after him, weren't there?"

"Well, you know how some people are about how things should be done."

Pavlina saw Bree hold back a giggle, and she understood why. *Sounds just like Finn.* The Irishman was known for his strict attitude with students and his hubris in general. The sirin could only imagine how insufferable a lightkeeper ghost full of criticisms must have been for his successors.

The next slide was of little spectral girls laughing at the woman they'd stolen a bracelet from. "Not all the ghosts at the lighthouse are—"

The door swung open, and Pavlina didn't even need to turn to know it was Principal Cailleach at the entrance. The woman's bracing breeze entered before she did. The real surprise was the girl at the principal's side.

If Pavlina could sum up the teenager in one word, it would be "golden." Her bouncing curls, playful eyes, and smooth skin were resplendent, as if she'd eaten the sunshine and taken all of its warmth as her own. Pavlina had never seen this student before; she would have remembered one with this level of charisma. The sirin half-wondered if she was just eye-catching or a god's secret child.

Pavlina gave her class a quick scan to make sure they weren't too distracted. Most were still scribbling notes, except for two students. Todd was giggling at something he'd drawn on his desk. Bree was staring at the golden girl with large eyes and a half open mouth. *Oh dear. This better not be another Tabitha Huey.*

Keeping a neutral expression, Pavlina turned to her boss. "Principal Cailleach, how can I help you?"

"We have a new student with us, today," the principal answered. "This is Ylva Heidelberg. She's an exchange student from Germany."

Ylva gave the class a nervous wave. "Hello."

"We just got done with all her paperwork, and she's ready to get started with her class schedule." Principal Cailleach gestured toward the one empty desk in the room, the one next to Bree. "That desk will do until we bring in a new one after school."

Pavlina watched Bree's astonished face as the German girl sat down shyly next to her. *She looks like she might pass out on the spot.*

"It's very nice to meet you, Ylva," Pavlina said. "We'll get you set up with class materials."

"Yes, you do that," Principal Cailleach said. "In the meantime, I need to talk to Miss Castille."

Bree pointed at herself. "Me?"

The principal nodded. "Yes, I need to make sure you understand your responsibilities."

"Responsibilities, Principal Cailleach?" Pavlina

asked. Can't this Chosen One business wait until after school?

The principal gave her a cold look. "Every exchange student needs a student partner they go to each class with so that they get accustomed to our way of things. Surely, the Chosen One is the best student to do that."

"Oh, don't you think we should wait until someone volunteers?"

Bree jumped up from her seat. "I'll get her materials. I can go after class to get them for what she's already missed today."

"Looks like she's volunteering right now," Principal Cailleach said. She cast a look at the slideshow. "Now get back to teaching your class about what happens to children who don't follow the rules and wind up getting hurt."

The principal closed the door behind her, leaving the class silent as stone.

Pavlina turned back to her class and noticed Todd was no longer absorbed in his school property defacement, and had his hand up.

"Yes, Todd?"

"W-what did Principal Cailleach mean by that?" Todd asked.

"Oh, well, these girls are dead because they went playing where they weren't supposed to," Pavlina answered. "Let's get back to the slideshow."

"Yes, ma'am!" the boy said and opened his notebook

immediately.

Every student in the class scribbled down notes in haste. *I guess there's something to be said for Principal Cailleach's approach.*

Bree found it hard to think with Ylva smiling at her. She had been briefly aware of a lesson involving the St. Augustine Lighthouse happening in Ms. Sirin's class. For the most part, her attention was on the way the exchange student penciled her letters perfectly into the little squares of her grid paper.

"It's the paper we write on back home," Ylva had explained when Bree had dared to ask her in a whisper. "It's easier for me to write this way."

Ylva's writing looked so tidy, even more so than Bree's, which was a high bar to jump. This level of organization showed in every other mannerism the German girl exhibited. Bree had never met anyone whose approach to school was so relatable.

As intriguing as that was, however, Bree knew the only reason she was so focused on it was because she didn't want to be caught staring at Ylva. The exchange student glowed. Golden locks coiled in perfect, bouncing spirals to her shoulders. She had amber for eyes. Her pink lips pouted prettily on sun-kissed skin.

I meet pretty girls all the time, even before I met Tabitha Huey. Why don't I feel like this about any of them? Bree

assured herself that once she got to know Ylva well, her heart would stop racing. After learning how superficial and inconsiderate Tabitha was, Bree's crush had quickly diminished.

When the last class wrapped up, Bree didn't know how she could possibly wait until tomorrow to see Ylva. They'd barely gotten to talk to each other, and then it had all been about school stuff.

The bell rang and Ylva gave Bree a beaming smile. "Thank you for your help today."

"Nice to meet you too!" Bree held her hand out, as if they had just finished a long business meeting, and immediately felt herself dying under the weight of her embarrassment. *Too late now, better commit to it.*

Ylva looked at Bree's extended palm and scrunched her eyes together. "Is this an American custom?"

"Yes!" Bree responded a little too enthusiastically. "We shake hands with new friends."

The German girl grasped Bree's hand, and the sensation of her skin was so delightful that the Chosen One almost forgot to shake it. The motion was weak and hesitant, as if Bree thought of Ylva's hand as an injured bird.

"Well..." Bree said, not sure what to follow that up with. "I guess you're ready to go home now."

Ylva's face fell. "My foster family can't pick me up for two more hours. I have to wait in Principal Cailleach's office until then." The exchange student shivered, and Bree knew exactly why. The principal's wintry powers kept that room an ice box.

Bree almost offered her condolences but then she remembered where she was headed. "Wait! I'm heading to the Magical Automaton Club! Why don't you join me?"

"Do they have room for me?"

They have room for you and probably fifteen more people.

"I'm sure we can fit you in. Come on." Bree nodded in the direction of the principal's office. "Let's tell Principal Cailleach that you're coming with me."

"Cool!"

The pair sprinted toward the office, each eager to get Ylva out of a miserable situation. When they arrived, however, the woman in the reception area told them to wait while the principal was on an important call.

"It's okay," Bree whispered to Ylva. "Club doesn't start for thirty more minutes. Gives Mr. Finn time to set up and stuff."

The two teenagers sat down on the plastic chairs in the reception area. The enthusiasm of their race to the office had halted, and now Bree had no idea what to talk about. Her brain froze up every time she tried to think of what to say. When Ylva spoke, the Chosen One fought back a sigh of relief.

"What kind of movies do you like?" Ylva asked.

Bree knew this was a desperate small talk maneuver to kill the awkward silence, but she didn't care.

"Mostly documentaries," she said. "About different cultures and stuff. I saw this movie about werewolves for my birthday last year. It was really good, so I've been trying to read up on them and stuff." *Though the stuff they have in the non-magical reality couldn't be less helpful.*

Ylva brightened up at this statement. "You like werewolves?"

"Oh, yeah! They have so many different societies and rituals," Bree answered. "Besides, who doesn't love a full moon, right?"

"Right!" Ylva's response came with a hefty helping of zeal. Her laugh wasn't the golden bell Bree had expected. It was a hushed, breathless bubble—entirely relatable and adorable.

Bree almost got lost in the girl's eyes, when the principal's office door opened.

"Hello, Miss Heidelberg," Principal Cailleach said. "And Miss Castille? What brings you here?"

Under the principal's no nonsense eyes, Bree wondered if she was in trouble for some reason. *Of course not. I've done nothing wrong.* "Oh, uh… Well, Ylva seemed interested in the Magical Automaton Club…"

"Oh, yes, take her there," the wintry woman said with a dismissive wave. "I have much to do this afternoon. I'd rather her do something besides sit still for the next two hours."

The two teenagers leapt out of their seats. They

raced to the door, but Bree stopped to give Principal Cailleach her appreciation. To her surprise, the principal was smirking at her. *Oh, gods… does she know? Does everyone know?*

"Where is the club?" the German girl asked.

Up until that point, Ylva's smile had been beautiful and happy but also shy. This time, Bree saw the real smile, the one you give without thinking. *Dimples. She's got dimples.*

"Um…" Bree pointed down a hall to their right. "It's down there. Better follow me closely. There's a pocket dimension by the water fountain that you could fall right into if you're not careful."

Ylva stayed by Bree's side the whole trip. With every step they took, the Chosen One's heart skipped a beat. As Ylva talked, Bree had to remind herself to breathe. When they finally reached Mr. Finn's room, Bree realized the horrible mistake she'd made. *Oh, gods, what will I do when she turns me down?*

"You should've been there, Pav," Finn said, twisting some Pad Thai noodles around his fork. "Every club member who came in had invited a friend to join. By the time everyone arrived, most of the lab tables were filled!"

Finn had to remind himself to taste the food he

was forking into his mouth. He hardly noticed the hectic but delightful atmosphere of the Asian fusion restaurant he and Pavlina were eating at. There wasn't a thing in the world that was more important than telling her all about that afternoon's experience he'd had with the Magical Automaton Club.

Pavlina smiled at him with a mixture of amusement and genuine joy for his delightful afternoon. "I wish I could have come, but I had to read through a bunch of freshman essays on Constantine and—"

"Gods, I don't know how you can deal with essays," Finn interrupted. "For me, it's projects and tests. No reading for me."

"Says the man who reads three romance paperbacks a week."

She's never gonna let me live down that second giant pile of books she found hiding in my closet.

"That's different, and you know it." Finn took a moment to eat another bite. "A freshman who's barely paid attention in class and slept through English every year isn't the same kind of writer as Gloria Vandiver."

Pavlina chuckled and took a sip of her wine. With her chin raised slightly for a sip, Finn got a nice look at her elegant neck. He'd spent many long nights letting his lips linger there. For a moment, he forgot his excitement about the Magical Automaton Club.

Why am I talking about this when I could be romancing this gorgeous woman?

"Was Bree there?" Pavlina asked, breaking the spell she had on Finn.

"Of course," Finn answered. "She also brought a friend."

"Can I guess who?"

Finn nodded.

"Ylva Heidelberg."

"How did you know?" Finn asked. The shine in Pavlina's eyes made him wonder if it was what he thought.

"Principal Cailleach assigned Bree to be Ylva's student partner." Pavlina took a bite of her spring roll. "Bree seemed much too eager for the position."

"She was also excited to partner up with Ylva to build a magical automaton."

Finn thought of how much the two girls giggled at their lab table while tinkering with gears and crystals. He wanted to feel happy for Bree, but he was also a little worried. "You don't think this is going to be another Tabitha Huey experience, do you?"

Pavlina shrugged, but her face was much less nonchalant. "Bree definitely has a crush on Ylva, but I don't know if it will be like last year. Tabitha is kind of, well… a bitch. Ylva seems very sweet. She'd at least let Bree down easy."

"Maybe she won't let her down at all." Finn was surprised at the hopeful tone coming out of his mouth. He'd spent decades living in pessimism. For Bree and

Pavlina, though, he let it go. He had to. *If anything bad happens to them, it's over for me.*

"That's something I'm a little afraid of too, though," Pavlina said. Instead of taking another bite of her spring roll, she dangled it in front of her wistfully. "What if Ylva feels just like Bree? What then? They can't go on dates. The moment Bree leaves the school, she'll be targeted and—"

A scream from outside caught their attention. Everyone in the restaurant turned their heads to look out the open window. A crowd of passersby rushed across the busy intersection toward Riverside Park.

A murder of crows swooped across the road toward the commotion.

Pavlina jumped up from her seat. "That's Corbin and his friends! Let's go!"

Before Finn could even leave his seat, Pavlina was out the door. Once again, the Irishman promised himself that he'd take up some kind of cardio exercise as he panted trying to catch up to his girlfriend. When he finally did, everything became clear.

A teenage girl, just about Bree's size, shape, and complexion, lay on the ground. Her head had split open and rivers of blood flowed from it. Next to her, a fallen streetlight's glass had taken on the same gory, burgundy hue.

"It happened so fast," a girl nearby whispered into someone's arms. "We were on our way home from the park and then... and then... It just fell out of nowhere. I don't... Oh gods... Tasha..."

Pavlina squeezed Finn's arm with a vise-like grip. "Finn, this isn't right."

"I know," he responded. "Streetlights don't just fall for no reason."

"Not that." Pavlina's big, brown eyes were wide with terror. "I didn't sense this, Finn. Not even a bit of nausea. I sat there happily, eating the whole time. Nothing."

The importance of this statement hit him at once. Pavlina's sense of impending death was hyper-sensitive. If anyone within a mile was going to die, she knew it.

"What does the girl have to say about it?"

Pavlina shook her head. "She's not here. There's no spirit at all."

That's when Finn understood what really had Pavlina scared. "That's not natural. That's not... Do you think it's...?"

He didn't need to say anything more.

"It's got to be *them*." Tears welled in Pavlina's eyes. "Why else would they pick someone who looks so much like Bree?"

Finn put a protective arm across Pavlina's shoulder. Usually, it was this beautiful sirin who comforted him, but there was no facing this alone. The dark sect hiding within the Council of Pantheons weren't so

secretly looking for Bree anymore. They didn't hesitate to do something as bold as killing a similar girl in such a brazen, unbelievable manner. They wanted their sacrifice. It was the only way for them to hold on to their immortality.

Worst of all, they'd somehow found a way to keep Pavlina from guiding this innocent teenager to the afterlife. No one deserved that. That didn't matter to them though.

We're all just pad thai and spring rolls to those monsters.

FIVE

The One Year Anniversary

Pavlina had barely slept the night before. How could she after such a tragedy? *And it wasn't just a young life taken. Where was her spirit? Why did my sense fail me?*

With enough coffee to fill a jug and a purse full of nicotine gum, the magical history teacher managed to trudge through her first class. When she handed back the graded Constantine essays, she didn't notice the groans of students seeing their disappointing grades. Her mind was somewhere between the previous night's dreams and the realization that she'd be seeing Bree soon. *Will I tell her? Should I?*

Bree had a right to know if whoever wanted her dead had kicked things up a notch. However, that information may not even be necessary. Annie Lytle High was safe, and the girl spent every second she wasn't in school in a reality where the gods couldn't travel without risking being erased from existence. Telling her might give her more to worry about, when she was already struggling to balance a new life with a student population that were hesitant to even look at her.

Pavlina went back and forth on this question as she monitored her students reading through the next chapter. She didn't have a chance to settle on a decision though, because Mrs. Selkie opened the door with a hesitant but curious expression on her face. The swim instructor waved Pavlina over.

When the sirin reached her friend, Mrs. Selkie said, "Hey, the front office sent me. There's a detective on the phone asking for you?"

Oh gods. Not again. When the police had arrived the night before, they'd had questions for everyone, especially Pavlina. They heard her last name and wanted to know all the details only a death harbinger would know. But she couldn't tell them anything. Unsurprisingly, that raised a lot of suspicions from them.

"Can you watch my class?"

Mrs. Selkie nodded. "Of course, but…" She whipped her Atlas phone out of her back pocket, and tapped on it. "I've got new baby pics for you when you get back!"

Pavlina smiled. "Of course." The selkie and her wife had adopted a child over the summer. Ever since then, Pavlina never went a day without an update.

Mrs. Selkie entered the classroom as Pavlina left it. Her nerves on edge, she tried to focus on the way her old Doc Martens echoed around the hallways. It reminded her of the 90's, when she'd gotten the shoes and when things had been simpler. She'd fallen in love with Henry. They were happy, *truly* happy. They had plans for a family one day, but made sure to spend enough time exploring life together.

These shoes had tramped all over the streets of New York. Despite the frequent instances of death, Pavlina's role as a harbinger hadn't pulled her into despair. No, she did her job with compassion and empathy. She understood how she was helping others, and most of her days were spent in a beautiful love bubble with Henry.

After Henry and their unborn child passed away within months of each other, Pavlina struggled with being a death harbinger. Death had become more personal. She knew the pain of that loss. As she walked the empty hallways now, she wondered how the girl's parents were doing. Pavlina tried not to think of it happening to Bree or Liz.

When she reached the front office, the secretary said Principal Cailleach wanted her to take the call in her office. *That makes sense. She'd want to keep this under wraps too.*

Principal Cailleach was waiting for her, standing just behind the office desk with her arms crossed. The cold woman usually looked stern and self-assured, but Pavlina could see cracks in that armor now. There was a shadow of worry across those pale eyes.

"Do you know what this is about?" the wintry goddess asked. "The detective wouldn't tell me."

Pavlina nodded. "Yes, I'll let you know everything as soon as the call is over."

That seemed to appease her, because she stepped away from the phone and waved in its direction. "She's on line one."

Pavlina lifted the receiver and pressed the button for line one. The school had never taken to modernizing their technology for some reason. Everything from the computers down to this telephone had been manufactured before Atlas tech had improved anything you could think of. So, there was no way of sharing the call or recording it, and that bothered her.

"Hello?" Pavlina didn't know why she always answered the phone with a question. *What am I expecting? Someone to say 'goodbye'?*

"Hi, is this Pavlina Sirin?" The woman on the other end of the line sounded tired, as if she had asked that question several times that day.

"It is."

"Thank the gods!" The woman let out a long breath that rattled the line with static. "I'm Detective Cassandra Troias and I'm calling about the girl who died yesterday."

No, really? I thought you were going to ask about my car's extended warranty.

"Yes, how can I help you?"

"You're a sirin, right? A death harbinger?"

Here we go again. "I am, but like I told the officers yesterday, I don't know anything. I didn't even sense her impending death. I'm afraid I can't help—"

"Wait!" Detective Troias said in a panicked voice. "You can. I promise. You're not the only death harbinger like this."

Pavlina stood silent for a moment, trying to understand what this call could possibly be about. "What do you mean?"

"There have been a few teenage girls in the county who died in a weird, sudden way like this," Detective Troias explained. "None of the death harbingers in the area had sensed their deaths and they all said there was no spirit to guide to the afterlife."

"That girl last night wasn't the only one?" *This is even worse than I thought.*

"I think there might be some kind of serial killer, one like we've never encountered before, going after these girls." The detective sighed and her voice shifted to an almost plaintive tone. "Please believe me. No one ever believes me when I'm right."

For some reason, Pavlina felt almost magically compelled not to believe this woman. The sirin was used to listening to her gut though, and that intuition told her to keep listening. "Tell me more. I think there's something going on too."

On the way home, Finn listened to Pavlina share the events of her day. Every sentence increased the anxiety within him. The night before had been tragic, disturbing even. The news from today made it even worse.

This wasn't even the first time.

"She described them to me." Pavlina's fingers picked at the thread loosening its hold on her purse strap's seam. Finn made a mental note to buy her a similar one, because at this rate it wouldn't make it through the night. "They all sounded like they looked like Bree. All of them."

"Jaysus…" Up until now, Finn had tried to keep his reactions to himself, but this time it slipped out before he could stop it. "I'm sorry, Pav."

"I'm going to help the detective. None of the harbingers will even believe her."

Finn was having a hard time believing the idea of a serial killer as well. Though there were compelling facts, for some reason, the idea seemed impossible. It felt like anything the detective said must be some kind of lie.

"You don't believe her do you?" Pavlina looked at him with such a hopeless expression that Finn didn't have the heart to tell her the truth.

"I believe her if you do."

Those words created some hint of relief on Pavlina's face, so Finn felt good about fudging the truth.

When they made it to his rental house, Finn handed Pavlina the keys. "Run on in. I've got to check the mail. I'm hoping for a postcard."

One of the highlights of his weeks were the anonymous postcards he received. They were always from some exotic location, often from different realities. They were carried to his mailbox by crows. The mail woman who brought all of the other letters seemed a little put out when a black bird came along and dropped something in while she was just trying to do her job, but Finn didn't care. These were obviously from Oísina, and every one of them meant she was happy and safe somewhere with Cal.

No postcard waited for him this time, and Finn's heart sank. He collected the stack of impersonal letters that waited within. Once inside, he set the letters on his kitchen counter.

"Pav?"

The sound of water coming out of the tap in the bathroom caught his attention.

"Taking a shower," Pavlina called back.

"Okay, let me know if you need anything."

Maybe the shower will let her wash away some of this worry.

Finn returned to his mail to sort it out. He opened his bills, each time with a sigh. A teacher's salary wasn't a hefty one and he'd be rubbing his last two pennies together after taking care of these. When he got to his final piece of mail, he was both relieved it wasn't another bill and disappointed that it was a letter from the Probation Office.

Over the last five years, his frequent visits had slowed down to annual meetings. The dwarf who had handled Finn's sentence over the centuries had grown quite lax in recent years, much to Finn's delight. All he had to do anymore was say he regretted his actions and wave his book around to show he was keeping his word.

When Finn opened the letter though, it wasn't the dwarf's name at the top. It was some woman named Delia Pace. *Feck.* A new person meant dealing with a new way of doing things. It made sense. Finn had known this day would come before his sentence was up. Dwarves lived for a very long time, but his old parole officer had been in his senior years even when Finn was first assigned to him.

After heaving a hefty sigh, Finn read the rest of the letter. Miss Pace had scheduled a meeting for them in six days. She would portal to his home. Finn scanned his rental house. He didn't have enough things to have a cluttered home, but Pavlina was right about him needing a bookshelf for all the books piled in the corner.

Finn knew his home's appearance might not make any difference to a new parole officer, but he didn't want to take any risks. He needed to prove he'd be ready to end his community service in nine years. That meant a flawless work history, the book his daughter was supposed to be trapped in, and obvious life improvements. A new look was in order.

But with what funds?

The bathroom door opened and a plume of steam escaped before Pavlina stepped out. The cheap towel hanging in there barely covered her body. That didn't bother Finn at all, as he eyed her generous curves. Unfortunately, cheap linen probably wasn't going to impress his parole officer if she needed to go to the bathroom.

"You look worried about something new." Pavlina placed her palm against his cheek. "What's going on?"

Finn shook his head. "It's not important. I don't need to put anything else on your plate."

"Maybe I need something not important right now."

Holding up the letter, Finn said, "I have a meeting with a new parole officer next week *here*."

Pavlina winced, confirming his worries that his

home might be less than adequate for an official visit.

"Time to buy some curtains…" Pavlina took a long look at her surroundings. "And maybe a lot more…"

"Yeah." Finn walked from her and slumped onto his couch. "I thought the same, but there's no way I can afford that on short notice."

"Well, there's another way we could do it."

Pavlina bit her lip and not in the sexy way that Finn liked. She didn't want to follow through on whatever idea she had. Still, he had to know.

"How?"

"We could bring some stuff over from my house."

That would do it, but I know why she doesn't want to.

"That would mean going over there, with all those memories waiting for you."

"I know." Pavlina sat next to him and laid her head on his shoulder. "But you'll be there. I know you say this isn't important, but it is. You doing well with your parole means a lot for your future—for *our* future."

Finn lifted Pavlina's head so that he could see her eyes. "Our future?"

Pavlina nodded. Finn was surprised at how much the thought of a future with her lit up everything within him. He was immortal; she wasn't. The future wouldn't be forever, but he wanted every possible second he could have with this compassionate, brave, beautiful woman.

Instead of answering, Finn wove his fingers through

her hair and brushed his lips against hers. She leaned into the kiss, and all at once, he put every bit of passion he had into it, only stopping to lift her up and carry her to the bedroom.

"Our future," he said with certainty, his eyes not leaving hers, as they lay down on the bed together.

The day should have been a good one. Ylva had opened up about her life in Germany, and Bree found every detail fascinating. Apparently, the exchange student's family was huge but also very close. She was the only daughter and the youngest of a family of six. While her brothers teased her for not being as burly and bold as they were, they did everything they could to make sure she never had to worry about anything.

Hearing about Ylva's family only made Bree miss hers, the one that had died, exactly a year ago that day. No one noticed it except for Bree and Liz. Their non-magical family didn't know when it had happened. Ms. Sirin and Mr. Finn were so busy with work, that Bree doubted they remembered the exact date. So Bree spent the day pretending her heart wasn't breaking all over again.

When Bree stepped through the door to the non-magical reality's home, it was quiet and the lights were off. The afternoon light was already dwindling, while everyone seemed to be off in their own corners of the house spending time alone—as usual.

There was homework to do, so Bree took her backpack up to her room. She left it on her bed, though. *I need to see how Liz is doing.*

Bree knocked on Liz's door. "It's me," Bree whispered, knowing that Liz was probably pretending to sleep so she wouldn't have to deal with anyone else.

A moment later, Liz opened the door and waved her inside. Once the door was closed and they were alone, Liz leaned in for a hug. "Gods, it's good to see you. It's really been a day."

"Yeah…" Bree ended their embrace and sat on the edge of Liz's bed. "One year ago today."

"Not just that," Liz said. "Grandmother is really on a roll today."

"How bad?" Bree asked.

"She's been coughing a lot." Liz sat next to Bree, biting her thumb like she needed to consider her next words. "Mother asked her to give me space so I didn't get sick. So of course that led to a speech about how Covid isn't real and how I need to build up my immune system."

Bree wanted to burst out of the bedroom and shake the old woman by the collar. *She has sickle cell anemia, you old hag!*

"Did she go away at least?"

Liz shrugged. "Eventually, but the whole thing wore me out. I already feel like going to sleep for the night."

Bree laid her hand on her sister's forehead. "You're a little warm."

"I've been under the covers for a while," Liz said. "I'm fine."

"Let me just take your temperature."

Liz pointed at a temporal thermostat on her bedside table. "I've been checking it all afternoon. This isn't my first trip to the sick kid rodeo."

The younger Castille's lips smirked, but her eyes were too weary to feign mirth. Liz was more than tired; she needed a break from hopelessness.

"I should have known. You're smarter than all the adults in this house."

"Well, Betty didn't have sickle cell," Liz said with a shrug. "They don't really know what that's like yet."

Bree nodded, but inwardly she struggled against the dim truth of their situation. They had run away from the dangers of one reality, only to encounter great risks in this new one.

While fudging old school records had been all they needed to enroll Bree in a school, no one there asked about death certificates. A hospital trip wouldn't be so easy. They could only hope things wouldn't get that bad. *We have to figure out a plan eventually.*

The door cracked open and their grandmother walked in holding a mug. She looked more tired than usual, but she wasn't coughing. *Maybe she had an allergy earlier or something.*

"My *daughter-in-law* says you've been tired," the old woman said. When she referred to Mrs. Castille like that, it usually meant she was holding back a nasty comment about her son's wife. "She suggested that maybe you caught my cough."

Liz shook her head. "I don't have a cough. I'm just tired."

The grandmother nodded. "That's what I thought, but I thought I'd give you some tea just in case."

Liz took the mug offered to her and sniffed it. Bree knew her sister's face well enough to understand it must smell putrid.

"This is very nice," the younger Castille said without taking a sip. "Thank you."

The old woman smiled. "You're welcome. Make sure to drink that down."

Liz glanced down at her mug. Bree was certain her sister was trying to find a polite way out of this. Eventually, the girl gave in and drank some. She failed to disguise her repulsion and gagged.

"You don't have to like it," their grandmother said. "It's medicinal. It wasn't made for tea parties."

Liz gave a pained smile and chugged the rest down quickly. Bree knew her sister had spent many years taking medicine in far worse ways than a gross drink.

Their grandmother took the mug back. "I'll let you get your rest now."

When the woman closed the door and left the sisters

alone, Liz grabbed a tissue and wiped off her tongue. "That was the grossest drink I've ever had in my life."

"At least she was trying to be nice?"

"I'd really prefer if *nice* came in the form of chicken soup or something." Liz scrubbed at her tongue again. "Like Abuela used to make." She stopped, hands slumping into her lap, and turned her tearful gaze to Bree. "One year today."

Bree nodded. "Yeah."

"It's so hard looking at these people and knowing we'll never see our real family again."

Bree pulled her sister close so that Liz could rest her head on her shoulder. "Well, you and I are a real family. At least there's that."

SIX

The Deep Stuff

Two weeks passed since the death anniversary of Bree's true parents. Though sad, Liz seemed fine physically throughout that period. Their grandmother still insisted on giving her the occasional sip of tea when she showed any weakness. Bree suspected it was more to prove she was right to her daughter-in-law than out of any real concern over Liz.

Still, it gave the older Castille sister some relief to know that preventative measures were being taken. With her birthday growing closer and closer, all Bree wanted was for her sister to feel well so that they could have a slice of cake and watch pixies flit about the backyard like they did as little girls. Even if her sister remained in good health, the non-magical reality had never once been graced by a single pixie. *Guess we'll make up for it with more cake.*

When not at home, Bree savored every last moment during her days at Annie Lytle Magical Magnet High. She also enjoyed every laugh and story she shared with Ylva. They came from totally different worlds, but had so much in common. The German exchange student also wanted to go into law so she could protect often misunderstood races such as dark fae and vampires from oppressive laws.

Ylva was especially interested in representing werewolves. Bree had never known anyone who knew as much about them in her life. Even with all the documentaries Bree had seen, Ylva expanded on her knowledge with additional details and facts. Underneath her sweet, innocent surface, the golden-haired girl had an impressive brain. *Ugh. I'm crushing so hard.*

During Magical Automaton Club, the two chatted and giggled as they worked on their creation. Most of their conversation was about how to improve their work and what would set it apart from the competition.

"Do you have plans for this day next week?" Ylva asked, turning the tiniest screwdriver with precise, delicate rotations.

Is she asking me on a date? No, of course not. "Wouldn't mind crushing the competition during our first automaton battle."

"That's definitely happening!" Ylva held out her palm but her eyes remained on the joint she'd just created with a small pin. "Can you give me the tourmaline?" When Bree handed it over, the golden-haired girl continued, "Anything else? Something special?"

It took Bree a moment to realize what Ylva was hinting at. "You mean my birthday?"

Ylva held up a finger and hushed Bree. "Don't say that word too early! You want bad luck?"

You brought it up. "I don't really believe in luck or fate or anything like that."

The German exchange student's face took on a forlorn shadow. "I wish you were right."

Before Bree could ask what Ylva meant, Mr. Finn approached their table. "You two are creating something very different. Going for agility over strength?" He waved at the other tables. The other automatons were gigantic compared to theirs, but Ylva had pointed out long ago that this meant they would have difficulty with speed.

"A giant can't swat a deadly bee," Ylva said with a devious sparkle in her eyes. To demonstrate, she snapped her fingers and a needle-like appendage protruded from the automaton's wrist.

Bree found it remarkable that the golden-haired girl could switch so easily from melancholy to mischief.

It was impressive, but it troubled her a little. She wondered if she knew the real Ylva.

When Mr. Finn moved on to another table, Ylva's improved mood continued and Bree felt tempted to let it go. Then she remembered all the times she wished her friends had asked if she was okay when she pretended everything was fine.

"Ylva, what did you mean by that?"

Ylva's eyebrows tented with confusion. "What do you mean?"

"About luck and fate," Bree said.

"It's nothing. I was just being silly."

Ylva pressed the tourmaline into the setting they'd created on the top of the automaton's spine, but Bree pulled their creation away.

"I know how you look when you're being silly. Your face showed the opposite."

The German girl sighed and cast a serious expression at Bree. "I know you've experienced a lot of pain, but there's one way you're much luckier than you think."

"What's that?"

"You were born a human."

"I'm not human. I'm a witch. I have a mageiathalamus."

"Passing for human, then," Ylva said. "It's a privilege."

Bree bristled at the last word. *Am I privileged for*

growing up in a poor neighborhood, for my parents dying, for being hunted by certain gods? "Wow… okay…"

"It's not a bad thing. I have privileges you don't… I mean other people… not just me." Ylva paused and swallowed. "Why do you think I want to represent misunderstood supernaturals? Fate wasn't kind to them. Just because they were born a certain way, people treat them like monsters. Many of them aren't even allowed at social events at night in my country! I mean they think werewolves are all wild, savage animals who can turn others into one with a bite, like it's a *curse*. They only stopped hunting season on them sixty years ago!"

"That's awful," Bree said. "But that's not fate. That's genetics and bigotry."

Ylva said nothing else. She only looked at Bree with disappointment in her eyes. She pulled the automaton back and clicked the tourmaline place. She grabbed another one from their kit and continued. For the rest of the afternoon, the golden-haired girl was all business.

Pavlina was glad she had helped Finn by bringing over stuff from her house to make his more presentable. When she'd left for work that morning, Finn's place looked respectable, perfect for convincing a parole officer that he'd turned a positive corner.

It hadn't been easy, though. The entire time she packed up items for Finn's place, she chewed at a giant wad of nicotine gum to manage her stress. Even her crow friends seemed to pick up on her mood. Every time she passed by a window, she spied Corbin and his murder watching her. *You know they pity you when they don't tap on the glass to beg for snacks.*

Despite seeing Bree frequently at school, the reminders of their life together still stirred a painful nostalgia in her heart. The traces of Liz throughout her home especially hurt. She thought of those small hands, ones that looked so childlike for a middle schooler. They would grow without Pavlina watching. She would never hold them again. She would never feel them becoming those of an adult. *Snap out of it. Things might change. Liz might come back.*

To reward herself for pushing through the pain and getting the job done, Pavlina decided to spend the afternoon with Mrs. Selkie while Finn met with his parole officer. For many months, Finn and Pavlina had existed in a bubble no one else could enter. It was a common mistake many couples made, but she didn't want to lose her friends. *I had no one but my mother and sister to turn to when Henry died.*

In the past, Pavlina had only seen Mrs. Selkie's house in passing. She'd chauffeured her there on occasion or stopped by to drop off something her friend had accidentally left at school. The magical history teacher had never seen beyond the entrance hallway before. She wasn't sure what she had expected, but it wasn't this.

Mrs. Selkie's house was the only one Pavlina had seen with a deck that acted as a ramp into the water. Long strands of Mika's hair, wet and caked with algae, could be found on surfaces, especially around the bathroom sink. This was far from the only mess in their home. Sports equipment cluttered the corners. Water stains on cushions and wooden surfaces were everywhere to be seen. Scores of Mrs. Selkie's many scrunchies were scattered around.

Is this what happens when you have a baby? How does someone live like this?

That afternoon's plan was to work on a gift for Bree's upcoming birthday. They planned on making a silk purse lined with magical thread for her fairy stones. The hope was that it would help the rocks hold their charges longer.

With very little space to work in, the two settled on working at the kitchen table while Mika fed their newly adopted son, Zennie. Unfortunately, this proved incredibly stressful. The baby howled in protest in his highchair, refusing the spoonful of avocado Mika was trying to feed him. He turned his cherubic cheeks away and used his tentacled appendages to pull himself out of his seat and crawled down the back of the chair until he reached the floor. His human face shone with triumph while his lower octopus half wiggled with delight.

Mika slumped in defeat and cast an exhausted look at her wife. "Erica, I don't think this is going to work."

"We've got to try," Mrs. Selkie said. "I know cecaelias prefer clams, but I doubt that will be on the lunch menu when he gets to elementary school."

Hearing Mrs. Selkie called by her first name felt strange to Pavlina. She knew it, but had become so accustomed to her friend's "teacher name" that anything else felt like a costume.

"You could maybe try gradually building up to human food?" Pavlina offered. "Like give him some imitation crab or something?"

Mika responded by giving Pavlina a withering stare, and then turned her attention to Mrs. Selkie. "I'm going to see if I can settle Zennie in his tank for a nap." With that, the rusalka scooped the baby off the floor and walked to his room.

Pavlina leaned in to whisper to her friend. "I'm sorry. I wasn't trying to overstep."

"Don't worry," Mrs. Selkie replied. "It's not you. Mika's still convinced you were hitting on me at that Yule party five years ago."

"That's ridiculous."

"I know!" Mrs. Selkie threw her hands up for emphasis, letting the ribbon she'd been working on fall to the table. "No matter how many times I tell her you're straight, she tells me I'm wrong."

"Well, I mean, I definitely don't think of you as anything other than a friend," Pavlina said. "But Mika's right. I'm not straight."

Mrs. Selkie laughed. "You're dating the most obviously cishet man I've ever seen."

Pavlina set the strip of magical thread she had in her hands on the table. "I'm bi. I've told you that. I was in a relationship with a woman for decades."

"And her husband," Mrs. Selkie said with an arched eyebrow. "Come on now. That was a phase. You were in it for the threesome, and then you settled down with a man when that ran its course."

Stunned, Pavlina could only sit there blinking at her friend for a moment. Until that moment, she'd always felt like Mrs. Selkie accepted her for her true self. All this time, it turned out her friend had only seen her as an ally.

The shock shifted to indignation soon enough, and Pavlina found words again. "Just because I'm with a man now doesn't mean I'm not bi. You don't get to decide who counts as bi and who doesn't. I know my own mind and my own heart."

"I'm sorry. I just… I mean it always seemed like…" Mrs. Selkie stammered.

"It wasn't just a phase," Pavlina continued. "Even if I'd never been with a woman, it doesn't change who I am or what's in my heart."

Mrs. Selkie was usually the peppy sort, but at that moment she looked serious and remorseful. "I'm sorry."

Ugh. She's like a puppy dog. I can't stay mad at her. "And I'm sorry we haven't spent more time with you, lately."

"Honestly, with Zennie, we wouldn't have much time to spend together anyway." Mrs. Selkie gestured around the house. "I mean look at our house. Having a baby who has the escape skills of an octopus and the stubbornness of a human leaves us too busy to even keep the house livable."

"Good thing he's super cute."

Mrs. Selkie's face lit up. "I know right? He's grown so fast since we adopted him. Cecaelias mature much faster than most kids. Right now, he's a baby, but in less than a year he'll be ready for preschool."

Pavlina wondered what that was like, to watch the baby you love grow up, discovering piece after piece of the puzzle this person was. She thought of the parents who just lost their teenage daughters. Their journey was cut too short.

"Take a million pics," the sirin said. "And a million more and hold him for as long as he'll let you."

"You okay?" Mrs. Selkie tore off a piece of paper towel from the roll on the table and handed it over. "You're crying."

"I am?" Pavlina grabbed the paper towel and wiped her cheeks. "Gods, it's been a rough few days."

With a comforting smile, the swim instructor pulled up photos of Zennie on her phone. "Want some cuteness to drown all that out?"

Anything to stop thinking about Bree or Liz dying. "Definitely."

Mrs. Selkie squinted at her phone. "Oh, that's weird. I guess I recorded us talking on accident. It's the last thing on here." The selkie blinked and shook her head. "And now it's gone. Must have been in my imagination. I need to get more sleep."

Finn's home didn't look like the cheap little house he'd rented when he moved to Jacksonville, FL. It looked clean and cozy with its generic, department store throw pillows and high thread count towels. This wasn't Finn's style at all. He was more of a rustic type, but it was perfect for convincing a parole officer he was more responsible now.

Still, he was worried. Finn compulsively rubbed the spine of the book which had once trapped his daughter with his calloused thumb. When Oísina escaped it, she cast a spell on it so that it would seem as if she were still inside. As talented as she was at magic, Finn feared this new parole officer would figure out Oísina was gone.

It seemed like an eternity before a portal finally appeared in his living room. Most portals resembled some ethereal magic or a mysterious door of some sort. This one was a manilla envelope that opened up a far larger opening for Delia Pace to walk through. She kept her eyes on the Atlas tablet in her hands with each step.

Finn cleared his throat and said in a rapid, perfunctory voice, he said, "It's nice to meet you, Ms. Pace."

The parole officer looked up at last and gave him a friendly, professional nod and smile. "Hello, Mr. MacCool." She glanced at the book and employment records in his arms. "I'm grateful that you were prepared for me, but I won't be needing those."

"You... you won't?" Relief and suspicion battled each other, and Finn had no idea how to feel about this revelation.

Ms. Pace waved at the book. "My records show that the Oracles reset the curse on your book when you communicated with them that it had accidentally been opened by a third party. There's no reason for me to believe you would lie about having it."

Well, that's logical. "And my employment records?"

Ms. Pace tapped on her tablet screen. "Are on record electronically, along with periodic reports from your employer."

Gods, I hope Principal Cailleach has been kind.

"Oh, well, I guess, I'll move on to the next step then," Finn said. "I regret my actions against the Council of Pantheons and will do my best to be a better citizen."

The new parole officer stared blankly at Finn for a moment with her head tilted to the right. "Is that what Mr. Digli had you do? Just throw some proof on his desk and regurgitate a memorized oath?"

"Well, I mean… What else do you do during a parole meeting?" As soon as Finn said it, he realized how little he knew about the whole parole process.

"My job is to rehabilitate you, not chew you up and spit you out," Ms. Pace said. "And if that oath is as genuine as your robotic tone, it's worthless."

Finn gasped. "No, I do mean that! I regret what I did!"

"Oh, I'm sure you do." Ms. Pace fished a binder out of her messenger bag and flipped through the pages. "It got you in a lot of trouble. I don't think you care a smidge about the Council of Pantheons, though. If I had to guess, I'd say you resent them for the situation you're in. Am I close?"

The Irishman said nothing. *I only had nine more years of this charade. Now this.*

"Yeah, that's what I thought." Ms. Pace tapped on the desk. "Look at me, Mr. MacCool."

Finn lifted his head and took in his parole officer's face with his burning eyes. *Stay cool, MacCool.*

"By the end of our time together, you're going to be a better man." Ms. Pace gave him the same professional smile she'd greeted him with earlier. "Given that I have most of a century of mismanaged parole, we have a lot to catch up on."

Oh, gods. Does that mean what I think it means?

"Now, I don't want to interrupt your work schedule. That's an important part of your rehabilitation and one that seems to be working." She pulled the rings in her binder apart and pulled a sheet of paper out. "I'll be portaling to Jacksonville every other Saturday so we can make progress. I'll be assigning homework at each visit."

Feck. "Please don't go through the trouble of working on a Saturday. It's really not—"

Ms. Pace held up a hand, stopping him. "I *care* about my job, Mr. MacCool. I care about helping ex-convicts find redemption. I'm not going to give up on you just because I enjoy free time on the weekends."

"R-redemption." Finn hated the positive emotional response that word stirred with him.

Ms. Pace handed over the paper she'd just taken out. It read "Exercise One" at the top.

"That's right, Mr. MacCool. Redemption."

SEVEN

The Birthday

It wasn't Pavlina's day to teach Bree's class, and she was glad. Keeping surprises a secret wasn't her strong suit, and she wanted to make sure that her former foster daughter didn't expect what was coming to her at lunch time.

With Mrs. Selkie's help, she'd made several gifts she was sure Bree would enjoy or would at least find helpful. There was the fairy stone purse, of course. She'd also made self-repairing book covers for the teenager's textbooks, a pencil case with a spell to reclaim anything that accidentally fell out of it, and a cute little werewolf stuffy. *I hope it reminds her of the documentary we saw for her last birthday.*

Finn had purchased the grid paper Ylva used,

because Bree kept talking about how much smarter it was to use than the lined stuff Americans used. As boring as that present seemed to Pavlina, she was sure Bree would love it.

To everyone's surprise, Principal Cailleach had offered to bake the cake. Mrs. Selkie had joked privately that their boss was so cold that it would probably be ice cream cake. Humor aside, they were all a little worried about the dessert's quality. No one had the guts to suggest they should buy one from the grocery store instead though.

When Pavlina saw what the principal created though, she felt bad for her assumptions. The wintry goddess had a hidden talent for baking. It was a sheet cake that looked just like a textbook. It read, "Great Birthdays 101." It smelled so good that Pavlina wanted to bury her head in it.

"It's lemon," Principal Cailleach explained in the most deadpan voice anyone had ever used to explain a birthday cake. "The frosting is orange and vanilla flavored. I seem to recall you got her a similar cake last year."

Mrs. Selkie stared at it with awe-widened eyes. "It's… it's… so beautiful."

"I watch a lot of baking shows."

From behind their boss's shoulder, Finn mouthed to Pavlina, "Can you believe it?"

"Lunch has a time limit," the principal said, her feet

already moving toward the cafeteria.

The other three chased after their boss, presents in tow.

There had been some debate about whether they should show up at lunch like this. It would surely look like special treatment to the other students, but pretending that Bree wasn't part of their found family hadn't worked. Most of the other students didn't regard Bree as one of them. The few that had warmed to her were already sitting at her table giving her birthday wishes.

When they showed up with the cake and presents, Pavlina was relieved to see that the friends Bree had made were just as pleased and surprised as she was.

Bree gasped with surprise. "You got me a cake?" Her eyes flashed wide again. "And presents?"

"Of course we did," Finn answered. "Did you think we'd just let it go by without doing anything?"

Principal Cailleach set the cake down on the lunch table and everyone, classmate friends included, sang the "Happy Birthday" song. The birthday girl blew out her candles and Mrs. Selkie set about cutting everyone a slice.

From her peripheral vision, Pavlina noticed the envious glances of other students who were stuck with mystery meat and apple sauce for lunch. Before she had a moment to feel bad for them, the cafeteria workers passed out plates of vanilla sheet cake to them. A pleased buzz of voices told Pavlina that no one would resent Bree's birthday surprise. *Principal Cailleach was prepared for anything.*

Bree opened the presents one by one, fawning over each. "I didn't think anything special was going to happen today."

"Well, what about at home?" Ben from the Magical Automaton Club asked.

Bree's smile falter for a half second. "Oh, they've been a little busy."

"Too bad you couldn't stay with Ms. Sirin," he mumbled and frowned.

The story they'd given the school district was that the system had found a distant relative of Bree's and Liz's who wanted to take them in. To those that cared, it was quite a sad tale. It wasn't far from the truth either. Today wasn't about what they'd lost though. It was a chance to celebrate.

Bree opened her last present, the cute werewolf stuffy. "Oh wow! Thanks, Ms. Sirin!"

While Bree's smile brightened, Ylva's fell.

"This makes werewolves look like animals," the German girl said. "Look, it's snarling and its clothes are in tatters."

"That's not a snarl; it's a smile." Pavlina traced the mouth to demonstrate, but as she did so she saw what Ylva was talking about. "Well, at least it was supposed to be a smile. It's harder than you'd think to make a

stuffie look happy with wolf fangs."

"You could have just bought a werewolf doll," Ylva said. "They sell them at stores. It normalizes them for non-werewolves by showing their human side."

The words wounded Pavlina with their honesty. She hadn't considered the human aspect of a werewolf when she made the toy. In her mind, it was like a cute, puppylike wolf. It was the same as if someone had made a blackbird stuffy of a sirin.

"You're right," Pavlina said. "I'll do better next time. Thank you, Ylva."

Ylva looked surprised by the apologetic response. "Thank you for listening. People don't usually listen."

Pavlina's phone buzzed in her pocket. Bree and her friends were busy stuffing their faces and moaning over the delicious lemon flavor, so Pavlina pulled it out to see a text from Detective Troias. The message was grim.

Another teenage girl had died, and no harbingers were nearby. The detective wanted to know if Pavlina could come to see if there was a soul to guide to the afterlife.

Finn sidled up beside her. "Is everything okay?"

Pavlina shook her head and tilted her phone at him. Finn's face darkened.

"I'll let Principal Cailleach know you need someone to cover your afternoon classes."

"What about Bree?" Pavlina asked. "It's her

birthday."

"You need to do this," Finn said. "Not just for those girls, but for Bree too."

Since their disagreement a week ago, Ylva had been a little distant from Bree. She wasn't unfriendly. In fact, she would joke around still. Bree could tell she was holding back though. She didn't share as much about her life in Germany as before. As trivial as having a difference in a simple belief seemed before, Bree wished she'd simply let her stance go. It wasn't worth losing her one good friend.

Bree had assumed it would be just the same on her birthday. Surprisingly, Ylva had warmed up to her a little. After she had opened her presents and eaten her cake, the golden-haired girl took Bree to her locker so she could give her a special gift—an antique book on werewolves.

It was unexpected. More than that, the gift showed her that this German exchange student understood her more than any other friend she'd ever had.

"I'm sorry that it's worn on the corners and the cover is faded," Ylva said, handing the book over to her. "I remembered you like werewolves a lot, but I didn't have money to buy you some newer books."

"Are you kidding me? This is a treasure!"

Bree applied a feathery brush of her fingers across

the golden letters on the cloth-covered hardback book. This was easily from as far back as the 1940s or 1950s, when anthropologists wrote about their experiences with werewolf communities that had remained hidden for centuries.

As she flipped through the pages, the detailed illustrations on yellowed paper almost blended together like an old movie. This wasn't something you picked up from the bookstore. People spent their entire lives hunting down limited-edition books like this.

"I feel bad accepting this gift," Bree admitted. "It must have been so expensive."

Ylva shook her head. "My family actually has three copies of it. I took the one in the worst shape with me here."

"Three copies! How?"

"When it came out, my whole town bought copies." Ylva lightened her backpack by placing several textbooks back in her locker. "The writer lived there, and we were all so proud."

"That's so cool!"

Bree scanned the Table of Contents. *Physiology p. 10. Traditions p. 43. Values p. 129. Power Dynamics p. 301. Common Misconceptions p. 445. This goes on for nearly 800 pages!*

"I know how I'm spending my weekend!" Bree slipped it into her backpack. "Can't wait to talk with you about it on Monday."

Ylva's eyes widened. "Monday? You're going to read all of that over the weekend?"

Bree shrugged. "Well, I'm going to start tonight, obviously."

"How does anyone read that fast?"

"I'm a fast reader," Bree explained. "You're super smart. You must read a lot too."

"No, I have dyslexia. It's part of why I won't switch from grid paper to lined."

The bell rang before Bree could find out more, and the two girls had to leave for their next class. Unfortunately for Bree, it was Gym. She groaned, while Ylva dashed ahead. The golden-haired girl loved anything physically active, and she was always the first one picked when it came to anything team related. Bree was the last.

Bree dragged herself into the gymnasium, hoping her cadence looked more like an amble than a march to the guillotine. The other students already avoided her since she was the Chosen One. In Gym class, they outright loathed her because she couldn't dribble a basketball.

By the time she got in her uniform and on the court, Ylva was already practicing her shots. With each swish of the net, the exchange student's smile widened and Bree wondered how anyone could be so perfect.

A whistle echoed across the gymnasium. Bree turned to see that Mrs. Selkie, not Miss Banshee, was

approaching. As always, the swim instructor and health teacher had her hair pulled up into a frizzy ponytail. With her seal skin tied around her waist and her shoes worn and scuffed, she looked absolutely delighted to be there.

"Sorry, kids," Mrs. Selkie said when she reached the group. "Miss Banshee called out from work with a sore throat. Looks like I'll be teaching today."

"That's okay, Mrs. Selkie," one of Bree's classmates said. "We'll still have fun playing."

The selkie teacher shook her head. "Sorry, but she left instructions that today was just pass and dribble practice."

Everyone groaned at once, except for Bree. *Maybe I can partner up with Ylva and no one will feel stuck with the girl who sucks at sports.*

"I'm calling out partners from this list she left; please form a line on your colored markers across from your partners." She pulled a folded up sheet of paper from her pocket and with a booming voice read names, one after the other, "Tamsin blue marker with Edward yellow marker. Bree blue marker with Ylva yellow marker."

Bree's heart leaped at those words and she nearly clapped with joy. She couldn't believe her luck. Not once during the school year had she and Ylva even wound up on the same team. She ran to her place and beamed at the golden-haired girl as the other pairings lined up.

Mrs. Selkie passed each pair their own basketball. When she reached Bree and Ylva, the German exchange student declined. "We have a ball already."

The teacher took the ball from Ylva's hand and walked to Bree's side. "I'd rather you use my ball." She placed the new ball in Bree's hands and leaned over her shoulder to whisper, "I put a special little crystal inside. It's illegal for official games though, so don't tell anyone." Mrs. Selkie winked. "Happy Birthday."

Energy, radiating from the ball, buzzed up Bree's fingers all the way up to her shoulders. Her body felt lighter and stronger. A euphoric spark lit within her.

From several yards away, Mrs. Selkie called out, "Three dribbles and pass!" A sharp whistle signaled the start.

The moment the basketball left Bree's hands, she could physically feel the velocity and angle of its departure in her fingers and palm, the direction it bounced from the floor. Like a magnet, it pulled up to her palm again. The next two dribbles were even more effortless. When it came time to pass over to Ylva, Bree saw the trajectory before she tossed it. It made a perfect arc toward the golden-haired girl and planted into her hands as if it had always belonged there.

For a moment, Ylva stared at Bree, absolutely gobsmacked at the Chosen One's sudden proficiency with a basketball. Obviously, Mrs. Selkie hadn't let her in on the secret, giving Bree an opportunity to impress her crush.

"How... how?"

Bree shrugged. "Lucky day, I guess."

With a bright smile, Ylva took up her part, and the two had a blast for the rest of class while everyone else performed the exercise like it was a pop quiz.

This is a good day. This is a great day! This might be one of my best birthdays yet.

The day had finally come, and Finn was brimming with excitement. As much as he had enjoyed the small lunch celebration he'd had for Bree's birthday, that afternoon would be even more thrilling. *The first magical automaton battle!*

Principal Cailleach's secretary had actually set up individual battle rings on the grounds right behind the school, but still within the safe confines of the magical barrier. They looked a little like table-top roller rinks.

The only thing that would have made the setting better was if the afternoon heat hadn't been so oppressive. Samhain was less than two weeks away, but Finn and the impartial referees from the Alachua district were still swatting away mosquitos. *Why did Principal Cailleach insist on this being outdoors when we could have done it in the gymnasium?*

When the other school's team showed up, the

reasoning became very clear to Finn. He pulled out the paperwork he'd received about the match, and cursed himself for not paying closer attention to the details. This was the same school he'd met at a track meet the previous year, and somehow their club sponsor was the same giant who coached their track team.

Mr. Colossus had grown up with centuries of family tales about Finn MacCool. None of them were flattering. This giant pushed every single one of Finn's buttons, and they'd wound up racing each other. Finn's loss had been humiliating, until Pavlina had turned it into proof that the giant's tales were lies. *Good old, Pav. Wish she was here right now.*

Finn didn't have time to worry about what new tragedy his sirin girlfriend was dealing with at that moment, because Mr. Colossus's booming laughter rattled the ground beneath them.

"Finn MacCool!"

Jaysus, I hate this eejit. "Hello, Mr. Colossus. Good to see you again."

"It is!" The giant clapped a hand on Finn's shoulder. As strong as the legendary hero was, he struggled not to stumble from the impact.

Finn rubbed the spot where he'd been hit. "What are the odds that you and I would meet under such different circumstances?"

"Well, not as great as you think." Mr. Colossus leaned in to whisper, but even the big man's voice couldn't be small. "When I saw that your school had also formed a club, I had a feeling it might be you."

There was no hiding the shock Finn felt. "You created a Magical Automaton Club just because I did?"

This time, Mr. Colossus didn't try to whisper. "No, no! I already had one set up. But I did request that ours be the first match of the season so you could watch me win again." The giant erupted into laughter.

Finn crossed his arms. "I think you'll find it difficult to outdo me when it comes to intelligence and magic."

"Oh, not between us!" Mr. Colossus said. "I only meant my club will beat yours."

"I'm pretty confident in my students' abilities. This *is* a magical magnet school, after all."

The giant smirked in response. "And my school is a robotics magnet."

Feck. "Tech without proper magic isn't enough."

"Well, we're about to find out."

Finn took a look around at all the students he'd gotten to know in this club. Each one of them was remarkable, and there was every reason to believe they would win. In that same moment, he realized something very important—it didn't matter if they did.

These teens were learning and having fun the whole time! They were staying after school to *work* on magical automatons. They were even warming up to Finn, the teacher everyone had been scared of at the beginning of the year. They'd already won what really mattered.

Still, I'd love it if we wiped off that giant's smirk.

Finn waited for everyone to take their seats and set up their magical automatons under black cloth. Beside them were the scrolls that the student pairs had written out with spells to animate their creations and ensure that they followed orders.

Once everything had settled, Finn clapped his hands to get everyone's attention. "The rules are simple! Read your scroll, uncover your automaton, and command it to fight the automaton across from you. The first automaton to fall is the loser. Whichever club wins the most battles, wins the whole match."

"May the best club win!" Mr. Colossus bellowed, and then snarled at Finn.

Ignoring that, Finn paced the grounds, monitoring each battle for fair play. This was a good competition. There was no telling who would win, because they were on similar skill levels and their automatons were all nearly identical. *Except for Bree and Ylva's.*

Finn hung back just a little ways from their table to keep a curious eye on what was happening at their match. The other pair was a girl who looked remarkably like Bree and a gangly boy. Based on the animosity between Bree and that girl, it seemed that's where their similarities ended.

Each pair read their scrolls and uncovered their

automatons.

"Fight that puny thing on the table, Megalossus!" the girl from the rival school commanded.

"Make their automaton fall, Leshy!" Bree instructed the automaton she'd created with Ylva.

The opposing pair laughed and the girl asked, "Leshy? What kind of name is that?"

Ylva gave the girl a wicked grin and said, "Leshy is a forest spirit known to defeat his enemies through trickery."

The gangly boy glanced at his teammate with a little less confidence than he'd had just seconds before. The girl only glared at Ylva.

A split second later, Megalossus hammered its fist down, but Leshy twirled out of the way. The other automaton was so powerful that its fist got stuck in the crater it made on the battle ring's formerly glossy surface. Finn winced. *I hope Principal Cailleach didn't pay too much for that.*

While Megalossus worked its fist out of the mess it had created, Leshy jumped on its back. The lumbering automaton righted itself and turned around in circles to reach its smaller opponent, but its arms were too thick to bend that way.

Ylva snapped and a spike protruded from her automaton's wrist. Leshy slid it between the head and neck where the metal joint connected the two. With one forceful motion, it punctured the joint holding

Megalossus's body to its head.

The gangly boy watched in terror as the automaton lost its noggin and Leshy swung around to hop on Megalossus's chest, pushing the automaton down to the ground.

Ylva wasn't kidding when she said a giant can't swat a deadly bee.

"What?!" the girl from the rival school yelled and jumped up from her seat. "That's cheating! It cut through his joint! That doesn't count!"

Upon hearing the accusation, Mr. Colossus walked over, giving Finn the stink eye the whole way. "Using dirty tricks like their teacher?"

Finn smiled at Mr. Colossus and opened up the rule book. He pointed to the list of accepted attacks. "Says right there that cutting through the opponent's automaton is approved. It's not our fault that you didn't look up what techniques your team could use."

Mr. Colossus rolled his eyes. "Whatever, we'll still win the match, even if you won this battle through a stupid loophole."

Finn nodded. "Maybe you will, but I'm proud of Bree and Ylva. They used their brains for this one."

Bree glowed under his praise. *It doesn't matter if we win. We're all learning valuable— Wait, did we just win another battle?*

All around him, referees were declaring winners. It was happening much faster than he'd thought it would. By the time he registered the cheers and groans at one table, another one had finished their fight. A couple went to Mr. Colossus's school, but more went to Annie Lytle High, and Finn's club was declared the winner.

Finn was proud of his students for demonstrating the behavior of gracious winners. *They have the right of it. I've been much too competitive my whole life. After all, it's not about whether we win. It's about —*

One of the referees handed him the award for his team's win, and Finn remembered the giant's smug face when he'd won the previous year's race.

Feck it.

"Booyah!" Finn cried out much to everyone's surprise. He pointed at Mr. Colossus's chest. "How do you like *that!*"

The giant growled, but that was his only response. To his club, he barked, "Let's go!" and they left with slumped shoulders and sallow faces.

While the other team shuffled toward their bus, Finn gathered his students to one spot. "I want to get a photo of you all for our first battle and first *victory!*"

When Finn pulled his Atlas phone from his pocket, he saw that it was unlocked and a voice recording app had been active for the last hour. *I've heard of butt dialing but butt recording?*

After taking several group photos, Finn put his phone away and tidied up. Then he realized something. *I don't have a voice recording app.*

EIGHT

The After School

Despite being a 140-year-old death harbinger, this was the first time Pavlina had ever been to a morgue. Once she guided a soul to the afterlife, her job was done. She didn't follow the empty body anywhere after that. There wasn't any point to it, other than to depress her.

This seemed to surprise Detective Troias who had to escort Pavlina to the teenage girl's dead body. The sirin hoped that she'd find her footing once she finally reached the victim. Unfortunately, that's not what happened.

"Anything you can do?" The detective looked at Pavlina with hopeful eyes, but the harbinger could see the doubt behind them. *She already knows.*

"There's no soul to guide." *Just like the others.* "But I do think we have a clue here. I wonder if you've picked up on it too."

"I'm a detective. I see all the clues. I want to know what you see."

Pavlina had a feeling that if the victim's hair hadn't been matted with blood from her skull cracking open, she would have had hair like the Castille sisters. Her skin would have been like theirs as well, but there was a grayness only seen in long-departed corpses. Her fingers, which were so small like Liz's, had lost their fingernails.

"When did she die?" Pavlina asked.

"The witness report says yesterday afternoon."

Detective Troias handed the file over, and Pavlina read the witness statement. The girl had been killed in a car accident, a grizzly one. She'd been standing at a bus stop when a car careened off the road out of nowhere and hit her. The driver had apparently stated that the vehicle had taken control of itself, but Pavlina dismissed that as a man trying to get out of a manslaughter trial.

Pavlina could see where the car had impacted her. It looked fresh, not like the rest of her body.

"She was already dead." The moment the words left Pavlina's lips, she wanted to recant them. *Maybe I'm not considering everything. Maybe… But this is what would make all the pieces fit.* She turned from the corpse to the detective. "She was already dead, wasn't she?"

Troias crossed her arms and offered a sorrowful expression. "That's what I think, but no one believes me. She was standing, after all."

"There are so many reasons why she could have been dead but standing, though." Pavlina handed back the file. "Why don't they believe you?"

"It's all there in my name. Troias." The detective placed the file in her messenger bag. "I come from a long line of seers that Apollo doesn't like."

"Wait... like Cassandra of Troy?"

The detective nodded. "That's the one. My mom even named me after our ancestor. I try not to predict anything, but sometimes the prophecies slide into my deductions. Then no one believes me."

That explains why everything she says seems ridiculous. "Are there any other clues as to why she might not have been alive?"

"They're all Jane Does, so we try to find their identity in our system." Troias pointed at the corpse. "This girl has been missing for about a month. The kid you witnessed had been gone for a couple of weeks."

"They're not really dying, which is why no death harbingers sense it coming, and why..." Pavlina choked down a small sob. "Why there's no soul to guide to the afterlife."

She took a long look at the poor, mangled girl laying there. Her life had ended too soon. Worse than that, her soul was likely lost somewhere, afraid and alone, a ghost.

"Can I trust you?" Pavlina asked.

Detective Troias shook her head in confusion. "What do you mean?"

"You're a cop," Pavlina said. "You report to the Council of Pantheons. Your loyalty is to an institution that may or may not want these murders solved."

"The police force is here to serve and protect."

Pavlina fought the urge to roll her eyes. "The police force is there to enforce laws. What are *you* here for? Who are you loyal to?"

She watched the detective consider these words in silence. Her eyes seemed to be searching Pavlina's, feeling out how serious the question was.

"I'm a homicide detective," Troias said. "I'm loyal to the dead and their loved ones. I may be a cop, but I'm not the system. If I were, I wouldn't keep pushing against it."

This might be a mistake but...

"These girls are zombies. A bokor made them."

Troias squinted. "Zombies strolling down sidewalks and standing at bus stops? Why aren't they attacking people?"

"Because they weren't commanded to attack. They were commanded to die."

The detective looked even more confused than before and Pavlina didn't want to discuss this any further in a government building.

Pavlina held a hand against her belly. "I didn't get a chance to eat lunch and it's nearly dinner time. Let's grab a bite somewhere and talk more."

Seeming to understand, Detective Troias nodded right away. "I know a good place. A little hole in the wall. Let's go."

The moment they walked out of the building together, Pavlina leaned over to whisper in the detective's ear. "This is bait. They're after the Chosen One."

Troias stepped away in shock. "The Chosen One?"

Pavlina hushed her and waved her into her car. Once the two were seated, the sirin continued.

"Bree Castille was picked as this century's Chosen One," Pavlina said, turning on her engine and buckling her seat belt. "I know her. She's a student of mine. Everyone who has died looked like her at least a little."

"So are these threats?" The detective clicked her seat belt into place.

"I think it's more than that." Pavlina pulled out of the parking space. "She's not accessible. I think they want to lure her out."

"Wouldn't that do the opposite? If someone was killing people that looked like me, I'd stay someplace with a thousand locks."

"You're not Bree. She'd see it as her duty to save all

these girls herself, even if that means giving herself over."

The light turned green and Pavlina pulled forward to cross the intersection, when a teenage girl charged her at full speed. The sirin slammed on her brakes, missing the girl by mere inches.

"Oh gods…" Detective Troias whispered.

"I wasn't going fast," Pavlina said, shaking her head. "Barely 20 miles per hour. She was able to catch up with us. She—"

The teenager waved at Pavlina with a bright smile and dead eyes. Then, she simply walked away, while every car horn nearby blew at her.

"That was a message if I ever saw one," Detective Troias said. "But I don't think it was for Bree. I think it was for you."

When Bree had left for school that morning, she hadn't thought it would be anything other than an ordinary day. She knew that Ms. Sirin and Mr. Finn would say something, but she hadn't expected anything special. But her day hadn't just been *special*; it had been *spectacular*. She'd had her favorite cake, gotten some truly incredible presents, and a whole group of friends had celebrated with her.

On top of all that, Ylva and she had absolutely

demolished the pair they were matched with at the magical automaton battle. This alone would have made Bree happy, but there was also a petty satisfaction in beating somebody like Maia Sisifo. *What a terrible last name. No wonder she's such an insufferable b—*

Bree stopped herself before she could finish the thought. She felt guilty even thinking swear words. Her experience with Maia though made it almost impossible for them to come unbidden into her mind. *Mami would be so ashamed.*

As Bree walked back to the house where she lived with the people that looked like her real family, she wondered what today would have been like if her Mami and Papi were there. How would they have treated her on a day like today? Would they have attended the battle? These questions threatened to tear her heart to shreds.

In order to avoid delving too far into that spiral, Bree directed her thoughts back to snotty-nosed Maia. She'd made her teammate carry everything over. She'd even snapped at him when it was time to set things down. The rude girl had sniffed and grimaced at the battle set up, and rolled her eyes the moment she deigned to look at Bree and Ylva.

Bree would never forget Maia's first words to her. "I thought our first battle would be a challenge. This isn't worth my time." The entire match, the rude girl had belittled them and their automaton. *We beat her, though.* Bree smiled at the memory of Maia's stunned expression when she lost.

When Bree arrived at her house's doorstep, she felt loved and victorious. Once she opened the door, that changed.

Balloons were tied everywhere they could be. A small pile of presents sat on the coffee table. All the signs of a birthday surprise assaulted Bree immediately. The birthday cheer didn't match any of the faces staring at her from the living room, though.

Gabby, Bree's non-magical counterpart, had a November birthday. She'd seen it on the birth certificate still framed and hanging in the upstairs hallway. Bree had done nothing to inform these parents that hers was different.

Bree hung her backpack on the hook by the door, and tried to place a grateful smile on her face. "You remembered!"

Mr. Castille's jaw tensed. "No, not really. Liz here told us."

Liz offered Bree an apologetic gaze and tepid smile. *Gods, why, Liz?*

"Thanks, Liz!" Bree said, forcing all of Florida's sunshine in her tone. "You didn't have to do that!"

The younger sister lowered her head, indicating that she knew the sarcasm behind those words.

"Yes," this reality's father said. "That was very nice

of Liz. She just wanted to make sure we'd have cake with dinner."

Bree felt a little guilty for her anger with her sister. She had only been trying to do something for Bree on her birthday. There wasn't much she had control over, especially with how ill she'd been feeling lately.

Their father rose from the couch he'd been sitting on and approached Bree. His face was grim, his steps deliberate. This wasn't how you approached someone to wish them a happy birthday.

When he got close enough to Bree that she had to crane her neck to look at him, he said, "But we wanted to go further than just a cake so we drove to your school to drop off a balloon and a card."

Shit. Sweat trailed from the edges of Bree's hairline to her throat.

"Apparently, your *'parents'* unenrolled you from Andrew Jackson High School, and filled out the paperwork for homeschool."

"I—"

"Just how did you think this was going to play out, huh?" Any pretense of this man keeping his cool evaporated under the heat of his glare. "Were you going to do your own End of Course exams? Where are you even going while we think you're at school?"

This reality's mother rushed over, looking more distraught than angry. "Is it drugs, Bree?"

Bree shook her head. "What? No! I'm not on drugs!"

Mr. Castille scoffed. "You'd have to be on drugs for you to think this dumb plan would work."

It did, though. For a little bit anyway. Bree's eyes flicked over to Liz, who had tucked her knees in so she sat like a deflated ball on the armchair.

This reality's father snapped in her face. "Hey! Eyes on me!"

With a flinch, Bree forced herself to look at this man whose resemblance to her Papi ended with his face.

"Since you went ahead and *forged our signatures* to get yourself designated a homeschooler, you now are one."

"It will be nice for Liz to have a classmate, even if you'll be learning different things," Bree's grandmother said from her armchair in the living room. The woman coughed into a tissue. "Might take things a little slow though. Not feeling too hot."

The reality of what was happening slammed into Bree like a train. This wasn't only going to mean dealing with angry parents, not even a long-term grounding. There would be no more Annie Lytle Magical Magnet High. No more friends or magical automatons. No more Ylva, Mr. Finn, or Ms. Sirin.

No more magic.

Bree considered raging against this. Every cell in her wanted to. Despite having a history as a goody two shoes, a teenage rebel had slowly begun to emerge over the last year. She was intelligent enough to know it wouldn't do any good, though.

Liz didn't deserve even more yelling and conflict. If anything, Bree should give her a long hug and reassurance that she'd love her forever.

Fighting back wasn't the answer, and they'd be even angrier if they knew the truth of her reality hopping. Bree wasn't sure what the solution was, but she had the patience to think things through. The next plan wouldn't fail. She wouldn't let it.

Finn returned home feeling proud and victorious. He couldn't wait to tell Pavlina all about it, but she was still out with Detective Troias. *I hope she's okay.*

Finn had texted her while cleaning up the mess left by the magical automaton battle. He'd let her know they won and he hoped all was well. She responded moments later that she was happy for him and she was fine. Nothing else.

The house was dark and quiet without her in it. Finn was tempted to wallow in anxiety and loneliness, but he reminded himself that Pavlina was a 140-year-old death harbinger. She would be alright. He had lived alone for decades too. Now was his chance to relax with a good book. *And avoid that depressing homework Ms. Pace gave me.*

He picked up *Loved by the Yeti Duke*. This book had been quite the scandal when it hit the shelves.

People wanted it banned for being too steamy. Nine chapters in, Finn felt certain all the outrage had been a marketing scheme. *Gods, kiss already or something.*

The sound of beach waves caught Finn's attention and he looked up to see a foam-ringed tear in reality opening before him, bringing with it the scent of brine and sun-warmed sunblock.

Finn tossed his book on the side table and stood up. As he did, a very familiar and welcome person stepped through the portal, gapped teeth, tumbled hair, and all.

"Cal!" Finn threw his arms around the portal-hopping book dealer who loved his daughter. She hugged him back with all the enthusiasm he'd come to expect from her. "It's so good to see you," he said when they finally parted.

"I'm glad to see you too!" Cal responded, all smiles.

Finn craned his neck to see through the portal. "Where's Oísina?"

"Oh, she's at a poetry circle," Cal said. "Those are pretty popular in the island reality." She turned to the portal and said, "And now we close just how we rose."

As the portal narrowed, the foamy bubbles popped. Within a heartbeat, it was as if the beach had never cast its sunshine in Finn's living room. His heart fell.

"Oh I thought maybe…"

Cal shook her head. "I'm sorry. Not this time. We'll figure it out, but it's still not safe."

"You're right." It hurt to admit it, but he'd rather miss his daughter than let harm befall her. She'd already suffered ninety years imprisoned in a book so the CoP could keep him in line. If they found out she'd escaped, they might do even worse to her. "Have a seat." He gestured at the couch, now graced with a throw blanket from Pavlina's house.

Cal plopped onto it, and stretched her legs out to prop her feet on the coffee table. Finn swatted at them.

"Hey now! I'm trying to keep this place clean!"

Cal held up her hands in relent. "Sorry. It's been a while since I've been somewhere like this."

"Like this?"

"You know," Cal said with a shrug. Her smile saddened. "Someone's home."

Finn nodded, knowing exactly what she meant. Cal was a nomad like him. Though lately, he'd felt different... almost domesticated, but in a pleasant way.

"What brings you here?" Finn asked and sat in his recliner.

"I wish I could say it was a social call, but I'm sure you know it's not."

Cal pulled a shaking hand through her wild, short-cropped curls. At that moment, Finn noticed the cracks in her cheerful, confident demeanor. *She's scared.*

"What's wrong, Cal?"

The bookdealer let out a forceful breath, causing her lips to blubber. "So, you know how I have this one reality where I dump all my junk."

"How could I forget? That's where you sent— Oh no." Finn slumped to the back of his chair, the weight of this realization pinning him down. "He got out?"

"No, well not yet." Cal pulled out a tattered sheet of paper from her jacket pocket. She'd hastily drawn something on it. It looked like a child's drawing of the sun.

"What is this?"

"This is what I saw when I cleaned up the mess from last night's party." Cal tapped on the sun. "I know this seems crude but this is *exactly* what I saw. It was a massive ball of light with bolts of… something shooting out of it."

Finn scratched his head. "I thought that was an empty reality. Well, I mean except for your trash."

"I never said it was empty," Cal said. "Just that the Big Bang hadn't happened *yet.* Whenever I pop over there, it's always in some random location. I never see any of the other garbage I've tossed in. I don't see anything at all, because nothing but my trash exists and it's too far away to see. I just wanted to find an easy way to clean without polluting other realities, but now I think I made a mistake."

"Why?"

"Think about it," Cal said. "The Big Bang was what happened when a giant mass of matter couldn't stay contained and exploded. I've tossed in more stuff to add to the pressure." She sighed and hung her head low. "And one of our more powerful gods."

"Feck."

"Exactly." Cal returned the drawing to her jacket pocket. "I mean he's not a creation god, but that's likely from lack of opportunity, not ability. Looks like he's got what he needed all along, and I was the one to give it to him."

"He could do anything. He could make his own world, he could climb out of that reality, he could... Oh gods..."

Grim lines formed between Cal's eyebrows as she said, "And there's nothing we can do to prevent him from doing whatever he wants."

Finn considered himself a brave man. He'd defended countless mortals. He was even a Chosen One once. This, though? This scared him.

"He could break through the boundary Principal Cailleach put on the school." The memory of Bree laughing with Ylva earlier that day switched to a nightmarish vision of Hermes looming above her, vengeance in his terrifying eyes. Before being tossed into nothingness, he was willing to kill everyone Bree loved to coerce her into martyrdom. What would he do now to the girl who had defied him, whose very life stood in the way of strengthening his immortality?

"I don't think we should shelter her anymore."

Finn opened his mouth to argue. Cal raised her

hands to stop him.

"I'm not saying we should give up on her," Cal said. "I would never say that. But she's a Chosen One, Finn. It's time to start treating her like one. She's made to take on battles most people would flee from. We just need to give her the tools to win."

"What do you have in mind?"

Cal smirked. She straightened up in her seat and pulled off a pouch from her belt. "Well, she has a pretty big interest in portals. I think we should start there." She loosened the bag and more fairy stones than should have been able to fit spilled out onto the coffee table. "I know a reality where these are as common as sand."

NINE

The Friday Scaries

After ninety-one years of teaching magical application at many high schools across America, Finn was used to having the Sunday Scaries, the dread of the approaching Monday that tainted any relaxation a weekend day should have. This morning, he had the Friday Scaries. He hadn't finished his parole homework. In fact, he hadn't even started it. All he'd done was look at the instructions. *I'm just not ready for this.*

It didn't matter whether he was ready. It was five in the morning and he'd be busy that evening figuring things out with Pavlina, Cal, and this new detective he had a hard time believing. Still, this piece of paper was asking for a lot from him emotionally. *Write a five paragraph essay explaining what events led to your incarceration.* He didn't want to relive those moments, even if it was a relatively short piece of writing.

"Can you believe they call it that?" Finn grumbled and waved at his homework on the coffee table. "Incarceration? That's what they call years of torture for simply meddling with mortal affairs?"

Pavlina, somehow already polished and ready for work, sat at the table between the kitchen and living room. She drank black coffee from one of the Victorian teacups she'd inherited from her father. When she'd moved her decor over for the parole officer's visit, she'd made sure to bring little touches like this. Finn didn't mind it one bit. In fact, it made him wonder what it would be like if this went on forever. *But it won't. She doesn't have forever. Not like me.*

"You're stalling," Pavlina said, spreading cream cheese on her bagel.

"What's the point? Even if I finish it now, it will be pure drivel."

Finn's beautiful sirin took a bite of her bagel, but maintained eye contact with him, with an expression that communicated that she saw right through his excuses.

"It's an F either way, Pav, and—"

"An F and a zero are two different things, Finn." Pavlina set her bagel back on its plate and came over to sit with Finn on the couch. "You've been a teacher long enough to know that. She may have you do this over again if it isn't to her standards, but she also may make *very* big decisions about your parole if you don't even try."

"I just... I just can't."

Pavlina picked up the paper and read the prompt. "The events that led up to your incarceration. That would be the Great War right?"

Finn nodded.

"Is it hard for you to talk about it?"

"It's hard for me to even think about."

The sirin sat the paper down on the table. "You were a hero to all those people you saved."

"But what about those that I didn't?"

Finn hated the hot tears welling in his eyes. Crying wasn't something he did, especially not in front of others. Pavlina encouraged him to cry when he needed to. She'd told him that working through his emotions made him a better, braver person. He still didn't want her to see him like this, though.

Pavlina laid her cool, comforting hand on his cheek. Finn always loved her calming touch. He'd come to learn this was part of her gifts as a death harbinger. After leading the dead to the afterlife, she returned to the living world and her touch offered the grieving some peace, at least for a short time.

"War isn't easy. I know. I've spent some time busy as a harbinger through a few." Pavlina picked up a tissue from the box on the side table and wiped his face dry. "You fought in one far more deadly than most, full well knowing the trouble that could land you in with the Council of Pantheons. The whole ordeal must have been terrifying and heartbreaking. Maybe you even feel guilty you survived."

"If I could have made them all immortal, I would have."

"I know." Pavlina picked up the pencil on the coffee table and placed it in Finn's hand. "You need to write this, though. Keeping silent won't bring them back. It won't make you feel better. Getting through parole means being with Oísina."

Finn looked at the assignment. One five-paragraph essay would bring him another step closer to being with his daughter. He took the paper from Pavlina's hand. "I'll do it, but…"

"But what?"

"Can you stay with me while I do?"

Pavlina kissed his cheek. "Of course I can."

The Irish warrior was an incredibly intelligent man, but Finn feared he wouldn't be able to put into words what happened. To his surprise, they flowed.

Finn wrote about watching the young men who lived in the village near him march off to war and never come back. He witnessed the grief that settled over those left behind. Worse, some of these soldiers returned missing limbs. Sometimes, their faces were unrecognizable, burnt or mangled until they hardly looked human anymore. Their haunted eyes were windows to their dimmed souls.

Tired of feeling useless to help them, Finn took on the guise of a mortal soldier and left with yet another troop sent to Europe. There he fought with his supernatural strength and he used the wealth of knowledge magically gifted to him long ago. It was easy for them to win, too easy. He knew it was only a matter of time before he caught the Council of Pantheons' attention.

Finn wouldn't hold back, though. Even with him pulling out every trick in his book, people who shouldn't have died did. Every single soldier there was sent to die for those who had some idea of how powerful they should be during their pitifully short human lives.

Then it ended, and Finn knew it wouldn't have happened without him. Everyone did. They heralded him as a hero. They gave him medals. No one knew how an ordinary Irishman could have done so much. The Council of Pantheons understood why, though.

It always seemed hypocritical how the gods handled the whole thing. They'd known early on that he was playing a big part in the war, that he was lending his immortality to meddle in mortal affairs. They let him do it anyway. No one wanted this war to drag on any longer. It wasn't until a peace treaty was signed that they arrested him and imprisoned his innocent daughter in a book.

Finn let his resentment bleed into his writing. He didn't care what the parole officer thought when she read it. It was the truth.

By the time he finished, the morning light filtered through the windows onto the paper, revealing his tear stains. Finn sat staring at it, feeling blank and immobile. He'd forgotten Pavlina's presence until she wiped his face with a warm, wet washcloth.

"Maybe you should stay home from work," she whispered.

The immortal hero shook his head. "No, I can't."

"You just relived some of your worst experiences."

"If I stay here alone all day, I'll do nothing but think about all this. I need crowded, noisy hallways full of life after spending an hour consumed by death."

Pavlina nodded. "Okay. Well, let's get going then. After everything that happened yesterday afternoon, I really need to see Bree's face as soon as I can."

Pavlina didn't see Bree when she arrived at school, but that wasn't a huge surprise. Students clogged up every hallway and the teenager's first class wasn't anywhere near the magical history teacher's.

Still, Pavlina worried. Yesterday's events had rattled her. Examining the corpse of a girl who reminded her of her former foster daughter and then nearly running over another one wasn't something she could recover from overnight. Once she and the detective had finally been able to park the car, the girl was already out of sight. They had no way of knowing who she was or even if she was a zombie like the others. In the back of her mind, Pavlina kept expecting to see that face every time she turned around. *Which is a ridiculous fear to have... But then again I never would have imagined that scenario to begin with.*

After leaving Detective Troias, Pavlina had returned to the house she shared with Finn. She'd hoped to hear all about the magical automaton battle. He'd skipped right past that to share the terrifying news that Hermes was amassing more and more power in the reality Cal had sent him to in the spring. That of course led to Pavlina sharing her own experiences that day.

At school, they both had to pretend everything was okay, at least until they could talk to Principal Cailleach. *Surely, she'll have some plan or at least some ideas.* The lack of confidence Pavlina felt in that saddened her. The school wasn't a sanctuary. It was a fortress that could come crumbling down with a big enough cannon. So when Bree didn't arrive for her class, the sirin's fears only increased.

As Ylva entered without her friend, Pavlina couldn't help but throw a thousand questions at her. Was Bree just taking a long time in the bathroom? Did she seem like she was coming down with something yesterday? Do you know any reason why she wouldn't be here?

Ylva seemed just as concerned as Pavlina. That didn't help at all.

When she arrived at the cafeteria to drop off her students for lunch, she caught Finn's eye from across the room. "Where's Bree?" he mouthed. Pavlina could only shrug and shake her head. The panic in his eyes matched the frantic beat of her heart. The two made their way to the exit together.

"Ylva has no idea what's going on," Pavlina whispered as soon as they met.

"No idea? Feck." Finn looked up the empty hallway in the direction of the front office. "We need to talk to Principal Cailleach right away."

"Let's go."

The two rushed forward, but stopped in their tracks when they saw their boss walking toward them with a woman dressed in the kind of business attire characteristic of those who worked for the Council of Pantheons. She had a long lion's tail, paws for hands, and paws for feet. *Oh no, a goddamn sphinx?*

Principal Cailleach waved at Pavlina and Finn to come over. With a gulp, Pavlina walked toward them.

"Ms. Sirin, Mr. Finn," the principal said. "This is Miss Sphinx from the Council of Pantheons. She's Bree's new representative."

The representative offered them a genuine smile.

"I'm so excited to meet you," she said. "I've heard wonderful things about the teachers who took care of her when her parents died." The sphinx shook her head. "That's far too common with our Chosen Ones. It's almost like a curse."

Or it's a tactic that a secret sect of gods use to manipulate their sacrifices. "It's nice to meet you." Pavlina took out her hand to shake the representative's.

"Oh, I'm so sorry." Miss Sphinx raised her paw. "I'm not very good at handshakes."

"Bree's new representative unfortunately arrived on one of the rare days our Chosen One is absent." A slight, almost imperceptible quiver in Principal Cailleach's voice told Pavlina her boss was also worried, probably more so with the Council of Pantheons showing up so inconveniently.

"Yes, it's such a shame, but I'm sure we'll have time to catch up later," Miss Sphinx said. "The CoP would have sent someone sooner, but they wanted to be more careful since Mr. Casmilus abandoned his duties. I promise you I have a reliable history of helping with Chosen Ones from as far back as ancient Egypt. I'm so excited that I get to be the guide this time."

"Well, we're happy to meet you," Finn said.

Pavlina was surprised at how well Finn pulled off this facade. He'd never been good at pretending to be friendly, preferring to intimidate rather than get in someone's good graces. *Then again, he has decades of practice keeping in good standing with the Council of Pantheons.*

"Since Bree isn't here, maybe you could show me the Magical Automaton Club, Mr. Finn," the sphinx said. "I hear it's something she's very passionate about and it's an important part of my job learning about her strengths since that will aid in her quest."

"And what is her quest?" The question came from Pavlina's lips without her even examining the thought.

Miss Sphinx shook her head. "We won't know until the time comes."

"Isn't it usually fighting a beast or something?" Pavlina asked.

"You know, it usually is," Miss Sphinx answered. "I don't know why. That seems so small-scale for an actual Chosen One, and most of them wind up sacrificing themselves in the process."

You have no idea how sacrificial it is. "Yes, that is strange."

"Strange and heartbreaking to witness." Miss Sphinx's sad tone and crestfallen expression put Pavlina somewhat at ease. This representative wasn't another Harold Casmilus. *Maybe she cares.*

"Well, what other kinds of quests could there be?" Pavlina asked. "She's a pacifist."

Miss Sphinx brightened at that. "Oh, well, that's splendid! I think we could all use a little peace. Perhaps she will bring the gift of healing or locate a relic."

"I like to call her a warrior of peace," Finn interjected.

"Oh, that means a lot coming from a hero like you!"

Miss Sphinx's enthusiasm surprised Pavlina. By the look of Finn, he hadn't expected it either. Council of Pantheons' employees typically looked down on him as a criminal.

"She's also got aspirations of working as an attorney representing sick children in battles against insurance companies," Finn went on. "Maybe her quest could lead to that?"

"It absolutely could," Miss Sphinx agreed. "I can't wait to meet her and find out more about such a special girl."

"Well, let's at least show you the club you asked about." Finn guided the representative toward his class and away from Pavlina and Principal Cailleach.

As soon as they were out of earshot, the principal whispered, "Do you have any idea where she is?"

Pavlina shook her head. "No, and it's even worse than that. Can we talk in private?"

"To my office." The wintry goddess didn't wait for Pavlina to respond and started walking.

Gods, can things get any worse?

Bree didn't know if things could get any worse. Not only was she unable to return to the school, but she was stuck with her grandmother as a teacher. The woman had given her multiplication and division worksheets, despite the teenager explaining that she'd taken and passed trigonometry the previous year. Now, she was working on a reading comprehension worksheet about Florida history. *This is baby stuff even for a middle schooler like Liz.*

It was three in the afternoon and Bree's sister had gone to bed. After finishing a small amount of work, Liz complained of having trouble understanding her math work. Tired, she slurred her words, asking for more tea. *It must be really bad if she's asking for that awful stuff.*

Their grandmother ushered Liz to her room with a mug of tea and came back.

"Maybe we should take her to an urgent care or something," Bree said. "That's not as risky as a hospital."

The old woman scoffed. "And have them pump her full of chemicals? No, it's better for her to drink the teas I make her. They have natural curative properties."

Bree stayed silent so as not to upset this reality's grandmother, but she had many thoughts about it. *But everything has chemicals. That's what all matter is composed of. Besides, the tea hasn't helped for weeks. Liz seems even worse.*

Within an hour, Bree finished all the worksheets given to her, and she was bored. When she asked what to do next, the woman gave her chores.

Bree was a tidy person, but this was a tall task even for her. This reality's mother didn't clean; she didn't even pick up after herself. She sat in front of a television, barely watching it in her depressed haze.

The only good thing about the drudgery was that slowly the clutter and mess disappeared, along with the sensory overload Bree felt in the house's common living areas. Her mother even thanked her every time Bree passed by. The mess must have weighed on her as well. *She cares, but all her grief keeps her incapable of doing anything productive.*

Bree rounded up the cleaning session by putting away the clean dishes. Looking at one of the dozens of book themed mugs her mother had, she came up with an idea.

"You like books, right?"

Mrs. Castille turned her attention away from the television. She seemed surprised to hear someone asking her what she liked. "I used to read all the time before..."

Bree nodded, understanding. "I love to read. Maybe we could do it together?"

A small smile flitted onto her mother's face. "You'd want to do that?"

Sure beats doing busy work and hanging out with an old woman who coughs every thirty seconds. "I'd love to! Here, let me grab a book I have in my backpack."

Bree rushed to retrieve the book Ylva gifted her and came back to Mrs. Castille. "I've been pretty eager to read this one. It's about werewolves."

"I used to love paranormal stories like that." Excitement lifted her mother's tone, she flipped through the book and blinked in confusion. "Oh, but it's all in German. Is there an English version?"

"Oh, I didn't think about that." Bree thought about the bookmark in her bag that helped her translate any human language in text format. "I can read in German, though. Maybe I could read it to you?"

"You speak German? Wow!"

"Well, read, not speak," Bree said, fudging the truth a little. "Speaking is much harder. But yeah, I do."

Mrs. Castille's small smile broadened. "That's so impressive. I didn't know that about you." She looked down at the book in her hands. "There's a lot I don't know about you. You're not… you know…"

"I'm not Gabby."

Her mother nodded. "Sometimes, I forget." She sighed. "Well, not really. But you know…"

"I know. That's how I feel about Mami."

"Is that what you called her?" Though she still smiled, a tear trickled down her cheek. She wiped it away. "Gabby and Betty called me Momma. I miss that."

Bree swelled with empathy. This mother wasn't a bad woman. She wasn't combative like their father or off-putting like their grandmother. *Maybe she just needs someone who really cares about her.* "We may not be the people we lost, but maybe we can be the people we need."

Mrs. Castille squeezed Bree's hand. "I would like that."

The front door slammed behind them, jarring Bree out of the touching moment. She turned to see Mr. Castille staring at the house in awe. "What happened here?"

Bree rose to her feet. "I finished my work early so Grandmother asked that I clean up."

"You did all of this?" he asked, gesturing at the tidy kitchen and living room.

"Yes."

His surprise shifted suddenly to aggravation. "Where's all my stuff? You didn't lose it did you?"

Bree gestured to the console table with drawers under the window. "It's all in there, boxed and labeled."

The father's jaw dropped. "You did that? Why?"

"I like things organized," Bree explained. "And I thought maybe you would like to find your things more easily." *Plus you're always stressed and yelling about how you can't find anything.*

"I… I don't know what to say." Mr. Castille walked over to the console table and opened the drawers to look inside. "This is so much better."

"I was hoping you'd like it."

He turned from the drawers to her with a stern expression on his face. "This doesn't mean you're not still in trouble. A clean house doesn't make up for what you did."

"Yessir, I understand."

Mr. Castille let out a short laugh. "Yessir?" He gave her a real smile, and plopped his keys on the basket Bree had placed on the top of the console table. "I'm going to be busy working in my office for a while. Maybe you could make dinner while you're at it?"

Bree knew he was probably joking, but she winced anyway. "I'm pretty terrible at cooking."

"Oh, I didn't really think—"

Before Mr. Castille could finish his statement, his wife got up from the couch and said, "I'm actually a good cook," the woman said. "Or… I was before…" Mrs. Castille took a deep breath. "Maybe we could do it together and I could teach you."

"That would be really nice!" Bree responded.

"Did someone cast some magical spell over the two of you?" Mr. Castille asked.

"No," Mrs. Castille answered. "I think Bree and I just understand each other a little better." She looked at her husband with hope in her eyes. "It's really helped."

The father's chin quivered for a moment and then he cleared his throat and composed himself. "Well, I'm very happy to hear that. Let me know when dinner is ready."

"We will," Bree said.

Mr. Castille made his way to his office, and for the first time, Bree wondered if this new family could work.

"Let's start with something simple," her mother said. "I'm thinking spaghetti."

Yum! "Sure thing!"

TEN

The Worries

Finn wasn't in the mood for a parole meeting. If this had been the previous weekend, he would have been stressed, but he wouldn't have felt like the world was crashing around him. But after Bree's mysterious absence and the threat of Hermes's possible return, this meeting was just another thing he had to wear a mask for, one that said everything was fine, when nothing was fine at all. *Except for having Pavlina on my side.*

Pavlina was at Annie Lytle, meeting with Principal Cailleach and Cal to discuss all the bad news that had recently fallen in their laps. Even if she didn't have a reason to be out of the house, they'd both agreed it was best if Finn saw his parole officer alone. Having his girlfriend there would only create the idea that he wasn't capable of improving on his own.

A manilla envelope portal opened in his living room, interrupting his churning worries. Ms. Pace stepped through, her eyes once again focused on the Atlas tablet in her hands. Before, he had assumed she was busy trying to catch up on his case, but at that moment, she had the air of someone making a power play. It put Finn even more on edge. After a few taps on her screen, she lifted her eyes to look at Finn.

"Hello, Mr. MacCool. It's nice to see you again." Ms. Pace set her bag on his coffee table, but held onto her tablet. "Grab the exercise I gave you and let's have a seat together."

As his parole officer sat down, Finn grabbed the tear-stained paper he'd completed the prior morning and handed it over before sitting on the edge of his recliner.

"Oh my," Ms. Pace said, feeling the wavy texture of the paper. "This seems to have brought out some deep emotions."

Ms. Pace took a photo of the exercise with her tablet and set the device on the coffee table, then leaned back and started reading it at once. Watching her read something so vulnerable in front of him made Finn so anxious that his knee bounced up and down like a rabbit on Adderall.

If the parole officer noticed this, she didn't say

anything. Instead, she read Finn's words with a calm expression, tracing each sentence with her fingertip until she reached the end. To Finn's dismay, she slid her finger back up to passages, tapping them thoughtfully. Finally, she finished and placed it on the coffee table.

"I can see why you feel resentment toward the Council of Pantheons," she said.

"I don't mean to. It's just that—"

She waved her hand to stop him. "No, your feelings are valid. No one said the CoP was infallible."

Except for the gods in control of it. Finn wanted to ask why he was still serving parole then and why the Council of Pantheons hadn't freed his daughter. However, he was an intelligent man, and he didn't need another century of community service.

Ms. Pace fished around in her messenger bag. "This essay tells me that you're dealing with untreated c-PTSD."

"No, I'm fine," Finn said. "I spent centuries in battles before the Great War. One war wouldn't suddenly break me."

The parole officer paused rifling through the contents of her bag to look at Finn. "Mr. MacCool, can you not see that those battles contributed? Every dangerous moment, every tragedy, builds into a staggering pile of trauma. You may be immortal, but you aren't impervious to emotions."

Ms. Pace slid the tablet back into her bag and pulled out a new sheet of paper that said "Exercise Two" at the top. "I need you to get this done before our next meeting. Have a seat with at least three people in your life and ask them to tell you how your actions have negatively impacted their lives."

I don't like the sound of that. "I'm going to ask people to tell me what I've done that they don't like?"

"I never said these exercises would be easy," the parole officer said. "But everyone has room for growth and always will. To redeem yourself, you need to realize you can hurt people."

"But I—"

"In addition to that, ask your employer to tell you one of your strengths and one of your weaknesses."

Oh gods, I don't want to have that conversation with Principal Cailleach.

"I don't know if—"

Ms. Pace held up a finger to stop him and she pulled out a business card from the front pocket of her bag. "This is a psychologist I frequently work with. Give him a call before our next meeting and schedule an appointment. Since this is paid for by the CoP, you have no excuse not to go. You *must* see him regularly or I *will* recommend an extended parole sentence to my superiors."

Finn gulped and took the card.

A portal opened in the living room. "I will see you

in two weeks, Mr. MacCool," Ms. Pace said. "Make sure you get this all done."

Finn watched his parole officer leave and the portal closed behind her. *Bree is missing, Hermes is gathering even more power and surely wants revenge, and zombified teenagers are roaming the streets. How am I supposed to fit a therapy session in there?*

Liz hadn't come down for dinner the night before. She hadn't felt well enough for it. As wonderful as it had been to cook with her mother, Bree couldn't help but worry. In the reality they came from, their parents would have rushed her to the hospital with these symptoms. When they lived with Ms. Sirin, Liz had seemed in pretty good health. *Until Hermes got involved.*

In this reality, though, Liz didn't have access to the kind of healthcare she needed as a person with a serious disease. There was nothing Bree could do but hope her sister just had a little cold and would get better soon.

Usually, Liz asked for Bree to cuddle her during the night, but it was the older Castille sister who needed to lay next to her sister this time, just to know she was there and breathing. When the morning light woke Bree, she saw her little sister's jaundiced skin and felt the shallowness of her breath. She tried to stir Liz awake, but the girl stayed fast asleep. That's when she decided she wasn't going to wait for the adults to do the responsible thing.

Bree got dressed and brushed her teeth. Then she headed downstairs to grab her backpack and make sure she had enough cash for a ride. Steps behind her stopped her shuffling, and she turned around to see her father.

"What are you doing?" he asked.

Removing her hands from her bag, she said, "I was getting out some weekend homework." As soon as the lie left her lips, she knew how much she was about to be in.

"Really? Homework for what? Certainly not the school you *weren't* going to."

Bree considered telling another lie, but he would see through it. Telling the truth was a risk, but he wasn't going to let her leave the house either way.

"It's Liz." Bree swallowed a lump forming in her throat. "She's so much sicker."

"How much sicker?"

"You know she didn't feel well enough to come to dinner," Bree said. "Now she looks yellow and I can barely tell she's breathing."

Her father worked his jaw, and Bree braced herself for an angry tirade.

"Goddamn it," he whispered. "If we take her to the

hospital—"

"They'll have a copy of her death certificate, I know," Bree interrupted. "But what if we take her to an urgent care clinic?"

"Bree, this isn't something a place like that could handle. It's the ER or…" He shook his head and let his eyes drop to the floor. "I don't know what to do."

Bree's heart plummeted. Everything could go wrong if questions rose about who Liz was. Would they claim the parents had faked her death for life insurance money? Would they accuse them of abducting a child who just happened to look like their daughter? Would she be pawned off to a family who treated her poorly?

Mr. Castille headed to the kitchen. "I'm going to find out what's in that tea." He grabbed a small mug from beside the sink and lifted it for Bree to see. "Mom gave her this before bedtime and didn't wash it out."

Before Bree could ask him how they would find out what was in it, the man wiped the residue on the bottom with one finger and tasted it. He grimaced and spit into the sink. "Ugh, Mom used to give me this stuff when I was sick."

Bree took the mug from him and sniffed it. It smelled nauseatingly sweet. "What is it?"

"One part store brand herbal tea, one part cough syrup."

"Oh no!" On reflex, the mug dropped from Bree's hand and shattered on the floor. She didn't even notice it. Instead, she sprinted up the stairs, shouting back to her father, "People with sickle cell anemia shouldn't use decongestants! It messes with their blood vessels! We're lucky she's just been tired!"

Bree bolted into Liz's room and shook her sister awake. "Are you okay, Liz? Are you in pain? Are you—"

Liz swatted at her sister. "Let me sleep…" she mumbled. "I'm tired…"

Mr. Castille rushed into the room as Liz slumped in Bree's arms. Mrs. Castille shuffled in behind him, wiping her sleepy eyes.

"I thought you were headed to the bathroom," she said, but then her eyes moved from her husband to Liz. "What's going on? Is Liz okay?"

"Mom's been giving Liz decongestants," her father answered. "Apparently it's really dangerous for people with sickle cell anemia."

Liz breathed steadily but softly against Bree's chest. It was a sign of life, but Bree didn't know how much longer that would be enough. "We've gotta take her to the hospital!"

Bree's parents gave each other a look. Mr. Castille nodded and Mrs. Castille shed a tear.

"I guess we have to risk it," Bree's father said.

"If only we could take her to a hospital in your old reality," her mother said, wiping away the tear trailing down her cheek. "But you said it's dangerous and you couldn't get back anyway."

I have to tell them. "Well, about that…"

Mr. Castille cocked his head to the side. "Were you lying to us?"

Bree shook her head in protest. "No, no! When we told you about how we got here, we didn't make up a word of it. But then something happened."

"What did?" Mrs. Castille sat next to Bree on the edge of Liz's bed.

I'm about to be in so much trouble. "Well, you know Public School No. 4?"

Bree's mother squinted. "That old, abandoned school everyone thinks is haunted?"

"Well, in our reality, it's a high school, a great one. It's where I went to school before we came over." Just the thought of it hurt Bree. "On the last day of school, I found out that there was a portal inside that school to the one I went to and… Well, I figured out a way to go there."

"What?!" Bree's father snapped. "You've been going there this whole time?"

"I'm sorry! I just missed it so much!" Tears flooded down her hot face. "Please, just punish me later. We can use the portal to get Liz to the hospital there."

For a mortifying moment, Mr. Castille stood there, his chest heaving with anger. "How could we possibly sneak into that school and get her there? Even if we made it inside, that building could collapse in on us."

"I learned how to create a portal at the fence." Bree dug into her pocket and pulled out a fairy stone. "Using these."

Mr. Castille took a look at Liz in her pale, sickly condition and his whole body deflated for a moment.

"We have to do this," Mrs. Castille said.

Bree's father wiped away a tear before it could fall onto his cheek. He pointed to his wife and said, "Get dressed and meet me outside in the next five minutes." He turned to Bree, "I'll help you get Liz to the car." Then he whispered, "I'm not losing another daughter."

Cal, Principal Cailleach, Detective Troias, and Pavlina sat at a table in the cafeteria. Without the students and the hot food, it smelled of antiseptic and every whisper echoed. With increasing issues and anxiety, their voices didn't stay low for long. Within minutes, every word bounced around the room like a ping pong ball.

"Maybe it's a good thing she's not here," Troias said. "If whoever is killing these girls is trying to lure her out—"

"We don't know that hasn't happened already," Cal interrupted. Noticing the horrified expressions on everyone's face, she added, "Sorry, but we have to consider everything."

Pavlina crossed her arms. "I'm not entertaining that.

We need to focus on this being a rescue mission."

Cal lowered her gaze and nodded. "Agreed. We can't assume she's in that other reality, though."

"Pause," Principal Cailleach said, holding up a finger. She stood up and moved toward the exit. "I think someone's banging on the front door."

Pavlina squinted. She couldn't hear a thing. By the confused looks on everyone else's faces, she wasn't alone. The principal walked away and left them alone.

"Are... are we just not supposed to talk while she's gone?" Detective Troias asked.

"Basically," Pavlina answered. "Well, not about Bree at least."

The sirin planted her elbows on the table and rested her cheek on one palm. The conversation may have taken a break, but her thoughts were still churning. She couldn't stop them; she didn't want to. Pavlina hoped that they were all overreacting and Bree had just had a flu or something. With all the other factors at play, however, she couldn't assume something so normal.

When Principal Cailleach returned, Finn walked with her. He waved at the group, and relief washed over Pavlina. Everyone here was reliable, but only Finn knew her heart in this matter.

The Irishman sat next to Pavlina and put an arm around her shoulder. "So, what have you figured out so far?"

Cal shrugged. "Not to assume she's dead or in the other reality."

Finn cocked his head to the side. "Haven't you all been talking for two hours now?"

"We're just as lost as before," Pavlina said, slumping against her boyfriend. "We don't even know where to start."

"Maybe we should go further back," Detective Troias offered. She took out a pen and a pad of paper. "Let's take some notes starting from when Bree was picked as the Chosen One."

"That's a lot to write by hand. Maybe you should type it out. Let me see what I've got." Pavlina rifled through her purse for her Atlas tablet.

Before she could find it, Troias shook her head. "No, I really prefer to write by hand. It helps me remember it better." The detective scribbled down a quick note and said, "Okay, what do you remember about that day?"

The group went over all their memories. Reliving them sent Pavlina on a wildly emotional trip. The tragedy of Bree's parents dying, the bond they formed, the terror of her disappearance, the relief of her rescue, the heartbreak of her departure.

Detective Troias tapped her chin once they'd finished their recap, and stared at her lengthy notes. "Some of this seems too convenient to be luck."

"Like what?" Pavlina asked.

Instead of answering Pavlina, the detective looked at Principal Cailleach. "How did you know there was a family just like Bree's that just happened to have lost their daughters so quickly? It's a non-magical reality that gods can't monitor. Besides, why would you even be looking for this information?"

Everyone watched the principal. The questions etched deeper and deeper into Pavlina's mind as her boss took her time answering.

"I'll answer your last question first," Principal Cailleach said at last. "I didn't arrive at Annie Lytle to simply be a principal, as you may know. I'm a minor goddess on the Council of Pantheons, often ignored. I'm invisible around more powerful members, and I use that to my advantage."

"How so?" Detective Troias asked.

"I catch secrets. I learn what I can to sway decisions, but one day I heard something I knew I needed to act on. It wasn't something I should use for my own gain." The wintry goddess looked at Pavlina. "They spoke about a little girl in Jacksonville, FL who had cursed a boy, and how they were certain she would be picked as this century's Chosen One the moment she reached the typical age quests are given."

Pavlina nodded. "I remember you mentioning something about that."

"That's when I started researching her," the principal went on, now looking at everyone. "I employed crows to travel across realities for every version of her."

"I thought you didn't like crows," Pavlina put in.

"I never said that," Principal Cailleach responded. "I just don't like your crows causing a mess inside the school. I was fine with renting Atlas crows for inter-reality errands."

"But why?" Cal asked. "I've been to enough realities to know that Bree could have been completely different or not exist at all."

"Because I wanted to find an empty spot where she could belong if things went wrong."

"You knew," Pavlina whispered.

The principal shook her head. "I suspected; there's a difference. I've lived for so long that I was even there when Finn was picked. I've seen the trend of Chosen Ones dying early on. That's not normal."

Detective Troias turned the conversation back to her questioning. "So, your crows spotted a family in a non-magical reality. How did you know those people would remain in Jacksonville or would be willing to take Bree in?"

"Because I left a spy," Principal Cailleach answered. "Someone who sent me regular communication through the crows. When everyone ran off to help Bree, I checked with her to confirm."

This revelation shook Pavlina. "A spy? Who?"

"The grandmother over there," the principal said. "I

gave her enough charged crystals and an Atlas device so that she could summon crows and keep tabs on Bree's progress." She frowned. "Unfortunately, her communication has dropped since the beginning of the school year. I assume she felt her job was done."

Pavlina bolted up from her seat, sending the plastic chair clattering to the linoleum floor. "Why didn't you ever tell us any of this? Why—?"

Pounding on the emergency exit door caught everyone's attention. A shout, shrill and indecipherable followed the thundering knock.

"Let me see what this is." Finn got up and headed to the window.

Pavlina didn't wait for him to check. She raced to the door, knowing exactly who was calling. She'd heard that voice at every conceivable pitch and volume. *Bree.* More than that, a strike of icy nausea shot right down her spine. Bree or not, impending death waited outside. The strong sirin busted the door open, causing the emergency alarm to blare. Pavlina didn't notice.

Standing on the other side was Bree, but not just her. Behind Bree were two people who looked enough like the teenager that Pavlina had to assume they were her parents. The father held a sleeping Liz in his arms. She was limp and looked even smaller than Pavlina remembered her.

"Liz is sick, really sick!" Bree's voice was frantic,

and she'd been crying for so long that her collar was wet. "We have to get her to a hospital! Please!"

ELEVEN

The Emergency

Bree knew finding help had been a gamble when they drove to the ruins that had once been an elementary school. It was Saturday. The school was typically empty on those days. Even if someone *was* there, it would likely be a custodian or some other person who would have no idea what was going on.

When Ms. Sirin opened the door, Bree almost screamed with relief. She didn't have time to celebrate her luck, though.

When she and her parents left the house, they'd had to get Liz into the car. That proved to be a struggle with a girl who flopped like a wet noodle when placed in the backseat. Then they had to drive away, but her grandmother ran out of the house with a thousand different questions and opinions. The old woman was certain that they were making a mistake, but Mr. Castille ignored his mother.

By the time the four of them reached the fence where Bree intended to cast the portal, Liz seemed even weaker. Frantic with anticipatory grief, Bree's multiple attempts to open a portal proved useless. Each fairy stone only bounced off or flew through the chain link fence.

After the sixth attempt, Bree fell to her knees and cried into her hands. To her surprise, Mrs. Castille kneeled next to her and rubbed her back affectionately. "You can do this," she'd whispered. "I know... I know what it is to feel hopeless, powerless. You don't have to. Breathe."

The woman demonstrated by taking deep breaths herself. Bree mimicked her and soon, the storm of danger calmed so that she could focus on what she needed to do. She got on her feet again, rolled a stone around in her palm, chanted, and tossed the stone.

The portal opened, this time looking like temple doors, making her parents gasp. Bree realized then that they hadn't quite believed in her plan, but they were willing to try it, because it was their only option.

"Let's go," Bree said and waved them through.

Once on the other side, she closed the portal and Mr. Castille stared at her, impressed. "You do that every day?"

Bree nodded. "It's worth it."

When Ms. Sirin opened the door for them, that seemed more like a miracle than their transportation from one reality to another. Even then, there were obstacles.

"Oh gods," Ms. Sirin rushed to caress Liz's cheek and kissed the top of her head. "This is the worst I've ever seen. Oh gods, what will we do?"

"Get her to the hospital!" Bree yelled again, trying to be heard over the blaring siren above the exit door they stood at.

Over Ms. Sirin's shoulder, Bree could see Principal Cailleach clap and then suddenly the alarm was off, leaving only the ringing in Bree's ears.

"We need to get her to the hospital!" Bree exclaimed again.

Some woman Bree had never seen before stood up, "That's much too dangerous right now."

Bree squinted at Ms. Sirin. "Who's that?"

As worried as Bree's former foster mother had looked a moment before, her eyes looked even more plaintive now, down-turned and framed by tented brows.

"This is Detective Troias," she said, gesturing at the woman. "She's a homicide detective investigating the deaths of girls in Jacksonville who look very much like you. There's a serial killer…" She swallowed down a shaking breath. "They're trying to lure you out."

The detective shook her head. "You know I disagree with that theory. I wish you'd hear me out."

Mr. Finn walked over and gently moved Pavlina aside, creating a wider entrance to the cafeteria. "Please come in. We should figure this out some place less…" He glanced around at the moss-laden oak trees and down the littered but empty road. "Outside."

Bree entered, with her parents walking behind her. Cal was there and Principal Cailleach too. They both looked tired. Bree hadn't ever thought of her principal as someone who *could* look tired.

The wintry woman stood and walked over to Liz slumped against Mr. Castille's chest. She pressed a hand against her back and examined the girl with her pale eyes. "We can't waste any time." She looked up at Ms. Sirin. "I'm sure you felt it."

Ms. Sirin hesitated but nodded.

"We can't take her to the hospital, though," the detective said. "I don't know if we'd even make it once it's known that Bree's sister is out of this protective boundary. Does anyone know a doctor we could bring here?"

"No, but I have another idea," Cal said. She rustled through her satchel and picked out a fairy stone, looking at Bree as she did so. "You remember that Timucua reality?"

A flash of hope brightened the room at once. "You think they can help her?"

"Kid, they fully healed your broken ribs in a matter of hours." Cal stood up and cinched her pouch shut. "I don't know if there's anything they can't do."

"You think they'll be safe over there?" Ms. Sirin asked.

"Well, not permanently," Cal answered. "If this group is tied to the Council of Pantheons, they can get to any reality. Well, apart from theirs, due to the lack of magic." The bookdealer gestured at the Castille parents. "It would take them time to figure out where she'd hopped off too, though. We'd have more than enough time to help Liz out."

Detective Troias stroked her chin, considering Cal's words. "There's still a small risk, but that certainly seems like the safest bet." She looked over at Bree. "I'd go a step further and split up the group. Whoever is after Bree will be watching any time she enters or exits a reality. They probably already know she's here. She needs to stay in the school while it's a sanctuary. A few of us will stay here with her and a few will go with her sister."

"That's the plan." Principal Cailleach's tone didn't hold a hint of negotiation. "Cal, Mr. Finn, and Mr. Castille. You three take Liz to the Timucua reality. Ms. Sirin and Mrs. Castille, you stay with Bree. Detective Troias and I will continue talking in my office. Come there if you need anything."

Mr. Finn, Ms. Sirin, and Bree's parents looked back

and forth between one another. No one wanted to leave anyone behind. Not each other, not Liz, not Bree. In an unspoken heartbeat, however, resignation flattened their features. As terrifying and possibly heartbreaking as this was, it was their best plan and hesitating any longer would only lower its chances of success.

Rather than sit in the cafeteria, which had grown eerie and cavernous without everyone else, Pavlina escorted Bree and her mother to the magical history classroom. When she flipped on the lights, Mrs. Castille gasped.

"This is such a beautiful classroom…"

Pavlina turned to usher them in and saw that Bree's mother had her arm holding onto Bree in a protective manner, but her eyes tracked the posters bordering the top of the walls. "Who are all these people?"

"Famous magical philosophers," Bree answered.

"And alchemists," Pavlina added.

Mrs. Castille squinted. "Is that René Descartes?"

Pavlina looked where the woman pointed. "Yes."

"He does magic?"

"Well, he was a famous alchemist and magical philosopher." The magical history teacher turned to Bree. "And Bree, he actually did a lot for the practice of traveling through realities."

Bree's mother shook her head in wonder. "I always just thought he was a mathematician. A religious one, a philosophical one. But magic?"

Pavlina made her way to her desk, where she kept some snacks she wanted to offer Bree and her mother. "He's not the same as the one from your reality. Magic doesn't exist there."

"Well, I wouldn't be so certain of that," Mrs. Castille said, her eyes still tracking the posters.

Bree and Pavlina exchanged a shocked glance and then turned their gaze to Mrs. Castille.

"What do you mean?" Pavlina asked.

"There are plenty of people where I'm from that believe in magic," Bree's mother said. She was now walking around the perimeter of the room, pointing at each poster as she inspected them. "We have people who profess to be witches and shamans. There are people who claim they've seen fairies."

Mrs. Castille stopped in front of one poster and turned to look at Pavlina. "This guy right here? Aleister Crowley? He's famous where I'm from for starting an occult sect. He preached that magic was real, wieldable, and desirable. There's some debate about whether he was a charlatan, possibly even a predator, but… If there was never any magic where I'm from, why would we have these kinds of stories?"

Bree had told Pavlina that even the air there lacked the buzz of magic. It had felt like a desert to her. By the time she got to school, she was usually parched for some drop of magic, after thirsting for it so long. *But then many deserts used to have lakes and streams. The climate just changed.*

"Have some cookies." Pavlina brought out a box of ginger snaps and offered them.

Mrs. Castille lowered her head and waved her hand. "I don't think I could possibly eat when I feel this scared."

"Of course." Pavlina lifted it in Bree's direction.

"No thanks, Ms. Sirin."

Pavlina placed the box back in her desk drawer and sat down. She was frightened too. A cloud of death had hung over Liz. It wasn't certain, but it did seem to be waiting there, ready to cloak the girl the moment there was no possibility of survival. *The Timucuan doctors can do anything, though.* The sirin hoped that was enough.

Clearing her throat, Pavlina continued the conversation, knowing that it was either talk or fall down a spiral of hopeless thoughts. "You talk like a scholar."

Mrs. Castille offered her a sad smile. "I used to be." She sighed and left her journey along the poster border to sit down at a desk marred by countless pen and pencil drawings, as well as nicks. "I have a doctorate in anthropology. I used to be a professor. And then..."

Bree sat next to her mother. "Gabby and Betty

died?"

The woman nodded. "It didn't seem to matter anymore. Nothing did. And now Liz is sick, and there's someone after you." Her tears came so fast, she didn't have time to wipe them away. She might as well have been fighting a tide with a broom. "Am I cursed? Is that why this is happening?"

Pavlina rushed a box of tissues over to Mrs. Castille. "This was happening whether you were involved or not."

"Yeah," Bree said and tapped on her mother's hand with a fresh tissue. "You didn't tell grandmother to put decongestant in Liz's tea."

"Wait…" Pavlina sat down sideways on a desk in front of Bree and Mrs. Castille so she could see them. "Your grandmother made Liz sick?"

"It was a home remedy she used to use when my husband was sick as a child," Mrs. Castille explained. She wiped her face and blew her nose into the tissue. "She's been getting eccentric as she's gotten older, and doesn't believe in modern medicine."

"I'd say she's been more than eccentric," Bree added. She squinted and shook her head, as she traced the grooves of someone's name on the desk she sat at. "She's always watching online videos telling her that vaccines cause autism and that Covid is a myth."

"Covid?" Pavlina asked.

"It's a deadly virus where we're from," Mrs. Castille

explained.

Pavlina shook her head. "Why would anyone think that wasn't real?"

Bree's mother sighed. "Because she's constantly glued to this tablet watching videos of people telling her it's all a conspiracy. I don't even know where she got that thing. It's not a brand I've heard of. But at least she keeps to her room when she's watching this stuff."

Pieces started coming together as Pavlina remembered what Principal Cailleach had told her about communicating with the grandmother.

"Is it an Atlas brand?"

Mrs. Castille nodded. "You've heard of it?"

Bree's eyes shot open wide. "I knew she had a tablet, but I'd never seen it up close. I just…"

"Is that bad?" Bree's mother asked.

"Atlas tech doesn't exist in that reality," Bree explained. "How did she get one?"

Because Principal Cailleach gave her one.

"We need to go talk to Principal Cailleach." Pavlina opened the door and gestured for the other two to join in her leaving the classroom. "And Detective Troias. Now."

Finn didn't like having a fish in his ear, but he'd

let Cal shove a dozen of them in there if he needed it to communicate with the Timucuan doctors. These were the best healers anyone knew of. Finn knew how lucky it was that, at least in one reality, this nation of Native Americans still existed in northeastern Florida. However, while they'd been quick with Bree's injury, they clearly understood that Liz's condition was much more extreme.

"Five hours..." Mr. Castille said, his voice sluggish with exhaustion. "We've been sitting here for five hours."

Why use the energy to bring up the time?

They sat in a row along the thatched bench that nestled against cool, rounded, mud walls. Across from them was a window framing a scene that could have been a postcard. Countless pine trees and palm trees lined the streets far below them. Ahead was the serpentine path of the St. Johns River. Its brown tannin contrasted against the leaves which nearly exploded with neon green. A few wispy clouds danced across the impossibly blue sky. Not one of them cared.

"It took three hours for them to heal Bree's broken rib," Cal said as she fiddled with the compass on her multitool. "It's going to take longer to help with Liz's long-term exposure to poison."

"Decongestants aren't poison," Mr. Castille insisted for the fiftieth time during their stay in the hospital waiting room.

Finn gave the man a blistering stare. "They are to someone like Liz."

"I. Didn't. Know." Each word from Mr. Castille's mouth was enunciated through gritted teeth, to communicate just how much anger he was holding back.

"You should have," Finn said.

Mr. Castille jolted from his seat, but Cal pushed him back into it. "If you two are going to fight, at least take it outside of a hospital where people are trying not to die. *People like Liz.*"

Cal's voice was just as firm as her features. A flat line replaced her gap-toothed smile. Dark circles framed her sparkless eyes. Even the curl of her short-cropped hair had lost its bounce. Finn knew to listen when this bookdealer was serious. She laughed in the face of so much danger that it was scary when she wore a frown.

"It's hard," Finn whispered as he slumped against the wall. He rubbed his face up to his hairline and twisted his long, blond hair into a bun on the top of his head. "I was able to protect her when she was here. She's so little for someone her age. So frail."

Mr. Castille nodded. "Sometimes I forget she's thirteen. She looks the same age Betty did when she died, and that was years ago."

Finn looked at Liz's father through kinder eyes. "Did your Liz have sickle cell too?"

"No, she was perfectly healthy." The man cast his

eyes to his feet. "Not that it mattered. There's no vitamin or vaccination that could have saved her and Gabby from drowning."

"Gods, I can't imagine your pain," Cal whispered. "I'd be crying all day after something like that."

"Crying is what my wife does." Mr. Castille worked his jaw while staring at some dark memory on the horizon. "I don't deserve to grieve. I let them go to the beach with their friends. I didn't check that there was a strong swimmer with them or even if anyone knew first aid."

Cal patted Mr. Castille's shoulder. "You made a small mistake, one that most likely wouldn't have resulted in a tragedy like that in most cases. Be easy on yourself."

Liz's father shirked away from Cal's sympathetic hand. "The moment I let things go is the moment someone else gets hurt. My wife is so weak now. If I slack off an inch, I don't know what she'll do to herself."

Cal shook her head. "You really can't take on the responsibility of your wife's—"

"No," Finn said. "I get it."

Mr. Castille looked away from the horizon and directed his questioning gaze on Finn. "What do you mean?"

"I have a daughter," Finn said. "She… she got in a really bad situation because I thought she would be fine no matter what decisions I made about my own life. She was grown, and still my world affected hers. I've been blaming myself ever since."

"Oísina is fine," Cal said.

Finn shook his head. "She may be out of her prison, but she's not fine. She may be happy with you, Cal, but there will still be moments where she thinks about her frightening past and it greys out all the color in her world for a moment."

"How do you know?"

"Because that's what life is like for me now," Finn answered. "I may be out of Tartarus. The wounds on my back may have healed."

Finn pointed at his temple. "But there will always be scars here." He pointed at his heart. "And here." His hand dropped to his lap. "Everything else is just a distraction from this burning hatred in my chest."

"Hatred?" Mr. Castille asked. "At the people who hurt you and your daughter?"

"No. At myself. I could have prevented it all if I'd just played it safe."

Finn let this statement settle on him, and understood what his parole officer had seen in his words. He may resent the Council of Pantheons, but he blamed himself. Oísina would have a scar she'd wear for the eternity of her life because he couldn't protect her.

"Yeah…" Liz's father whispered. "It's like you can either be angry or you can sit with this hate you feel for yourself."

Finn and Mr. Castille locked eyes, seeing the mirror in each other.

Before Finn could say anything, a woman opened the door to the waiting room with a kind and confident grin on her face. "Thank you for waiting. We're nearly done. The poison was difficult to draw out."

"It wasn't really poison—" Finn started.

"No, it was," Mr. Castille relented. "It was to her, but now we know better. I need to learn more about sickle cell."

"Oh! No need!" The woman's smile brightened. "We actually realized a better solution was to simply remove her sickle cell condition. Fortunately, one of our best magical surgeons was on call today."

"What?" the trio said in unison, bolting up from their bench.

"You can just... *cure* someone of sickle cell anemia with magic?" Liz's father shook his head in disbelief.

"No, not at all," Finn said. "Liz went to the best hospitals in our reality. They'd have cured her by now."

"Any blood disorder can be healed here," the woman stated.

"Why isn't everyone from every reality coming here for health care?" Finn asked.

"Well, as the head of the Council of Pantheons authority, the Greek pantheon overruled our gods and implemented a strict policy on not allowing anyone to travel to our reality," the woman explained. "With exemption for people like Cal here."

Finn blinked. "Cal?"

"Yes, she's—"

Cal jumped in. "I'm a bookdealer. It's like I have a VIP pass to any reality."

The woman squinted at Cal for a moment, but then returned her attention back to her chart. "Liz will be ready to leave after a few hours of rest," the woman said. "In the meantime, please have something to eat in the food hall on the first floor."

The Timucuan woman closed the door behind her, leaving Finn and Mr. Castille staring at Cal.

"Bookdealers travel through realities?" Bree's father asked.

"Of course they do!" Cal said. "Best way to get rare books."

Mr. Castille chuckled. "And Bree goes to school every day knowing people in her life are having all these adventures?"

"Well, she has them too," Finn responded.

"Yes, I'm still coming to terms with that," Mr. Castille said. "I wish her biggest problems were a bad test score or an unrequited crush. That I could help with, but this all seems beyond me."

"I'd wager not many parents have hopped across multiple realities to take their kid to the doctor," Finn responded. "So, maybe you're doing better than you give yourself credit for."

TWELVE

The Morning Revelations

Bree woke up stiff and sore from sleeping on a cot in the school basement. Before she even opened her eyes, she gagged at the scent of glawackus dung. *They couldn't put us in the area with all the board games?*

Fortunately, the pens had been covered for their protection. No one could afford to forget a single thing given their currently very dangerous circumstances. When Principal Cailleach had guided them down to the basement for their own safety, she'd made sure to explain all the precautions taken against an incident.

Unfortunately for Bree's mother, this was the first time she'd heard about monsters who could wipe your memories if you looked into their eyes. She seemed to think it was an extreme measure to enforce the Family

Educational Rights and Privacy Act, but Principal Cailleach assured her that it only deleted details about grades and such. Bree doubted the woman had gotten a moment of sleep, even though she'd kept her eyes shut tight the moment she laid down. Given that Mrs. Castille wasn't on her cot when Bree woke, she felt more certain of her assumption.

Eager to leave the scent of feces behind, Bree sprinted up the stairs to find Mrs. Castille in the cafeteria picking at a fruit cup. Though the woman hadn't eaten since lunch the previous day, she still didn't seem to have an appetite.

Without looking up to see whose footsteps were approaching, Mrs. Castille said, "There are a lot of differences between this reality and mine, but the one that's strangest to me out of all of them is the presence of a basement."

Bree squinted as she sat down across the table from her mother. "Why's that? There are basements where you're from. I've seen them on TV."

Mrs. Castille set her plastic spoon down on her napkin and looked up at Bree. "But not at our house, right? Basements aren't a thing in Florida. The water table is too high, especially near rivers, lakes, and oceans. And this school is what… a fifteen minute walk or less to the river?"

"That's right," Bree answered.

"So how is it possible that it's not flooded down

there?"

Bree shrugged. "I'm not an architect."

A chilly breeze caught Bree's attention and she knew Principal Cailleach was nearby. She brought two styrofoam cups of coffee with her and handed one to Mrs. Castille before sitting down.

"Thank Christ," Bree's mother whispered before chugging it down.

Principal Cailleach arched a brow. "I don't know who Christ is, but I'm the one who got you coffee."

"Christ is a title they have for Jesus over there," Bree explained.

"Oh!" Principal Cailleach seemed surprised, which was just about the strangest thing Bree had ever witnessed. The woman's face, which normally looked like ancient stone under frost, stretched to the point where Bree thought the old woman might crack. "Jesus exists over there? But he's a god!"

Mrs. Castille laughed. "Your reality doesn't own religion."

"No, it's not that," Bree explained. "She's surprised because your reality isn't supposed to have enough magic to support a god's existence."

"Well, you know what I have to say about *that*." Mrs. Castille looked into the bottom of her now-empty cup and frowned. "Is there any more coffee?"

"In the kitchen behind that wall." Principal Cailleach pointed. "But, first, what is this about magic?"

"She thinks there's magic there too," Bree explained.

"I want to hear from her what her thoughts are," the principal said, giving Bree her infamously stern face.

"Well, it's like Bree said," Mrs. Castille said. "We have thousands of years of people telling tales of magic, believing in it. People have claimed they wielded it. We even have stories about similar creatures as yours."

"Really? Like what?"

"Well, Bree and I started reading her book about werewolf creatures. We have books and movies about them where I'm from." Bree's mother bobbed her chin a little in thought. "Well, they're a little different here than where I'm from. No alphas and fated mates."

"They're not creatures," Bree said, tapping her mother's shoulder. "They're supernaturals, people like you and me. Remember?"

"Oh, yes." Mrs. Castille nodded. "I remember you said your friend Ylva is very vocal about supernatural rights."

Principal Cailleach tapped her chin while her cloudy eyes peered right into Mrs. Castille's. The non-magical woman didn't seem intimidated by this, which surprised Bree since everyone else was terrified of her principal.

"This is interesting, very interesting indeed."

For a moment, the winter goddess seemed lost in

introspection as she drank her cup of coffee. Just as Bree was about to ask where she could find a fruit cup like her mother's, Principal Cailleach spoke again.

"I suppose it's possible that there was once as much magic there as here, at least the kind that would exist over there. And something just… leached it out."

Mrs. Castille nodded. "That's my thinking."

"Let me accompany you to get more coffee," the principal said, rising from her seat.

Before the two women could walk to the kitchen, however, the sudden appearance of palm fronds spreading apart from each other opened a portal. Cal, Mr. Finn, and Mr. Castille stepped through. Liz was there too with a cheery smile on her face as she held on to both Mr. Finn's hand and Mr. Castille's.

"Liz!" Bree flashed over to her sister and squeezed her tight.

"Oof!" Liz croaked.

Bree pulled away at once. "I'm sorry, I forgot for a moment about your asthma."

Liz laughed. "Oh Bree! Bree!" Joyful tears splashed from her sparkling eyes. "It's… it's *gone!*"

"What's gone?"

"*It!* The sickle cell… It's just not there anymore."

By this point, Mrs. Castille had caught up with Bree, and grabbed Liz for a happy embrace.

"How is that possible?" Bree directed her question to the adults who had returned from the Timucuan reality.

Cal nodded at Finn and carried on closing the portal behind them.

"They can do that there," the Irishman explained. "That's how advanced their medicine is. We just didn't know because they have a strict policy about who can even know they exist."

Bree couldn't stop the laughter bubbling from her. She only stopped to cry and hold her sister tight. All those years of worry, all the times she'd looked up the life expectancy for someone like her sister. Those moments were in the past. The future wasn't an epitaph she'd memorized for some horribly certain path for the person she loved most in the world.

But that's not the only danger now. We can't run forever. We can't even hide, not when the other reality may not be as safe from the gods as we thought.

Pavlina hadn't been able to sleep in the basement with everyone else. Too many thoughts and worries somersaulted in her brain. That along with the snoring coming from the glawackus pens had ruined any chance of rest. So she'd gone to her classroom once everyone else seemed asleep.

Mrs. Castille's words had intrigued her. It wasn't unheard of for realities to have overlaps, but a non-magical reality sharing so many of the same magical

concepts seemed far-fetched. After the revelation that Principal Cailleach's last-minute escape plan had actually been an orchestrated Plan B years in the making, Pavlina found herself questioning anything she'd assumed was the truth.

At some point, while reading Descartes' essays on reality, "I think, therefore I am" turned into "I blink, therefore I sleep." When the magical history teacher finally woke, she found a puddle of drool on her desk and winced at the crick in her neck. She looked at the clock and panicked for a moment seeing that it was nearly eight in the morning. Then she remembered it was Sunday.

With a yawn and a stretch, Pavlina rose from her chair. She recounted yesterday's events as she walked to the cafeteria. The scent of coffee was meager solace against the grim thoughts she battled. *Is Liz okay? Is Bree? Gods, the world is darker than my own feathers right now.*

When Pavlina opened the door to the cafeteria, she shouted with joy and ran toward the group. With one swift motion, she scooped Liz up in her arms. The girl was so light, even her aura had lost its weight. Not even a hint of nausea bothered the sirin.

"You're okay, you're okay. Oh, Liz! You're *alive*!"

Finn stroked Pavlina's back and gave her a peck on the cheek. "More than that, my love. She's healed."

"*Obviously!*"

Pavlina set Liz down. The girl looked at her former foster mother with an amused spark in her eye. She caught her breath for a moment and then laughed.

"Wait…" Pavlina turned her gaze to Finn. "What do you mean by healed?"

"Completely. No more routine medical treatments for this kid."

Finn reached to ruffle Liz's curls, but the girl smacked his hand away. "It takes a while to make my hair look nice!"

Pavlina gawked, too scared to believe it but also too desperate not to. As she did so, Mrs. Castille walked over to hug her daughter before guiding her to sit next to her at the table.

"Sit down," Mrs. Castille said to the others. "We were just about to explain what we figured out last night."

"I've called Detective Troais," Principal Cailleach said. "She'll be here momentarily. Hopefully she'll have more ideas on this when she comes back." She held up a pot of coffee. "Would you like a cup, Ms. Sirin?"

"Yes, please," Pavlina said, relief spilling out of her words as she sat next to Bree's mother. "Should I start?"

After Mrs. Castille nodded, Pavlina detailed the revelations from the previous evening. With every word, Cal's, Mr. Castille's, and Mr. Finn's eyes grew wider and wider. Just as she finished, Principal Cailleach got up from her seat announcing that she'd heard a knock at the front door and left to answer it.

Mr. Castille looked as though someone had hit him straight in the chest with a cannonball. "So, my mom... She's what? Possessed?"

"We don't know exactly what's going on, but it sounds like something flipped just about the time this sect started going after girls to lure Bree out," Pavlina answered.

"How would that lure her out, though?" Mrs. Castille asked. "Wouldn't that make Bree stay in hiding?"

"I'm not sure anyone's told this to you," Pavlina said, "but Bree was picked last year as this century's Chosen One by the Council of Pantheons. That's only given to true heroes."

Mr. and Mrs. Castille shared a quizzical look and turned back to Pavlina. "You mean like she was destined to save the world?"

"Well, more like she was the most highly qualified candidate to make a big positive change in the world," Pavlina answered. She wavered her hand with uncertainty. "Though, the last few Chosen Ones were just given a questing beast and the CoP called it a day."

"Well, we know why now," Finn said.

The grim bitterness in his tone didn't surprise Pavlina, but it did seem to rattle Bree's parents.

"I don't suppose Bree explained why she needed to move to your reality," Pavlina said.

"She just told us it wasn't safe to live here," Mrs. Castille said. She looked at her husband for confirmation and he nodded.

Pavlina sighed, hating to be the one to tell them this. *Harbinger of death, bearer of bad news.* "It turns out there are some gods part of a secret group who use quests to sacrifice Chosen Ones so that they can lengthen their immortality."

"And she's been coming to this school here Monday through Friday, knowing that people wanted her dead?" Anger burned in Mr. Castille's cheeks as he turned to his daughter. "Bree! What were you thinking?"

"I just wanted to learn—"

"And you!" Mr. Castille pointed a shaking finger at Finn. "You *let* her?"

"There are extra protections here. She's perfectly—"

"That doesn't make any sense." Mrs. Castille interrupted. "Immortality means living forever. You can't lengthen eternity. That means they lost it, and if the gods are so powerful to track a girl across realities, then how could they lose that?"

"I think we all assumed they were immortal because they'd lived for so long," Pavlina said. "I guess they only had the ability to live for a long time and some of them are just now figuring that out."

"I must admit that it was quite sobering when I learned that my life is finite," Principal Cailleach interjected. "To know that the only difference between me and the mortals I encounter is that I've been around longer." She cast her pale eyes on Bree. "And that I am the past, while heroes like you are the future."

"I wonder if they're scared of her, of all the Chosen Ones," Mrs. Castille said. "Mortals becoming powerful enough to change the whole world? Sounds like stiff competition to me. I mean, isn't that why the Titans fought Zeus and his siblings?"

"Titans?" Cassandra Troias said as she entered the cafeteria with Principal Cailleach. "Like Atlas?"

Detective Troias nodded at Pavlina in greeting. "I was thinking about what you shared all night. Bree's grandmother held onto that thing for years, and since the Castille girls arrived, she's gotten more radicalized against medicine to the point where Liz almost died."

"That's a lot of people her age these days," Mr. Castille said.

"But how many of them have access to magical technology?" Troias asked and then she looked over at Pavlina. "And why did she suddenly stop communicating with Principal Cailleach when school started?"

Mr. Castille turned a questioning gaze toward the principal. The wintry woman opened her mouth to speak, but Cassandra wasn't done talking.

"The timing was what really irked me," Troias said. "I had my suspicions, but I didn't want to give into them and if I fell asleep I might have a vision, and then no one would believe me. So I spent the whole night researching Atlas tech's capabilities."

"What did you find out?" Pavlina asked.

"Even though there are no public records of who owns or created it, the CoP gave all Atlas tech blanket permission to monitor more than its users' locations and purchases."

Despite the dread growing in her, Pavlina knew she had to ask. "Like what?"

"It can listen to, watch, and record its users," Troias answered. "Anywhere that it functions as a communication tool. *Anywhere*."

Finn stewed, wondering how long this had been going on. He and Oísina had been granted immortality for fulfilling their roles as Chosen Ones, but some centuries ago, that reward had been taken off the table, replaced with a prestigious internship and acceptance into any school of their choice. It was by no means an even trade for risking your life.

Had the Council of Pantheons truly put Oísina into a book to keep Finn beholden to his community service, or was that to keep her power contained? Had his sentence to Tartarus actually been to use torture as a means of correction or had it been to break his will? Was his time as a teacher only to give the appearance that they weren't trying to harm Chosen Ones?

Hermes had forced Bree into a quest that he knew she'd have no hope of succeeding at. He'd made Finn an accomplice. It was only through luck that they'd saved Bree. With every minute, he knew Hermes was building up enough power to shatter their reality if he wanted to.

Before the greedy god had fallen into Cal's portal, he'd said that his "boss" was far more powerful than Zeus. A Titan could possibly have more power than a god losing his immortality without his knowledge. Atlas would certainly have a grudge against the King of the Council of Pantheons, as well. After all, it had been the Greek gods who had punished him with an eternity of quite literally bearing the weight of the world on his shoulders.

When Detective Troias revealed the trail of clues she'd followed, Finn felt a strong urge not to believe her. Every fact, though, weakened that instinct. It all made sense, it all clicked into place. The very company that created all the devices and services that were meant to help, had built the perfect machine to monitor and even control the world. *Even other realities.*

Finn's anger did nothing to help the situation,

though. He couldn't punch and kick his way through a problem like this. This wasn't a war he could win. Of course, that only magnified his rage. When the detective finished revealing everything, Finn excused himself and left the cafeteria. He didn't even pause to explain. He simply marched out.

It wasn't until he reached the gymnasium that Finn realized that was where he'd felt compelled to go. He grabbed a basketball and bounced it with all the force he could muster against the basketball court floor.

With Finn's mageiathalamus blocked by the Council of Pantheons, there was no risk of him breaking anything with his previous supernatural strength. Another realization punched him in the gut. They'd neutered him. They'd taken away a part so integral to his identity so that they could ensure he was harmless, no threat at all to the power they held over the world. *They said I'd have it back once my sentence was served, but that could have been another lie to control me.*

"Those bastards! Those bastards!"

Finn flung the basketball as far as he could, causing it to bounce off a distant wall and soar back at him. He dodged out of the way, but it slowed down and fell a few yards short. The immortal warrior, not feeling even a little like the hero he had once been, lowered to his knees on the floor. Exhausted by the limit of his very human physical capacity, Finn only had one outlet left for his pain—tears.

This wasn't a beautiful, melancholy moment like he'd witnessed with Pavlina's tears. This also wasn't anything like the burning pricks at his eyes that he wiped away immediately. It was ugly. His screaming sobs flayed his throat as the tears fell from him like rivers of grief.

Then, a familiar, cool palm swathed him with a calm that only a harbinger could provide to a person who had suffered a great loss. His roars of pain softened to gasping breaths. His heaving chest sank as he slumped onto Pavlina's shoulder.

"I feel your pain, my love," she whispered and pressed her lips against the top of his head.

"How? How could anyone?"

Pavlina lay her cheek where her lips had just touched and wrapped her strong arm around his shoulder. "Because I feel all of you in my heart every moment of every day."

"I used to be able to protect the defenseless."

"And you still can," Pavlina said. "But you don't need to right now, because none of us, not one of us in here, is defenseless."

Finn pulled away from Pavlina's embrace to take a better look at her. There wasn't a hint of doubt on her face, only the calm he felt at her touch. "Yeah?"

"Bree's mother said something earlier, and I think she's right. The gods view all Chosen Ones as competition."

"Except me." Finn hated the sulk in his tone and hoped Pavlina wouldn't think less of him for it. *I should be more concerned for Bree and Liz right now than my own ego.*

"Are you kidding me?" Pavlina looked at him with creased brows, shaking her head.

Finn felt certain that she was calling him out for his childishness, and prepared to apologize, but then she continued.

"They should be even more scared of you."

This was the last thing Finn had expected to hear. He was sure there'd either be pity or admonition in her words.

"Why should they?"

"You've spent ninety-one years shaping young minds," she said. "You haven't buckled to their punishment or submitted to them. You've never once wavered on your choice to save lives at the risk of your own. Finn, even without your former powers, even without their countless threats and tortures, you've stood your ground against them."

A sharp glint shone around the edges of her usually soft, languid eyes. "And worst of all for them, you've only grown more resentful. They have every right to be terrified of you, and I bet they haven't even considered the nightmare you could unleash upon them."

The burning that had wracked Finn with grief lit up

again, but this time it flickered with determination. "We're done hiding."

Pavlina nodded. "It's time to fight."

THIRTEEN

The Curriculum Change

It didn't feel right setting up desks in a semi-circle for a guided discussion using the Socratic method when the Castille family was hiding in the basement. When Pavlina had planned this lesson some weeks before, she hadn't realized just how strange events would turn out. A few quick revisions to the plan, however, made this perfect for new purposes.

Yes, Pavlina's students would learn the valuable skill of cooperative argument and gain a more personal understanding of some of the most famous magical philosophers in history. However, they would walk from this class with even more important knowledge. They would know their own worth and power, and hopefully measure the Council of

Pantheons with critical thinking instead of blind subservience. *I just hope that's enough to keep them out of harm's way.*

It was difficult to keep the ferocity out of her countenance and to disguise the pounding of her heart, but Pavlina knew it was worth it. Who knew how many gods were intent on ending more innocent lives to remain immortal cowards? She would make sure not one of her students left this school defenseless.

Pavlina's focus was so intense that she didn't even notice Mrs. Selkie had entered the room until she felt a tap on her shoulder. She jumped in response, startling the swim instructor.

"Hey, relax! I come in peace!" Mrs. Selkie exclaimed, holding her hands up in defense.

Catching her breath, Pavlina said, "I'm sorry. I was lost in thought."

"Yeah, I can tell." Mrs. Selkie passed Pavlina a clipboard. "I want you to remember that I'm only a messenger when you read this."

Pavlina groaned as she read the words. "Are you kidding me with this bullshit?" she said, tapping the clipboard with the back of her hand.

Mrs. Selkie shrugged. "Sorry. I have to pass it out to everyone."

Scanning the paper again, Pavlina grew increasingly irritated. The head of the Florida Board of Education had decided it was time to reinvent the wheel *again*, and October hadn't even ended yet.

"I mean… Scripted lessons? Fifteen minutes of mandatory SAT prep in every class?" Pavlina looked up from the paper at her friend in disbelief. "They don't even test for magical history on the SAT!"

"I know," Mrs. Selkie said with a sigh. "I wish I could stay here and bitch with you about this, but I've been tasked to hand this out to every teacher who will now spend the day screaming about it."

"Gods, I'm sorry…"

Mrs. Selkie turned to leave, but then looked over her shoulder. "Oh, and by the way, they're cutting off all funding to swimming programs and canceling *all* health-related classes."

"What?!" Pavlina yelled, her voice ringing throughout her room. "Are you fired?"

Mrs. Selkie shook her head. "No, the Calculus teacher just quit over the weekend. So now I'm in charge of a curriculum that I have no expertise in at all. Good thing they're giving me scripted lessons!" Pavlina's friend had a sarcastically cheerful shine to her words, but it couldn't hide the pain in her eyes.

Pavlina wrapped Mrs. Selkie in a tight hug. "I'm so sorry. I know how much you've loved coaching."

The selkie was usually the most optimistic person Pavlina had ever known. She infected everyone with positivity. When Pavlina had been at her lowest, Mrs.

Selkie was there to pick her up and stop the sirin's self-sabotage. At that moment, however, Pavlina's friend sank into the hug, needing all the support the world had to offer.

"Thanks." Sniffing, Mrs. Selkie pulled away from her friend and forced a smile. "I'll see you later."

As Pavlina watched her head out the door, she felt some of her fiery energy slip away. Yes, she was determined to protect the students at Annie Lytle in every way she could, but she also had a job to do. Teaching was never easy, and often Florida politicians made it even more difficult.

The magical history teacher let out an exasperated puff. "Been teaching for almost twenty years and they can't even trust me to do anything other than work from a manual? Gods, these assholes."

Pavlina couldn't help but wonder if this was another tactic to weaken non-deities. *Stop it. Not everything is a conspiracy. Idiots have been ruining education since forever.*

Just when Pavlina made peace with the fact that she'd have to find creative ways to give her students a real education despite these last-minute changes, her door swung open. The sirin could feel Finn's rage before he even spoke a word.

"Can you believe this complete garbage?"

With a deep sigh, Pavlina turned, prepared to placate her boyfriend so he could actually teach that day. "I know. I'm sorry. A last minute change to curriculum really sucks."

Finn shook his head. "That alone is insulting, but it's far from the first time that's happened to me. No, it's this!" The magical application teacher waved the paper above his head. "They're cutting all funding to extra-curricular activities."

Pavlina nodded. "Yeah, Mrs. Selkie told me she can't coach swimming anymore."

"We just started the Magical Automaton Club, Pav."

Finn looked like he was on the verge of tears, and Pavlina had to fight the urge to cry with him.

"The kids. *My* students. They were learning so much. We just won our first match."

The giant of an Irishman slumped into one of the tiny desks in Pavlina's classroom and dropped his papers onto it. Planting his face between his two palms, he stared at the papers and whispered, "I can't believe it's already over."

Pavlina kneeled next to him. "It's just the funding that's cut. Maybe Principal Cailleach will find another way?"

Finn lifted his head and turned to look at Pavlina. "You think?"

"You should ask her. The worst she can say is she can't do anything."

Finn took Pavlina's hand and tenderly kissed the back of it. "Have I told you lately how much I love you?"

"No," The sirin said with a shrug, "but we've been a little busy saving lives and discovering truly disturbing things."

Finn shook his head. "That's no excuse. I should be telling you every hour how precious you are to me."

"You've been reading too many romance novels," Pavlina said with a laugh.

"There are *never* too many romance novels."

Finn made this bold declaration with such noble indignation that Pavlina's laugh turned into a snort. The sirin slapped a hand over her mouth in mortification.

"Aww," Finn said, laying a hand over his heart. "That's adorable."

Pavlina blessed her olive-skinned genes, because without it she was sure her blush would be obvious. "Stop it, I'm such a dork."

"The most beautiful dork in all the land!" Finn exclaimed with a sweeping gesture. "The dork that holds every atom in my heart."

A chorus of giggles drew Pavlina's attention to the doorway. A group of freshmen stood at the threshold laughing at them. *Oh gods… Not in front of teenagers…*

As Pavlina expected, one of the boys mimicked big, sloppy kisses, and another one said in the best falsetto impression he could muster, "Oh, Mr. Finn! You're such a dreamboat!"

Finn cleared his throat. "Well, it's time for me to

head to my class." He stood up, but not without taking the desk with him. With a grunt, he unstuck himself from it and let it fall to the ground. All of this caused the crowd of teenagers to laugh even more.

"Are you seriously leaving it to me to quiet this down?" Pavlina whispered.

"Seems to me that staying is just going to make it worse." Finn offered her his most charming smile before he walked out of the classroom.

The students whistled at him as he walked down the hall.

"Enough, enough," Pavlina called to them in exasperation as she put the desk back into its former position. "Class has started and we've got a temporary seating chart to sort out." The class groaned all at once. "I promise. This will be worth it."

This might be the last fun lesson you get once we switch over to the new curriculum.

Bree had experienced many strange school days at Annie Lytle Magical Magnet High. She wasn't sure anything could match knowing her parents were hanging out in the basement playing old board games with her little sister. She wasn't sure she could concentrate on school work with all that had happened over the weekend. Her sister had almost died, her parents from the non-magical reality hopped over to hers, and then she'd discovered just how closely everyone was being monitored by the gods.

On top of all that, Bree had to pretend everything was normal. She had to sleep in the basement next to the glawackus pens. In the morning, she had to wash herself using the ice cold water from the restroom sinks. She was grateful that Ms. Sirin had enough of her clothes from her freshman year. The only problem with that was that these clothes belonged to fifteen-year-old Bree and didn't fit sixteen-year-old Bree.

The teenager was still incredibly uncomfortable in any clothes that showed off any hint that she'd reached puberty. Bree longed for loose clothing that would allow her to feel comfortable and androgynous. She already got stares for being the Chosen One; she didn't need anyone ogling her because she was shaped like a girl.

When the school opened, Bree pretended to come in with all the other students, which she found difficult as she pulled her pants waist up and her shirt hem down. When Ylva arrived, Bree forgot all about her discomfort. Seeing her friend lent her a comfortable normalcy she desperately needed.

"Oh, gods, it's good to see you!" Bree said, rushing over to Ylva.

The German girl seemed just as happy to see Bree. "I really missed you on Friday. Were you sick?"

Bree laughed nervously as she lied, "Oh, just a little

twenty-four bug."

Ylva squinted, confused. "There was a bug?"

"Oh, that's a saying here for a virus that only lasts for a day," Bree explained. "Your English has already gotten so good, I keep forgetting you don't know all of our idioms."

"I'm sure you'll have taught me all of them by the end of the school year," Ylva said with a big golden smile.

The two girls walked toward their first class together in an unusual silence. Most mornings, they had so much to catch up on from when they'd last seen each other. Even if they didn't have that much to share, they at least buzzed with excitement when their first class of the day was Magic in the Humanities with Mr. Reynaud. Bree couldn't help wondering if things were still awkward because of their fight.

So, she blurted out the first thought in her head. "Um, so I read the book you gave me over the weekend."

"Did you like it?" Ylva asked. Her tone was light, but there was a noticeably nervous tremor to it.

"Of course, I did! It's about werewolves!"

Bree truly had loved every page of it, and wished that she could be in the basement right now reading it again. "I've been reading it with my mother. She said she really likes werewolves too so we figured we would talk about it with each other."

Ylva jolted and she whipped her head to the left to stare at Bree straight on with her wide, terrified eyes.

"Your mother is reading it?"

"Y-yes," Bree stuttered. "Is that... okay?"

A pained smile stamped onto Ylva's face. "Yes, it's fine. Does she like it?"

Okay, obviously sharing it with my mother was the farthest thing from fine ever. "Yeah, she loves it too. She said she's learned things about werewolves that she never knew and it changed the way she sees them."

Ylva's nervous features relaxed. Though she wasn't smiling anymore, her face seemed softer, calmer. "She did?"

Bree nodded. "Yeah, me too! I kind of wish I could get to know some of them now, but there aren't many who live in this area because you know..." She grimaced. "All the anti-werewolf folk in Jacksonville."

The golden-haired girl lowered her head. "Yeah, I know..."

"You've met enough people here to get a sense of who lives here, huh?"

"I mostly spend time with my host family. That's enough to know."

"That bad?"

Ylva shrugged, offering Bree only a forlorn expression.

"So I guess school is the only place you can talk about supernatural rights."

"And you're the only one who listens," Ylva said.

Bree now understood why her friend had been so upset about their disagreement. She'd become the one person Ylva felt comfortable being herself around. That wasn't just a difference of opinion to her, that was a seed of doubt about whether she could trust Bree.

The German girl resumed walking and Bree followed, all the while wondering if there was anything she could say to help Ylva feel better.

As they settled into their desks and Bree pulled stuff from her backpack, Ylva tapped her on her shoulder.

"Oh, do you need a pencil or something?"

"No." Ylva wore a sweet, genuine smile. She wasn't exactly beaming, but she was nothing like the sad girl in the hall. "I just wanted to thank you for what you said out there about werewolves and how you and your mom feel about them. I…" She chewed her bottom lip a little guiltily. "I don't know if you've noticed, but I can be a little moody. That's just how my family back in Germany is and I forget most people aren't like that."

Bree shook her head. "Hey, we all get that way sometimes. If it helps, you're one of my favorite people."

Ylva's eyes shone with the promise of tears and her smile spread. A soft blush spread pink over her golden tan. "Do you mean that?"

"I wouldn't lie about something like that."

The German girl wiped her eyes. "You're one of my favorite people too. I... Well, I've been wanting to tell you—"

"Hello, class!" Mr. Reynaud called out, catching Bree's attention. "Happy Monday! Hope you all had a great weekend. Today, we're going to start a new unit, so get ready to write down a *lot* of notes."

Bree turned back to ask Ylva what she was going to say, but the golden-haired girl was already writing down the date at the top of her grid paper. *I guess it wasn't that important.*

Finn spent the morning navigating a battle of emotions. Anger and fear churned in his guts. At times, he thought he might vomit into the trash bin. Other times, he thought of the moment he'd shared in the gymnasium with Pavlina. *"Because I feel all of you in my heart every moment of every day." She really said that.*

The Irishman already knew he loved her, but that moment went a step above. This was more than a sweeping romance. When Pavlina had told him that, when she'd rallied him, she felt like the other half of him, a feeling he hadn't had in many centuries. Time had worn away many memories of his wife, but one thing remained clear no matter what. She felt like *this.*

For months, Finn's main concern about their relationship was how much it would hurt when she died and he was left to grieve her. What the conversation about immortality the day before got him wondering about was his own. If it was slipping away, many things made more sense.

Finn had lived for many centuries. Most of it, he appeared to be a robust, wrinkle-free twenty-year-old. In the last couple of decades, his face had lost that youthful roundness, his joints were stiffer, and, as Pavlina sometimes pointed out, his cardiovascular health could use some improvement. For a while, he'd simply blamed it on the tamper on his mageiathalamus. Now, he suspected it had more to do with what Mrs. Castille suggested.

The idea of his possible death frightened Finn. He had no idea what it would mean for him. Was there an afterlife for those who were never supposed to die? Yet there was also a small relief there that this could mean a life with Pavlina that didn't end in centuries of grief.

Before Finn could consider any kind of future with her, he needed to concentrate on the present. He knew he should focus on solving the situation with Hermes or taking on the sect within the Council of Pantheons, but he didn't have any solid plans for that yet. One thing he *could* do was talk to Principal Cailleach about the new changes from the Florida Department of Education and what that meant for his club.

When he reached the front office, the door was propped open by another teacher waiting not-so-patiently to fully enter the room.

"What's going on?" Finn asked.

The teacher rolled her weary eyes. "We're all in here trying to find out stuff about the new changes to the curriculum and everything."

Of course. This doesn't just affect me and my club. "Gods, this isn't going to resolve itself by the end of lunch is it?"

"Probably not," the teacher said and she slumped against the door frame. "My planning period is right after lunch break, but I'm probably not going to talk to Principal Cailleach before that's over either. But I mean... I don't even know where this new *script* is right now or when I'll have it. Should I even be planning anything right now?"

Suddenly, Finn's club didn't feel nearly as important as everyone else's issues. These teachers were concerned about how they were even supposed to teach. He just wanted to know if he could keep playing with automatons.

"Well, I think I'll wait until things slow down a bit," Finn said. "Maybe by then my question will be answered through the grapevine."

The teacher waved as Finn walked away, and she returned her attention to the packed office.

Going to his classroom to test lab reports didn't seem possible in his distracted state so he wandered over to Pavlina's room. He found her sitting at her desk, flipping through a binder. She looked just as weary as he felt.

Finn knocked on the door frame to catch Pavlina's attention, bringing a small smile to her lips. "Come in," she said, waving him in. "I could use a break from all this."

Leaning over Pavlina's shoulder, Finn took a look at her binder. It was full of organized, thorough notes about her future lessons. "You've got a lot of creative ideas in here. Do the kids respond well to them?"

"They've worked for years." Melancholy tinted Pavlina's words. "A lot of these I got from my mentors when I was a new teacher. So there are decades and decades of proof that students learn better with stuff like this, but…" She shrugged. "Scripted lessons don't usually allow room for creativity. I remember about five years ago when they tried it out. It didn't work and they canceled it for the following year. But not without students missing out on a year of real education."

Finn nodded. "These politicians treat children like guinea pigs."

"Yes! That's exactly it! If it was just me not wanting to change my methods, I wouldn't be so upset, but their futures are being gambled by people who don't even care about them." Pavlina sighed. "Gods, I wish I could be in the basement catching up with Liz."

"Principal Cailleach is right, though." Finn kissed

the top of her head. "If we go down there during the school day, we'll only make the other teachers curious about what might be down there. A small risk, but still…."

"Yeah, I know." By Pavlina's tone, this reasoning hadn't improved her mood.

"Besides, she's more than healed now."

"Who knew they could solve something as complicated as a genetic blood disease over there?" Pavlina asked. "It's like a miracle. It's… well, like Detective Troias says, it's awfully convenient."

"What do you mean?"

Pavlina turned in her seat to look Finn straight in the eyes. "I'm having a hard time believing they healed her. One moment, she's dangerously ill. I mean I felt death rolling off her before I even opened the door. Then she's back fully healed of everything that's hurt her physically her entire life?"

"Sometimes good things happen."

"That doesn't seem like the norm these days."

Finn cupped his beautiful sirin's cheek. "You're right. It's one thing after the next. Things get worse and worse. Statistically, that means at least one truly wonderful thing had to happen."

"You think?" The doubt in Pavlina's voice didn't match the desperate hope in her eyes.

"It's got to be." Finn got down on his knees so that he wasn't hovering over Pavlina. "Something truly perfect has happened to me."

"What's that?"

"Finding you."

Pavlina laughed. "You're such a mush. First this morning and now too?"

"I mean it," Finn said. "Pav, I think I want to marry you one day."

That stopped the sirin's laughter. It stopped her despair as well. "Yeah?"

Finn nodded. "Yeah."

FOURTEEN

The Lesson

It had been two weeks since Bree and her family took up residence in the school basement, and it looked as though that wasn't going to change any time soon. During that time, Principal Cailleach had reached out to the grandmother who lived in the non-magical reality. According to her, the elderly Castille had seemed gruff, but satisfied that everyone was at least safe, and she didn't seem to be exhibiting the same strange behavior as before. None of Bree's family bought that for a second.

Principal Cailleach explained that she was working on a pocket reality that would contain beds and a fully functional bathroom. The wintry woman had spent the whole summer creating a few pocket classrooms within the school, though. A full suite was a little more difficult.

The Castilles spent Samhain in the damp space instead of around a bonfire. They didn't share stories about the dead either. That wasn't the worst thing in the world as far as Bree was concerned, considering they avoided that topic most days.

Unfortunately, without the distraction of Samhain's traditions, the reality of their dank and dreary environment was inescapable. Bree had very little hope that things would get better, and felt certain that it was their fault they were in this situation. *If I'd just done as Hermes wanted, everyone would be safe.*

After getting an update from Mr. Finn and Ms. Sirin, Bree knew better than to think of the school as a sanctuary. Hermes was adding all of Cal's garbage to a dense ball of matter and using the powers of one of the highest level gods to create something out of it. Whatever it was, it wouldn't be good for Bree, and probably everyone else in her reality. No one in her close-knit group of confidants knew if the boundaries Principal Cailleach had placed on the school would be able to hold up to Hermes once he inevitably escaped his prison. Though the principal was a winter goddess, she had nothing on the son of Zeus.

At least the weather had taken a pleasant turn with November's arrival. Bree felt grateful for that when she made her way to the school's grounds in the back.

It wasn't just because of the cooling temperatures or the crunch of leaves under her feet. The very fact that nothing had exploded yet was a blessing.

Even the murders had paused. No one knew exactly why, but they had their theories. Detective Troias thought it was because they'd all tossed their Atlas devices away. She thought that most of these murders were to send a message since they typically happened where they could be seen, and it was all too easy to track everyone's location using Atlas tech. Ms. Sirin said it was because they were thinking up something worse, since this idea hadn't worked so far.

Bree knew that was the truth. The only reason why they would have killed all those girls was because it was an easy way to scare everyone who knew about the dangers Bree faced. It hadn't worked as well as they thought it would, and they were cooking up something worse.

Bree's enemies had known her altruistic side, but not her wisdom. Bree understood not one person would come back to life if she walked out onto the street and yelled, "Here I am!" She could only do so much, but she put all her heart into it. *Better to try than to give up.*

As Bree took in a lungful of fresh autumn air, Cal called out to her. "Hey, kid! You ready?"

"Yes!"

Bree ran over to her adventurous friend, eager to

resume portaling lessons. This was the one activity that made her feel in control of her life. She could create little tears in reality with a small stone, and it turned out she could do it almost as well as a bookdealer—the one profession specifically trained to portal hop in their quest for books.

"Okay, so this time let's take it a little slower. We need to be more careful." Cal placed a few fairy stones on what used to be an automaton battle table.

Bree rolled her eyes. "You don't need to baby me."

Cal crossed her arms. "Just weeks ago, you couldn't even close a portal without my help."

"Yeah, but now I can create portals to just about anywhere!"

"Look, you may be a quick learner and may have gotten better than pretty much anyone at the Council of Pantheons really fast, but you're still not on bookdealer level yet." Cal held a fairy stone up at Bree's eye level. "Remember, these may be small, but they're dangerous when you break their limits. You need to treat them with respect."

"Yes, Cal."

Bree stroked one of the fairy stones on the table. During her first lesson with the bookdealer, they hadn't opened even one portal. Cal spent the afternoon explaining exactly what a fairy stone was, what it could do, and what it *couldn't* do.

There wasn't a charming reason for their name.

Fairy stones were the rusty remains of what had once been a fairy. As gross as that seemed to Bree at the time, she learned that wasn't the same as a corpse.

Unlike pixies, fairies couldn't be caught, because they had no physical form. These sentient beings existed as colorful flickers in the air, coming and going in unpredictable ways. They delighted children the same way a red laser dot amused a cat. Their breathtaking form was due to the tiny windows into other realities they created when the power within their spectral bodies overwhelmed them. Oil companies vented energy with gas flares; fairies tore open reality.

When they died, they didn't leave a body behind, because they didn't have one. They left a solid form of concentrated energy. When it struck matter in just the right fashion, with just the right spell, it split the seams open of whatever you perceived to be there.

"Let's go over the rules."

Bree groaned. "Gods, Cal! We do this every day!"

"And we'll keep doing it every day," Cal responded.

Together, the bookdealer and the Chosen One parroted the rules, "One, always set proper, detailed intentions, otherwise you could get terribly lost. Two, never throw a portal at a living being, or they might implode. Three, always close your portals in a timely manner in case someone or something is following you. Four, only share portaling magic knowledge with people you've known for at least five years; that should probably be long enough to trust them."

Bree grabbed a fairy stone from the table. "You know you've broken every single one of these rules, right?"

"Do as I say, not as I do," Cal said, rolling her fairy stone around in her hand. "Where to this time, super important Chosen One girl?"

Cal's question reminded Bree of all the times someone had asked her where she wanted to eat and her mind went completely blank. She looked around her current surroundings, in search of something she wished were better. Kicking the brown leaves beneath her feet, she said, "What about a reality with *real* autumn scenery?"

"That's just a trip to Vermont. You can do better than that."

Bree's lips vibrated as she let out a frustrated breath. "Okay, what about a reality where autumn is the only season there is?"

Cal tapped her chin. "I like that, but keep going. Detail it more. Paint a picture."

Bree closed her eyes. "The trees are all shades of red and gold and orange and school bus yellow!"

"School bus yellow? That's really specific."

"It's safe there," Bree continued. "No monsters, no natural disasters. Just trees and streams and trails for as far as you can see." The vision in her head was the perfect escape from her current living situation, and she felt grateful all over again that there were as many realities as her mind could randomly dream up. The possibilities were endless.

"Okay," Cal said. "Keep that thought in your mind. Try not to think about anything else, because that would mean we have to break through *multiple* realities, and you know how bad that would be."

"Yes, I know. You don't have to keep telling me."

"Well, you did it that one—"

"Cal! Do you want me to lose this picture in my head?"

The bookdealer went silent, and Bree recreated her perfect vision. An impromptu chant flowed from her lips like a song, and she tossed the fairy stone, opening her eyes to see a crisp breeze send fiery leaves spiraling through the air.

"How is it possible?" Bree asked, watching the flame-like leaves flurry across a stream like a flock of birds.

"How is what possible?"

"I just imagine a place and it already exists as a reality somewhere?" Bree shook her head in wonder. "Is magic really that powerful?"

"It's because deep within you, you already know all the realities," Cal explained. "Some people can remember them and make portals to them. Ninety-nine percent of the population can't, though. That's why people from the Council of Pantheons can only go to specific locations. That's all they know, and usually someone else makes it for them."

Bree squinted at her mentor. "Really?"

"This is probably something you hear all the time as a Chosen One, but you're special, Bree." Cal pointed at the autumn paradise Bree had created. "Time to dip our toes in and jump back over here again."

The awe Bree felt for the world across the portal disappeared when she remembered all over again that she couldn't explore all these fantastical realities. "Yeah," she said. "Let's go."

When Henry had proposed to Pavlina, she'd had no inkling it was coming. Theirs was such a whirlwind romance, that she hadn't really had time to realize it was a possibility. The moment the ring box opened and the words came out of his mouth, though, she knew she wanted nothing more. She danced on clouds all the way to the courthouse.

Finn hadn't truly proposed to her, but she felt that same excitement. Immortals didn't choose their spouses lightly, especially when it came to mortals. They knew they'd watch the person they loved grow old and die. Most chose to stay single forever. Finn hadn't even been in a steady relationship for nearly one thousand years. *But he wants to marry me one day.*

Pavlina knew she should feel frightened when every horrible thing was waiting to spring out of the shadows at them. Instead, she felt one hundred years younger. Finn seemed younger too.

Since he'd told her he wanted to marry her, things escalated quickly. Whenever they came home, they didn't waste a moment ripping each other's clothes off and jumping into bed together. They would order pizza and eat it naked in bed while watching their favorite shows. It was rare when Pavlina went without a shower buddy. She'd even taken to wearing scarves to work to hide her hickeys.

Whenever they left Finn's house, however, their little love bubble burst. Every worry attacked her at once, and all Pavlina wanted to do was search for solutions or at least make life more bearable for Bree and Liz.

Every day, before the school opened and after the last student left for the day, she would visit Liz, Bree, and their parents. She gave the girls fresh, new clothes. She'd even set up an old television with a VHS player so they could watch movies without worrying about Atlas spying on them.

If it weren't for the certainty of Hermes' return and an all-knowing force out to get them, Pavlina would have believed life couldn't get any better. Time was running out, though, and deep inside, she felt the clock ticking. *I need to plan and prepare. Teaching teenagers critical thinking only goes so far.*

It wasn't until Miss Sphinx showed up at the school again that something rustled around Pavlina's brain. This was a woman with noble intentions, who wanted nothing more than to help Bree reach her full potential. Though she wouldn't trust someone from the CoP with Bree's full situation, the magical history teacher could certainly appreciate someone with that type of motivation.

When Pavlina saw her heading toward the school's front exit, something struck the sirin like lightning. She wasn't exactly sure what it was, but she knew she couldn't let the representative walk away before sharing a few words with her.

"Miss Sphinx!" Pavlina called out as she raced toward her. "Miss Sphinx!"

The representative turned with a confused furrow to her brow. "Ms. Sirin?"

Pavlina stopped to take a deep breath when she caught up. "Hi," she said, still a little winded. "I wanted to check with you on Bree's progress."

Miss Sphinx shrugged and lifted her lips into a sad smile. "She's fine. I haven't really gotten much time with her, and when I do... Well, I have a feeling that Mr. Casmilus put a bad taste in her mouth."

"Yeah, he was rather off-putting, if I'm being honest." *Understatement of the decade.*

"If only they'd assigned me right from the start."

The sphinx's patient expression did little to cover the obvious pain she felt from the Chosen One's rejection. "Every century, they've passed me up and I played a supporting role. Look how things worked out this time."

"She takes time to warm up. You should ask Mr. Finn how their relationship started off."

Miss Sphinx chuckled. "Principal Cailleach mentioned something about mystery meat."

An idea popped into Pavlina's head. "Maybe it would help if I sat in with you and her at the next session? An adult she already trusts being friendly with a new person could turn things around."

The representative tilted her head thoughtfully. "It couldn't hurt. I'd love to bring her out of her shell a bit, and explore some of her ambitions. I want to give her any support and resources she needs."

Pavlina nodded her head, perhaps with a little too much enthusiasm. "I mean, Bree can tell you herself, but she feels very strongly about protecting young people. Maybe some legal history on that or something?"

"I'll consider it. Thanks." Miss Sphinx checked her watch. "Gods, I'm already late. Look, I'll be back in a week, maybe we could meet up before I check in with Bree?"

"Absolutely!"

Miss Sphinx waved and walked outside. As she did,

Pavlina's thoughts sped along like a horse on a track.

Bree was a pacifist. That was a quality the sirin admired. Even if Bree was willing to change something like that about herself, Pavlina wouldn't want her to. The teenager could think her way through most problems, though. While her bravery and wits might only get her so far against someone like Hermes, she could persuade the non-corrupt in the Council of Pantheons to join them in the fight against his sect.

A familiar hand tapped Pavlina on her shoulder, and she stirred from her planning.

"Have you visited Liz yet?" Finn asked. "Bree's already out back taking a portal lesson with Cal, so we might not get much time with her."

Pavlina shook her head. "Not yet, no, but let me talk to you about something first."

"Go ahead."

"Principal Cailleach is a god. She's a member of the Council of the Pantheons. I'd say she's a good one, right?"

"Of course."

"Not all of them are bad. Maybe most of them are decent people."

Finn scrunched his brows together. "Where are you going with this?"

"We don't need to fight the whole Council, just the sect." Confidence lifted Pavlina's shoulders and spread a smile across her face. "We're going to get them from the *inside*."

"Them meaning the sect or the CoP?"

Pavlina sighed. "Gods, that *is* confusing, isn't it?"

"Maybe they need their own name," Mrs. Selkie said from down the hall.

Finn and Pavlina jumped at her voice.

"Oh, I didn't realize you were there," Pavlina said, holding a hand over her hammering heart.

Mrs. Selkie shook her head. "You two don't know how to have a private conversation. This is probably one of the most used hallways in the school. I mean…" She sighed with exasperation. "I'm really tired of pretending I don't know anything and waiting for you all to tell me what's happening."

"What do you mean?" Pavlina's feigned ignorance wouldn't have fooled anyone, certainly not her friend.

"You two, Principal Cailleach, and Bree keep heading down to the basement," Mrs. Selkie said.

"Well, we—"

"And I hear your whispers. Liz is here and needs new clothes? Atlas is a spy or something? Also, the Council of Pantheons is full of evil people?" Mrs. Selkie raised her hands in defeat. "If I didn't know any better, I'd believe you both joined a cult or something." She squinted. "You didn't, did you?"

"No, look…" Pavlina looked up and down the hallway. Then she nodded in the front office's direction. "Come with us and we'll fill you in with

Principal Cailleach."

Finn held up a hand. "Leave your Atlas stuff behind though. This is going to be a *private* conversation."

Weekends hadn't been relaxing for Finn since Ms. Pace entered his life. All Saturday, Finn felt closer and closer to vomiting right there on his living room floor. His parole meeting was about to start and he hadn't finished his "homework." He hadn't even thought of it since their last meeting. He didn't think Ms. Pace would understand any of his excuses, because he couldn't exactly tell her the truth. *Hey there, parole officer! I know you work for the Council of Pantheons, but right now I'm hiding children from them so I got a little sidetracked.*

Finn didn't trust anyone, especially a Council of Pantheons employee, with his true worries. He'd only opened up his circle of trust to include Mrs. Selkie the previous day, and that was because she had figured out enough on her own. He felt grateful for her help, though. She'd already come up with a name for their true enemy. *The Shadow.* It sounded corny, but it worked. "A secret sect of the Council of Pantheons" didn't exactly roll off the tongue.

Knowing he didn't have enough time to even slap some words onto a piece of paper, Finn sat in his recliner, with his elbows on his knees. He stared where the portal would show up as he bit his thumb searching for some way to get out of the situation.

When Ms. Pace stepped through the portal, she wasn't looking at her tablet like she had the previous two visits. Instead, she came into the room with disappointment stamped onto her face. "You didn't make the appointment."

Finn glanced at the floor like a chided boy. "No, I'm sorry."

"Did you at least finish your homework?"

Finn winced, and the parole officer heaved a long sigh.

"I didn't expect a backslide this early, Mr. MacCool." She sat down on his couch and tapped on the coffee table. "At least respect me enough to look at me."

Doing as told, Finn sat upright and looked at the woman who had far more power over his life than he'd like to think about. She seemed kind and understanding, but then a lot of bad people did too. Her job was to make sure that people stuck to the rules of their parole, and if they didn't... *I can't think about that right now.*

"You look like you've had a rough couple of weeks," Ms. Pace said, as she pulled her Atlas tablet out and sat it on the coffee table.

Finn couldn't take his eyes off the device. He wondered if his parole officer had any idea what kind of danger she'd brought into his home. He was supposed to share so many personal things with her in this room. *She took a picture of what I wrote about the war. This thing, these people, they know all about one of my most vulnerable moments.*

"Yeah," Finn said, finally tearing his eyes away from the tablet. "The FLDOE suddenly changed the curriculum."

"I'm sure that's been difficult."

"Well, yes, it can be *difficult* when you have to suddenly dump months of careful study and work to parrot some watered-down garbage about crystals."

The bitterness that escaped Finn surprised him. Ms. Pace only nodded.

"I'm sorry you're going through that, and perhaps I can understand why that would have made your exercises more difficult to complete."

Thank the gods, that excuse worked.

"However," the parole officer continued. "Your growth is just as important as your students' education."

Ms. Pace handed him another sheet of paper that read "Exercise Three." Finn stared at it in disbelief.

"But I haven't finished the other one…"

The parole officer's face held not one hint of sympathy. "Tell me, Mr. MacCool, if a student doesn't turn in their homework on time, do you stop giving out assignments?"

"Well, no."

"Even if they're going through a really difficult time?" Ms. Pace asked. "What if another class gives an extra big assignment? What if they suddenly had to take on extra work to help their family with the bills? What if their mom gets sick and they have to take care of their siblings?"

"I do still give them homework, but if they came to me with a situation like that…"

Finn paused. Not one student had ever come to him to tell him about the hardships they were experiencing. After ninety-one years of teaching, he statistically would have had many students who went through incredibly difficult times. Yet none of them had ever wanted to tell him. Even with Bree, it took surviving a magical storm with him for her to open up even a little. *And it's because of what an arse I am.*

"If anyone ever *had* come to me, I would have given them an extension," Finn said. "As long as they needed. I'd even offer to help."

"Are you lying?"

Finn shook his head.

Ms. Pace chuckled softly and sardonically to herself. "Not that you'd tell me if you were." She tapped into some fields on her tablet. "I was going to give you an extension anyway. I just wanted to make sure you added this to your to-do list."

Relief washed over Finn. "Thank you."

"It's not all out of the kindness of my heart," Ms. Pace said as she packed her tablet into her messenger bag. "I have a conference in two weeks in Atlantis and another in Asgard right after that so I'm having to push out our parole meetings until December."

"Oh, I see."

The parole officer raised two fingers, almost pinching, at eye level. "Try a little harder to look disappointed you won't see me." She stood up and hoisted the messenger bag's strap onto one shoulder.

Finn stood as well, raising the paper she'd just given him. "I'll get this done. I promise."

"Be careful what you promise, Mr. MacCool," Ms. Pace said as the portal opened. "Especially when you haven't read the instructions for the next assignment."

Once Ms. Pace exited and the portal closed, Finn took a thorough look at the exercise.

The Irish warrior gasped and wrinkled his nose. "Make some art?" Finn scanned to the bottom of the page to find a voucher for a paint and sip class. "Oh, gods..."

Finn was good at many things. He was such a fantastic hero that he'd led the Fianna. He used his intelligence to help his countrymen for centuries. He wasn't bad with a tune and could read endlessly. But the thought of lifting a paintbrush and trying to create anything pleasant filled him with anxiety. *Who wants to do something they're bad at?*

FIFTEEN

The Gifts

The Shadow, as they'd taken to calling the gods coming after them, hadn't made any moves, allowing them to attempt to have an operational school. There were moments when Pavlina's life felt *normal*, and then something would remind her of how unstable everything was. It felt like that moment when she'd be drifting off to sleep and suddenly feel as if she was falling, which woke her immediately.

On this late November morning, Pavlina felt very much awake. She stood in the pocket reality accessible from the basement where Bree and her family were living. It had all the charm of a low-budget hospital room.

Pavlina had come to congratulate the Castilles on

their big move from the space beside the glawackus cages, but this didn't seem much better. Four twin sized beds took up the main living space. To the right of the room was a door to a bathroom that had one toilet, one sink, and the kind of shower Pavlina imagined prisoners used to get clean. *They must really not trust the grandmother over in the non-magical reality to choose this over their own house.*

The sirin lifted the shopping bag in her hand and forced a smile onto her face. "I got you a few housewarming gifts!"

Mrs. Castille held a hand over her heart and grinned. "You're too sweet."

"What did you get?" Liz jumped off her bed and ran over to peek inside.

Pavlina pulled out a mirror with a frame of wood-carved tentacles. "I thought Bree might like this."

The Chosen One took it and melancholy drooped her eyes. "Reminds me of Johnnie." She sighed. "I miss Johnnie."

Oh, gods, I've gone and made her sad. Pavlina pulled out a fake succulent plant in a monkey-shaped planter, and handed it to Liz. "I thought you might like some fun little decor."

Liz snatched it with a giant smile on her face. "I'm gonna cuddle this all night!"

Pavlina thought about mentioning it wasn't a stuffy toy, but decided it was best to let Liz enjoy it in whatever way she wanted. Instead, she pulled out a mug with the words "I'd rather be reading" painted in gold. She handed it to Mrs. Castille.

"I heard you like reading *and* mugs, so I thought you might enjoy this."

"Oh, isn't this lovely!" the woman said as she took it. "I'll just put this…" She looked around the room with only beds for furniture. "Well, I'm sure I'll find a place for it soon."

"Maybe I could bring a table or something next time I'm here," Pavlina said, but she couldn't see room for anything other than end tables.

Pavlina pulled out the last item—that day's newspaper. She really hoped this one did the trick, because no one had been able to improve Mr. Castille's mood. According to Bree, he had been quite a hothead in his reality. Though he didn't show much anger outside of his spats with Finn, he hadn't warmed up to anyone.

"I thought you might like an idea of what's happening outside of the school, Mr. Castille."

Bree's father took the paper from her, with a subtle smile. "Well, this looks very interesting."

"I subscribed to the daily paper, and I can bring them here when I come to work."

Mr. Castille's smile broadened. "Even the Sunday paper? I love comic strips and crosswords." He flipped through the pages. "This looks so much like our paper back home, except… Well, I mean we don't have headlines like *Vampire Bar Shut Down Due to Zoning Violations.*"

A pounding against the wall caught Pavlina's attention. Bree was banging a nail into the wall, using the spine of a twenty-year old textbook. *Well, I guess the junk in the basement has its uses.*

Bree hung up the mirror and took an appreciative look at it. "Now, I can remember Johnnie whenever I make sure I look clean for school."

Mrs. Castille exited the bathroom. "That mug is perfect for holding our toothbrushes. Thank you for the gift."

Relieved that everyone had found something they liked about their gifts, Pavlina shared why she was really there. "So I've been sitting in on meetings Bree has with her representative."

Bree groaned and flopped onto her bed so that she stared at the ceiling. "Don't remind me."

"She's a very nice person."

"She's one of *them.*" If Bree wasn't such a tidy person, Pavlina imagined she would have spit to emphasize that last word.

Pavlina sat next to the teenager. "Look, we have to keep up appearances. If you refuse to meet with your representative, that's going to raise some alarm bells with the Council of Pantheons," she said. "Besides, not everyone who works with the Council is a bad person.

She's really excited about what *you* want to do."

Bree sat up. "Mr. Casmilus didn't seem like a bad person, but you saw how that turned out."

"Really? Him?" Pavlina asked with an arched brow.

"I know he was super sketchy, but he seemed like a *normal* kind of sketchy."

The magical history teacher patted Bree's hand. "Remember that talk we had last year? About dealing with people when you're an attorney one day?"

"I'm not fighting with her, Ms. Sirin," Bree said. "You've seen me; I've been super polite."

"Absolutely, you've been quite civil. You need to start working with her, though."

"Come on, Ms. S—"

"Listen to your teacher, Bree!" Mrs. Castille interjected. She wasn't the kind of person to yell. Her husband did enough for the both of them. So even her shout at this point sounded more like a suggestion than a command.

"Oh my gods..." Bree looked back and forth between her mother and Pavlina. "You two have been talking about this without me, haven't you?"

"Only because we wanted you to understand why it's important," Mrs. Castille explained.

"This wasn't the kind of parent teacher conference I thought you two would ever have," Bree grumbled.

If I ever doubt Bree is a teenager, I should just remember this conversation.

"Do you want to live here in secret forever?" Pavlina asked. "Even if you do, it's not going to last and that's because someone who could pick his teeth with you could climb out of his reality at any minute."

Bree said nothing to that. She only stared at herself in the mirror with a tragic expression on her face.

"Miss Sphinx is willing to part with a lot of information you can use, Bree," Pavlina continued. "Stuff that you have the skills to turn into a powerful and *non-violent* weapon against The Shadow."

Liz snorted.

"Hush, Liz," Bree said, shooting her sister a look.

"It's just such a stupid name!" Liz laughed even harder.

Pavlina ignored Liz's snickering and continued, "With her help, you could find out just how the CoP's legal system works, their barriers and loopholes. You could find out who in the system might side with us in a battle, and Bree, there's definitely going to be a battle. There's no avoiding it."

Bree sighed. "Fine."

"You mean it?"

The teenager nodded.

"She's supposed to come tomorrow afternoon and—"

A knock on the door interrupted her.

"Come in," Mrs. Castille called out.

The door creaked open and Finn's head poked

through. "Hey, they just opened the doors."

"Oh great, I haven't even gotten my class organized for the day yet." Pavlina got up and gave Bree a pointed gaze. "Remember. Tomorrow."

"Yes, Ms. Sirin, I can do this. I promise."

Pavlina smiled at Bree. "I know you can. There isn't much you can't do."

Annie Lytle High had countless safeguards in place: magical barriers, pocket reality classrooms, sigils on doorways, even wand detectors. Yet, they just let a representative from the Council of Pantheons roam right in whenever she wanted.

Principal Cailleach had said there wasn't any choice in the matter, and Ms. Sirin had said Miss Sphinx was a good person. Bree didn't care. It wasn't their little sister living in the basement so she could hide from the Council of Pantheons.

Ms. Sirin had been right, though. She had to at least pretend to like this woman. The fate of the world relied upon it. *No pressure or anything.*

Bree normally liked most people she met, but once she decided someone was bad news, it was impossible to change her mind. She also didn't have the ability to keep her thoughts off her face. Miss Sphinx definitely knew Bree didn't like her.

After a day and a half of stewing over this

unwelcome assignment to be friendly with the representative, Bree was sitting across a cafeteria table from Miss Sphinx.

"Did you have a good day?" the woman asked in the friendliest voice, clearly desperate for Bree to like her.

"Yeah, it was fine."

Bree leaned back in her chair, only half present in the conversation. The clack of a broom falling across the empty and silent cafeteria jarred her out of the meditative state of playing with her shirt sleeve cuff. She blinked and sat up in her chair, forcing herself to look at Miss Sphinx.

"How was yours?"

The sphinx brightened at the question, and Bree realized this was probably the first time she'd ever asked the representative how she was.

"Lovely, thank you! I was hoping we could catch up on how your portal research is going."

During all the talks Bree had had with Miss Sphinx, she'd kept information shallow. She discussed learning about portals, but not creating them. She talked about playing cards with her sister, but not how their games took place in the school basement.

"It's going fine."

Ms. Sirin's words from the previous morning nagged at Bree, and she forced herself to say more. "I was thinking we could talk about law history."

Miss Sphinx nodded with the enthusiasm of a puppy when their owner returns home. "Give me a second, I'll get my Atlas—"

"No!" Bree was halfway across the table with her hand outstretched before the representative had even unclasped her messenger bag. "I prefer paper. Technology is just *so* not cool anymore."

The representative squinted. "It's… not cool?"

Bree rolled her eyes. "Yeah, duh, all the kids at school know it. Atlas devices are what our parents use."

"Unfortunately, I'm not sure if there's another way to give you the historical records I thought you might be interested in," Miss Sphinx said.

Bree shrugged. "Just look up the paper files or something."

"Paper files?"

"With the Council of Pantheons. Principal Cailleach does…" Bree realized she was about to blow her principal's cover, and rushed to correct herself. "She does it with her school records."

"Okay, well, I don't have access to those right now," Miss Sphinx said, placing her messenger bag on the ground. "I suppose we could explore what you would like to learn about law. It would help me figure out more about what kinds of information I should find for you."

"I want…" Bree considered telling her about her

future goal of helping kids like her sister get what they needed from their insurance company, but she knew that wasn't going to help with their current situation. "You know, I'm keeping my options open right now."

Miss Sphinx rested her elbows on the table and smiled patiently at Bree. The Chosen One paused, considering how she could explain herself without giving away her intentions.

"I know you work for the Council of Pantheons, but they can't *always* be right about everything," Bree said as she watched the representative's eyes for any sign of suspicion.

"Everyone is fallible, even the CoP."

Though Bree knew the cafeteria was empty, she still took a visual sweep of the room. "Has anyone ever convinced them in court that a god committed a crime?"

"I don't know," Miss Sphinx said. "I'll have to look it up."

"Is it possible, though?"

"No one is above the law. Not even Zeus."

Bree spent a moment studying the representative's face.

Before she'd met Miss Sphinx, she'd never seen a sphinx in person. In the drawings, it was a woman's face with a lion's body. This woman was a little more complicated than that. She had tawny eyebrows that lifted into a fine fuzz on her forehead. Her lion's mane had been styled into a swing bob. Her round, furry ears wore diamond studs. She stood like a woman and had a mostly humanoid body, except for the tail and the paws.

Like Bree, the representative was terrible at keeping her emotions off her face. When she'd mentioned Zeus, Bree noticed the way her gaze lowered. She didn't very much like the tip top of her company's hierarchy.

"So, basically, if a god committed a big crime, a mortal could take them to court, and possibly win?"

"Where are you going with this, Bree?" Miss Sphinx's smile flattened and worry shadowed her eyes.

If I tell you, you might go running to your boss. Bree paused again, wondering how to tell the truth without putting anyone in danger. "It's just… I want the world to *actually* be fair, and it isn't," she said. "If the world was fair, the most powerful would still experience consequences for hurting even the least powerful."

"Oh, I see." Miss Sphinx nodded slowly. "And you want to see just how possible that is. Well, hold on."

The representative's paws struggled to open her messenger bag. For a moment, Bree feared the woman would put her Atlas tablet on the table. Instead, Miss Sphinx tossed a handful of business cards on the table.

"These are all organizations that fight for justice," Miss Sphinx said. "Even when the government is at fault."

Bree's eyes wandered over the scattering of connections. *Mortals for Equality. Pandora's Hope. The Minotaur Society.* The Chosen One lifted a card and turned it to show Miss Sphinx.

"What's the Good Grifters?"

The representative chuckled. "I forgot that card was in there. I wouldn't take them seriously."

"Who are they?" Bree asked.

"It's a group of minor trickster gods run by Reynaud Fox," Miss Sphinx explained.

"Who's that?"

"See? *Minor* trickster gods," the representative said. "To answer your question, though, he's a fox god who mostly plays tricks to humble people in power."

Sounds like the kind of person I want to meet. "Tell me more."

"The Good Grifters have this whole message about how power corrupts and there shouldn't be a world government."

"Thanks for this. I'll look into these." Bree pulled out the pouch she kept her index cards in and scooped the business cards into it.

"I hope they help!"

"I'm sure they will," Bree answered with a smile.

***

That afternoon had been excruciating. Though the therapist Finn talked to was so bland he practically blended into his unremarkable office, just the thought of him listening and scratching down notes gave Finn the shivers. The man's little recorder had whirred as Finn spilled out every last horror in his brain, including those he'd taken part of while at war. Now any subtle sound reminded him of his guilt, and he wallowed in self-loathing from the awful things he'd committed in the name of good. *If that's what therapy is like, I don't know how I'll get through my parole.*

On the tail end of that, he had to attend the painting class from Ms. Pace's exercise. Being immortal had given Finn a life of feeling safe in public. With the questions swirling around his small group of confidants, that had changed. Every minute of the painting class he'd attended had sent his anxiety reeling.

It wasn't just that he hated to be bad at something in front of others, and he was *terrible* at painting. It wasn't that he possibly wasn't as immortal as he previously thought. What brought a nervous sweat to his brow were all the Atlas phones.

Couples all across the room took selfies and offered to take photos of each other. When the instructor asked Finn and Pavlina if they wanted him to take a photo of them with their paintings, he had been surprised to learn neither of them had a phone and neither of them wanted a photo.

When the class was over, Finn felt like he could

finally breathe. He marched away with a canvas under each arm. Pavlina walked by his side chewing an ever-increasing wad of nicotine gum.

Once they reached a street corner just a block away from his car, a light mist of rain began falling on every surface. Finn pressed the crosswalk button over and over, as if the laws of traffic would bend to his impatience.

"Gods, it's nights like this that make me wish I'd never given up smoking." Pavlina reached her hand over and waved at the paintings. "Give me one of those. I feel ridiculous not helping you out."

"Not a chance. I need you prepared for anything." Finn mashed the button again.

Pavlina rubbed her naked upper arms. "I should have worn a cardigan or something."

"I'd offer you my jacket, if it weren't at home."

Florida was usually warm during autumn, but once in a while the weather decided to pretend there were actual seasons in Jacksonville. Between the unexpected, temporary dip in temperature and the moisture everywhere, even Finn was shivering.

"We both used to live up north. We can handle temps like this." Pavlina let out an exhausted laugh. "Who am I kidding? We've already been conditioned. Our very cells have become Floridian."

"Gods, I don't want you to be right but..." Finn leaned on the crosswalk button with as much force as his thumb would allow.

Pavlina popped another piece of nicotine gum into her mouth. "The funny thing is," she said, her words garbled by her chewing, "I would have *loved* coming to something like this with you a few months ago. But all those Atlas devices all over the place gave me the heebie jeebies."

Finn chuckled. "Heebie jeebies? You're adorable."

Pavlina smacked his arm playfully and he almost dropped one of the canvases.

"Can we please just leave these somewhere?" Finn asked as he regained his grip on it. "At least mine? I don't see why we need them, and mine is absolutely hideous." *And all I can see in it now are the sins I admitted to this afternoon.*

Pavlina shook her head. "Not a chance. You need evidence you went to this thing. Besides, I kind of like our flamingos. They make a heart when you put them side by side."

"Except one side of the heart looks like it needs a cardiologist." The crosswalk sign changed, displaying a little man walking. "Jaysus, that took an eternity. Look both ways now."

"I'm not a kid, Finn," Pavlina called after him as he dashed across the street before she'd even stepped off the sidewalk.

A squeal of tires of wet pavement jolted Finn and he turned to see Pavlina halfway across the street, frozen with terror. He expected to see a car, but there wasn't a vehicle in sight this far from the Five Points area. Whatever sound they'd heard had happened on another street.

Finn waved at her. "Pav, let's go!"

The sirin shook her head. "Look." She pointed at the sky.

A murder of crows flew just overhead. Corbin swooped down and landed on top of the No Parking sign next to Finn. Pavlina sprinted over and stroked the sleek black feathers on her crow friend's head. He dropped a piece of broken amber bottle glass in her hand.

"Thanks for the tip," Pavlina said. "Here's a treat." She dug around in her purse and found a dog treat. Corbin gobbled it down quickly and left them to rejoin his murder.

"What's that?" Finn asked.

"I don't know, but we need to follow them and find out." Pavlina trembled. "Feathers are bristling all up and down my back. Wherever they're going is where a death harbinger should be."

"Okay, look, we're almost at the car," Finn said. "I'll put these in the boot really quick and I can drive you there."

"Just meet me there." Pavlina pointed at the crows again as they descended on some shrubbery hiding the private parking area of a temple.

Finn nodded and the sirin raced toward the gathering crows. *I knew something would happen. I just knew it.* As promised, he put their paintings in his car and drove to her location.

When Finn got there, he saw Pavlina's back first, no wings this time. He wasn't sure if that was a good sign or a bad sign. Something furry lay on the crook of one of her arms. "Please don't be a dog."

Pavlina turned at the sound of his voice. He wasn't sure if it was the mist or tears that made her cheeks so wet. "We need to call 911, but we don't have phones."

"Oh gods..." Finn walked around to see the full scope of the situation.

A young werewolf lay against Pavlina's thighs, with her head resting on the sirin's extended arm. Her golden fur was matted with blood, but also dusted with what looked like glitter. After a blink, Finn realized it was actually small shards of glass.

"It's shallow, but she's still breathing," Pavlina said. "I can feel it in her back. Can you go to that bar across the street and get them to let you use their phone?"

Finn nodded. As he turned to sprint away, Pavlina called out to him to wait. "Before you go. Look."

With her free hand, she pulled a black backpack forward. On one of its straps was a label for the owner's name—Ylva Heidelberg.

SIXTEEN

The Confession

Bree had spent years of school without Ylva, but as her friend convalesced in the hospital, nothing about the school day felt natural to her. She wished she could go and visit her, and hoped Ylva didn't feel abandoned. *Especially after what we all found out.*

Ylva's passion for defending those who suffered the worst prejudice made so much more sense now. Everything did. *Of course, her family had multiple copies of a rare book about werewolf communities. Gods, and I actually chalked up the mention of werewolf hunting season as an unfortunate coincidence. For all I know, her grandma's head could be mounted above some creep's mantle.* Bree thought about the werewolf plushy she'd received right in front of Ylva, and realized why it had hurt her.

It made her feel like her one friend in America thought of her as a dangerous creature.

After being absent for a few days, the golden-haired girl was returning to school. Bree hoped that she could make her feel comfortable and cared for. Yule Break was coming in a week, and Bree feared the German girl might return home instead of coming to school in January.

When Ylva showed up, she had hints of bruises on her jaw and chin. Bree had a feeling there were more hidden by clothes. She wore a scarf over her head, but it had slipped back just enough to reveal a small patch on the girl's head where golden curls had once been.

Usually, Ylva would see Bree and skip over to her bubbling with energy. That morning, she gave Bree a weak smile but lowered her gaze as she walked over.

"Did I miss any tests?" Ylva whispered.

"Nothing, except for Mr. Jessup making us all sing a song about imaginary numbers."

Ylva winced. "I'm not sorry I missed that."

Bree would have normally laughed at a statement like that, but her friend still hadn't lifted her head yet.

"Hey…" Bree placed her hand on Ylva's shoulder. "I'm sorry I didn't come visit. I'm not really allowed to explain why, but I can't leave home."

Ylva lifted her head and squinted. "But you're here right now."

"Well, except for school, obviously."

"So, you can go to school, but not the hospital?"

Ylva's eyes, which usually shone like lucky pennies, had lost their copper glow. What had happened to her had more than hurt her body, and Bree wasn't surprised. She had imagined what the attack must have been like, and every instance involved slurs and worse.

"Like I said, I'm not allowed to explain it." Bree sighed. "I probably shouldn't have said that much."

"I know what it's like when you need to keep a secret," Ylva said. She scanned the crowded hallway, where more than a few heads turned to look at her. "Even though I don't have mine anymore."

The German girl shrugged her backpack higher. It was new, still just a regular black backpack like the last one. This one didn't have her name on it though. *Probably because she doesn't want anyone knowing it belongs to her and doing something awful.*

"You never needed to keep it from me," Bree whispered. "You can always trust me."

Ylva returned her gaze to Bree. Her eyes were tired, resigned, and not at all consoled by Bree's kind words. "But you can't trust me? Or maybe this is just an excuse for not coming to see me."

"No, Ylva—"

"Let's go to class so I can pick up the work I missed."

Ylva moved ahead, not waiting for Bree to agree.

The Chosen One chased her.

"It's not like that Ylva! Please, stop!"

As the German girl kept walking, Bree saw her one true friendship leaving with her. Yes, the teenager loved her sister, but she was family. That was a different kind of bond. Ylva was the first friend to ever make Bree feel like she was more than a brain with a future, like she wasn't just a Chosen One.

"I'll tell you!"

Ylva stopped. After an agonizing second, she turned to look at Bree. The dark rings around her eyes seemed deeper under the shadow from her tented brows. The fluorescent lines created trenches around her frown.

"Just... just..." Bree looked around for anywhere private. She could only think of the grounds out back, which would make her late for class. *I'm going to get in a lot of trouble for this.* She beckoned Ylva with a wave. "Come with me, okay?"

The two teenagers walked against the tide of students, until Bree ushered Ylva out the cafeteria exit. It was comfortably warm outside, and not too humid. This was the kind of weather that made Bree wish she could spend time strolling along the river.

They walked a few paces from the school's exterior, and hopefully any accidental eavesdroppers.

Bree tried to find the right words to explain as her stomach churned with anxiety. She wanted to tell Ylva just enough so that she didn't worry, but not enough to put her in even more danger. She kicked at the decaying brown leaves on the ground, while Ylva stood there with her arms crossed and her head bent.

"So, I'm the Chosen One, right?"

Ylva nodded.

"And what they don't tell you about Chosen Ones is that not everyone on the Council of Pantheons likes them."

"Many of them don't like werewolves either."

"It's a little different."

Ylva puffed out a bitter half-laugh. "Yes, we are very different in their eyes."

"I'm not trying to say I have it worse than werewolves or anything." Bree reached out to touch Ylva's elbow, but the girl shirked away. She still hadn't looked up from the ground. It was going to take a fair heap of the truth for her to understand.

"Ylva, a *lot* of them are committed to sacrificing me."

The golden-haired girl lifted her head at that. Mixed with the sorrow still etched into her features was a shock that couldn't be feigned. "Sacrifice?"

Bree nodded. "My representative last year came pretty close to succeeding."

"Is he in prison?"

"No." *Not really.* "I'm not sure where he is. He could come back and even if he doesn't, he made it really clear that there are more powerful people than him that want to sacrifice me."

Ylva's features opened up into perfect circles of horror. "Have you told the police?"

"What could they possibly do against the gods?" Bree wiped away a tear and lowered her voice. "Even if they could, I don't know if I can trust any of them. I-I don't know who to trust, but my family says I can only be at school or home. Anywhere else isn't safe."

"You can trust *me*."

Ylva put her arms around Bree, and the Chosen One leaned into it.

It wasn't as if the two girls hadn't touched before. They were good friends, after all. They'd never hugged before, though. In this position, Bree could smell the honey-sweet scent of Ylva's hair, and feel the warmth of her skin against hers.

Heat rushed through Bree until her cheeks burned from it, and she let go of her friend. There was a pretty pink bloom on Ylva's face. The golden girl's eyes were wide with wonder and her lips had opened just a little. *I bet her lips feel like rose petals.*

Bree cleared her throat. "We should get to class."

"Yes," Ylva whispered and then took a deep breath and nodded. "Yes, we're already late."

"We might still make it."

Ylva shook her head. "The bell just rang. Didn't you hear it?"

The only thing I could hear was my heart.

This was the third meeting Finn had had with Principal Cailleach regarding the Magical Automaton Club. He wasn't sure why he kept trying. There was no loophole or secret fund they could take advantage of. The Florida Department of Education had made it plain that there were only two extracurriculars that would receive any school funding—football and cheerleading. *They couldn't have at least one magical extracurricular?*

Still, Finn had once again found himself in the icebox that was Principal Cailleach's office during his planning period. There were many more pressing matters, but this club remained a high priority to him. He didn't know how many years were left of his "immortality," but he wanted to make the most of it. That included teaching kids how to use magical application in fun ways.

Principal Cailleach sat at her desk, with her arms crossed and her cloudy eyes void of any compassion. Her unmoved face was framed by the wall of Hummel figurines behind her. The contrast of sweet porcelain figures of children and an ancient winter goddess would have made Finn laugh under different circumstances. This meeting wasn't going well, however.

"Nothing has changed since we spoke a week ago," the principal said. "I used up all the funding on the tables. Besides, the next match was supposed to be at another school. Bree couldn't go to that."

"This isn't just about Bree," Finn argued. "I love her, truly, but she's not my only student. These kids are already subjected to the farce of the curriculum the state shoved onto us. They deserve some real education. This would count."

"Your impassioned speech is moving, but hasn't magically produced a credit card."

Finn shook his head in defeat. "Fine, I'll just use my own money."

This cracked the wintry woman's icy exterior. "You will do no such thing!"

"I can do what I want with my money," Finn said, as he stood with his proud chin held high. "If the school can't provide it and the state refuses, I must use my own funds."

Principal Cailleach got out of her seat as well. "Don't be ridiculous. You make a teacher's salary. *Less* actually, since the Council of Pantheons capped you a decade ago."

Don't remind me. "I'll figure something out. I'm not letting these kids go without a proper—"

Principal Cailleach dropped a heavy binder on her desk. "I'm not letting you spend your money on this." Principal Cailleach pointed to the label on the binder's cover. "Fundraiser Ideas."

Finn flipped through the contents of photocopied

pamphlets, printed emails, and laminated newspaper clippings. "You think this will work?"

"It might," she said. "Especially if we work together with the other regional clubs. They all lost funding too."

Finn's whole body lifted along with his spirits. "I'll work on this right away!"

Principal Cailleach held up a finger for him to wait, and then typed something on her computer. After a few clicks, the printer whirred. "I'm getting you a contact list of the other clubs in the area. I put this together when Mr. Colossus called me."

"Mr. Colossus..." The name sank Finn's mood like an anchor.

The principal nodded. "Yes, he called me within a few days of the state making the change. He's very distraught for his students. I'd say he's desperate for any support at all."

The printer spit out a fresh, hot sheet and the woman extended it in Finn's direction. "I think he'd even work with you if it meant saving his club."

Finn waved it away. "I'd rather raise the money myself."

"You know how you needed me to tell you a strength and a weakness for your parole officer?" Principal Cailleach asked.

"You said you'd get back to me."

"Well, I'm getting back to you now."

Principal Cailleach stepped close enough to Finn to where he could smell the cold rolling off her, and goosebumps rioted across his chest, neck, and face.

"Your strength is your determination," she said. "Your weakness is your stubbornness. Learn the difference and work on it."

Finn's boss slapped the paper onto his palm and he grabbed it, knowing better than to argue with her again. "I'll do that."

He scanned the list as he walked out of the office. There were roughly a dozen clubs in northeast Florida. Most of them seemed to be from schools he knew were under-funded due to their school grade.

After ninety-one years of teaching, Finn had seen many changes. One of the few things that remained true was that the system punished schools from lower-income neighborhoods. He knew this was why Bree had fought so hard for her spot at Annie Lytle High School. Many of these students had been forced into their role in the school to prison pipeline. It was an absolute tragedy.

Finn knew the teachers running these clubs must be trying their best to do what they could for their high schoolers. It's possible that they didn't even have funding to begin with. He wouldn't be surprised if they were already forking over their meager paychecks to make it happen.

To his surprise, Finn noticed another trend. Under

the listings of many of the underfunded schools there was a line: Alec Colossus - cosponsor. *He's helping sponsor clubs that aren't even at his school. That obnoxious giant actually cares?*

After school the Irish warrior would have his second appointment with the therapist Ms. Pace wanted him to see. He imagined explaining that he let an old grudge get in the way of helping kids. That wasn't the kind of thing a hero did, and the kids certainly didn't deserve it.

With a sigh, Finn turned and walked back into the front office's waiting area. "Can I use the phone? I need to make some calls to these schools." He waved the paper Principal Cailleach had given him.

The secretary tsked at him. "You need to buy a new phone, Mr. Finn."

"I will. I just need to find one I can afford." *And doesn't use Atlas technology.*

"The moment someone calls in, I need it back."

"Of course," Finn said with a smile. The first number he dialed was the one he was most reluctant to call.

"Hello, I was wondering if Mr. Colossus was available."

After spending some time with Bree and Liz in their

strange pocket reality of a home, Pavlina was ready to go home and relax. Finn had an appointment with a therapist after school, though, and she hated the idea of being alone even for a second after all that had happened before Yule Break even started.

When Mrs. Selkie offered to have her over, Pavlina took the invitation at once. A screaming cecaelia baby and a gloomy rusalka wasn't the sirin's idea of a good time, but spending time with an old friend would be a welcome break from the upside-down life she'd had for the last several weeks.

To Pavlina's surprise, the household was tidier and more peaceful. Mika was practicing vocabulary flashcards on the floor. Zennie kept grabbing them to chew on them.

"Teething," Mrs. Selkie explained when Pavlina glanced in that direction.

"Can you get me a frozen waffle?" Mika called out to her wife.

The selkie grabbed one and handed it to the rusalka. Zennie's eyes grew wide and slobber rolled down one corner of his mouth. One of his tentacles shot out like a whip and snatched it. He gnawed at it, pressing as hard as he could with his gums, all the while making happy little grunts. *So gross, but also… actually pretty cute?*

Mika shuffled the cards together and put them back in the box. "I'll just let him enjoy that. I was tired anyway. There's only so many times I can say *bus* and point at a picture while making vroom vroom sounds."

"Go relax for a bit," Mrs. Selkie said. "I can see Zennie from here."

"If he starts whining, please put him in his tank."

Mrs. Selkie gave her wife a thumbs up and the grateful rusalka walked off to their bedroom.

"Having a good day?" Pavlina asked.

"It's been nice." The selkie smiled and pulled a sports drink out of the fridge. "Want one?"

Pavlina shook her head. "You both seemed stressed out last time I was here."

"Well, that was before we got a night nurse." Mrs. Selkie sat down at the table between the kitchen and the living room. She opened up her blue drink to take a long sip of it. "Seems my parents might actually care about their grandchild. Not enough to get over their homophobia of course, but enough to hire someone to help."

"Well, that's something, I guess." Pavlina sat across from her friend.

Mrs. Selkie chuckled a little. "They'd hate knowing it's helped our marriage."

"Oh yeah?"

Being a pale, freckly type, Mrs. Selkie's blush might as well have been a neon sign. "Mika is very grateful for a night of sleep. Very, *very* grateful."

Pavlina waggled her eyebrows. "My, my!"

"Ma ma ma!" Zennie called from his spot on the floor. His face was covered in remnants of the frozen waffle he'd demolished.

Mrs. Selkie got up from her seat to scoop him up. He laid his head on her shoulder and immediately fell asleep. "I should put him in his tank but..." She kissed the top of his head. "Maybe I could just hold him for a bit."

A familiar ache dug into the pit of Pavlina's stomach. She wanted that. She wanted the tender moments and the long hugs that came with having a child. Parenthood wasn't always a walk in the park, but any of that would have been worth it to her.

"Hey? You okay?" Mrs. Selkie sat back down at the table, with her son still drooling on her shoulder.

"It's just... I wish..." Pavlina waved at the cecaelia child.

"It's not too late, you know," Mrs. Selkie said.

Pavlina scoffed. "I'm one hundred forty-one years old. I'd really be pushing it if I tried for one now, and I don't think Finn and I are exactly ready to bring a kid into the world yet."

The selkie arched an amused brow. "Yet?"

"Oh, gods..." Pavlina lowered her head and laughed at herself. "Don't listen to me."

"Get talking, lady."

"He said... you know... he might want to get

married one day."

With every word, Mrs. Selkie got visibly more and more excited. "I'm gonna put Zennie in his tank. I'll be right back!"

Mrs. Selkie whizzed off, leaving Pavlina to think about that moment and all the passionate ones that followed. Just remembering the last few weeks stirred longing in her and she checked her watch to see how much longer until Finn would be home.

"Okay, I'm back," Mrs. Selkie whispered as she slid into her seat. "What happened?"

"Well, you know, the whole damn world is falling apart, right?"

Mrs. Selkie nodded. "Right. Continue."

"And I think that got us both thinking about the happiness we have," Pavlina explained. "We love each other, but it's more than that... It's..." She stopped to consider exactly what *it* was.

"Like you click?"

"Like... we *always* clicked." Pavlina offered her friend an awkward smile. "Does that make sense? I don't know how to say it."

"Sometimes, that's the way love is," Mrs. Selkie said with her hands raised as if in prayer. "Beyond words."

"But the thing is, I have years of true, meaningful love," Pavlina explained. "Bridge, Baron, Henry... All of that was real. They'll always have a spot in my heart, even if those relationships are over. But this?"

She tapped on the table for emphasis. "It stirs up some nostalgia for a past that I don't remember."

"Mr. Poetry is getting in your head," Mrs. Selkie said before taking a swig of her sports drink.

Pavlina laughed. "Maybe he is."

"So, what are you going to do about it?"

"What do you mean?"

Mrs. Selkie set her drink down and rested her elbows on the table. She laid her hands on top of Pavlina's. "My dear, beautiful, tragic friend. There are powerful people that don't like you. You're dealing with some pretty scary shit."

Pavlina held up a hand to stop her friend. "Okay, I don't need the reminder, thanks."

"I'm not saying the world is ending. It isn't. Hermes doesn't get the immortality he wants if that happens."

"What are you saying?"

"Life is short," Mrs. Selkie said. "Why are you saying 'I want to marry him someday' and not 'I want to marry him now?'"

SEVENTEEN

The Accident

The temptation to wear seasonal sweaters and buy hot cocoa during December had gotten the better of Finn. When he'd stepped out to run some errands that morning, there had been a pleasant bite in the air. So, he put on his nicest reindeer knit and threw a plaid scarf around his neck.

By the time he was supposed to meet Mr. Colossus for coffee, it was over eighty degrees fahrenheit. The yarn of his sweater scratched at his sweating skin, and Finn had to pull it off and tie it around his waist. The sleeves were bulky, so he had to keep retying it. He stuffed the woolen scarf into a shopping bag and hoped it didn't make all the gifts he purchased smell like his body odor.

When Finn entered the coffee shop, he forgot his former craving for hot chocolate and ordered a frappuccino instead.

"Extra whipped cream and caramel drizzle please," he called out to the barista as she walked over to the espresso machine.

"Is your girlfriend here or something?" Mr. Colossus said.

Finn turned to see the giant bent awkwardly so that he didn't plunge his head through the cheap ceiling tile.

"Er… We can sit outside, if you want." Finn waved at the small tables just outside the windows flocked with snow-like foam.

Mr. Colossus grunted. "I want a drink though."

"I can pick it up for you," Finn offered. "What do you want?"

The giant squinted at the menu. "I don't see anything with bourbon so I guess I'll have the hot cider." He gave Finn some dollar bills and stumbled outside, trying not to bump into anyone.

Gods, I can't imagine having to live like that. As impressively tall as Finn was, he didn't have to worry about bowling strangers over. Finn ordered the giant's drink as well, and then met the rival teacher at the table he'd claimed.

Mr. Colossus took his cider and gulped it down. As he wiped the last of it off his bottom lip, he waved at the wintry paintings on the cafe's windows. "Happy Holidays!" he harrumphed. "Why can't they just say Blessed Yule? Everything's so politically correct these days."

"I mean, some of their paying customers observe Saturnalia," Finn said. "Maybe they want them to feel included."

The giant grumbled but let the subject go. "So, you want to talk about fundraising?"

Finn nodded. "Yeah, I know we don't exactly get along, but I think we have something pretty important in common."

"I suppose we do." Mr. Colossus stared at his empty cup. "It isn't even just my students that I want this for."

"I saw that you're cosponsoring groups from other schools," Finn said. "That's very generous of you."

"I grew up in Appalachia," Mr. Colossus said. "We weren't exactly poor, but we weren't rich either. It wouldn't matter if we were. Schools in my town didn't have two pennies to rub together. I was lucky and got a track scholarship for college. I saw things there that I wished I'd had as a kid, that I wish my friends had too."

"Is that why you became a teacher?"

"That and I actually like teaching."

One of the cafe's employees came out to wipe down a nearby table, and Mr. Colossus waved at her. "Hey, could I get a refill on this?"

The worker shook his head. "Sorry, we don't do refills. You'll have to come in and order another one."

The giant lowered his eyes to his cup and frowned. "Never mind, then."

Finn raised a twenty dollar bill. "Sorry, we're not able to come inside, but if you could put in the order for us and bring it out, I can give you a tip."

The cafe employee looked at the bill for a moment and then took it. "I'll bring you back your change."

"Keep it," Finn said. "Get me another frappuccino while you're at it."

When Finn turned to look at Mr. Colossus, he expected gratitude, but was met with an annoyed glare.

"You don't have to show off how much money you have like that."

"I wasn't. I don't have enough money to show off, honestly."

When that didn't change the expression on the giant's face, Finn tried to explain himself better.

"We got off on the wrong foot the moment we met. If we want to make good things happen for these kids, we need to learn to get along. A cup of cider isn't much of an olive branch, but I'm hoping you'll take it."

Mr. Colossus stared at Finn with a flat expression for far longer than the Irishman was comfortable with, but finally he said, "Fine. Let's see if we can do this. What are you thinking we should do?"

"Well, it's Yule Break already," Finn said. "Not much we can actually do right now, but maybe we could plan some stuff out. What about we do a donut sale? Those are pretty popular."

"Except in a lot of the schools we need to help," Mr. Colossus pointed out. "Some of those kids don't even have money for lunch."

"I hadn't thought of that."

Mr. Colossus tapped his chin. "What we need to do is something that would get rich people interested." He smiled wide, showing off every one of his yellow teeth. "Let's auction off something."

"Like what?"

"Maybe a date night with you."

"*Hard* pass," Finn said, shaking his head. "Pavlina would kill me."

"Pavlina? You still with that pretty little sirin?"

Unfortunately for Finn, legendary Irish warrior and leader of the Fianna, he was an easy blusher. Mr. Colossus howled with laughter.

"Oh, she's got her hooks in you *good*!"

Finn shrugged. "I mean… You saw her…"

The giant pounded on the table, rattling every particle of dust that happened to lay there. Tears sprang from his eyes as he struggled to regain his breath. "Good for you! She's quite a looker!"

"That she is," Finn said, glowing with pride.

Mr. Colossus's guffaw stopped short and his attention suddenly moved to something behind Finn, so the Irishman turned to see what it was. The girl who had battled against Bree at their match waved. The giant teacher waved in response. As soon as the exchange ended, the girl stepped into moving traffic, not caring to look at the vehicles zooming left and right.

As one, the men jumped from their seats. The table fell to the sidewalk the moment they did, but neither of them noticed as a truck barreled into the teenager. As she fell, she kept her eyes focused on Finn's.

Bree was a quick study, especially for what she loved already, and she had a passion for portals. Ever since she met Cal, portals intrigued her. You could go anywhere and learn so much. If she didn't have the desire to become a lawyer one day, she'd consider becoming a bookdealer.

This surprised Bree in the beginning. Order and predictability helped her get far over the years. Adventures seemed to be the opposite. During her lessons with Cal, however, she realized just how vital her organizational skills were to portal-hopping.

Cal came off as carefree, but she believed in doing things the right way. She also liked to say, "When you know and become proficient in all the rules, then you know the best ways to break them." That didn't make sense to Bree, but it *felt* right, so she wrote it down in her journal.

The only thing Bree didn't like about portal lessons was the anti-climactic nature of them. She prepped the fairy stones, reviewed the rules, envisioned the location, opened the portal, stepped through for all of three seconds, and then returned to her original reality. She wanted to explore, but there was no safe way to do it. If she took longer than the blink of an eye, The Shadow could swoop in and it would all end.

"Come on! You've done this a hundred times!" Cal looked at Bree with an encouraging smile. This usually worked on her, but the Chosen One had run out of get up and go.

"It doesn't matter."

Bree set the fairy stone in her hand down on the leaf-covered table, and leaned back to look at the oak branches above. Ms. Sirin's crows waited there. Bree didn't understand why. It was Sunday; their favorite person wouldn't be back until the next day. *Maybe they don't know that.* Corbin gave her a pointed look from one of the lower hanging branches. *Okay, they know. Something else is going on.*

"Why are you giving up?" Cal approached Bree with genuine worry etched into the lines around her eyes. "You've gotten so good at this. If things were different, I'd tell you to take the bookdealer test."

Bree turned her attention to her mentor. "That's the thing, Cal. *If things were different.* When will they be? When will I get to experience these entire worlds I never knew existed until they were right there in front of my face?"

Cal shrugged. "I don't know, but one day." She tugged at Bree's arm. "Come on. Just think of a place. I'll give us a whole minute this time. You're gifted enough to portal out of there if things get really bad."

None of the pulling on Bree's arm budged her. For a small teenager, she knew how to stand her ground. When Cal offered a full minute, though, she'd piqued the Chosen One's interest enough for her to try again.

"Okay, fine, I'll make another portal." Bree picked up the fairy stone. "I need to make this count though."

"Okay, let's go over the rules again."

Bree tilted her head so that she could give Cal an annoyed look. "Really?"

Cal held up her hands defensively. "Okay, okay!"

Closing her eyes and taking deep breaths, Bree allowed her mind to wander. *Where would I most like to be right now?* At first she thought of a winter wonderland where she could experience a real Yule, but what would be the point of staying there for one minute? That wasn't even long enough to sing a carol.

Being cramped in a white room with only beds and a bathroom hadn't been ideal. It had been longer than she could remember since she'd felt free.

Bree wanted somewhere quiet with plenty of space. She imagined a starry sky. The only time she spent outdoors anymore was under the canopy of old, moss-covered oak branches. In the non-magical reality, she spent most of her time hiding in her or Liz's bedroom. She hadn't seen a star since their summer trip to Virginia.

I need to be careful that I don't fling myself into outer space, though. Bree kept thinking, detailing the image. Quiet, spacious, starry, safe and life-sustaining. It would be a place where she could sit long enough to enjoy one full minute of celestial beauty.

"You got it?" Cal asked.

"Yeah," Bree whispered. "Fairy stone, fairy stone, listen to my request. Take me to the place of my dreams, to the world that knows me best. Quiet, room, and starry skies. A place where I need no disguise. My breath will not falter, my heart will not cease. I just want a place where I can find peace."

When Bree tossed the stone, it struck the air and exploded. At first, it reminded Bree of fireworks, then she saw it for what it really was—the birth of a star. She gasped in awe of the shining portal opening before her. This was the most beautiful one she'd seen so far, and she'd seen many.

"Wow! Good job on whatever this is!" Cal said, laughing.

Bree stepped through, beckoning Cal to join her.

Once they passed through, the Chosen One realized this was as close to perfection as it got.

She cast her gaze everywhere that she could, fearful that time would move too quickly. A swirling *something* caught her attention. Soon it joined a group of others.

Bree pointed at the gathering forms. "What are they?"

Cal shook her head. "I don't know. I don't like it; feels off. We should go." The bookdealer pulled at Bree's arm. "Quick. We need to hop back and close off the portal!"

Bree tugged her arm back, and Cal lost her grip. "No, I see faces, Cal."

The more she looked, the more she saw. Pale blue lines formed the rounded cheeks that belonged to the young. Curly tendrils of hair came into view and Bree could even tell that some were in styles that were popular at school. They gazed at each other with round eyes that reminded her of what she saw in the mirror while getting ready for the day.

"Faces a lot like…" She whispered with a fearful breath. With a gulp, she turned to her mentor. "Faces a lot like mine. They're spirits. They're… oh gods, Cal… I think this is where the bokor is keeping their souls."

Cal held her hand over her mouth. "You mean the victims from our reality?"

"We need to tell Ms. Sirin," Bree said. "Will we be

able to come back?"

"As long as you can remember this place."

"I don't think I could ever forget it."

One of the faces turned to look Bree directly in the eyes. Bree gasped at the spirit's recognizable features. "Oh gods, it's that girl Maia from the automaton match!"

Cal tugged on Bree's arm again to leave, but she patted her away.

"Hold on. She needs to tell me something."

Pavlina finished stringing together dried cranberries and orange peels, and then went about draping them over the curtains and archways. The festive colors and delicious scent could fool anyone into believing winter happened in Florida.

With Finn gone, she could wrap his presents and that was the next item on her Yule prep agenda. But before she could even grab scissors and tape, the phone rang. It was an old-fashioned thing, a relic from her life in the nineties. No caller ID, no cell service, and most importantly, no Atlas.

The drawback to having a phone like this was that she had no idea who was calling. So when she picked up the receiver, she half expected to have to hang up on another robocall. Instead, she heard Detective Troias on the line.

"It happened again."

"Oh gods… I was hoping it was over…"

"Sometimes, these types of killers take a break," the detective said. "It won't be over until we catch whoever this is. Meet me at the hospital."

"Hospital? Not the morgue?"

"She's still technically alive."

Pavlina gasped. "How? I mean…"

"I don't know, but maybe there's a chance we could save her."

"If we can find her soul, I might be able to." Pavlina checked her watch. Finn would be home any moment, but she could leave a note saying where she was. "Can you give me about thirty minutes?"

"I'll be here."

The call ended and Pavlina rushed to hide all of Finn's presents. Before she could grab her bag to leave, the phone rang again. This time when she picked up the phone, it was her Irishman.

"I'm so glad you called," Pavlina said "I wanted you to know I'm heading to the hospital. A girl—"

"Got run over?" Finn asked.

"Yes," Pavlina asked, perplexed. "How did you know?"

"I'm at the hospital with Mr. Colossus. She's his student. We saw it happen."

"Finn…"

"I know."

"What are the odds?"

"This has to be orchestrated, Pav." He took a long breath that shook with more than the static of the line. "Get here. I think we should talk this over with him. I think a *lot* more teachers need to know what's going on."

"I'll see you in a little bit. It might have to wait until I see Detective Troias."

"I love you."

Pavlina thought of Mrs. Selkie's parting words the last time they hung out. *What are we waiting for?*

"I love you too."

Hanging up the phone, Pavlina slipped some flats on and grabbed her purse. As soon as she headed out the door, she immediately regretted wearing long sleeves. She wished she could spend Yule Break someplace that experienced winter, but travel was out of the cards until this whole thing blew over. *If it ever does.*

The sirin got into her car and buckled up. This was the only thing in her life that had Atlas tech in it, and that was only because she couldn't afford a new car. Even if she did find something in her budget, the chance was slim to none that it wouldn't have Atlas tech in it as well. Not everyone could snag a classic like Finn had.

This thing could track wherever Pavlina was traveling. For that very reason, she almost always rode with Finn. She didn't have time to think of any other options, though, so she got going.

As Pavlina drove, the little dot that represented her car moved down the roads on the car's map screen. She tried not to look at it, knowing that it was a distraction she didn't need to have during a time like this. She wasn't able to ignore the radio suddenly flipping around stations without her control.

At a red light, Pavlina pressed the off button, but it did nothing. "Gods damn it…" She turned the volume knob all the way down and it turned itself all the way up until it felt like her eardrums would rupture. "Fuck off, Atlas!"

Pavlina almost didn't hear the horn blaring behind her, until several others joined in, and then she saw the light had turned green. Knowing she couldn't drive safely in these conditions, she turned the corner and parked in the nearest spot she could find.

The sirin turned off the engine, popped a piece of nicotine gum in her mouth, and got out of the car. She leaned on the side of it, staring in the direction of the hospital. *If I were a crow, I could fly there. Or if I transitioned right now, I could.*

Pavlina's groan of frustration flipped to a gasp when a giant clock appeared a few yards down the road from her. The face of it opened, and out walked Cal.

The bookdealer waved. "Hey, I heard you need to get to the hospital." She pointed at Pavlina's car. "And

I figured that wasn't going to be much help."

"Thank the gods, Finn got ahold of you."

"What?" Cal asked, as she scanned the street.

"Finn told you to come get me, right?"

"Oh! No, Bree did."

"Bree?"

"I'll explain later." The bookdealer let out a blubbering sigh. "Can't see any steel. I'll have to use a burner bar to make this doorway." She pulled a steel bar out of her messenger bag. "Hold my hand, would you?"

Pavlina remembered the doorway spell Finn had taught her and Bree in the desert reality more than a year before. After a short recap from Cal, it was easier than before to bring up the hospital door and step through to the other side.

EIGHTEEN

The Yule Break

The day had not gone at all as Pavlina had planned. Things had been so calm for so long, she hadn't thought anything would have gotten in the way of simple Yuletide traditions. Being lulled into a false sense of security wasn't a mistake she wanted to make again.

The girl on the bed was named Maia. According to Mr. Colossus, she was a bright kid, a little too competitive, but she had her soft side. Of course, Pavlina kept seeing all the similarities to Bree in the girl's features. Fortunately, her breath was even, but it made little difference. Whoever Maia was, she wasn't there. The death harbinger had no idea where the girl's soul could be. *Since they didn't manage to kill this one completely, maybe there's a chance we can save her.*

On top of that, the crushing sense of impending death made Pavlina want to vomit. Her face was a mess of black feathers. Wings had sprouted within an hour of arriving. Detective Troias left before it got that far, knowing that her time would be better spent tracking how far back Maia had gone missing.

Finn and Mr. Colossus stayed, though. Pavlina was certain no one could have made the giant leave, even though the room was clearly far too small for him.

"I should have known," he said, wringing his hands. "She wasn't at school the day before Yule Break."

"Take it easy on yourself." Pavlina laid her hand on top of his, letting her calming magic soothe him. "Lots of kids don't come to school the day before a break. That's why we usually give them something fun and easy to do."

"I know but…" Mr. Colossus shook his head. "Home wasn't a good place for her to be. I'm pretty sure her parents were abusing her. I kept calling the Department of Children and Families when she'd come in bruised. One time, her eyes were red and veiny, like someone had choked her. The Department of Children and Families did nothing."

"You did everything you could and you're here now," Finn said. He sat in the other corner of the hospital room, trying to give the giant enough space to have at least a little comfort.

"I wish there was something I could do about this. I feel so useless."

Pavlina glanced at Finn with a questioning gaze. He nodded in response.

"You know," she said to Mr. Colossus. "There may be something you can do, but we need to have a long talk. Just the three of us, outside of this hospital, and with no phones, nothing."

Mr. Colossus eyed her suspiciously. "A secondary location with no way to call for help."

"We're teachers, not murderers," Finn interjected.

"Fine," the giant said, "but only because I need to stretch and I could take you both down easily."

Finn opened his mouth to argue, but Pavlina shot him a look. *Now is not the time for a pissing contest.*

By the sound of the giant's creaking joints as they exited the hospital, he really had needed to stretch. When they got some distance away from the building, Finn asked Mr. Colossus again if he had any devices on him. The man grumbled about how he'd left them and wished he hadn't.

"It's for the best," Pavlina reassured him. "What we're about to tell you needs to be kept private. For our safety, your safety, your students' safety."

Those last few words shifted the giant's mood. He gave up his harrumphing and gave Pavlina his full attention. It was a risk to let another person in on the secrets, but Finn had been right. Other teachers needed to know so they could protect their students. Besides, playing it safe hadn't accomplished anything.

Pavlina and Finn filled in Mr. Colossus with as many details as they could. They explained that the reason they felt Maia was targeted was because she both looked a lot like Bree and had a personal connection to her. They told him about the secret sect of gods so scared of losing their immortality that they'd taken to sacrificing Chosen Ones.

"The Shadow?" Mr. Colossus asked. "What a dumb name, but… I guess I believe you. You'd be a fool to make up something like that. What can we do about it, though? They'll just keep at it until they sacrifice the Chosen One."

"We can't let that happen," Finn jumped in.

"Of course we can't!" the giant shouted. "I don't want kids to die because some powerful assholes don't value mortal lives."

"Currently, Bree is learning about the legal system and how to approach—"

Mr. Colossus shook his hand to stop her. "Wait a minute, wait a minute. You have the *Chosen One* studying law to do what? Somehow convince the Council of Pantheons that there's a secret group intent on killing innocent kids so they can live another hundred years? Something tells me that's not going to win anyone to your side."

Pavlina shrugged. "It's the best idea we have right

now."

"Sometimes you have to fight," Mr. Colossus said. "We need to gather allies. People who care, even supernaturals and immortals. This is going to be a war."

"That's tantamount to treason," Finn said.

"So what? You're scared to go back to Tartarus? I'd be more scared about someone you love dying, if I were you." Mr. Colossus squinted at Finn. "Unless you don't really care about her."

"Hey, now!" Pavlina rubbed Finn's arm to comfort him. "He cares very much, but let's not jump to *war* without trying everything else first. Besides, Bree is a pacifist. There's no way she'd go for that."

The giant blinked. "A pacifist? Gods, no wonder they chose her. They didn't want a fight." Mr. Colossus let out a resigned sigh. "Fine, we'll try your way first, but I still think we need to get as many people on our side as possible."

Our side? We're winning him over. "You can help with that," Pavlina said. "You have connections with a lot of schools. Spread the news and let's see who will help us."

Mr. Colossus grinned. "I can do that."

Just as Pavlina was about to make further plans, Cal showed up, stepping through a portal that looked like a mirror with an oak tree for a frame. It stood in the middle of the parking lot like a sore thumb. *Again? Are you kidding me?* Just as quickly as the portal appeared, Cal closed it again.

"Hey, if you're done here, Bree needs you," Cal said, pointing her gaze at Pavlina.

"Who is this?" Mr. Colossus asked.

Cal turned to him and, in a very matter of fact tone, said, "I'm a bookdealer." She turned back to Pavlina. "We gotta go. It's related to this."

"What about me?" Finn asked.

"If you want to be there, go for it," Cal answered. "I wouldn't leave your car behind, though."

The bookdealer didn't even look around for a piece of steel this time, but pulled out another bar and created the front door to Annie Lytle High. *Now we're going to school? What's going on?*

Cal opened the door and beckoned Pavlina to follow. The moment the sirin stepped through, she felt all her feathers retreat and her wings return to their hidden spot.

The school's air conditioning blasted. As always, Pavlina's wings had torn the fabric of her shirt, which left her skin bare to the artificial breeze and sent a shiver down her back. The moment Pavlina saw Bree, though, she forgot all about her discomfort.

Beside Bree, a figure hovered. She looked much like Bree, but she was clearly ethereal. Pavlina had seen many people who looked like this—spirits waiting to go to the afterlife—but this girl was more corporeal.

"Where…" Pavlina looked from Bree to the girl and back. "Where did you find her? Was she at this school?"

Bree shook her head. "No, we were doing a portal lesson and I saw them in another reality."

"Them?"

"There were probably a dozen." Bree looked at a ghost next to her. "Is that right?" The spirit nodded in response.

Pavlina stepped toward the ghost. "I can guide you, all of you, to the afterlife. I can bring you peace."

The ghost shook her head and shifted away.

"Ms. Sirin, they don't want to go yet," Bree said. "They want to stop this guy before it gets worse. Plus, Maia here still has a body she can go back to."

Pavlina gasped and took in the sight of the spirit's face. She saw the resemblance now. "I just saw you."

"Sorry I didn't tell you what was going on earlier," Cal said. "We needed to get everyone out of the portal and wanted you to make sure she was okay at the hospital while we did it. If you'd known, you would have come here instead."

Damn right I would have! Pavlina's face burnt with rage, knowing she'd been held back from protecting Bree when she had been so close to those who wanted to sacrifice her. The sirin decided to keep her mouth closed for now, though, because fighting wouldn't help things progress at all.

Instead, Pavlina asked, "Do they know who the bokor is?"

"He's not a bokor." Bree turned to Maia. "Tell her what you told me."

The spirit stepped forward with shy, hesitant eyes. Maia was nothing like the girl that Mr. Colossus had described. *Being murdered can change you like that.*

"He just plucked me out of my body and put me on his back," she said with a voice that sounded like a soft, distant echo. "It got bigger and bigger until I couldn't even tell I was on someone's back anymore. There were other girls like me there. We were all so scared. And then I heard someone talk to him. He called him Atlas."

Pavlina froze. "Atlas?"

"Yeah," Bree said. "Atlas."

"The other girls were killed," Maia said. "I don't know why I wasn't, but if you can keep my body alive... I'm too scared to come back yet, but maybe when he's been caught I can?"

Pavlina nodded and stroked the spirit's ethereal cheek. "Keeping souls safe is what I do best."

The moment the words left her mouth, lights flickered around her, forming into the other girls. It hit Pavlina then why Bree and Cal were able to see them. *They've chosen to stay. They're ghosts now, and only resolving their murders will allow them passage to the afterlife. Until then, they'll haunt the living.*

Pavlina turned her attention back to Bree. The girl had told her about all the disturbing ghosts she'd encountered sitting on the city bus or meandering around her old neighborhood. Back then, she'd been so frightened of them that it had put her off magic entirely.

Over the last year, all that had changed. Not only had the Chosen One embraced magic, but she was also using it to risk her life in an effort to save ghosts. Pavlina's terror over Bree's situation ebbed for a moment, making room for the pride she felt for her former foster daughter.

The arrival of Yule usually sparked joy in Bree, but today she was a bundle of stress due to her new living situation. The Chosen One wasn't the most introverted person in the world, but she did like to have her space. Living with a dozen teenaged ghosts didn't allow her much privacy. You couldn't lock your door when someone could just glide through it to talk to you.

The elder Castilles weren't fans of this development either. Her parents came from a reality where stories and movies painted ghosts as malevolent beings who could and would kill anyone they met. Bree knew better.

Ghosts just wanted to show off their wounds and

hurl insults at you. They were mostly a nuisance, and one that Bree and Liz were accustomed to from once living in a neighborhood filled with them. A couple of years without spirits lurking around had spoiled them, though. Also they weren't just roaming the streets anymore; they were roommates.

Even while she was getting ready in the bathroom, one of them often marched right in. Maia liked to strike up conversations with her there so Bree's family wouldn't be around to listen.

"Is Ylva coming today?" Maia asked for the thirtieth time that morning, as she wafted right through the locked bathroom door.

Bree groaned, tired of this pestering. The ghost was more interested in the Chosen One's social life than even she was. *I know Maia's bored, but there's got to be something more interesting for her to do than annoy me.*

"You know, I could have been on the toilet," Bree grumbled.

"Well, is she?"

Bree pumped some face wash liquid into her palm. "Like I said before, she *might*. Her host family isn't exactly keen on her leaving the house since she got attacked."

"Must be nice."

"What's nice?" Bree asked as she washed her face.

Maia looked at Bree with the mournful eyes that only the ghost of a murdered girl could achieve.

"Having people who care about you."

While they were antagonistic during their brief interactions before Maia's death, Bree understood better now. The Magical Automaton Club at her school was Maia's only family, and she wanted to make them proud. Bree had gotten in the way of that.

Bree rinsed her face and patted it dry. "Mr. Colossus cares about you a lot. Ms. Sirin too."

That last part pricked a little jealousy in Bree. Ms. Sirin was *her* former foster parent, but she'd taken to Maia like a mother hen. It made sense, given that the sirin was a death harbinger and Maia was the soul of a wronged teenager. *Still, what about me?*

"Are they coming today?"

"Ms. Sirin will for sure," Bree answered. "I don't know about Mr. Colossus. I didn't ask."

"At least I can spend Yule with you and Liz."

All annoyance washed away with those words. Maia *liked* them. She might be a pain in the rear, but only because she always wanted to hang out. It was a little like having a clingy pet.

"Wish I could give you a present." Maia held up her translucent hands. "But it's a little hard right now."

"We stand a much better chance of staying awake all night with you, though," Bree pointed out.

Maia laughed. "I suppose so, but then again, I'm a ghost. Technically, I would be the thing to watch out for on Yule night."

"I'm more scared of the living than I am of the dead, right now."

Bree opened the bathroom door to see their pocket reality suite was empty.

"Everyone's up in the cafeteria," Maia said, floating toward the exit.

As soon as Bree left her suite and entered the school's basement, she could hear faint echoing upstairs. "I guess the festivities have begun."

Maia didn't wait for Bree to catch up; she flew straight through the basement ceiling. Bree dashed up the stairs, taking the slower path of a mortal.

For many reasons, the school had to be somewhat empty for the party. Custodians still visited on a weekly basis and they had to make the place look less lived-in for those occasions. Still, Bree could smell the aroma of a winter feast and picked up on select notes from a common Yule carol.

Bree was humming along to *Porridge for the Tomte* when she entered the cafeteria and saw everyone. She'd expected Ms. Sirin, Mr. Finn, and Principal Cailleach. She *hadn't* expected Mrs. Selkie, her wife, and her baby to be there too. She was also pleasantly surprised that Mr. Colossus had made it. The only other person she could hope to see was Cal, but she knew the bookdealer was having a romantic Yule day with Mr. Finn's daughter, Oísina.

Every single ghost was there as well, mostly

gawking at the beautiful Yule tree. Maia, though, was talking with Mr. Colossus. It warmed Bree's heart to see that someone really did care about the teenage ghost. *This has got to be the most wholesome haunting in history.*

Just as Bree was headed to the sweet potato casserole, she felt a tap on her shoulder. She turned to see Ylva's beautiful, golden face beaming at her.

"Blessed Yule!" the girl said, holding up a red gift bag.

"Blessed Yule!" Bree replied and shook her head at the bag. "You didn't have to get me anything. I'm not able to shop for any gifts, so I don't have anything for you."

"I know that, and I don't care." Ylva pressed the bag against Bree's hand. "Take it."

Knowing that turning down a gift would make Ylva sad, Bree pulled her present out. She had expected another book or maybe an ornament. She hadn't expected a fat stack of letters.

"What...?"

Ylva tapped on the top letter. "Look at who they're all from."

Mortals for Equality, Pandora's Hope, the Minotaur Society, and more had written to Ylva.

"I remember you telling me how you couldn't find a way of contacting them without drawing attention from The Shadow," Ylva explained.

"You did this for me?"

"Ylva nodded. "I thought if I wrote them, it might not raise suspicions. I'm just an exchange student writing letters. It's what we do."

"Can I open them now?"

Ylva laughed. "They're Yule presents! Of course you can!"

Bree ripped the envelopes open right away. Each letter shared information about their causes and experience defending those wronged by the Council of Pantheons. Then Bree opened the one from the Good Grifters. This was something completely different.

"How...? How did they know?"

"Know what?" Ylva asked.

"Dear Bree," Bree read. "Very clever having your friend write to us. A tactic worthy of a grifter, but not what we'd expect from a Chosen One. The Good Grifters is a society of tricksters who understand that the establishment should always be questioned. While you seem like a very good person, your role is a major part of upholding what we're trying to take down. We wish you the best in your endeavors, and hope you find the right organization for your needs. Sincerely, Mr. Fox."

"You have all these other organizations I can write to for you, though."

"Yeah, but..." Bree tapped the letter from the Good Grifters. "I'm pretty sure these are the only ones who would really be on my side."

Ylva squeezed Bree's free hand. "It's Yule. Let's enjoy ourselves before our break is over."

Bree laughed. "Come on, you love school as much as me."

"Even the smartest students need to give their brains some rest."

"You're right." Bree set her letters on the nearest table and walked with Ylva to get a plate of food.

Despite the tree still standing in the corner and the holiday movie marathon on the television, it was hard to believe it was only the day after Yule. It felt more like May that afternoon, as they sprawled out on Finn's living room furniture, him on the couch and her on the recliner. Finn and Pavlina had swapped their itchy holiday sweaters for light t-shirts and shorts.

"The Yule Cat will just have to eat us up," Finn had said as he tore his off and tossed it onto the living room floor.

"Technically, all we have to do is *receive* new clothes by Yule Eve," Pavlina said. "Objective achieved."

Finn got off the couch and headed to the kitchen. "Come on, let's stuff ourselves with more leftovers and I'll turn the channel to that comedy about the thirteen Yule lads."

Pavlina didn't seem to hear him. She stared at the

Yule tree with a mournful expression on her face.

"Pav, what's wrong?"

"I hate this feeling," she answered.

Finn returned to the couch and reached over to stroke Pavlina's hand. "What feeling, my love?"

"I should feel nothing but gratitude right now." The sirin wiped away a tear. "Yule wasn't guaranteed to us at all. Every single day we have is a gift, but…"

"But what?"

"Seeing the Castilles like that, getting to be parents again. Do they realize how lucky they are? They must."

Ah, so that's it. Pavlina's heart opened to everyone and it got hurt time and time again. She wanted a family more than anything else, and it had been denied to her multiple times.

"They're very lucky," Finn agreed. "You have every right to feel the way you do."

"What good does it do, though?" Pavlina wiped more tears off her cheeks. "It's not like I'll ever have that."

Finn grabbed the remote and turned off the television. The room was quiet now, no more lulling buzz to drown out doubtful whispers.

"Why can't you ever have that?"

Pavlina arched a brow. "Finn, look at me. I'm no spring crow. I'm halfway through my lifespan. Having a child at this age would be a miracle."

"First of all, you're not that old. I've known middle-aged *humans* who have gotten pregnant."

"That's a—"

"Second," Finn said, holding up a finger to stop Pavlina's protests. "Even if you can't, we can adopt."

"We?"

Silence took hold, leaving the two to search for clues in each other's faces.

I just said that out loud. I didn't even think about it.

It was too late to take it back. Finn knew he'd meant it, even if he hadn't even thought about it before. He'd always been content with Oísina as his only child. Then again, the only other time he'd wanted to marry since his wife had died had been for very political reasons.

Looking at Pavlina's glistening eyes, Finn felt that familiar longing again, the kind he'd felt all those centuries ago. He was a hero, not one for staying put anywhere for long. Yet with his sirin, he wanted something permanent. He wanted a home in her heart. He even wanted a family, not just for her, but for them.

Finn broke the silence. "Well, I mean we hadn't talked about it, but it seems like a possibility if we get married, right?"

"I didn't want to assume anything. I don't want you to have a child just to make me happy. That wouldn't be fair to you or her."

Pavlina's words protested against it, but there was a

lamplight of hope in her eyes. If Finn said he wanted a baby right then, he knew she would be on the phone with a fertility clinic within minutes.

"I'd have to be an entire fool to think children were completely off the table with you." Finn stroked her cheek. "I'm not saying it's certain, but I don't want to say it's never happening."

"Alkonosts and sirins aren't the easiest children to raise."

Finn chuckled. "Oísina gave me plenty of experience handling a difficult child."

"No! Oísina?"

"She was *always* sneaking out to go on some adventure!"

Pavlina laughed. "Okay, tell me more."

"When she was little, I'd tuck her in and not three minutes later I'd hear her playing with brownies in her bedroom."

Finn shook his head, remembering all the times he'd find his chubby-cheeked, flaxen-haired daughter pulling out candy she'd hidden under her pillow to feed her fae friends.

"That was nothing compared to her teen years, though."

"Oh, I'm sure."

"She used to run off to Tir na nÓg," Finn said, beaming. "I didn't know why for a long time, but it turns out she had a sweetheart over there named

Niamh. Poor dear had a pig head, but Oísina's a poet and fell in love with her for her heart. And with a little fae magic they even wound up having kids! *Kids!* Three of them!"

Pavlina gasped. "You're a grandfather?!"

Finn's smile fell. "They were mortal. They…" He shook his head. "I *was* a grandfather, yes."

"Gods… And now you're in love with another mortal." Pavlina rested her forehead against his. "I'm so sorry, Finn."

"Don't be sorry, Pav."

"I don't want to be another loss in your story."

Finn scooped her into his lap and kissed her, tasting apple cider on her lips. Though she'd quit smoking long ago, she still smelled like cloves.

"The true loss would be never having met you or loved you," Finn said after ending his kiss. "And it's not just about my story. I want to be more than a passing romance in yours. There's no one else in any reality like you, Pav."

"Oh gods, I'm crying again." Pavlina wiped at her face. "I swear I've cried so much since meeting you and the girls."

"It's hard to hold that much compassion in," Finn said. "I guess it just leaks out."

"You should tell yourself that the next time you refuse to cry."

Finn nodded. "You're right. You're always right."

Pavlina let out a soft laugh, despite wiping away her remaining tears. "I love it when you tell me that."

"Then, you'll hear it every day for the rest of your life."

Finn lifted her hand and laid a sweet kiss on her knuckles. *Gods, I hope the rest of her life is at least another century. The Shadow might not even let us have tomorrow.*

NINETEEN

The Lupercalia Dance

Despite the unpleasant way Finn and Mr. Colossus had met, they'd gotten fairly chummy over Yule Break, and by January they worked well together. They'd even reached a first name basis, which was rare for the Irishman. It helped that Alec was far easier to say than Mr. Colossus.

A surprise to both of them was how well they worked together. They both had remarkable determination, a fair amount of skill and talent, and a strong desire to make sure teenagers got what they needed to succeed in the world.

Even with their camaraderie, though, their two missions weren't exactly all that easy. They needed to raise thousands upon thousands of dollars to continue holding magical automaton matches and send whichever school won regionals to the state tournament. On top of that, they needed to inform and prepare teachers all over the district so that they could protect their students.

Alec and Finn did have a few tools at their disposal, however. The giant had been in a fraternity and many of his frat brothers were able to donate money. The magical application teacher was able to convince Principal Cailleach not to cancel the Lupercalia dance, and instead use it as a fundraising opportunity. If things went well, they would be able to make sure every school in the region had what they needed to bring their Magical Automaton Clubs back to life.

It was somewhat more difficult to convince other teachers that their teenagers were at risk because a powerful Titan wanted to sacrifice the Chosen One. Finn didn't blame them. He wouldn't have believed it either. However, when he invited these teachers to Annie Lytle High School for meetings about club fundraising, he was able to introduce them to the ghosts of Atlas's victims. A haunting on that scale was hard for them to ignore.

Unfortunately, it was one thing to convince teachers that their students faced a very real danger. It was another to come up with solid plans to protect those teenagers. They couldn't expect *everyone* in their schools to give up their Atlas phones and other devices. The spirits didn't feel safe leaving Annie Lytle either. So, Finn couldn't exactly parade them around to every high school in the district.

On a brisk January day, Finn and Alec discussed these difficulties while walking along the river after a good run. Occasionally, Finn would look at the water and wonder if Bree's tentacled familiar, Johnnie, was still swimming around so deep that not even the mermaids, selkies, and rusalki saw him.

"Finn, are you here?" Alec asked.

The Irishman laughed. "Mostly. Sorry, I got caught up in a memory." Finn pointed at the blue bridge in the distance. "You know that bridge?"

"Everyone knows the Main Street Bridge," Alec said. "I drive over it every time I head to work."

"That's where we caught Hermes with that portal."

The giant took a long look at it. "Do you think he'll show up there?"

"I figure he can show up wherever he wants. He's a god."

"Well, at least for now, he's quiet. I suppose it takes time to escape a reality like that without a portal."

Finn nodded and continued walking. Despite the truth of Alec's statement, the legendary hero knew that peace never lasted forever, and the shadow of dread that always lurked in the back of his mind remained in place.

"How's Pavlina doing?"

Alec's change in subject made Finn smile. Every day, he fell even more in love with his sirin. Yule had been a beautiful experience. They'd shared presents and dreams. Their visions of a married life in the future almost made him forget that the dangers surrounding them now could ensure none of their hopes ever came to pass.

"She's good. We're good."

"You two make a nice couple. How long have you been together?"

"Depends on what you'd call the beginning of our relationship," Finn said with a laugh.

"Seems like you were both sweet on each other at the track meet." Alec puffed up his chest with mock pride. "Otherwise she would have fallen to my charms."

Finn laughed even harder at that, and the stitch in his side from their jog returned. "Can we sit on that bench over there?"

"It's a good thing you've taken up weekend runs with me," the giant said. "You need to get in shape."

You have no idea. Finn wondered how many years of his immortality he'd lost and how soon he'd be an old man.

The two men sat and watched the afternoon light dazzle like diamonds on the river's waves. It brought Finn a sense of longing. He wanted to spend forever enjoying moments like this with Pavlina, but nothing was certain and forever was a long shot for anyone.

"You ought to marry her," Alec said, shaking Finn out of his reverie.

"Well, we've talked about doing that one day," Finn said and twirled a finger in the air. "You know. After all this is over."

"You think this is all ending sometime soon?"

Finn turned his gaze from the river to see a grim expression on his friend's face. "You don't?"

Alec shrugged. "Maybe it will, maybe it won't. I'm not going to assume it either way."

"What's the point of all this if things don't get better, then?" Finn asked. "The fundraisers, the cardio, the movies and presents, and hanging out with friends?"

"To enjoy what we have when we have it."

Finn ruminated on the giant's statement. There was hope in it. Even if everything fell apart in the future, there was always the present. After all, his daughter was on the lam and still in a romantic relationship with Cal.

"You're right."

Alec grinned. "I usually am."

"If I save up, I could probably get her a ring by Lupercalia…"

"Oh, that's quite a romantic day for it, but isn't that when you're doing the fundraiser dance?"

"Yeah," Finn said with a smile. "I knew I'd fallen for her at last year's dance. Maybe this time I could show it by getting down on one knee."

"Those cheesy books you read are coming in handy," Alec said. "Chicks dig stuff like that." The giant looked out over the river and squinted. "Do you see that?"

Finn looked in the direction where his friend pointed, and an image of a tentacle flickered. "Did I just imagine that?"

"If you did, we imagined it together." Alec laughed. "Maybe it's a sign. For what, I don't know, but I wouldn't take any chances. Better propose to that woman before I do, Finn!"

Pavlina had Finn's house to herself while he was with his therapist. From what she understood, his December meeting with his parole officer had been rushed and she had only said she would get back to him when she had a better handle on her schedule. Finn had a good excuse not to go to therapy for that very reason, but he chose to anyway. Pavlina couldn't be prouder.

Unfortunately, that also meant he wasn't around when Pavlina's mother and sister showed up. Neither of the alkonost women were good at keeping their thoughts off their faces, and the sirin knew she was in for it. She had been too busy to make a trip up to Savannah for a visit, and she had tossed her Atlas phone. So all communication was rushed and done through the school's landline.

"We brought presents," Luda said as she entered.

"Yes, they've been sitting in our house since before Yule," Pavlina's mother grumbled. The old woman pushed past her daughters to sit on Finn's recliner. "Harper kept trying to get into them, but we kept her away from them. For *two months* we kept her from it."

"I'm sorry, Mamushka," Pavlina said. "I really wanted to be there."

In the past, the sirin would have gone out of her way to avoid spending time with her family, but it hurt her heart knowing she couldn't spend time with them this year. All the death and danger kept her tethered to Jacksonville. She was fearful that her family visiting her would put them in the same boat.

Luda set the presents on the coffee table and gave her sister a peck on the cheek. "I'm sure you did."

Pavlina looked at her sister with appreciative eyes. "This is such a sweet surprise."

"We get it. It must be tough doing anything when your car is busted and you don't have a working phone."

Their mother harrumphed in her seat. "Who lives without a phone anymore?"

"It's tough on a teacher's salary, Mamushka!" Luda said, giving their mother a look that Pavlina knew meant they'd discussed all of this on the way over.

"Well, maybe in a couple of—"

"Which is why we came through for you!" Luda interrupted with a giant, beaming smile.

Oh no.

Luda grabbed a smaller box from the stack. "Sorry, I'm bad at hiding stuff. Open it up!"

Pavlina didn't need to unwrap it to know what was inside, but she still hoped she was wrong. Her stomach sank when saw the box for a brand new Atlas phone.

"Luda, this is too much. I—"

"I told her the same!" their mother jumped in. "You're an adult. You should buy your own phone. It's not like you have the expenses that come with being a mother."

"Ma!" Luda yelled.

"I… I have to go to the bathroom…"

Pavlina laid the phone box down on the pile and sprinted to the bathroom to cry. She thought about the little girl who almost lived, but never would. She remembered those months when she hoped she was going to be Bree and Liz's mother forever. *I would rather spend all my money on them than anything else.*

There was a soft knock on the door, but it wasn't for permission. Luda stepped inside and closed the door behind her. Her usually happy face was painted with sympathy and concern.

"She wasn't thinking, Pasha."

Pavlina sat on the toilet and tore off some toilet

paper to wipe her face. "I know."

"She's just mad, because she misses you."

Nodding, Pavlina repeated, "I know."

"And... Well, I'm a little hurt myself."

"I'm sorry. I really *did* want to be there."

Luda sat on the edge of the bathtub and stroked Pavlina's back. "Does it hurt too much when you see Harper or something?"

"What? No! Harper brings me nothing but happiness."

"Then what's holding you back?"

Pavlina didn't have it in her to go over all her excuses again. The more she had explained her situation, the less believable it became, even if it was the truth. They knew these were things Pavlina could have solved by now.

"I can't tell you," Pavlina whispered.

Luda frowned. Pavlina could almost see the wound in her sister's heart. "You can't tell *me*?"

"I don't want you to get hurt."

"Pasha, are you in some kind of trouble?"

Gods, I've already said too much. Pavlina wadded up her tear-soaked toilet paper and tossed it into the trash can.

"I love you and Mamushka and Harper," Pavlina said and continued with a shrug, "I kinda like your husband too."

A soft chuckle escaped Luda, but she still looked

injured.

"I'm a death harbinger, Luda."

Luda rolled her eyes. "Not this again. You know we don't care about that."

"No, that's not what I'm saying. I…" Pavlina sighed. "You help people find their greatest treasure, and I work with death."

"So?"

"Luda, there's a serial killer in Jacksonville."

The alkonost's eyes widened to perfect circles. "What?!"

Pavlina hushed her sister. "Don't upset Ma. Gods, she'll pack up her carpet bag and move in with me and Finn."

"You say that like I wouldn't welcome a break."

This caused a real laugh to bubble from Pavlina. "I love you."

"I love you, too." Luda scrunched her eyebrows together. "At least use the phone to call us."

"I can't! I…" Pavlina gave her sister a once over. "Where's your phone right now?"

"With Ma in the living room. Why?"

"Try not to use it."

"What do you—?"

"Try not to use any Atlas tech."

Luda squinted. "Pasha? Are you becoming a conspiracy theory nut or something?"

"The detective I've been working with told me the

killer might be monitoring activity."

"We live in Savannah," Luda said. "We'll be okay. But… I guess I see why you can't."

"I can still call you from work. Maybe we can even send letters and pictures?"

A loud pounding on the door caught their attention. *Here comes Mamushka.*

"Stop talking behind my back and open the rest of the presents!" their mother called from the hallway.

"I'll figure out an explanation for the phone," Luda whispered before opening the door.

Their mother waited for them both with crossed arms and a stern face. In the past, this would have pulled a long groan from Pavlina, but this time was different. She looked at the old alkonost, knowing it was very possible she might not ever see her again.

Pavlina threw her arms around her. At first her mother reacted with shock, but then slowly returned the hug.

"I've missed you so much, Mamushka," Pavlina whispered against the kerchief hiding most of her mother's fading red hair.

Her mother squeezed her as tightly as she used to when Pavlina skinned her knee or had a nightmare.

"Then come visit me, Pasha."

I wish I could.

Because of mid-year testing and Magical Automaton Club fundraisers, the weeks after Yule Break came and went in a blink. Then, it was suddenly Lupercalia. Thankfully, the school didn't organize a pairing again. They still held a dance, however.

To Bree's surprise, Ylva had asked if they could go to the dance together—as friends, of course. Living in a pocket reality in the school basement meant she didn't have anything nice to wear, but she accepted the invitation anyway.

The night of the dance, Ms. Sirin came to visit and handed her an outfit covered with an opaque plastic drape from the dry cleaners.

"No thanks, Ms. Sirin." Bree tried to push the gift away. Though she didn't have anything nice to wear, she'd rather wear her regular school attire than anything as frilly as her former foster mother got for special occasions the previous year.

Ms. Sirin tsked. "At least look at it before you decide you don't want it."

Bree rolled her eyes and laughed. "Fine, but only because I like you."

When Bree uncovered her gift, she felt guilty that she'd assumed anything. This was formal and high quality, but it certainly wasn't pukingly girlish.

Instead of a lacy dress, Bree's fingers slid against the lavender silk of a long-sleeved button up top that went all the way up to the neck. In contrast, the wide-legged slate-colored pants had a velvety texture. A narrow silver belt cinched it at the waist. Ms. Sirin had even given Bree fancy white and gray saddle shoes.

The teenager threw her arms around Ms. Sirin, and gave her an enthusiastic squeeze. At first the teacher croaked from the impact, but then she relaxed into the embrace. "I'm glad you like it," she said. "I saw it and thought of you."

Mrs. Castille helped Bree get ready. After inspecting herself in the small mirror she'd received from Ms. Sirin, Bree headed upstairs, prepared to meet Ylva.

Bree had expected to wait for her friend, but the golden-haired girl was already there wearing a cream-colored dress that made her look like a daisy. The blush colored balloons tied along the archway to the dance looked more like a frame of rosebuds behind the pretty girl.

Bree's heart thundered. *We're just here as friends.*

"You look so nice," Ylva said, approaching Bree. "I feel like I should have worn something fancy now."

"No, you look so beautiful!" *Way to play it cool.*

"Look what happens when I spin!"

The German girl twirled and her skirt fanned around her as she laughed. Ylva stopped spinning and took a moment to finish her giggling. Bree forgot to breathe for a moment. *Just friends. Just friends. Just—*

"I have something for you! Let me grab my purse."

Ylva ran over to a chair near the ticket table, where

they collected funds for the Magical Automaton Club. She rushed back with more than her purse in her hands. The golden-haired girl handed Bree a clear plastic box with a spray of baby breath flowers attached to an elastic wrist band.

"I hope this is okay," Ylva said. "I've never been to a dance before, but I heard this is what you give someone at one."

Bree opened the box and slid the corsage onto her wrist. "I wish I had something for you."

Ylva waved a dismissive hand. "I just want to have fun. Let's go dance!"

The German girl pulled Bree by the arm, past the ticket table and into the dance. The lights were low except for the sparkle from the charged crystals on the tables and the disco ball hanging from the ceiling.

Some volunteer's playlist blasted over the speakers with a sappy song about love at first sight. It was cheerful and didn't match the romantic energy of the room at all. Bree made a go of dancing, even though she knew how awkward and inexperienced she was at it.

When the music shifted to a slow dance, it got even more difficult. At least with the last song's high tempo, she could pretend she was dancing by bouncing along. Now she had to move her body with graceful strides.

Ylva giggled at her, sinking Bree's spirits. *Gods, I'm so clumsy.*

"Let's go get a snack or something," Bree said and took a step away.

Before Bree could get beyond Ylva's reach, the golden-haired girl tugged at her. "No, let's keep dancing. I'll show you how."

The mirth in Ylva's eyes held a special sparkle now that Bree couldn't say no to. So, Bree gave in.

Ylva put Bree's hands onto her waist before she looped her own hands behind Bree's neck. "Now, we just sway side to side."

Touching Ylva at all sent a warm buzz through Bree, but feeling the curve of the golden-haired girl's waist beneath her hands made her tremble. Because of their position, the two were so close that Ylva's amber eyes hypnotized her.

"This is nice," Ylva whispered.

"Yeah…"

A pretty pink blush spread across Ylva's glowing skin. "I've been meaning to tell you something for a while."

"What?"

Ylva said nothing, but pressed her lips against Bree's, and everything in the whole world bloomed. Bree was transported to a world that smelled of honey and was cast in the perpetual warmth of a summer sunset.

This is happening. It's really—

A boom shook the room. Students and school staff

alike screamed.

The girls pulled apart, terror mirrored in each others' faces. Bree raced to the window to see the magical barrier around the school flashing.

"What's doing that?" Ylva asked.

"I don't know."

Bree wasn't lying; she didn't know. She had her suspicions though, and they were confirmed within seconds.

Where the boundary had just flashed, a hot red line tore through it. Whatever the barrier had been made of seemed to melt away from it, dripping like lava and torching the ground where it fell.

"Run!" Bree cried at Ylva.

The golden-haired girl shook her head.

Instead of arguing, Bree turned to the rest of the room. "Run to the pocket classrooms! Get out of here!"

The other students didn't protest. They nearly stumbled over each other fleeing from the dance. Bree wasn't surprised to see who remained: Ms. Sirin, Mr. Finn, Principal Cailleach, Mrs. Selkie, and Maia.

The ground shook again, this time causing the disco ball to crash, sending a spray of mirrored glass everywhere. Ylva winced and Bree turned back to her friend to see that several pieces had nicked her cheeks.

"My eye," the German girl whimpered.

"Principal Cailleach, help her, please!"

The principal shook her head. "If this is Hermes,

you need me here."

Mrs. Selkie ran over. "I'll get her to my class! I've got all my first aid gear there!"

Just as she grasped Ylva's arm, a howl more terrifying than Bree had ever heard in her life stopped her breath. It was somewhere between a growl and a scream, a harvest of every terror imaginable.

Ylva and Mrs. Selkie were out of the room by the time Bree looked out the window again. There was Hermes, wedging his giant helmeted head through the hole he'd burnt through the boundary. He was glowing with the light of whatever star he'd formed in the prison he'd escaped from.

Where's Cal?

Hermes turned his flaming eyes to look directly through the cafeteria window at Bree. A too-wide smile split his incandescent face, revealing daggers for teeth. *He's going to rip me to shreds if I don't die in flames first.*

The latter seemed more possible at that moment. The centerpieces wilted from the heat, even though he was still squeezing through the barrier half an acre away.

Ducking behind a table did nothing to help against the sweltering temperature. A hot stinging tear didn't even make it to Bree's cheek before evaporating from the impending flashover. Her skin blistered. Soon she'd be nothing more than a mote caught in a star.

Ms. Sirin grabbed Bree around the waist. "We've got to get you out of here!"

A blast reverberated through them, causing everyone to tumble to the ground. Bree's head bumped the floor hard enough for her ears to ring and her vision to blur, but she still witnessed the window glass shattering.

"Oh gods," she squeaked, knowing that there was no escaping.

Hermes was all the way through the boundary. The giant god crawled on his hands and knees so that he could be closer to the ant-like mortals staring back at him through the window frame.

"I'm a *god!*" Hermes shouted, each syllable cracking the cement brick wall between them. "You don't fight a god; you don't *win* against a god. When you try, you just get *burned!*"

Hermes whipped his arm forward and a flare of sizzling plasma sprayed from his hand. It should have killed Bree, but instead time stopped, leaving the tip of the blast mere yards away. Just past the god's shoulder, a giant clock face closed and a pocket watch floated through the air toward her. The Chosen One lifted her hand and gripped it tight. Despite its ticking, the long hand and short hand were frozen.

Knowing that Hermes' attack could resume at any moment, Bree didn't have time to wonder what was happening or figure out what the strange watch in her hand was for. Instead, she reached into her pocket and pulled out a fairy stone. Cal had told her to always keep at least three on hand, because even in the most unlikely cases, Bree might need one.

She struggled to picture anywhere a god could be contained. Only a more powerful entity could overpower him. *Hermes isn't even one of the top Olympians. He's a child.*

Bree thought of Zeus and she latched on to that granule of hope.

Maybe it's time Hermes got grounded.

Gods could withstand the cosmic intensity that Hermes had harvested, but he wasn't a creation god, just a thief. He wouldn't know how to control the intensity of a star like his half-brother Apollo. He wouldn't stand a chance if he attacked the Council of Pantheons, and a violent act like that wouldn't be easily forgiven. The gods would see his treachery for themselves.

Reaching back to her social studies lessons, Bree remembered all the slideshows and textbook photos of the Council of Pantheons. She pictured it in as much detail as her mind could manage and rolled the charged fairy stone in her palm. The rock grew hotter and hotter with each thought.

"Fairy stone, fairy stone," she whispered. "Send Hermes to the place that he calls home. Send him to his mother; send him to his father. Carry his violence to those who can withstand it, to those who can disband it. Let him see their seat of power, in a place where he must cower."

With a deep breath and a throw more forceful than she'd ever managed before, Bree sent the stone flying. It didn't stop until it struck the god's forehead. When it bounced right off, the air rushed out of Bree's lungs.

Before Bree could fall to her knees in defeat, a portal framed by ornate columns opened wide, and Hermes landed perfectly at the center of rows and rows of gods gasping at the intrusion. The god of thieves remained frozen in time.

At that point, Bree didn't know what to do, until she heard the tick tock of the frozen pocket watch in her hand, and saw the little dial at the top. Though she still didn't quite understand how she'd gotten it, she suddenly had an inkling of what it could do.

Bree pressed down on it and suddenly the flare from Hermes' hand sprayed out, melting the seat directly in front of him—Zeus's throne.

For the briefest moment, Bree felt triumphant. She had protected everyone from Hermes's wrath. Then Zeus turned his eyes, filled with righteous anger, directly to Bree.

"Guards!" he yelled, pointing in Bree's direction.

The King of the Gods didn't need to say anything else. Dozens of heavily armored guards swarmed into the school cafeteria with their weapons ready.

Bree attempted to flee, but fear had locked her joints and given her tunnel vision. Instead, she stumbled backwards into Mr. Finn's arms.

"Corbin!" Ms. Sirin called.

The sirin's crow familiar and the rest of his murder swarmed in through the broken window and attacked the oncoming guards. Their vicious beaks pierced like short daggers into the intruders' eyes, sending sprays of blood everywhere. Their claws left long gouges in their faces, leaving flayed skin hanging like fleshy curtains. Bree doubted she could ever lose the memory of that horror.

Mr. Finn grabbed Bree tight and slung her over his shoulder. She knew the Irish warrior was strong, but Ms. Sirin was always teasing him about how quickly he ran out of stamina while running. Despite that, he raced down Annie Lytle's halls while carrying Bree, and he never stopped for even a second to catch his breath.

The moment he got her to the basement, he swung open the door to her pocket reality where her family lived. The Castilles gasped in shock at the sudden intrusion.

"Lock the door!" Mr. Finn yelled. "Don't let *anyone* in! Even if they sound like me."

"What's going on?" Liz asked.

Mr. Finn didn't answer; instead he slammed the door closed. *He's going to try to save Ms. Sirin.*

"Bree?" Mrs. Castille asked.

"Hermes… He came and now the gods—"

A blast shook the whole room and Bree stumbled to her knees. The door to their once hidden location busted open to reveal Council guards pinning Mr. Finn to the ground. Before Bree could even process what was happening, they swarmed her family, while one grabbed her and cuffed her hands behind her back.

"Bree! No!" Liz screamed. She tried to run for her big sister, but a guard pushed her to the floor.

"Leave my sister alone!" Bree yelled at him.

These were the last words the Chosen One spoke before a thud to the back of her head knocked her unconscious.

TWENTY

The Cells

Two weeks had passed since the incident at the Lupercalia dance, and the glowing green of March leaves sprouted everywhere. At least Finn imagined that was happening. From inside of a holding cell in Olympus, it was hard to tell.

Finn's parole had been going well for months. He had made sure to get his homework done and see his therapist. He had been open and honest with his parole officer, despite how uncomfortable his vulnerability was. All that good fortune had a limit though, and he'd reached it.

Still, Finn knew it could be worse. Meals came at predictable times. The food hardly qualified as ambrosia, in fact it resembled Annie Lytle's cafeteria lunches. It was better than starving though. Since they knew he was immortal, the Council of Pantheons representatives didn't have to feed him at all. *Except that none of us are really immortal, not that anyone here believes me about that.*

Ms. Pace was responsible for his regular meals, and occasionally she came to visit. These weren't social calls. She always came with disappointment in him, wondering how he could be so foolish. When he explained everything, she simply didn't believe him, just like everyone else.

So far, the worst thing about his time in the holding cell was that he missed the little family he'd gained as a teacher at Annie Lytle. Many of them were imprisoned as well. He was certain Bree and Pavlina were alone in their cells too. Ms. Pace had told him that Principal Cailleach had been freed due to her status as a goddess.

At least Liz and her parents are off the hook and allowed to live at the school where Principal Cailleach can watch over them. Plus this isn't Tartarus. The brief thought of Tartarus stirred up a new fear. *Oh gods... What if they've sent Bree to Tartarus?*

When the door opened, Finn didn't move. He remained on the ground staring at the ceiling. His thoughts were focused on just how terrible the Chosen One's punishment would be for the crime of defending herself from a god. Wrapped up in his dark worries, he didn't notice Ms. Pace until he saw the triangular toe tips of her black heels.

Once again, Ms. Pace greeted him with a sad and disapproving stare. Her voice remained kind, however. "How are you doing, Mr. MacCool?"

Finn considered responding with something snarky, but he didn't have the energy to antagonize the one person he got to interact with.

"Well, I'm sitting here wondering if an innocent girl is currently being tortured."

The parole officer sat on the ground next to him and laid her messenger bag down. "Bree Castille isn't being tortured. She's still in a holding cell like you, until the Council of Pantheons agrees on the best way to hold the trial."

The legendary hero sat up and gave Ms. Pace a weary look. "It's only a matter of time. Nobody believes her or any of us. Why would they? Hermes is a god. Bree is the one who opened the portal."

"Bree does have some protection as a Chosen One." Ms. Pace's features held some sympathy that Finn hoped was a good sign. "But a portal into the Council of Pantheons should be impossible. If she could explain how she did it, they might take it easy on her."

She'll never never tell them how Cal trained her. "I'm not sure she knows how she did it," Finn said. "It was something she did in a moment of panic. I doubt she even thought it would work."

Ms. Pace sighed. "That's what her representative says too."

"There's no avoiding the trial. Our only hope is that someone finally listens to us."

"Mr. MacCool, you have to know how ridiculous you sound."

"I'm telling the truth, though!"

The parole officer arched a brow. "You have no proof. Forgive me if I don't believe that Hermes is part of a secret group of Titans who have been sacrificing Chosen Ones for centuries, because gods have lost their *immortality*."

"He attacked an innocent child!"

"You mean the teenager who was powerful enough to toss a god into an alternate reality and then portal into the most guarded facility in *any* reality?" Ms. Pace tilted her head. "*That* innocent child."

Finn shook his head. "Why do you even visit me if you won't listen?"

"To see if you can explain something to me." Ms. Pace pulled her Atlas tablet out of her messenger bag.

On instinct, Finn slid away from it.

"It's *not* a spying device, Mr. MacCool."

Finn didn't believe that for a moment, but he realized Atlas had already gotten what he wanted. There was no reason to avoid it now.

Ms. Pace opened up a video file, displaying security footage of Pavlina's cell. The sirin was covered head to toe with black feathers. Broad wings had torn her shirt to shreds. Her head sat upon an elongated neck, and just above her void-like eyes was a beautiful crown.

"This is apparently how a sirin looks after fully transitioning into a death harbinger," Ms. Pace said. "Why would she do this? Is this a message?"

Tears slid down Finn's face. He didn't bother trying to wipe them away. "It is a message, but not from her. She can't control this. It only happens when she senses someone's impending death."

"But whose death?" Ms. Pace asked. "She's always alone."

Finn fought against the urge to vomit and scream. There was only one person's death she could sense in that scenario—her own. He thought of the times she'd voiced her worries that she would die alone, because of the vision she'd had when she experienced her first transition as a sirin.

"She's going to die. Alone. And I won't be able to do anything about it." Finn choked on his sobs. "I won't even be there to comfort her. And no one can go inside. So she won't even have someone to guide her to the afterlife."

Ms. Pace's eyes fell to the floor. "I'm so sorry."

"We're not lying," Finn said. "She doesn't deserve this."

"Mr. MacCool, she intervened during Bree Castille's arrest," Ms. Pace said. "She attacked the police. There's nothing I can do about it. There are consequences for that."

"Even if we're proven innocent in a trial?"

Finn couldn't help the desperate tone in his voice. The parole officer responded with piteous eyes, and he felt his heart shatter.

"If she dies, please just execute me. Please."

"I don't carry out the sentences, Mr.—"

"Then tell someone who does!"

Ms. Pace sat in silence a moment, before she turned off her tablet and slid it into her messenger bag. "All I can promise is that I will check in on Ms. Sirin. I can even carry a message to her. A *verbal* one. I'm not passing notes."

"Tell her she's not alone," Finn said. "Not really."

The parole officer nodded and got to her feet, taking the messenger bag with her. "It will probably be a week or so until your trial, and she likely will only have to serve some time in prison." Ms. Pace looked down at Finn, the same mixture of pity and disapproval on her face. "For what it's worth, I don't want any of you to die, and I still think you can find redemption."

With that, Ms. Pace walked out of the room, leaving Finn alone with only his pain. A short memory played on loop in his mind. Just as he had told Alec, he'd planned on proposing to Pavlina during the Lupercalia Dance. But when Hermes arrived and the whole room shook, the ring fell from his hand, rolling out of sight. The moment he was finally able to shake that memory, another memory from over a year ago replaced it—the night Pavlina had shared her past with him for the first time.

"You see your own death. In mine, I'm old and alone and it's so dark. That's when I gave up on the idea of finding The One, you know? Why look for that when you know it won't matter in the end?"

If they sent Finn to Tartarus for eternity, Pavlina really might die alone one day.

Balled up in the corner of the impossibly bright white room, Pavlina did everything she could not to vomit again. She kept her eyes squeezed tight and tried to shoo away any thought that entered her mind. Even mental visuals could send her hurling.

Pavlina had a strong constitution on most days. She could count on one hand the number of times she'd had to stay in bed sick for more than a day. The longer she stayed in this cell though, the more every last bit of sensory input was too much for her delicate state.

Closing her eyes at least took care of one of Pavlina's senses. The others weren't as easy to shut down. She couldn't seem to stop sobbing and the sound echoed around her brain like a parade of hammers. Vomit coated her tongue so that the taste and scent of it overwhelmed her. Even without these discomforts, the skull-cracking pain of her crown wasn't something she could ignore.

The sense of impending death was so terrible that in the few moments Pavlina was capable of thought, she had to wonder who was dying. When her thoughts turned dark, the overwhelming nausea was almost welcome. Anything to distract her from what tragedy was coming.

The door to her cell opened softly but it might as well have slammed into the wall. Pavlina's head pounded and she roared from the agony.

"Sorry, sorry," Detective Troias whispered.

The detective took a step, and the click of her shoe stabbed at Pavlina. At the sound of her scream, Troias slipped her shoes off and tiptoed over to the sirin.

"I brought you something."

Even these few words ached and that was all it took for Pavlina to lean over and vomit again. It joined the caked remnants of the rest. No one had cared to give her a bucket. They never even picked up the food they left by the door. The trays sat there with the food rotting on it.

"It'll be okay," Detective Troias whispered. She pushed the sirin up to a sitting position. "Oh gods, this is so gross."

Pavlina was too weak to rebel against this new position she was certain would lead to more puke.

Worse, the detective had opened a jar and the scent of it stung her nostrils. It was possibly the worst thing to smell when sick—rum and hot peppers. *Wait… Rum and hot peppers?*

The sirin's eyes flew open and she immediately regretted it. With a wince, she shut her eyes again and slowly, carefully opened them into slits. Sure enough, Detective Troias was holding a bottle of Maman Brigitte's favorite drink. *How did she get my ex-girlfriend's pepper rum?*

Pavlina coughed and, from her bile-seered throat, she croaked, "Why are you bringing me this?"

"When I was interviewing death harbingers over the summer, I met two very interesting people who recommended that I talk to you, and…" The detective gagged. "Okay, if we're going to talk, we need to do it away from your puke corner."

Troias set the bottle on the floor a few feet away and dragged Pavlina to another spot along the wall. Then she grabbed the bottle and sat cross-legged next to her. "That's better. Okay, these two people said you were the best death harbinger they'd ever come across. That was big praise, since they were death loas. Honestly, I kind of fan-girled a bit when I met them."

"Maman Brigitte and Baron Samedi?"

The detective nodded and shook the bottle in Pavlina's face. The sirin moaned and leaned over as she fought not to vomit again.

"Sorry, sorry," Detective Troias whispered. "Look, the bottle belongs to Maman Brigitte. I told her about your predicament, and she said to give it to you and to make you drink the whole thing down."

Pavlina shook her head and craned her neck away. If she'd had any energy, she would have flung the bottle across the room. The thought of even touching her lips to it clawed at her guts.

Detective Troias turned Pavlina's head back to her original position. "Look, I just saw her and I told her what was going on with you in here. *You have to drink this.* It's the only way to pause these symptoms."

Pause? Pavlina looked at the bottle. It looked absolutely rancid, but the promise of a break from her agony was enough to muster strength to speak again.

"I'm afraid I won't be able to keep it down."

"I won't let you throw it up," the detective said. "You may hate me, but I'll make sure you swallow it down."

The sirin gazed at the bottle. The longer she did, the more it seemed to undulate, her vision gurgling just like her stomach. She lifted her eyes to Detective Troias and let her mouth hang open.

Without even a half-second's hesitation, Troias grabbed Pavlina's face and tossed the liquid down her throat. The drink felt like lava on the tender membranes of Pavlina's flayed throat. Before she could spit it out, the detective used all her strength to keep the sirin's mouth shut.

"Swallow it. The faster you do, the faster this will be over."

Pavlina's chest heaved in protest, but the sirin forced the liquid down, hating every drop of it. Though it left a burning trail down her esophagus to her stomach, gratitude lifted her heart. With every breath, her symptoms alleviated.

The detective still had a firm hold of Pavlina's jaw and her eyes wandered all over the sirin's features, looking for a hint of success. "It looked like you swallowed it? Did you swallow it?"

I can't talk. I can't even nod my head like this. How do you expect me to answer? It was the first thought Pavlina had managed that didn't have to do with her physical or emotional pain in days. Even with her mouth forced shut, she was still able to lift the corners of her lips into a smile.

Troias nodded. "I'm going to let you go, but if you throw up on me I'm *out of here*. Got it?"

Once the detective released her hold, Pavlina rubbed her sore jaw and took a deep breath. "Gods, it smells so bad in here."

"Yeah, let me ring for the maid."

Pavlina let out a weak chuckle. "I'm pretty sure the smell is part of my torture."

Detective Troias responded with a grim nod. "Yeah, seems like something they would do." She looked up at the vents in the ceiling and then at the security camera. Leaning close to Pavlina, she whispered, "Look, I know I said not to puke on me, but can you pretend to?"

The death harbinger's symptoms had abated, but the smell of the room was enough to make anyone gag. Angling her head behind the detective's back, Pavlina folded over her lap and dry-heaved.

Troias groaned in disgust. "That death loa lied! Never trusting a trickster again!" Her words were loud and clear and obviously for whoever was watching over the security camera.

Once again leaning close, the detective whispered. "I'm about to tell you something and you're not going to believe me, because it was a vision."

Pavlina met the detective's gaze and saw the earnest hope in her eyes that the sirin would believe anyway. *I'll try.*

"They're keeping crows above those vents," Troias whispered. "They're feeding them poison so that they're dying slowly."

"You're wrong," Pavlina said, shaking her head. "I don't feel animal deaths."

"Not even if it's your faithful murder?" the detective asked. "Not even if it's Corbin?"

Pavlina screamed and Troias held her hand over the harbinger's mouth to hush her. "It's slow-acting. There's still time to try to save them. They don't want them dying right away; that would end your symptoms."

"What should I do?"

"For now, act miserable."

That shouldn't be hard to do.

"And try not to believe anything that anyone else tells you."

The empty room didn't have even one steel bolt. Bree's beautiful clothes from the dance had been replaced with a brown jumpsuit that scratched at her weeping blisters. It had no pockets for fairy stones. Not that it would have mattered if Bree had any.

The first thing the Council of Pantheons did to her was put a blocker on her mageiathalamus. Until the last few weeks, Bree hadn't considered how Mr. Finn must have felt when they tampered with his. Now she understood him better. It felt like someone had chopped off a limb she'd never noticed until it was gone.

Bree had only known she had the magical gland for over a year now. She'd never known she had any magic in her until then. She hadn't felt any more *special* after the news, but now she realized that was because magic was her natural state. The world lost its color and the air lost its energizing vigor the moment the blocker locked onto her brain.

There was one thing the Council of Pantheons couldn't take from her, though—her fight. They'd certainly tried to crush her spirits. They showed her videos of her sister and parents begging her to confess the truth. There were letters written by Mr. Finn and Ms. Sirin asking her to do the same. Not one word sounded like any of them. Even without her magic, Bree could see the lies for what they were.

Ms. Sirin had attacked the police with every protective inch of her body. She had called on her crows, who came flying through the shattered window. The fight had been so ruthless that Bree often had to shake away the image of small black claws shredding faces.

Mr. Finn had swooped over like the hero he was to hide Bree in the pocket reality with her family.

None of it had been enough. When Bree created the portal to the Council of Pantheons, she thought her plan was a masterpiece of genius. The gods couldn't refute the evidence of Hermes's violence if he was blasting it at them, or so she'd thought. Within seconds of the god of thieves blinking with confusion, Zeus saw past the portal and looked straight at Bree. There was no chance of escape.

The door opened and Miss Sphinx entered the cell. As much as Bree distrusted the Council of Pantheons representative, she felt relieved every time the woman entered the room. She always came with useful news and kind words. *She could still be buttering me up for information that I don't have.*

Bree walked to the sphinx with what she hoped was a thankful expression. "How are you?"

"I should be asking how you are," Miss Sphinx said. She opened up her purse and took out a peanut butter and jelly sandwich. "Your mother made it for you."

The teenager snatched the ziploc bag and ripped it open. The sandwich was mushed and purple in places from its time in the representative's purse. It reminded Bree of all the sandwiches she'd brought to elementary school in a lunch box. Ugly, simple, but delicious and comforting. Instead of scarfing it down, Bree savored each bite as she called on memories of better times.

"I've made sure the guards will allow an Olympus doctor in today to heal those burns."

Bree swallowed her bite and gave the representative a grateful look. "Thank you so much." The doctors at Olympus knew how to treat supernatural injuries like the ones Hermes had inflicted on her with his divine flames.

"Also, I made a petition for you," Miss Sphinx said.

"To Themis?" Bree asked, her voice muffled by more peanut butter.

Miss Sphinx nodded. "I don't know about this plan, though, Bree. If what you're saying about Atlas is true—"

"It is."

"Themis may not be willing to help you out," the sphinx continued. "She's a Titan."

The Chosen One finished chewing her sandwich and wiped the residue off her lips. "Gambles are really all I have right now."

The representative took the plastic baggie from Bree and handed her a napkin. "I've also looked into your other request."

"The Good Grifters?" Bree asked.

"Yes." If Miss Sphinx was trying to hide her poor opinion of the organization, she'd failed.

"Anything?"

"Well, it's a little difficult getting a hold of them, especially when I don't have an Atlas phone anymore," the sphinx said. "I can't use the landline at work, obviously. So I just got one hooked up at my house. Anyway, by the time I had a way to call them, all I got was their voicemail and I didn't think it would be a good idea to leave a message."

If anything was going to convince Bree that Miss Sphinx might be on her side, it was the fact that the woman had believed her about everything and willingly gave up her phone. *Unless she's lying.*

The two shared a tired look. Bree had been in this prison for weeks now, awaiting trial. Neither of them had any idea what that would look like, but they both would do everything they could to prepare.

"Would you like some advice?" Miss Sphinx asked.

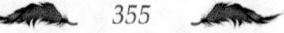

"I'll take all you've got."

The Council of Pantheons representative glanced at the security camera and leaned in to whisper. "Don't rely on Themis. She's the goddess of justice, but only between humans. If you want someone to go after the gods, talk to Nemesis."

Bree backed away, squinting at her. The Goddess of Retribution was the gods' messenger of vengeance, hardly the person she'd think would be on her side. "She's… a little extreme."

"That may be what some people believe, but it's just what Zeus wants you to think." Miss Sphinx looked at the camera and then beckoned Bree to come back. When she did, the representative continued. "Look, she and I have been friends for a *really* long time, and I'm telling you she's just misunderstood. There are so many mixed up stories about her that no one really knows the truth, but you know what sphinxes are good at? Finding out the truth. Please take my advice here."

This time, Miss Sphinx took a step away, leaving Bree to consider her words for a moment. During one of their meetings earlier in the school year, Bree had noticed the representative's subtle dislike for the King of the Council of Pantheons. She clearly knew something that he couldn't deny, something bad.

"Why are you helping me, Miss Sphinx?"

The representative offered Bree a soft, genuine

smile. "I was born to guard royalty. You are a Chosen One. That's royalty, even if we just call it an internship these days. And honestly Bree, after centuries helping representatives with their Chosen Ones, you're the only one I've met who has impressed me."

The sincerity of the sphinx's statement touched a heavily-guarded part of Bree's heart. *Maybe I've been wrong all this time.*

"I'll be damned if you die like the others." The sphinx's face took on a ferocious light, one that Bree had read about in history class. "Especially so that the powerful can take advantage of your potential."

TWENTY-ONE

The Likeliest Outcome

Themis never responded to the message Miss Sphinx sent on Bree's request. Even the Chosen One could be ghosted by the goddess of justice. A week passed without any news of progress, until Miss Sphinx arrived with a letter from the Good Grifters.

Bree's heart leapt at the sight. Their last letter had been to officially tell her she should buzz off because she was part of the establishment. She hoped that being under arrest by the Council of Pantheons would mean that they were willing to help her now.

She snatched it from Miss Sphinx with glee and tore it open.

"Dear Chosen One," Bree read. "It seems that we were wrong about you. The news is filled with stories about your terrorist attack."

Bree squinted at Miss Sphinx. "Terrorist attack?"

"That's the way the Council of Pantheons is framing it," Miss Sphinx said. "I mean, you did toss the violent fury of a flame-wielding god into the most protected facility in the universe. So…"

With a wince, Bree continued reading. "Perhaps you do belong among us and we can support your endeavors to create more justice in the world."

Elated, Bree almost stopped reading the letter there. She kept going, however, excited for more good news. "Contact us once you've won your trial and we'll welcome you with open arms. Yours In Solidarity, Mr. Reynaud. P.S. Please tell your girlfriend to stop writing us."

Bree gawked at the letter and then at Miss Sphinx. "How completely useless."

"Told you," Miss Sphinx said, shaking her head. "I just can't take them seriously."

"Yeah…"

"Well, you know my advice."

The idea of asking Nemesis for help scared Bree. The goddess wasn't known for a gentle approach to justice. Most called her wrathful. As a pacifist, the Chosen One didn't think she could associate with someone like that.

"I know what you're thinking, but you're wrong," Miss Sphinx said. She rummaged through her purse and brought out a letter. "Look, I know you told me not to reach out to her, but she and I were having coffee and—"

"You have coffee with the goddess of retribution?"

"Like I said, we've been friends for a very long time." The sphinx extended the letter. "She asked me to pass this note. At least read it before writing her off." She glanced up to the security camera. "But maybe not out loud?"

Bree shoved the rumpled letter from the Good Grifters into her pocket, not wanting to leave correspondence like that sitting around. Within the first sentence Nemesis wrote, the Chosen One felt her assumptions about the goddess crumbling. There were so many confusing stories about the gods that Bree's teachers never seemed to understand themselves. This letter made sense of some of them.

Nemesis was created to bring justice to those who showed arrogance before the gods. She had felt righteous in her calling until Zeus changed her mind. She didn't describe much of it, probably because Bree was still a kid. Zeus wanted her. She didn't want him. She wound up bearing his child anyway. What did the King of the Council of Pantheons do then? He gave Nemesis's daughter to his new romantic interest to raise.

The Chosen One's heart ached for the goddess who wrote the letter. "This is awful..."

"Do you know who her daughter was?" Miss Sphinx whispered.

Bree shook her head.

"Helen of Troy."

"But her mother was Leda… Oh… I see…"

"Want to know how I met Nemesis?" Miss Sphinx didn't wait for Bree to answer. With another look at the camera, she returned to whispering. "Helen was a Chosen One. I was an assistant to her representative. Nemesis wasn't allowed to help her. Zeus didn't want his daughter to know. Helen didn't die, but she also lost everything she ever cared about, including her freedom."

"Why hasn't Nemesis ever done anything about it?"

"She never had any hope. No one ever stood against the gods in any meaningful way."

Miss Sphinx held Bree's face between her paws. "Do you understand what's happening here? Zeus is scared of you. You've done what no mortal should be able to. You portaled into his sanctuary. You conquered his son, a powerful god himself, *twice*. There are *many* gods and immortals who have been looking for someone like you for a long time."

When Bree had created the portal, she hadn't thought about how impossible such an idea would be to carry out. No one got to Olympus without a summons. Even then, a person had to go through several bureaucratic steps. Multiple security screenings kept anyone of any threat level away. Even Council of Pantheons employees spent an hour of their day gaining entrance to their office.

The police officers who arrested Bree treated her like a bomb. They could have roughed her up, but they didn't. Over time it became clear to the Chosen One that it wasn't because of her title that they left her unharmed. They were afraid that touching her the wrong way would lead to catastrophe.

Meanwhile, they treated Hermes like the real victim in all this, taking his word over hers. They'd hidden him away to protect their "witness." Not even other gods were allowed to see him until the trial was over.

"Like Principal Cailleach?"

Miss Sphinx nodded. "She believed in you before most of us had ever heard of you."

"I'm not a violent person. I'm not a warrior."

"You know what Mr. Finn told me when I met him?"

The mention of her magical application teacher made Bree's heart swell. "What?"

"He called you a warrior of peace."

So far, Bree had shown a brave face during her time in her prison cell. She didn't want to show weakness to her captors. She didn't want them to think they were breaking her. Hearing these kind words from someone she so admired opened the floodgates, and she scrubbed away tears.

"Bree, you and I have been trying to find out what

your quest is for months now," Miss Sphinx said. "This is it. You've already been on it for a while. Your mission is to protect the innocent from some of the most powerful entities in any reality."

Miss Sphinx was right, and Bree knew it. The truth terrified her.

Hermes's plan the previous year had been for her to lose her life fighting a beast during the quest he'd given her. This year, The Shadow seemed intent on sacrificing her by luring her out to save all the teenage girls they were turning into zombies. However, the Chosen One's true quest was far more perilous than slaying a monster or saving damsels in distress. She had to dismantle a whole corrupt system to end a cycle of violence, and she could still wind up dying as a willing sacrifice for that.

While Maman Brigitte's pepper rum hadn't gotten rid of the physical characteristics of Pavlina's full transition, it had assuaged her of the cold nausea that had wracked her body for weeks. Because of that, she realized how hungry she was, having barely eaten. She had no mirror, but she was sure she looked gaunt.

When new meals were dropped off, Pavlina tried not to look eager for the food. She ate a few bites with slow, reluctant chews. It was difficult to hold back from eating more, but she knew better than to let anyone think their torture wasn't working.

After a week of that, the effects of the rum started to wear off. It wasn't much, just enough to make Pavlina queasy. Still, she longed for Detective Troias to return so she could have another swig before it grew as violent as it did before.

The next time the door to her cell opened, Pavlina fought the urge to race for it. She was glad she'd tampered that impulse when it was a guard and not Detective Troias.

"Wrists up," he said as he held out a pair of handcuffs.

"Am I going to trial?"

The guard said nothing. He only took her hands and cuffed them behind her back. Together, they walked out of the cell. The events of Pavlina's capture had blurred together so much that she didn't recognize the hall they walked through.

As expected, everything was marble, the preferred material of Olympians everywhere. Despite the expensive construction materials, it still had all the dread and depression of a prison. *Did they specifically create fluorescent lights that would flicker when a criminal passed under them?*

Eventually, the guard stopped at one of the many unremarkable doors and opened it. Inside was a table with two chairs. Pavlina had seen enough police procedurals to know this was where prisoners either met with their attorney or suffered an interrogation. By the look of the gloomy middle-aged woman in the business suit sitting in one of the chairs, Pavlina assumed this was her attorney.

The guard didn't wait for Pavlina to sit. He pulled her to the other chair and pushed her down into it. Since the sirin's wings were still at full width, this pinned them awkwardly behind her.

"Harvey," the woman at the table said, "They blocked her mageiathalamus. She's not able to fly."

The guard gave the woman a cold look and said, "And?"

The woman rubbed at a spot between her eyebrows and motioned to the door. "I'll knock when our meeting is over."

The guard left the two alone, and the woman extended her hand.

"I'm Ann Brown. I'm your court appointed defense attorney." When Pavlina wasn't able to reach out to receive her handshake, the woman swore under her breath. "Harvey didn't even uncuff you, did he?"

"No."

Ann got out of her seat. "Hold on, I'll go—"

"Don't bother. I'd rather not deal with him again."

The attorney chuckled. "Yeah, he's not what I'd call a charmer."

Ann sat back down and straightened her worn brown tie. Her whole outfit looked like she'd purchased it from a yard sale twenty years ago, and had been patching it up since. She was making less money than Pavlina was, which meant she wasn't getting many cases.

"You were the only one who would represent me, weren't you?"

For a second, Ann only looked at her with the kind of sad smile that came with seeing injustice served repeatedly in court.

"Yes."

"What are my chances of execution?"

The attorney shook her head. "No, I wouldn't worry about that. You didn't murder anyone."

That doesn't mean they don't want to murder me. "Well, give me the most likely outcome, then."

Ann lifted a briefcase onto the table and opened it up. She pulled a file out and reviewed the long list of charges Pavlina had accumulated. "Twenty years, maybe more." She looked up from the file. "A lot less if you tell them what they want to know."

"What do they want to know?"

"Explaining why the Chosen One attacked a god and broke into the Council of Pantheons would be a good place to start."

"I already told them that."

"You told them that Hermes is part of a secret group sacrificing Chosen Ones so that they can maintain their status as immortals."

"Yes."

Ann closed the file and leaned forward. "That sounds like you're crazy or you're lying. If the other two weren't sticking to the same story, I could make a case for insanity but—"

"We're all saying the same thing because it's the truth."

"My job isn't to prove the truth," the attorney said. "My job is to get you out of as much trouble as possible."

"Well, I'm not going to make up some story that will hurt an innocent girl," Pavlina said, wishing she could do something dramatic like bang her fists against the table or lean back with her arms crossed.

"Would you really call her innocent? I mean she—"

"Experienced an actual miracle, Ms. Brown," Pavlina interrupted. "A *god* was ready to use the power of a star to roast her alive, and she somehow managed to send him somewhere that his powers could hurt no one."

"Which happened to be directly in front of the King of the Council of Pantheons," the attorney responded. "That's a lot of miracles."

"Have you seen Bree?" Pavlina asked.

Ann nodded. "In the papers, yes."

"Well, let me tell you how she looks in real life, how she looked that night." Pavlina steeled herself, knowing how emotional this would make her. "She was dressed so perfectly because it was her first date ever. Bree is on the small side so her pants dragged a little on the floor. I don't think she noticed, though. She was having a really good time."

"Sounds delightful."

"It was," Pavina agreed. "There were a few minutes where I'm pretty sure Bree was having the best night of her life. And then a wrathful *god* crashed the party. Just his entrance injured people, but he was focused on Bree. The closer he got, the more she burnt. I watched her skin blister and her satin shirt blacken. The pretty little corsage on her wrist was reduced to cinders."

"Why would he attack a kid like that though? He has no reason to."

Pavina scoffed and shook her head. "You're wasting your time with me."

"I'm late on rent," the attorney said with hard, determined lines stamped onto her face. "I'm not quitting."

Pavlina shrugged. "Then just tell them all that I did it. It just looked like Bree did. I attacked Hermes and threw him through the portal."

"No one's going to believe that."

"Why can't they believe that, but they *can* believe the Chosen One is basically a terrorist?"

Ann leaned back and stroked her chin. "Because that's what Hermes said happened."

"And gods never lie, right?"

The attorney didn't say anything for a while. Pavlina watched her thinking and saw the shift in her expression. She knew Ann was remembering all the times a god backtracked on a public statement, all the rumors she'd heard about certain dirty dealings, and all the times she'd seen them back injustice.

"We're going to lose," Ann said at last.

"Probably," Pavlina agreed.

"I'll give it my best shot."

"That's all I can ask for."

Once again, Finn's only visitor entered the room. This time, she didn't look disappointed. She was harried and frustrated instead. Her heels click-clacked impatiently across the room where he'd nestled into a corner to wait for whatever further torture the Council of Pantheons had in store.

By the time his parole officer got to him, she looked down with a face red from exertion. She reached down to pull him up.

"Stand up, Mr. MacCool. I'm not getting on my knees to talk to you."

Finn thought about rolling over and closing his eyes. *What's the point in talking with her? The worst is already inevitable.*

"Do you want to know about Pavlina or not?"

That was all the motivation Finn needed to move.

Getting to his feet proved difficult. Grief had planted him solidly on the ground for days, and his muscles had grown weak from disuse. Still, he wobbled until he stood high enough for her to need to tip her head upward to meet his eyes.

"Did you give her my message?"

Ms. Pace nodded. "She said that sense of impending death started when Bree attacked Hermes at the dance and had only gotten worse."

Though Finn was dizzy from the blood rush that accompanied standing up after a long sit, he still had enough capacity to understand he'd just heard a lie. That wasn't how Pavlina's gift worked. *This isn't a virus. You don't pick it up and take it to your sick bed.*

"So perhaps it doesn't mean her own death," Finn said, knowing that calling out the untruth would be a big mistake.

"Yes. In fact, I think this might be a good sign!"

Ms. Pace smiled. The sincerity of it impressed Finn. He didn't think he'd ever met someone who could put on such a good act. *She probably has never cared as much as she's put on over the years.*

"How so?" Finn asked.

"Well, she said that she thinks it wasn't just Bree's attack."

Another lie. Pav would never call it Bree's attack.

The parole officer continued, "She said that she could tell there was some kind of spiritual disruption happening in the school at the same time. Our police have even said that there seems to be a poltergeist of some sort causing problems while they try to investigate the crime scene."

As soon as Ms. Pace mentioned a poltergeist, he realized how wrong she was. There was a spiritual disruption, because Atlas's victims had lost their sanctuary. They were either trying to escape or fight for their safety.

"Well, you know it's a high school," Finn said. "All that teenage energy. Bree's a powerful girl, that would be enough to whip something up."

"That's what Ms. Sirin said. We're thinking if you can write something to Bree to convince her that she needs to come forward with the truth—"

"I thought you didn't pass notes."

Ms. Pace blinked. "Well, in this case, I think a written statement is best."

Finn felt tempted to play along. He had uncovered just how deceptive his parole officer was and he knew he was close to figuring out what she was after. Yet if he did as she requested, it would endanger Bree, and he'd sworn to protect her long ago.

"I've already shared the truth with you. Bree isn't responsible for what happened, Hermes is and he's under the guidance of Atlas."

The parole officer's jaw clenched and her eyes grew cold. "I'm tired of your lies."

And I'm tired of yours. "I'm not lying."

"Oh yeah?" Ms. Pace scoffed. "Where's your daughter right now?"

Finn's breath halted, and Ms. Pace smiled. She knew she had him.

"That's right, we went through the book. Oísina isn't in it. You've broken your parole. But… There's a way to get back in our good graces."

The parole officer stepped close enough to Finn that he could smell her expensive perfume, one he'd only smelled on gods, one that a parole officer couldn't afford. Though she was significantly shorter than him, even with heels, her proximity intimidated him.

"Just tell the Council of Pantheons what they want to hear, Mr. MacCool."

"Even if it's not the truth?"

Ms. Pace didn't answer. She simply smiled again. This time, it was cruel. She'd given up her pretense of compassion.

"You know I have all these tear-stained essays confessing your guilt. There's also copious notes from my therapist friend about how unhinged you are. Maybe the Council of Pantheons will want to lengthen your sentence. Maybe they'll think you need more time in Tartarus."

"I'd like to speak to an attorney."

It wasn't the first time he'd made the request, but each time they informed him that no one had taken up his case yet.

"Okay," the parole officer said as she backed away. "They actually got some poor schmuck for your defense team." She knocked on the exit door and a guard opened it. "Has Ms. Brown left yet?"

"No, she just finished her interview with the harbinger."

Finn's heart leapt with desperate hope. If Pavlina had spoken to a lawyer, maybe there was some hope for her. That meant she had enough energy to at least walk with a guard's guidance.

Ms. Pace nodded in Finn's direction. "He's requested an attorney. I think it's time to see who we were able to drum up for him."

The guard nodded and waved to Finn. "Let's get you cuffed."

When the Council of Pantheons had arrested him for his participation in the Great War, nothing had happened with ease. At least he'd seen an attorney right away, though. He remembered little of the man, but he'd been professional and competent. Without him, Finn was sure he wouldn't have received a short sentence followed by community service.

By the tone and expressions of the two at the doorway, Finn knew not to expect that this time. Before, he'd simply broken a law. He'd gotten too heavily involved in mortal affairs. This time, they accused him of abetting a terrorist in an attack against gods, not just any gods, powerful Greek gods.

Finn walked to the guard and let the man clasp the cold cuffs around his wrist. *Time to see who was desperate enough to take up my case.*

TWENTY-TWO

The First Day of Trial

Bree knew Nemesis couldn't meet her directly at the prison. That would give away too much of the tattered plan she and Miss Sphinx had pieced together. Her representative had assured her though that the goddess of retribution would provide Bree's attorney with helpful communication.

The unkempt interview room the CoP had built for these types of meetings in no way resembled the polished, marble halls of every other facility in Olympus. Bree knew that was on purpose. They could afford to do better, but instilling the accused with dread was easier in a dim room where everything sported scuffs and stains.

Any confidence that Bree had coming into the

space dipped low when her attorney showed up. She blended in with their drab surroundings. Her clothes were worn and faded from too many spins in the washing machine. She looked like she hadn't slept in days.

Still, the woman greeted Bree in a friendly way, extending her hand to shake Bree's as soon as she sat down.

"I'm your attorney, Ann Brown," she said as soon as their handshake ended. "I've heard so many wonderful things about you!"

"About me?"

"I spoke with your two teachers yesterday."

Tears sprang to Bree's eyes. She didn't try to hide them. Any pride and pretense of strength flew out the door at the mention of Mr. Finn and Ms. Sirin. "Are they okay?"

Ms. Brown seemed confused about whether she should nod or shake her head. She held her hands up in an *I don't know* fashion. "Well, they're not dead. They're eating, well at least Finn is. Pavlina's a little queasy."

The attorney's casual use of their first names heartened Bree somewhat. This woman was personable, perhaps she even cared.

"Ms. Sirin's queasy? Is she… Is she…?" Bree couldn't bring herself to finish the rest of that sentence. The sirin's nausea usually meant one thing.

Ms. Brown nodded. "Yeah, full blown transition."

Bree cast her eyes to the table. "That's not good, Ms. Brown."

"Yeah," she said with a sigh. "She told me, but she's still strong. She hasn't given in. In fact, she gave me a hard time." The attorney opened a file folder with a number of formerly crumpled papers barely holding together with paper clips. "Okay, we've got a lot to go over, Bree."

The Chosen One pushed her emotions aside and met Ms. Brown's eyes. *The only way I can help anyone is if I get to business.*

"Currently, the Council of Pantheons has a list of charges against you that could roll down to the floor," the attorney said. "Chief among them is that you attacked a god and illegally portaled into the Council of Pantheons during a major session."

"Major session?"

This was news to Bree. Yes, she'd been surprised at the mass of gods she'd seen through the portal, but in her mind that was how they always were. *That doesn't really make sense though, does it? After all, Principal Cailleach is almost always at school, not there.*

"Yes, they were discussing expanding Florida's new education curriculum internationally."

For weeks, Bree had heard grumbles from the teachers at Annie Lytle about the new curriculum. They said it was "scripted" and "dumbed down."

Ms. Sirin had riled against it and Mr. Finn griped endlessly. Since it had taken over, Bree felt like she wasn't learning anything new. Teachers had stopped challenging her to reach higher, even in her advanced placement class.

"But why would they do that? I've heard nothing but complaints."

Ms. Brown shrugged. "They like what it teaches."

Bree wanted to ask more questions, but she knew there were more important matters to address. "Well, I guess they know best."

The attorney squinted at her. "Do they? Is that how you feel?"

"Well, I mean…" Bree shook her head. "No, not really. They aren't paying attention to my warning and I've heard some things lately."

"Like what?"

Gods, I can't give Nemesis away. The Chosen One shook her head. "It's nothing. Don't worry about it."

"Is it this?" From beneath the stacks of legal papers, Ms. Brown slid a hand-written letter forward.

It was a message from Nemesis.

"Where did you—?"

Ms. Brown shushed Bree and whispered, "Miss Sphinx stopped me in the hallway. We have attorney-client privilege, Bree. *This* is a big deal and I want it just between us. Read it quick."

Bree did as instructed, trying to absorb as much as

she could without taking too much time. Nemesis was going to give the attorney as much ammunition as possible—information, tactics, and allies.

Up until that moment, Ms. Brown had seemed weak and defeated, a mouse of a woman the lions had sent in as a sacrifice. As an intended sacrifice herself, though, Bree knew that sometimes the small were quite mighty.

"I'll be honest," Ms. Brown said as she took the letter back and hid it under her papers. "I didn't have much hope before this. I also got the impression that you and your teachers would give in under enough pressure. You *are* a Chosen One, after all. Your role is integral to the establishment's grip on world power."

A gong rang in Bree's head. She'd heard those exact words before, or rather read them. She'd seen similar ones in the letter she'd received on Yule from the Good Grifters, declining to help her.

"And you have hope now?" Bree asked.

Ms. Brown shrugged. "Some. By the way, have you received any communication from an organization called the Good Grifters?"

"I have no idea what you're talking about," Bree lied.

Client-attorney privilege or not, this communication was probably the most likely to convince the CoP she was treasonous at best.

"You sure?"

"I'm sure."

The attorney nodded. "You aren't exactly what I pictured. You're not a terrorist; you're not a tool. You're a hero, a real one. You have my support."

Bree squinted at the attorney. "Are you who I think you are? Are you part of—?"

"I have no idea what you're talking about," Ms. Brown interrupted, repeating Bree's earlier response with a smile.

Bree silently urged her heart to stop thumping so hard. Getting her hopes up terrified her. *Is it possible that both Nemesis and the Good Grifters are on my side?*

"Thank you, Ms. Brown."

"You're welcome, Bree." Ms. Brown put her file folder back into her briefcase and clasped it shut. Before she stood, she gave Bree's hand another shake. "I look forward to seeing you soon, Chosen One."

Finn's meeting with his new attorney hadn't instilled him with confidence. It wasn't hard to understand why the Council of Pantheons had allowed such a woman to represent him. He'd never met someone so unintimidating in his life. They'd only give such a meek creature this position.

For the entirety of their interview, the woman kept explaining how her job wasn't to prove the truth but to make sure her clients got the lightest sentence possible. Something told Finn the woman had never succeeded at that.

To her credit, she didn't grow frustrated at Finn's insistence that he'd been telling the truth. In fact, she seemed to appreciate it. She had even told Finn that she admired his resolve. *She said I was the immortal hero she'd always hoped I'd be.*

In the past, if Finn had heard such a compliment it would have brightened his spirit considerably. However, it would take a lot more than that to unburden him from the mountain of pain he was under now.

The immortal warrior, fatigued by his own grief, returned to his miserable corner expecting long days of mental anguish ahead of him. Within moments, he fell asleep. Without any windows or a clock it was difficult to know what time it was, but he didn't feel all that rested when his door swung open and a guard stood there holding handcuffs. "Let me go back to sleep," Finn grumbled.

"It's morning, MacCool," the guard said. "Come with me."

"I just saw my attorney yesterday," Finn explained. "You don't need to come and get me again."

The guard's face remained expressionless. "Wrists up."

Confused, Finn returned to the entrance and let the

guard cuff him. "What's going on?"

Met with silence, Finn could only assume the worst. As the guard led him down the hallways, Finn's memory took over. He'd walked this way before, over a century ago. *They're already sending us to trial.*

Sure enough, around a final corner, a familiar sight greeted Finn. He stood in an arena, surrounded by gods, with Zeus sitting on the biggest throne of them all. All of the divine peered at him from their high vantage point, many of them with stony expressions.

Unlike mortal courts, there was nowhere for the accused to sit. Here they had to stand through the entire proceedings, which could go hours between breaks. The trials could take days or longer. After spending weeks wallowing on the floor, Finn wasn't sure he could take it. The once strong, muscular hero felt frail.

Yet, he wouldn't give in to his fear. He wouldn't let helplessness take over. They might execute him, but he'd fight for the truth and the people he loved until his last breath.

Ms. Brown the timid little attorney scurried over, puffing from exertion. "Boy," she whispered. "They sure called this faster than I thought they would. I hadn't even brushed my teeth when I got the summons."

"They've got enough evidence to end this, I guess." Finn kept his eyes on the giant that was Zeus. The gods could control their size and forms. The king of the Council of Pantheons had created a visage that sent a message. *He's powerful, unconquerable. I'm an ant compared to him.*

"Eh, I wouldn't be so sure," Ms. Brown said, snapping Finn's attention away from Zeus.

"What do you mean?" Finn asked.

"There's power in numbers."

Before Finn had a chance to ask what she meant, Pavlina was dragged into the arena. She was still in full transition. He knew how much physical pain she must be experiencing. Yet, she kept her head high and smiled at him. Her strength impressed him beyond measure. Despite all she suffered, she still offered him solace. *How is it that I keep loving her more than I already did every day?*

A moment later, Bree entered. She kept her gaze on Zeus. Her eyes shone with righteousness, instead of fear. *My warrior of peace.*

To Finn's surprise, another figure walked in with her. The woman wore the traditional chiton of a Greek goddess. She looked similar to Nike, because of the wings on her back, but that's where the similarity ended. In one hand, she held a measuring rod, in the other a sword.

"Nemesis, I haven't summoned you," Zeus said, his voice booming with such force that could cause an earthquake. "Themis is presiding over this trial. I don't need your assistance."

"I'm not here for you." Nemesis held up her chin in response to her king's genuine shock. "I've come to represent the Chosen One."

Zeus's face grew red, with lightning sparked along every centimeter of his skin. "She already has representation."

This didn't seem to intimidate Nemesis at all. She held her gaze steady, not once glancing away from the god who could easily crush her. "Even mortals are allowed more than one attorney in a trial, my king."

"This isn't who you are, Nemesis. You know your role. You bring retribution against those who wrong the *gods*."

"I punish those guilty of hubris against the gods, those that deserve it," Nemesis countered. "I represent those that are wronged. Bree Castille is innocent. Your *son* is the one guilty of attacking the Council of Pantheons."

"How dare you imply—"

"I'm implying nothing. I'm directly accusing Hermes of hubris in the face of gods, even against you."

"You are *not* to talk over our king!"

Another figure stepped forward, now standing next to Zeus, one that Finn recognized. *Ms. Pace?* She wasn't dressed in the garb of a parole officer. She wore expensive robes and a shimmering chiton, looking every bit like a Greek goddess.

Zeus took her hand and kissed it. "Themis, my love, I appreciate your support, but I can more than quash someone like Nemesis."

Gods, his second wife. I've been dealing with a Titan for months now.

"My apologies," Nemesis said. "I will act with more decorum for the rest of the trial, but I will ensure that the guilty are punished and the innocent are vindicated."

"Then you will punish our treasonous Chosen One."

"We'll see at the end, my king."

There wasn't a hint of defeat in the goddess's face, and suddenly Finn felt more than a flicker of hope. *We have a chance, a real one. She's a Greek goddess. She holds more sway than half the gods here.*

When Pavlina had entered the arena, she was certain that this was her last fight. While Ms. Brown had been friendly, she hadn't instilled her with much confidence. She had even said that they were going to lose. *But at least she believes us.*

Seeing Finn had given her at least one moment of peace. No one could or would tell her how he fared. Though his eyes were red and his skin had lost all color, he still smiled at her and that was more than she'd hoped to see.

When Bree joined them, Pavlina's heart swelled with pride. Her former foster daughter greeted all the gods, including Zeus, with dignity. No shadow of fear crossed over her eyes. The sirin didn't know where her confidence came from, but she was glad to see it.

What Pavlina hadn't expected was for a Greek goddess to accompany them. Compared to their tattered attorney, this woman exuded power. For a brief moment, she wondered if the goddess was there to skip the trial and jump right to executing the three of them. Then, she countered Zeus. *She's here to represent us.*

Pavlina glanced at Ms. Brown. She didn't see the same shock in the attorney's face. *She expected this. She knew.*

Themis had control of the trial, unfortunately. As one of Zeus's most respected wives, she certainly wouldn't rule in their favor. The Titan had a reputation for her fairness, but she would never side against the gods.

The first people called to the witness stand were Bree's parents. Pavlina wanted to cry for them. Themis grilled them relentlessly, accusing them of faking their deaths. When they tried to explain who they really were, she asked them to prove they came from a magicless reality, and they couldn't. Not one person in that room believed that the Chosen One could live in such a place and still come to a magical school. *Even if she can portal into Olympus.*

Still, this wasn't enough to prove Bree was guilty of a terrorist attack against the gods. Nemesis argued as such.

Then Themis presented something unexpected—a pocket watch.

"We found this at the scene of the crime. Do you know why it was there, Miss Castille?"

Bree nodded. "Yes, someone I didn't see tossed it to me from a clock portal."

Clock portal? Pavlina recalled seeing Cal stepping through a portal like that. She'd helped her get to the hospital when all hope seemed lost. Cal had intervened again, just when Bree would have died.

"Someone you didn't see tossed it from a clock portal?" Themis shook her head. "I've heard some wild lies, but this is one of the biggest."

"I have no way of proving the truth to you about this," Bree said. "But I didn't lie."

"You used this to stop time, didn't you?"

Bree shook her head. "Actually, whoever tossed it to me stopped time. I just got lucky."

"Another lie."

"But I did use it to start time again."

Themis smiled as if she'd caught Bree with a gotcha moment. "If Hermes really was attacking you, then why did you start time again?"

"Well, I figured keeping time frozen forever

wouldn't be a good idea," Bree answered.

Ms. Brown chuckled softly. Pavlina looked at her to see a mischievous sparkle in her eye. The attorney noticed Pavlina's attention and turned to whisper, "She's some kind of kid, isn't she?"

Themis continued her interrogation. "It was to ensure he attacked his own father wasn't it?"

"I did portal him to Olympus..." Bree looked around in awe at the massive arena. "Somehow... But not so he could attack anyone. He was already attacking me. I knew if he unleashed here, no one would actually get hurt, because you're all gods. Nothing can hurt you."

"You knew a major session was happening, didn't you?" Themis asked.

"I didn't know that until earlier today," Bree answered. "Apparently, you all were deciding whether you should expand Florida's curriculum internationally? Why would you do that? I heard it's—"

Themis held up a hand to stop Bree. "I do the asking. You do the answering."

They were going to push our curriculum everywhere? Pavlina searched for a reason as to why. It was terrible, scripted and limited. Kids memorized facts. Most of the magical history teacher's classes had turned into shiny, happy stories about how powerful and perfect the gods were. *Which is far from the truth. But then the truth doesn't matter, does it?*

Pavlina leaned over to whisper to Ms. Brown, "Does anyone know who created the curriculum?"

"The Titan Initiative," she answered.

"But didn't the Titans lose their power?"

"Well, I mean, not all of them." The attorney gestured at Themis who continued her baseless accusations. "Titan or not, if you kiss up to the Z man, you get to hold on to your power and immortality."

"Except they're not immortal anymore," Pavlina said. "You saw that in my records, right? It was the first thing I told them."

Ms. Brown shook her head slowly, a true look of confusion on her face.

"I guess they omitted it." *Wouldn't want anyone knowing how weak they actually are.*

"The sun is setting," Zeus said. "I'm ready for my feast. We'll continue this tomorrow."

"Yes, my king," Themis said with a bow of her head.

A guard tugged on Pavlina's still cuffed wrists. "Time to go back."

Pavlina gave her attorney one last glance. There was a confident tilt to her head, one that hadn't been there when she'd met her. *There's more to this than Nemesis, isn't there?*

TWENTY-THREE

The Witnesses

A full day of standing before the gods and holding up to Themis's constant attacks had exhausted Bree. When a guard woke her the next day however, she wouldn't let him see even a hint of what the trial was doing to her body and psyche. She clung to the hope that between Nemesis and the Good Grifters, they could still win.

Zeus didn't seem to want that outcome, though. Bree wasn't sure if he cared that his son was a murderer. He cared more about appearing powerful, and that meant not being anyone's fool, including Hermes's.

But Bree couldn't give in to worrying. She had studied law the whole year, knowing in the back of her mind that she might wind up in legal trouble. *Maybe not this much...*

As soon as Bree entered the arena, Nemesis was already waiting for her. Just as before, she held a measuring rod and sword. The gods were busy chatting with each other, and Bree took the opportunity to talk to the Greek goddess standing beside her.

"Why do you have a measuring rod?" Bree asked.

Nemesis arched an eyebrow. "Of all the questions you can ask me, that's what you chose first?" She lifted the rod to eye level. "I'm not measuring centimeters or anything earthly. I'm measuring hubris on one side and guilt on the other."

"How does that work?"

"When I stand beside someone, it indicates their level."

Bree moved to get a closer look at it. "I don't see anything."

"I'm the only one who can see it."

The teenager turned her attention to the goddess. "What does it show now?"

"Well, it's not high," Nemesis answered. "Nothing on the guilty side, but just enough to show you have a Chosen One's hubris."

Bree blushed, feeling the sting of those words.

"You don't need to feel bad," Nemesis said. Her voice and her face weren't kind, only speaking facts.

"No one is free of hubris." She nodded toward Zeus's currently empty throne. "Especially not in that direction."

Emotion crossed Nemesis's face for a brief moment. There was resentment in her eyes.

"I'm sorry about what he did to you."

The goddess shook her head. "You're not the one who should be sorry." She sneered. "I'm more upset at myself. I let him dictate who I am all these centuries. I let him spread his lies."

"He's scary. I can't blame you."

"You're scarier."

Before Bree could ask what Nemesis meant, Mr. Finn and Ms. Sirin came in. If she hadn't been handcuffed under the watchful gaze of dozens of guards, Bree would have rushed over to give them each a hug. Her heart broke at the sight of her former foster mother still in full transition. She knew it was painful, and she couldn't help but wonder who was going to die.

Ms. Brown came in next, looking more confident than the day before. She approached Nemesis with a bow.

"You need not bow to me, trickster," she said. "You are a god, as well."

"Shh…" Ms. Brown gave a look around the arena to see if anyone had heard her. "I still need everyone here to think I'm just some idiot human." She gestured at Bree. "No offense."

Bree rolled her eyes. "Not a human, a witch."

"Eh, that's just a human with a mageiathalamus," the attorney responded.

"What have you come here to say?" Nemesis asked.

"They're gonna let me bring some folks to the stand," Ms. Brown said with twinkling eyes. "You three have a lot of friends, and they have a lot to say."

"I will help you question them." Nemesis held up her rod again. "This will measure whether or not they speak the truth."

"So that's what it does!" Ms. Brown glanced down at the sword and pointed at it. "What does that do?"

"What a sword does," Nemesis answered and Ms. Brown gulped.

The buzz of thousands of chatting gods quieted at once, and Bree knew Zeus was near. Sure enough, he stepped into the arena, with Themis holding his hand. He gave her a kiss and then sat on his throne. The goddess smirked at Bree.

"Why is she the goddess of justice?" Bree asked.

"Because Zeus said she is," Nemesis answered.

Themis stepped into the arena and gave Nemesis a glare before turning her attention to Ms. Brown. "I understand you have character witnesses today," she said in the most condescending voice Bree had heard in a long time.

This didn't phase Ms. Brown, though. She gave the goddess a friendly smile and bowed. "Yes, there are several people who will give testimony on behalf of my clients."

"You understand that tomorrow is the last day of the trial," Themis said. "Are you sure you want to waste time on character witnesses? It won't do anything to disprove Bree's attack."

"Alleged attack," Ms. Brown said. "They've asked to testify, and would like to be here tomorrow for sentencing, along with the Chosen One's many other supporters."

Themis nodded. "Fine, but I do feel bad that they will witness something so tragic."

"Who am I to judge?"

"I'll let you get on with it."

Themis walked away and took a seat next to Zeus.

Ms. Brown walked to the center of the arena and gave all the gods surrounding her a big smile. "Today, we will be hearing from several character witnesses, who I think you'll all agree have important things to say. I will get testimonies from Council of Pantheons' representative Akila Sphinx, Jacksonville Sheriff's Department detective Cassandra Troias, and Calliope."

"Excuse me," Themis spoke up. "Calliope who? We need surnames."

The attorney shook her head. "Just Calliope. Like you, she has no surname. Gods usually don't."

The color drained from Themis's face. "You mean-"

"My *daughter*!"

Zeus's voice nearly tumbled Bree over, but Nemesis caught her.

"Thanks," Bree said as she straightened herself. "Gods, what's another Greek goddess doing here?"

"You have more Greek support than you know," Nemesis answered.

The crowd of gods in the arena gasped as one. Pavlina joined them. Another Greek goddess was going to defend Bree. She hadn't expected any Greek support during this case at all, now they had two goddesses on their side. *And one of them is Zeus's daughter. I wonder what got her to turn on her dad.*

Of course, Ms. Brown didn't call on her first. Pavlina knew she wanted to save the best for last. Despite her impatience to see the goddess, Pavlina was glad that Bree's representative was doing her job and taking up the right side.

The sphinx walked into the arena. Despite her lion-like visage, she had always seemed sweet and soft-spoken. Pavlina got to see her steel backbone now as she swore to tell the truth. Ms. Brown took over the questioning while Nemesis stood by with her measuring rod.

"Miss Sphinx," Ms. Brown began. "When did you take over as the Council of Pantheons' representative for the Chosen One?"

"During the fall," the sphinx said.

"And why were you picked for the role?"

"Well, I was supposed to get the position originally, but Harold Casmillus got it unexpectedly." Miss Sphinx shrugged. "I'm not sure why. No one had ever heard of him and he disappeared months later."

"Bree Castille has testified that he was actually Hermes in disguise," the attorney said. "Could that explain a sudden change in assignment?"

"It's possible."

"It seems his disappearance also aligned with Hermes's disappearance as well."

Miss Sphinx nodded. "That's correct."

"Does our Chosen One strike you as a violent person?"

"Oh, not at all!" Miss Sphinx gestured at Bree. "The moment I got to the school, everyone told me how she was a pacifist and asked that I not give her any quests that involved fighting." She looked at Finn and Pavlina. "Remember?"

Pavlina nodded enthusiastically. This was a good line of questioning. It cast doubt on Hermes and showed that it wasn't in Bree's nature to hurt someone.

"What kind of quest did our Chosen One want?" Ms. Brown asked.

Miss Sphinx cast Bree a glowing smile. "She wanted to help sick kids like her little sister by defending them in legal cases against insurance companies."

"But her sister is well now, correct?"

The representative cast her eyes downward. "It seemed she was."

Pavlina threw her hand over heart, certain it would shatter otherwise. Liz had seemed completely healthy the last time she'd seen her. The Timucuan doctors had worked a near-miracle.

"Oh, what happened?"

The sphinx looked up at Themis, blame burning in her eyes. "Some of our gods felt that getting healing from a restricted reality was cheating, and that an alleged terrorist's family didn't warrant that kind of help. So the Council reversed her healing."

Ms. Brown tilted her head. "I'm so sorry to hear that a god would allow harm on a child like that, even if she is the sister of someone they dislike."

Themis stood up from her throne. "End this line of questioning! The gods are not on trial here!"

The attorney looked up at the goddess of justice. "Is this not a case about whether or not Bree acted in self-defense when attacked by a god?"

"Hermes isn't here to defend himself."

Ms. Brown scratched her head and looked around the arena. "Yeah, I noticed that. I thought maybe I wasn't able to see him in the crowd or something. But I see some other big name gods pretty easily."

The attorney pointed at four impressive Greek gods to the right of Zeus's station. Hera, Poseidon, Demeter, and Hades sat in objective silence looking down their noses at the mousy attorney.

"Gosh, usually Hera sits beside her husband, but I guess she didn't want to be anywhere near you, Themis."

A small chuckle rippled through the crowd, and Hera shot Themis a poisonous look, confirming what Ms. Brown had suggested.

The attorney continued, "I gotta ask. Why wouldn't Hermes be here to testify against his alleged attacker?"

"He declined," Themis said. "Victims are allowed to avoid time in court with those that assault them."

"Oh, so we wanted to make sure Bree didn't have to melt under the gaze of the person who tried to kill her."

"Enough!" Zeus bellowed. "Next witness."

The attorney thanked Miss Sphinx for her time, and Detective Troias entered the arena. As she did so, she gave Pavlina a nod of acknowledgement. *Maybe they'll listen to someone who works with law enforcement.*

Troias swore to tell the truth and Ms. Brown took up her line of questioning. "How is that you know Pavlina Sirin?"

"I'm a homicide detective. Since she's a death harbinger, I asked for her help as a consultant."

"Did she look like that when you worked with her?"

Ms. Brown pointed at Pavlina, and the sirin felt the thousands of eyes staring at her in her terrible state.

The embarrassment was so brutal, it overtook the nausea slowly regaining its power.

"Not at all," Cassandra Troias said. "She looked like any woman."

"Why's that?"

"Well, she only transitions to her full sirin form when she's in proximity with death."

"Oh." Ms. Brown looked around the room. "So, you mean, someone here could die?"

The arena roared with thousands of gods suddenly concerned about their safety.

"Wait, wait." Ms. Brown waved his hand dismissively. "What am I thinking? Almost everyone here is immortal."

"Well…" The detective glanced at Pavlina. "There's some question as to whether that's true."

"What do you mean?"

"During our investigation, we learned that there's a conspiracy amongst some gods." Troias looked around the room frantically. "A small group! Just to be clear."

"Tell us more," Ms. Brown prodded.

"Hermes told Miss Castille, Ms. Sirin, and Mr. Finn that Chosen Ones are sacrificed now to extend their immortality," Detective Troias explained. "You can't extend immortality. You can only lengthen mortality."

"What did your boss say when you told him that?"

"He didn't believe me." Cassandra looked over to Apollo. "A lot of people don't believe me because of a disagreement one of my ancestors had with a god."

"Okay, back on the subject," Ms. Brown said, directing the detective's attention back to the questioning. "Why would you take the defendants' statement over a god?"

"There was proof."

The attorney's eyebrows shot up almost to her hairline. "Proof! We haven't seen *any* of that in this case so far! What proof?"

Detective Troias pointed at Pavlina. "The case we were looking into was about a series of teenage girls dying. Death harbingers never sensed them and there were no spirits to guide to the afterlife. During our investigation it became clear that someone was stealing their souls ahead of time. A Titan. Atlas."

"Isn't Atlas in Tartarus?"

Cassandra shook her head. "No, Miss Castille found him in his own world. Along with all the spirits who had gone missing."

"Where are these spirits now?" Ms. Brown glanced around the room nervously. "Are they here with us?"

"They're hiding at Annie Lytle High School."

"Hiding from Atlas?" Ms. Brown asked.

"Well, him and Hermes, because of the way he killed all those people."

"Wait a minute… *Killed*?"

Pavlina clasped her hand over her mouth. Tears sprouted at once. She'd seen everyone in the cafeteria make it to safety. *But what about the people who may have been on the street or on the school grounds?*

Themis stood up again. "Those were accidental! He was defending himself against the Chosen One!"

Ms. Brown squinted at the goddess of justice. "You know what's really strange to me? How can a powerful god, one of Zeus's most beloved children, be so scared of a *teenage girl*?" She waved her hand at Bree. "Look at her! She's five foot nothing and one hundred pounds. She's a vegetarian and a Buddhist." The attorney nodded at someone behind Pavlina. "Yeah, one of your followers."

"Some people are more deadly than they seem," Themis said.

"And some people are weaker than they seem," Ms. Brown responded, letting her gaze flicker to Zeus for a fraction of a second.

Miss Sphinx and Detective Troias had given eye-opening testimonies. Finn knew that more than a handful of gods were beginning to question Themis's allegations, but he wasn't sure it would be enough. With a Greek goddess on the roster as a character witness though, they might be in a much more powerful position by the end of the day.

When Ms. Brown called for Calliope to enter the

arena, everyone watched with anticipation. Finn almost fell at the sight of her. He knew that short, curly hair, bright eyes, gapped teeth, and an infectious smile anywhere. *Cal, short for Calliope.*

Cal wasn't wearing her usual adventurous bookdealer outfit. She had on the delicate robes and silky chiton of a Greek goddess. She looked so uncomfortable that Finn wished he could throw her a jacket.

Zeus glowered at her. "Calliope, what is the meaning of this? First you disappear for decades and now this?" He shook his head. "Always the rebel. I gave you such a nice position as the goddess of poetry and harmony."

The bookdealer looked at her father with genuine empathy. "I'm grateful, Dad, but you know I wasn't made for that. I've always wanted to be a bookdealer."

"I gave you books!"

"But not the adventure in them." Cal sighed. "I'm not just here for Bree, you know. I'm here for you too. I want to protect you from—"

Zeus stood up and instantly grew several meters taller. "I'm the King of the Gods!" Lightning shot from his head in the form of a crown. "I need no protection!"

Cal nodded. "Of course."

During this whole interaction, Finn had only one thought on his mind. *Does Oísina know who she fell in love with?*

"If I may, can your daughter give her testimony?" Ms. Brown asked.

Zeus stewed but finally said, "Get on with it." As he sat, his white hot gaze followed Cal.

Once the room calmed down, Ms. Brown asked, "Calliope, how long have you known the defendants?"

"I met them over a year ago."

"How did it happen? Did they come to Olympus?"

Cal shook her head. "I'm a bookdealer. I travel through realities collecting books to sell."

Zeus scoffed, but Cal continued.

"I was in a desert reality of Jacksonville, Florida. I had just gotten this beautiful book with a wild story about a Chosen One named Oísina."

"Oísina? Like Finn's daughter?"

"Yes, she's Finn's daughter. It turned out this book was the one his daughter was trapped in." Cal winced. "And by reading it, I accidentally set off this countdown to her death."

"Yikes! What did she do for that kind of punishment?"

"It was to punish Finn, not her. Sometimes..." Cal looked up at her father. "Sometimes, gods are a little overzealous." She sighed when her father didn't respond. "Anyway, Finn was trying to get his book from me so he could rescue her. He actually wound up saving my life from a death larvae."

Zeus's eyes widened. "You almost died?"

"I'm okay, Dad."

Finn saw a father's panic in the Greek god's eyes, one that he could relate to. Zeus had almost lost his child, just as Finn almost lost his.

The King of the Council of Pantheons looked at Finn. "You saved my daughter? I—"

Themis laid her hand over his. "We should hear more of her testimony."

"So, you gave him back his book and went on your merry way?" Ms. Brown prompted.

"No, Bree's ribs were broken," Cal said. "So I helped her get healing from a Timucuan doctor. They like me over there."

"Isn't that a restricted reality?"

Cal gave her father an apologetic look. "Not to gods."

"Okay, so you gave Finn back his book and fixed Bree up and then you were on your way, right?"

Cal shrugged. "Maybe I should have, but..." She looked at the three. "The sirin lady was so nice and I just adored the kid." She looked longest at Finn. "And I'm pretty sure I was already in love with Finn's daughter."

Ms. Brown took a step back. Even she seemed surprised by this declaration. "Already in love? With a woman in a book?"

Still looking at Finn, Cal said. "I'm sorry, I swore to

 404

tell the truth."

The warrior wiped away his tears. *They'll probably find her anyway. They already know she's out of the book.*

"We got her out of the book," Cal said. "She's um…" She gulped and gave Finn another apologetic look. "She's my wife."

Finn jutted forward. "She's your what?!"

Before he could do more or say more, guards grabbed and gagged him.

"You're married, Calliope?" Zeus asked. "To a Chosen One?"

"You'd like her, Dad. She's really into poetry too."

The crowd of gods were wild at this point. There had been revelation after revelation, and Finn doubted they would ever quiet down. Themis stood up, however, and with a wave of her hand, everyone sat down and zipped up. It didn't seem voluntary. It reminded him of the spell Principal Cailleach used to get people to listen in her office. Thinking of his boss stirred up envy he didn't feel proud of. The winter goddess had immunity in this matter due to her station, but they still couldn't use her as a witness since she was aiding the three defendants during the incident.

Ms. Brown cleared her throat and continued her questioning. "What about your relationship with Bree Castille?"

"Like I said, the kid is awesome. I couldn't care

less about her being the Chosen One. She's *cool*, you know?" Cal shrugged. "And she likes portals, so I thought maybe I could mentor her."

"So she learned how to make portals under your guidance?"

"Yes." Cal took a deep breath. "I know you're not going to ask this question and I don't care. I can't let the kid go down like this. I know Oísina doesn't want me to say this, but..."

She's going to confess. Oh, gods, she's falling on the sword for Bree.

"I was there the first time Hermes tried to kill her."

"The first time?" Ms. Brown asked.

"Yeah, he admitted right there and then he was going to sacrifice her. So I..." Cal lifted her hand and flicked in demonstration. "Threw him through a portal to a reality where the Big Bang hadn't happened yet."

Zeus and Themis gasped at once. Finn watched all the gods struggle against their magical bindings to shout as well.

"So Bree *didn't* toss him through a portal?" Ms. Brown asked.

"That's correct."

"And you saw him try to sacrifice her."

"Yes, and I also was there when she rescued all of Atlas's victims. I saw it all."

The attorney stared in awe at Cal. Several times her mouth opened to say something, but at once she'd close it.

"I… I rest my case…"

"No, wait," Cal said, holding up a hand. "As far as Bree being able to open a portal into the Council of the Pantheons goes, she's good, but she's not that good. I saw what Hermes was doing. I've been tracking him for a while. I have, well *had*, a pocket watch that can stop time for a few minutes. So I paused everything, placed some fairy stones already charged and ready to open a doorway here. Then I whispered the idea into Bree's mind while she was still frozen."

"But she said she came up with the idea."

Cal gave a long, sad look at Bree. "She said what she remembered. I set up the whole thing to protect her."

Zeus, looking weary and heartbroken, stood up from his throne. "Oh, Calliope… My rebel…" With a sigh, he gestured to the guards. "Put her in a cell."

Cal ran toward her father, but guards grabbed her at once. "Dad!" she screamed, but Zeus ignored her as he exited the arena.

Before she could call for her father again, she was gagged and the guards dragged her out.

Zeus wasn't known for being a good father. He had a million children, but he only knew a fraction of their names. Yet, Finn had always assumed that he loved the ones he knew. *How can he do this to his child?*

TWENTY-FOUR

The Great Escape

While everyone in the arena reacted to Cal's arrest, Pavlina noticed that Nemesis remained focused on Zeus. The goddess of retribution held her rod up at the King of the Gods, and grew to nearly his height. She glowered at him in such a way that made Pavlina want to hide under a rock. She'd heard of the goddess of retribution before. It wasn't a secret that her fury was terrifying and her justice was swift. It still managed to shock Pavlina. Even the other gods in the room were gathering as far away from the pair as possible.

"Your daughter defended a Chosen One from a god who sacrificed innocents," Nemesis said.

Zeus lifted his chin and looked down his nose at Nemesis. "I am the King of the Gods. I don't need to justify anything I do."

"Yes, you do. The Council of Pantheons created a justice system so that *no one* would be above the law." Nemesis' face darkened further. "I can barely hold onto my rod, because the magnitude of your hubris is too powerful for it to handle."

Though not one hint of emotion affected her tone, it was clear that Zeus wouldn't come out of this interaction unscathed. *Even if he is the King of the Gods, the Council of Pantheons combined has more power than he does. They won't like that he can lock up any of them without a fair trial.*

"Your job is to bring justice to *mortals*, not gods," Themis said.

Nemesis turned her black eyes on Zeus's second wife. This time, emotion did color her words.

"My purpose and my actions are my own," she said with seething finality. "I am a *goddess*, not a mule."

Rustling behind Pavlina caused her to turn. There she saw a gathering of guards ready to act, only waiting on a word from Zeus.

"Oof," Ms. Brown said. "This is about to get scary. Totally thought the trial would work on its own, but…" The attorney gave a long, sweeping gaze around the room. "Well, I guess the battle has begun."

The mousy woman stretched out her arms and craned her neck, until they grew. Her brown hair lengthened into flaming red braids. Her eyes shifted from hazel to bright green, slanting upwards as they did. The unremarkable nose on her face pointed, as did her ears. The most noticeable change of all was that Ms. Brown seemed to be a man now.

The attorney smirked in response to Pavlina's gawking. "Recognize me?"

Pavlina shook her head slowly, and the shapeshifter frowned.

"Well, that's disappointing. I thought I was a bigger deal than that."

"Loki!" a blond, Scandinavian looking god shouted from the crowd of gods who were currently avoiding the encounter between Zeus and Nemesis. "Again?"

Loki shrugged. "The Good Grifters needed me. Plus, I felt like being a woman again."

"The Good Grifters?" Pavlina asked, but no one answered.

Bree gasped. "I *knew* it!"

Loki winked at Bree and turned his attention back to the fair haired god. "Bragi, what the defendants are saying is true. You must join our side."

"You're a liar and a scoundrel!" the Norse god replied, but there was a hint of doubt in his eyes.

He saw enough of the trial to question things.

Loki nodded. "I am, but Nemesis is not." He pointed at the goddess of retribution, still locked in a staring contest with Zeus. "We are losing our immortality. You can't tell me you haven't felt it too."

Bragi lowered his gaze to Finn and then looked at his own hands. "But we'd be battling Zeus…"

"And the Titans, possibly a lot more gods," Loki agreed with a nod. "But we've been preparing for that for a while now, in case war is what it came down to."

Still, the Norse god of poetry looked hesitant.

"Are you truly afraid of a battle?" Loki looked around the room.

The god of poetry puffed up his chest. "Of course not, but I don't support causes blindly."

Seeing that Loki alone wasn't swaying anyone, Pavlina decided to speak up.

"This doesn't just concern immortals!" she said.

Every god, except for Zeus and Nemesis, turned to watch Pavlina. She regretted her bravery, but it was too late to back out.

"I heard Hermes himself," she continued. "He likened *Zeus* to circus peanuts compared to his sect. Which… now that I think of it… any of you could belong to…"

Pavlina gulped. As she did so, she felt a wave of nausea roll within her, powerful enough to bring her to her knees.

Finn rushed over and grabbed hold of her, sinking to the floor so he could cradle her there. "No, you can't give in. Not yet. Not now."

Pavlina's nausea grew so intense that she went blind. "The gods… Someone's going to…"

Just as suddenly, it was over completely. Not a trace of queasiness remained. Her vision returned clearer than ever, and above her she saw hundreds of crows swarming in. A tug at her heart told her that Corbin was among them. It was her murder, and more. They'd called in reinforcements.

"How…?"

Loki tilted his gleeful face at her, like he had surprised her with a present. "Your detective friend went on a rescue mission."

Pavlina's crown sank away and her neck shortened, ending the migraine that had plagued her for days. Soon enough, the rest of her returned to its human-like appearance. Finn cried over her, kissing her cheeks and lips as much as he could.

"Oh, gods, Pav," he whispered. "I thought I'd lost you forever."

"If we don't get out of here right away, you might," Pavlina said, shaking her head. "I think the crows only stalled impending death for maybe a few more hours."

"Guards!" Zeus bellowed. "Get these crows!"

Pavlina turned to see Corbin and his friends swarming the King of the Gods, but never harming him. They were merely preventing him from harming Nemesis.

"Right as always, my love!" Finn said, lifting her up to her feet. "Now, to figure out how we're escaping."

Finn's mind raced with possible solutions, but just as soon as they entered his head, he realized how easily they'd fail. If they tried to leave through the exits, they'd only wind up back in prison. *And anyone could be waiting for us there.*

Loki seemed to be rallying quite a crowd of similarly-minded gods. In the past, Finn had a special kind of jealousy for the trickster. Loki was from the powerful Norse pantheon, and it made sense that he received a better reception than an immortal warrior, but even the god's lesser known children were more popular than Finn was. As a relatively vain Chosen One, that had never sat well with him.

Allies are allies, though.

"Got an idea of how we're getting out of here?" Finn asked their attorney-turned-god.

"Yes."

"How?"

"We're fighting our way out."

"Gods, I was afraid you were going to say that," Finn whispered.

After weeks barely eating or receiving much in the way of basic necessities, they weren't up to the task of a battle at all. There was also the matter of Bree being a pacifist.

At that thought, Finn looked up to the crowd of gods. Each one of them was roaring with debate over whether they were ready for a civil war. Silent among them was Buddha. Finn had met Buddha before, but only in passing. He seemed just as peaceful as anyone would expect. During this fray, he looked a little more confused.

"Bree!" Finn called to the young Chosen One.

"What?" Bree was shaking, her pretense of fearlessness had disappeared.

"I know you're a pacifist but—"

"Yeah, I heard what Loki said."

"If you don't want us to fight, we won't," Finn said. "We can figure out another solution."

Bree shook her head. "There's nothing else we can do. We would've won any fair trial, but that's clearly not going to happen with Zeus and Themis. We have to fight our way out of here."

"Right, yes…" Finn let out a long puff of air. "But how?"

As soon as the words left his mouth, Miss Sphinx leapt down to the arena with a terrifying roar. For half a second, Finn thought she might eat him up, and then he remembered she was dedicated to protecting the Chosen One.

"I *dare* anyone try to attack the three of you."

As if rising to the challenge, several guards rushed them. However, they were only mortals gifted by the gods with certain temporary powers pertaining to their station, and another roar from Miss Sphinx sent them running in the opposite direction.

"Jaysus…" Finn whispered.

Miss Sphinx smiled. "They've seen me defend royalty before. *I* am not a pacifist."

Finn gulped. "Glad you're on our side."

"We've been setting up a sanctuary for a while now, in case this trial didn't go well," Miss Sphinx said. "If we can escape the arena, we can get there."

"How?" Finn asked with a nod at Pavlina. "She's a little weak from throwing up most of what she's eaten."

"Well, Zeus is busy with a city's worth of crows and Nemesis isn't going to let him off easy," Miss Sphinx said. "I say we rush up in his direction and fly out the window above him."

"Pavlina's too weak to fly, much less carry any of us."

"You think she's the only one with wings here?"

Miss Sphinx tore off her business casual attire, revealing bronze armor beneath it and powerful eagle wings springing magically from her back.

"I… forgot sphinxes had those."

"I don't usually show them off." Pointing at Pavlina, Miss Sphinx continued, "She can ride on me along with Bree, but I'm not sure I can do a third person."

Finn gave a resigned nod that he hoped looked brave. "I'll stand and fight here."

"No, you'll fly and fight with me," called out a new voice.

The sphinx waved at someone behind Finn's back. The Irishman turned to see one of the more frightening gods of his life, one he knew from wandering Olympus in the past. Even the mightiest of gods made room for this person whenever they saw him.

The god of death flew down to the arena, his black wings leaving a wake of black smoke behind him.

"I'm flying with Thanatos?" Finn asked.

"Who else is going to help escort Nemesis out of here?" Miss Sphinx responded. "He's her brother."

Thanatos said nothing. He only nodded at the sphinx, then held his hand out to Finn. Taking death's hand wasn't something that the legendary hero ever wanted to do, but it seemed to be his only option now.

As soon as Finn touched the god's fingers, he was swept up in Thanatos's arms so tightly that nothing could have parted them. *There's no escaping death.*

"You must be very close with your sister if you're willing to do this," Finn said.

"More than that," Thanatos said. "Your sirin friend inspires me. Death immortals should work with compassion, and she's never lost hers."

"Pav isn't immortal."

"She's immortal for as long as I wish her to be."

With that, Miss Sphinx leapt into the air, Pavlina and Bree holding fast to the armor on her back. Thanatos and Nemesis joined her.

It wasn't easy, though. Soon enough, harpies were

soaring at them, screaming at the tops of their lungs and determined to rend their flesh apart.

Thanatos pulled out his scythe, slicing the nearest two in half. Nemesis got another three with her ruthless blade. Finn had been embroiled in many battles and seen the worst deaths imaginable, but after ninety-one years of teaching at public schools, he'd lost his apathy for violence. Finn shut his eyes so as not to see any more blood and dismembered body parts.

"You cannot fight now, warrior," Thanatos said. "But soon you must."

"I know."

Being carried away from the fray on the back of a sphinx made Bree consider how wrong she had been about many things. The world wasn't as black and white as she'd like it to be, and sometimes you couldn't outsmart your adversaries. *Also, I shouldn't be so quick to judge.*

Miss Sphinx had proven her loyalty in every way possible. Bree felt guilty about every moment she'd doubted her, and wished she'd treated her with more kindness.

They flew further and further from Olympus with Corbin and the other crows somehow able to keep up. Bree had never traveled this fast anywhere, and she'd been on an airplane before. It surprised her that she wasn't vomiting into the sky. Magic more powerful than she encountered in her daily life had allowed Miss Sphinx, Nemesis, and Thanatos to travel through realms with the ease of driving down the street.

Within an hour, the harpies had either given up their chase or died trying to catch them. There were other terrifying flying creatures coming for them, but they were far enough away for Bree's group to touch ground again. Just as fiercely as Miss Sphinx had fought to protect the Chosen One, she showed her gentle side by delicately landing on the road in front of Annie Lytle High School and lowering her passengers to the ground.

Bree looked up with apologetic eyes. "You've done so much for us. I'm so sorry for—"

"I appreciate this, but we need to get you to safety," Miss Sphinx said. "It will be a while before our allies arrive to put up a protective boundary around all of New Olympus, and we need to get you inside where The Cailleach has repaired your school's barrier."

"New Olympus? *The* Cailleach? Where is my principal?"

"We can talk about all this later, but you need to go *now!*"

Bree and Ms. Sirin turned to see Mr. Finn leaving the arms of the scariest guy the teenager had ever seen.

"Get them indoors," Miss Sphinx instructed Nemesis. "I'm pretty sure I saw minotaurs headed in this direction."

As Bree and her teachers were rushed to the school, the representative stood her ground, wings extended and claws out.

"Miss Sphinx!" Bree yelled, but her guardian didn't hear her.

A rumbling shook the ground beneath her, and around a corner came a stampede of minotaurs. They were more frightening than anything Bree had seen in a textbook. Taller and wider, with fangs and impossibly defined muscles, they raced toward Bree.

Nemesis swept Bree up in her arms, and the Chosen One could no longer see her protector. Once inside the school, the goddess let her go and pressed her hands against the doors, whispering a spell.

"Why did you need to do a spell?" Ms. Sirin asked. "I thought Miss Sphinx said they'd repaired Principal Cailleach's boundary."

"They did," Nemesis answered. "I'm locking what I just unlocked. This is the second one. Let's get past the fourth one."

"Fourth one?" Finn asked, but Nemesis didn't bother answering him.

The goddess of retribution pulled Bree forward. Her teachers and the black-winged god sprinted along with her down the hall.

Within a minute of passing the school entrance, a sensation like being yanked through transparent gelatin suctioned along Bree's limbs. Nemesis stopped to whisper another spell with her palms pressed against whatever boundary they'd just passed. As she did so, the school doors burst open, letting in several minotaurs.

"Oh, gods!" Pavlina screamed. She scooped Bree into her arms protectively.

The moment Nemesis finished her spell, they continued fleeing, but Bree kept glancing over her shoulder at her pursuers. To her surprise, a dozen ghosts, with Maia leading them, blocked the minotaurs screaming as loudly as they could. They were limited in their ability to fight against anyone, and Bree knew it wouldn't work for long.

However, these ghosts surprised her by pulling together items from around the school to create what looked like a magical automaton. An arm made out of several desks swiped at the minotaurs, knocking several over. *Maia must have planned this. It looks just like the one she used for battle.*

Then she saw someone else join the ghosts—a golden-furred werewolf.

"Ylva!" Bree screamed.

Nemesis yanked Bree along. "If you fall, your allies will give in to their fear of the King of the Gods and we'll lose this battle. So run!"

With great reluctance, she tore her eyes from her friends and ran at Nemesis's side. They fled past another boundary. This one sizzled, burning Bree's recently healed skin. She winced and stumbled, but Nemesis pulled her through, while her black-winged brother did the same with Mr. Finn and Ms. Sirin.

Once on the other side, Bree was shocked to see her skin hadn't suffered any burns at all. Nemesis cast another spell on this boundary, and Bree took the opportunity to look behind them. Miss Sphinx was within view again, standing over a pile of all the slain minotaurs in the hallway.

Ylva was licking blood off her paws, not seeing Bree as she did. The ghosts were celebrating. Several large and armed individuals were among them. She could only assume they were more gods who had come to their rescue.

One of those gods took Ylva by the arm and pulled her past the gelatin-like barrier. Some of the other gods joined him. The ghosts continued to swirl as though they were dancing, while the gods who remained with them were cheering each other on.

The moment Ylva saw Bree, the two waved at each other. The wolf shifted to the golden-haired girl Bree was more familiar with.

Ylva pressed her palm to the final boundary and winced from the burn. "Can you pull me through?"

Bree slipped her hand through, reminding herself that the pain wasn't real. Once she had Ylva's hand, she yanked her in, but with too much force. The two teenagers sprawled on the floor only an inch apart.

"Oh, Bree, I was so worried," Ylva whispered.

This close, Bree could see the long cut scabbing over near Ylva's eye. "I should have never let you get close to me. You could have died."

"You think you could have kept me away from you?" Ylva giggled and placed her palm on Bree's cheek. "I had a crush on you the moment we met."

Beyond Ylva, where Maia, the spirits and the other gods reveled in their victory, the floor beneath the gleeful group erupted. The sudden blast sent everyone toppling several feet away from the impact. A giant maw of a thousand cracked red teeth burst through the linoleum. Before Bree had any time to react, multiple gods were already free falling down its throat.

The mouth tilted so that its head could surface. A monster of a man focused on Bree with crazed eyes swimming in the chasmic hollows of his skull. Every inch of his face was a mismatched piece of patchwork sewed together with black cord.

"Cronus..." Nemesis whispered. She sounded frightened, small.

Only the most powerful gods had been able to overpower their Titan father, and none of them were in this school.

"How did he get out of Tartarus?" Thanatos asked no one in particular.

Ylva held Bree tight. Soon enough, Ms. Sirin and

Mr. Finn were part of the embrace. Just as sure as Bree had been that they had succeeded, she was certain now that they were all going to die. *Even Liz.* Bree wondered if the pocket dimension she lived in was safe from a Titan tearing the school's floor apart.

The linoleum tiles buckled further, and Bree expected to see the Titan's shoulders emerge. Instead, Cal climbed out from a hole from just beyond the crazed immortal, her face no longer holding its usual carefree nature. She glared at Cronus with vengeance in her eyes.

"Cal, you're here!" Bree yelled, but her friend was still focused on the savage Titan.

Beside her, a crowned man with dark hair and dark eyes climbed out. Though he fit in the hallway, his head brushed the ceiling. His black robe left long shadows on the tile. Beyond him, where the school doors had fallen from their frame, three more equally impressive figures arose. One of them wore a towering crown, golden silk robes, and a chiton bound by a belt of diamonds. Another wore a crown of wheat and roses, and a dress sewn together with every beautiful flower imaginable. The other, a man, had a crown of corals and sea green robes lined with creamy ribbon.

No one could deny who these people were. All school children had seen their faces in their most important textbooks. Stories about them were on every news channel every day. Their image was chiseled into countless temple walls.

Hades, Hera, Demeter, and Poseidon circled their father. Losing all their godly elegance, they turned feral. Hissing and growling, they attacked Cronus, tearing off chunks of his flesh and cracking his skull with their legendary weapons. Anyone else would have died instantly, but Cronus only screamed and retreated into the hole he'd risen from.

"Follow him!" Hera shouted at Hades. "We'll catch up with you."

With a nod, the King of the Underworld jumped down after their father.

Then the Queen of the Gods cast her eyes on Bree. "Chosen One, come here!"

"No!" Pavlina yelled. "You can't have her."

"Hold your tongue!" Hera countered, her voice thundering. "If I wished harm on the child, she'd already be dead. She must come here to receive my blessing."

"B-blessing?" Bree sputtered out.

Cal looked away from the exit Cronus had taken and turned to Bree. The serious lines on her face loosened in relief. "It's okay, Bree. You can trust her. She's the one who freed me."

Bree forced herself to pass through the blinding hot barrier that had almost defeated her before. Then she pushed through the suction of the next one, until she was within a yard of Hera. The Queen of the Gods had shrunk to human height and climbed out of the hole she'd appeared from. Poseidon and Demeter had as well.

Hera placed her shining palm on Bree's shoulder. "Chosen One, I have never seen such bravery from a human. You stood against gods and Titans to protect mortals and immortals alike. Never once did you even raise a blade, only your voice."

Bree shook her head. "Only because I didn't have to."

"I am still speaking, child."

Hera's face held no anger, but Bree committed to keeping her lips zipped at once.

"I just watched my father eat my husband in one gulp," Hera said. "The moment you fled, that whore Themis allowed Cronus access to the Council and helped him escape before any of us could reach him. I will *not* let that treason go unpunished. Though Zeus was flawed and has often hurt me, he is still my king."

A diamond tear spilled from Hera's eye. "At least, he *was* my king. I'm not sure he'll survive our father this time." The queen composed herself and continued, "Themis commanded Cronus to come here next. It seems she has control over everything dark you shared with us."

Bree gasped. All this time, they'd assumed it was Atlas, but it was another Titan all along.

"You have my blessing," Hera said. "As a young

woman, you have my gift of protection. My sister and brothers have given you their gifts as well."

"I… I don't know what that means," Bree said, and then realized she'd spoken without permission. "I'm sorry, my queen."

"It means that Demeter has given you insights into the mysteries of life, Hades has given you the ability to visit the dead, and Poseidon has given you safe passage to any part of his oceans."

The god of the seas spoke up at this. "And that means that you can be with your tentacled friend once again."

Tears streamed down Bree's cheek and she fell to her knees. "Thank you," she managed to squeak out. "Thank you so much."

"Don't thank us yet," Hera said. "This comes at the cost of taking down the most dangerous group we've ever encountered. You'll need much more than our gifts to succeed."

Bree nodded. "I understand."

Hera looked at the group who had come to stand a few yards behind Bree. "Now all of you rest, while we assist in putting together more powerful protections around this city of New Olympus."

With that, the three Greek gods jumped down the hole that Cronus had once occupied, leaving an uncomfortable silence and emptiness behind them.

"Now what?" Bree asked herself, not expecting an

answer.

Cal squeezed Bree's shoulder. "Now we recover."
She gestured to Ms. Sirin, Mr. Finn, and Ylva. "And we
spend time with the people we love."

TWENTY-FIVE

The New Olympus

Pavlina sat beside Finn in bed scrolling through rental listings as he wrote things down on a notepad. As much sentimental attachment as they had to Finn's cheap little rental house, it would provide nowhere near enough room for all of Pavlina's stuff. Summer was weeks away, and they needed to make a decision soon.

"What about this one?" Finn asked, pointing to a blue house overlapping the bottom of the screen.

Pavlina scrolled down some and clicked on the image. "It's in Riverside."

"Oh, that's nice!"

"Looks like it's one of the more college student populated neighborhoods."

Finn shook his head. "Changed my mind."

Pavlina groaned. "Gods, we've been at this for an hour."

"We'll figure it out."

"It's gotten so crowded here," Pavlina said, laying her head on Finn's shoulder. "It's so hard to find something we can afford on our salaries."

"Surely, someone will give us a discount as some of the Chosen One's top advisors."

They both laughed. With many gods now moving into town, they were less than ants in importance.

"Who knew Jacksonville would become such a popular place to live?" Finn asked.

"You mean New Olympus."

Finn rolled his eyes. "Why rename it? And with that name of all things. So unoriginal."

"What god wants to say they live in *Jacksonville?*" Pavlina closed her laptop and put it on the side table. "That's enough screen time for today."

"Do you still feel weird around technology? I know I do."

"I know they said they got rid of all the Atlas tech, but…" Pavlina opened her palms outward, gesturing at the world around her. "Whether or not they're part of The Shadow, I don't exactly trust most of them. I mean they put a restriction on a reality where anyone could be healed of anything. I'll never understand that."

"The gods are good at staying in power," Finn said as he got out of bed. "And that means making sure we have bigger things to worry about than how we're being governed."

Pavlina got up and put on a bathrobe. She wasn't naked, but if the Castilles showed up early, she didn't want them seeing her in her lacy nightgown. The very thought of all the work they were going to go through in moving Bree's family into Pavlina's old home exhausted her.

"Maybe I should get a storage unit instead," she said.

"You know that's not the answer. If we're moving in together for good, we're doing it right." Finn gestured for her to follow him. "Come on, I'll pour us each a bowl of cereal."

The thought of breakfast sent a wave of nausea through Pavlina. "No thanks. My nerves are too much today."

Finn stopped and held a gentle hand against Pavlina's cheek. "You've barely eaten in weeks, Pav. You've got to get your strength back."

Pavlina knew he was right, but every day was a struggle against her rumbling guts. She knew death must be around the corner somewhere. Nothing happened, though. She just experienced this low-grade but unignorable nausea that didn't even reach feather-sprouting level. As relieved as she should have felt that no one had died, she found herself guilty of wanting it to just happen already so she could move past this consistent misery.

Despite this, Pavlina would make an effort to ease Finn's worries. "Fine, I'll—"

Something chunky pushed up her esophagus and all Pavlina could do was dash to the bathroom and lean over the sink to release. *Gods, I am so tired of this. Why does it have to be part of my whole sirin schtick?*

Before Pavlina even finished vomiting, the front doorbell rang. The sirin groaned. She wasn't ready at all to talk logistics with Mr. and Mrs. Castille, while making sure to spend quality time with Bree and Liz. As much as she wanted this, she currently wanted an ice pack on the back of her head more.

With a heavy sigh, Pavlina resigned herself to her responsibilities and rinsed her face off. When she straightened up, she saw her gaunt face. She hadn't gotten thinner, but her skin was sallow and the dark circles under her eyes showed just how little sleep she was getting. Nausea or no nausea, she needed to eat and rest more than she had been. She made a mental note to see the doctor soon.

All the Castilles greeted her when she made it to the living room. Liz barreled into her with the full force of one of her ferocious hugs, and for half a second Pavlina thought she might have to run to the bathroom again. Even if it hurt, she felt grateful Liz had this much energy at the moment. Hera had sent word that Liz could go back to the Timucuan reality as soon as it was safe to travel again, but no one knew when that would be. Portaling anywhere was dangerous for Bree's loved ones, as they'd likely be targets of The Shadow. No one wanted to put Liz through that kind of jeopardy.

Mrs. Castille held up a giant plastic dish of chopped up watermelon. "Saw these at the grocery store. I thought we all could use some on such a hot day."

Finn winced and glanced at Pavlina. "Maybe we should hold off on that. Pavlina can't even think about food without—"

"Oh gods, that sounds *amazing*!"

Pavlina pried herself from Liz's vise-like grip and snatched up a fat wedge of watermelon. She shoved as much of it as she could into her mouth and moaned when its refreshing juice slid down her throat.

"Without vomiting…" Finn finished, as he stared at Pavlina with confusion plastered on his face.

Mrs. Castille laughed. "I can't blame her. Watermelon is one of my favorite things. In fact, I used to eat heaps of it every day when I was pregnant with this one." She pointed at Bree. "It was the only thing that could keep the reflux at bay."

A wave of peace washed over Pavlina as she swallowed down the last of her wedge. "Gods, I should just live off this stuff until this nausea goes away."

"Nausea?" Mrs. Castille asked.

Pavlina nodded.

"And this is the only food you've wanted for a while?"

"Thank you so much for…" Pavlina trailed off mid-apology. "Oh."

Finn squinted. "Oh?"

"Oh…" Pavlina repeated. "Oh! Oh! Oh my gods! Oh!"

"What is all this oh-ing about?" Finn asked, sharing confused glances with everyone *except* Mrs. Castille.

Bree's mother shook her head at Pavlina. "I thought he was supposed to be some kind of smart guy."

"He usually is, but neither of us really thought it was possible."

Mrs. Castille nodded. "Maybe we should come back in the afternoon."

Bree and Liz protested in unison, but their mother ignored them.

"I'll leave the watermelon," she said as she laid the container on the coffee table. "Let's go shopping for a bit. We'll see Mr. Finn and Ms. Sirin in a few hours."

Obviously reluctant, the girls dragged their feet after their mother. Mr. Castille gave Finn a salute on the way out and said, "Good luck, Finn."

Once the door shut behind the Castilles, an easy silence blanketed the room, made all even calmer by the temporary abatement of Pavlina's queasiness. *Thank the gods for that watermelon.*

Pavlina stroked her beautiful Irishman's cheek before running her fingers through his blond hair. His gorgeous green eyes held a thousand questions that she needed to answer right away.

"Finn, I'm not transitioning."

"That's what I've been saying. You need to see a doctor, Pav."

"You're right," Pavlina said smiling. "I definitely need to see a doctor. I need to see how far along I am."

"How far along..." Finn held a hand up to his forehead and let out a soft chuckle. "Gods, I'm an eejit. How much more obvious could it be?"

A worry wriggled its way into Pavlina's heart. "Are you changing your mind? About us?"

Finn's eyes widened. "What?!"

"I mean, there's a lot going on and this is just another—"

Finn cupped Pavlina's face in his palms and stopped her words with a kiss.

"I will *never* change my mind about us."

Pavlina wrapped her arms around her love and laid her head on his shoulder. "I love you."

"I love you too," he whispered. "I love you so much that I kissed you even though you just puked, which is so gross. So, so gross, Pav."

"You're a jerk, Finn MacCool!" Pavlina chided as she

slapped his arm.

Finn laughed. "I know. And yet, you still love me."

With testing season over, Finn was ready to go into summer mode and focus on his life with his girlfriend and the daughter that would soon join them. As he packed away his supplies and class decorations to empty his classroom until the next school year, he kept thinking about all the excitement they were about to experience with Pavlina's pregnancy. Sirins could only give birth to girls, so there was no need for an ultrasound to reveal that. Finn still found himself looking up how soon they could get an ultrasound anyway.

I can't wait to tell Oisina, though! She'll be so excited to have a little sister.

Remembering his daughter almost brought tears to his eyes. Finn felt renewed gratitude that Hera had promised Oisina could keep her freedom. She was even moving to Jacksonville. As a goddess targeted by The Shadow, Cal had to move to New Olympus, and her wife would be coming with her. Soon, he'd be spending *real* quality time with her, after decades fearing for her life.

Finn was wiping away his tears when Mrs. Selkie walked in. She was smiling so wide, Finn thought for a moment that Pavlina had broken their agreement to keep things quiet until they knew if her pregnancy was viable. It turned out that the selkie was happy about something else.

"Guess what's back in the budget!"

Finn bolted up from his seat. "No, really? Extracurriculars are back?"

The frizzy-haired woman bounced up and down with glee.

"How much?"

"Right back to where we started!" Mrs. Selkie held a hand up to her heart. "When Principal Cailleach told me to start planning for swim meets next year, I thought I would pass out right there. Gods, I've missed it so much!"

"And with Poseidon hanging around Jacksonville Beach, I'm sure you're going to have a lot of fun practicing!"

Mrs. Selkie shrugged. "Well, my team practices at a pool."

"Doesn't mean *you* have to," Finn said with a wink.

"I may be dipping my toes in those god-blessed waters already."

Finn looked at the piles of materials from his last club meeting. Because of the attack at the Lupercalia Dance, they'd never raised enough money for any more matches. All the teachers agreed that it was more important to focus on their students' safety instead. He was also able to continue growing in friendship with

Alec.

This news meant they didn't have to worry about finding the money to keep these clubs running, while also making sure the children of New Olympus were safe.

"I'm honestly surprised it happened," Mrs. Selkie said.

"Me too. I thought for sure they wouldn't have funding for anything other than eliminating The Shadow."

Mrs. Selkie shook her head. "No, not just that. I didn't think they'd want to."

"Why?"

"They're sticking with the stupid new curriculum."

Finn groaned and ran his fingers down his face. "Are you fecking kidding me?"

"Nope," she said. "Unfortunately, we haven't managed to magically fix governmental incompetence."

"Well, I'm going to take this victory and celebrate it while I can."

"Good idea." Mrs. Selkie looked at her watch. "Hey, I gotta share the news with some other folks."

Finn nodded. "I'm headed out anyway. I have therapy."

"How is the new therapist?"

"Fine so far," Finn said. "It's a little early to tell, but she hasn't made me feel like shite when I talk to her about my past."

Mrs. Selkie offered him a sympathetic smile. "I hate that Themis did that to you, but I'm proud of you for still working on your mental health."

"The thing that really made her believable was that she wove some truth in with all her lies, and she was right about my c-PTSD." Finn finished packing up his messenger bag and slung it over his shoulder. "I'm not about to let my trauma affect my future. Pav deserves better." *Our daughter does too.*

"Well, don't let me make you late. I'll see you later!" The swim instructor waved and headed out.

Once Mrs. Selkie left, Finn locked up his classroom. Before he could head down the hallway, he felt a cold draft behind him. *Oh gods, Principal Cailleach's come to stop me from leaving.*

Finn turned to face her. "Hello, Principal Cailleach."

"I see I caught you just in time," the winter goddess said.

"I have a number of errands I need to get done, so I'm taking my paperwork home tonight."

She held her hand up and shook her head. "No need for explanations. I just wanted to speak to you for a brief moment."

"Oh? What about?"

"I just talked to Ms. Sirin about this," Principal Cailleach said. "As Bree's advisors, as well as Annie Lytle teachers, I felt that you should both be the first to know."

Oh gods, what horrible thing has happened now?

"Hera has called on me to join the effort to get the original Olympus back from Themis and The Shadow, which means that I will no longer be able to uphold my responsibilities as principal here," she said. "A new one will be assigned over the summer."

"You're leaving us?"

"Yes."

Finn was surprised at the disappointment that hit him at that revelation. Principal Cailleach was a strict and intimidating woman. On occasion, she'd given him reason to fear for his job security. Over the two years they'd gotten to know each other, however, he'd grown to like her. She was a winter witch and a goddess, but she was also a woman who cared deeply about her students, especially Bree.

"I'm going to miss you," Finn said.

Principal Cailleach shook her head. "No, you won't. You'll be too busy to miss anyone."

"I'm sure."

"I'm not just talking about school and keeping Bree safe, Mr. Finn," the principal said. "I'm talking about you. You've spent more than nine decades serving community service for a government that has been secure longer than you've been alive. Things are about to get very unsteady, and you'll need to focus on keeping up with your community service despite that.

Just because the Council of Pantheons has split into two factions doesn't mean Hera's going to let you out of your probationary period."

"Another reason that I don't want you to leave."

She arched a serious eyebrow. "I'm certain Ms. Sirin can keep you in check. Go attend to your errands, Mr. Finn."

With that, Principal Cailleach walked away, taking her chill with her.

Even with this unexpected news, Finn felt optimistic. A war was brewing and he was charting unknown waters, but he could handle it. Finn was in love, he had his daughter back and another on the way, the god of death didn't have any plans to reap anyone he cared about, and he was finally working on the trauma he'd tried to ignore for so long. Life was

headed in the right direction for once.

After the trial followed by a rigorous testing season, Bree was glad that the school year was ramping down. She wanted to spend as much time with the people she loved as possible. *While I still can.*

Bree had been tempted by the Council of Pantheons' offer to withdraw from school so that she could focus on taking down The Shadow. But even with the promise that she would still be able to attend college later, the thought of leaving school behind was too painful. She wanted to learn, she wanted to put together automatons and hang out with her friends, and she wanted to see Mr. Finn and Ms. Sirin every day.

More than all that, Bree wanted at least one part of her teenage years to feel *normal*. She did have another thing in common with the average teenager, though.

When the doorbell rang, Bree jumped off the couch, letting her book fall to the floor. When she opened the door, she was almost too breathless to greet her girlfriend.

"Sorry, I'm late," Ylva said with an apologetic look. "Packing took longer than I expected."

The reminder hurt, and Bree found herself bringing up the same points she had since Ylva revealed she was going back to her family in Germany when the school year ended.

"It's not safe for you to leave New Olympus. Everyone knows you're the Chosen One's girlfriend."

Ylva responded as she always did. "Werewolf communities successfully hid from the entire world for centuries. I'm probably safer there than here."

"But I'm going to miss you," Bree sulked.

"We can write and call," Ylva responded. "My family even said we could all come visit for Yule."

It's not enough. Not nearly.

Mr. Castille walked inside from the backyard. He was sweaty from mowing, and wiping his face with a towel. When he saw Bree, he squinted.

"Why are you still here? Your movie starts in thirty minutes."

Ylva waved at him. "It's my fault. We're leaving now."

"I'll let you know as soon as the movie's over," Bree told her father.

He waved a hand dismissively. "Take your time. It's your last day together."

Mr. Castille had changed so much since he came to this reality; so had Mrs. Castille. Bree was sure the grief they held for Gabby and Betty was still there. Hers for her birth parents hadn't left, after all. However, danger had brought them closer together, and they realized they could be a loving family, and they would protect each other through anything.

Despite having to start all over again with new jobs and new customs, her parents had opted to remain with Bree in this magical reality rather than return home. They wanted to provide a safe, comfortable space for the teenager most people only saw as the Chosen One. Bree wouldn't have expected that loyalty from them the previous summer.

Bree waved at her father and left with Ylva. The German girl's annoyed host mother dropped them off at Sunray Cinema, and asked that they walk back to her house since it was only a couple of blocks away. Despite the woman's rude attitude, Bree buzzed with excitement. It had been so long since she'd gotten to leave hiding to do anything so simple as go to a movie.

"This place is amazing!" Ylva said, peeking through the window.

"Just wait until you get inside!"

Bree tugged her girlfriend along. Once inside, she showed Ylva all the wondrous things there. She dazzled the golden-haired girl by pointing out the floating pinball machines, the giant white moth, the flying books on film. She also introduced Ylva to the joys of curry powder popcorn.

They'd come to watch a documentary on the history of civil rights for supernaturals. While Bree had been excited about seeing it, she barely caught a minute of it. Her eyes kept wandering back to the girl sitting next to her. No matter how many times she looked at Ylva, she never got less beautiful.

Afterwards, they shared some cheese pizza, and Bree walked Ylva back to her host family's house. Bree used to walk home in the dark all the time, but things had changed. She wasn't just another nameless student lugging a backpack after getting off a city bus. Along every street corner was a New Olympian guard. They all knew her by sight, and every one of them had been ordered by Hera herself to protect the Chosen One with their lives.

When Bree reached the doorstep, she wished she had Cal's stopwatch. She wanted to freeze time forever. The Council of Pantheons had decided that a device like that was too dangerous in the wrong hands, though. It had been cast into a fire hot enough to melt anything, one left behind by Hermes when he'd run away from Olympus.

There was no stopping the inevitable. This was it. *Time to say goodbye.*

Bree held Ylva's hands in hers and took in a moment to appreciate how the outdoor sconces made her girlfriend's face glow even more.

"I promise," Ylva said. "You'll get so many letters, you'll be tired of my handwriting."

"I could never get tired of that. Your little letters are so perfect."

"You'll get lots of calls too."

"I better."

The girls laughed.

"Thank you for giving me the best school year of my life," Ylva said before placing her lips against Bree's.

This time, there wasn't a sudden, dangerous interruption. Bree got to enjoy the honey perfection of it for as long as possible. They shared a few more, until Ylva broke it, wiping tears from her cheeks as she did.

"Goodbye, Bree," she whispered.

"Goodbye, Ylva," Bree whispered back.

With that, the golden-haired girl went inside, leaving Bree alone.

Suddenly, the world seemed that much darker. Bree

wasn't sure if it was because so much time had passed that the last of twilight had disappeared, or because Ylva had said goodbye.

Mr. Castille had offered to pick up Bree wherever she needed him to, but she didn't feel like going home yet. She was near the river now, and wanted to walk along it for a while as she processed how much she was going to miss Ylva.

After only a few minutes beside the lapping waves of the St. Johns River, Bree leaned over the concrete barrier to cry. She was a brave girl, a Chosen One. She'd survived so much trauma in the last two years. However, the whole world was on the precipice of a war like no other, and she was its catalyst. So many people would die, simply because she hadn't. Her existence put her loved ones' lives in danger, and Ylva would be nowhere near the protections of New Olympus.

Bree was on the brink of spiraling into depression when something slid against her cheek. Normally, this would have alarmed her enough to jump away from whatever was touching her, but this was soothing. This felt like love. It took a moment, but she realized what was happening.

Lifting her head, she saw the multi-colored tentacle reaching from the river to stroke her cheek. Soon enough, a brilliant opalescent head and more shimmering tentacles emerged above the waves.

"Hello, Johnnie," Bree whispered, tears streaming down her face.

Though no words left the creature, Bree felt her familiar's greeting in return just like she had when they first bonded over a year before. The beast that Hermes had wanted her to fight in her quest had connected with the Chosen One on an emotional level that transcended any verbal communication. Though they hadn't seen each other in many months, their spirits were just as entwined as before.

Bree didn't bother to tell Johnnie how much she'd missed her and all that had happened since the Main Street Bridge. Bree knew she didn't need to. Johnnie already knew it all, and she intended to be at Bree's side as long as possible, even when she inevitably had to fight The Shadow in the battle to come.

I can do this. We can do this.

A splash of light barely visible from her viewpoint caught her attention. Somewhere far to the east, there had been another attack on the dome barrier over Jacksonville. It was a common enough occurrence now, but it shook Bree every time she saw it.

A New Olympian guard walked over. "Miss Castille, we need to get you home," he said.

Bree nodded. "I know."

She pressed her cheek against one of Johnnie's tentacles, letting the cephalopod know they'd see each other later.

"Miss Castille."

"I'm coming."

The Chosen One walked with the guard to the black vehicle that always showed up when they suddenly needed to get her to safety.

I can do this. I can do this. I can do this.

Inside the car, she sat beside another guard on an expensive leather seat. She looked out the window to watch Johnnie slip back into the river. In the distance there was another soundless blast. This one lit up the whole sky.

I think.

Epilogue

Without her son and daughter-in-law, Edna Castille's home was empty enough for her voice to echo. She refused to feel lonely, though, opting for resentment. Those two girls, the ones that looked like her grandchildren but weren't, had taken her real family away. She regretted rescuing them. *Should have let Hermes take them. That's what I get for being charitable.*

The online videos on her tablet confirmed her bias. The world was full of leeches, lazy louts living off the hard work of others. Her son had toiled day and night to provide for his family and in return he had a wife who lounged around all day and two kids who disrespected him. Yet, he hadn't listened to her wisdom in the end. He'd snubbed her home remedy, which she'd given to the youngest girl out of the kindness of her heart. Then he left her alone for the sake of those who didn't appreciate him.

A flicker interrupted the commentator she'd been listening to on her tablet, and she knew an important message was coming. A familiar, golden face with a winged helmet and a too-wide smile filled the screen.

"Hello again, Edna," he said. "I hope you're doing well."

The elderly Castille harrumphed. "Can anyone really do well in the hellscape liberals have turned this world into, Hermes?"

"True, true," Hermes replied. "I have a message from my boss."

"What does *she* want?" Edna didn't like Themis. The hoity toity Titan never deigned to talk to her directly.

"She wants you to send a message to The Cailleach."

Edna's cheeks burned with rage. "I already talked with that b—"

"Now, now, Edna!" Hermes interrupted. His voice was syrupy sweet, but his eyes were deadly serious. "You're a lady. I'm sure you wouldn't refer to a goddess in a disrespectful way."

"Why should I help you?" the old woman asked. "I gave you everything you wanted. I kept you updated the whole time the girls were here, and look where it got me." She gestured around her empty home.

"What if I could promise you your youth back?

What if I could give you immortality?"

Edna rolled her eyes. "You've promised that before."

"And I couldn't give it to you, because you're in a reality without magic," Hermes said. "But if you were to tell The Cailleach you're desperate to be with your family, that you're sorry for—"

"I'm *not* sorry!"

"Of course not, of course not. But…"

"But what?" the old woman asked. She tried to look disgruntled by folding her arms, but the messenger god had softened her up by making new promises, and she wanted to hear more.

Hermes must have picked up on her shift in interest, because he continued, "If you lied, she would trust you enough to let you come over to her reality where you could see your son again, and I could fulfill my promise."

"And what would you want me to do over there?"

The god shrugged. "Nothing complicated. A pretty fun task, really. Take Bree and the rest of your family on a short trip outside of Jacksonville."

"That's all?" the old woman asked.

"That's all," Hermes said with a smile.

Acknowledgements

A big "thank you" to the amazing authors I've found in the online Writing Community. Across social media platforms, we have found and supported each other. Without you, I simply wouldn't have any published books to my name.

I would also like to thank the Annie Lytle Preservation Group. This is a very real school which has suffered a great deal of damage and vandalism. They're striving to restore it and keep it safe from trespassers.

Please see their website if you'd like to make a donation: https://www.savepublicschoolnumber4.com/

About the Author

ARK Horton is a small woman made of round shapes and long sighs. Her vice is hoarding responsibilities, and she has the tired eyes to prove it. They still have a sparkle, though, seeing the next project ahead.

She began writing as a child because of her obsession with the most obscure fairytales, folktales, and myths. Now, she blogs extensively about them. ARK Horton is the author of Struggling With the Current, Flirting With the Tempest, Racing With the Serpent, and Heroes & Harbingers as well as a contributor to multiple anthologies.

You can learn more about her and find her other writing at arkhorton.com.